SIXTY ACRES AND A BRIDE

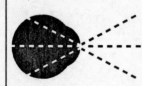

This Large Print Book carries the
Seal of Approval of N.A.V.H.

SIXTY ACRES AND A BRIDE

REGINA JENNINGS

THORNDIKE PRESS

A part of Gale, Cengage Learning

Detroit • New York • San Francisco • New Haven, Conn • Waterville, Maine • London

GALE
CENGAGE Learning®

LIBRARY OF CONGRESS CATALOGING-IN-PUBLICATION DATA

Jennings, Regina.
  Sixty acres and a bride / by Regina Jennings.
    pages ; cm. — (Thorndike Press large print Christian
historical fiction)
  Includes bibliographical references.
  ISBN-13: 978-1-4104-5056-2 (hardcover)
  ISBN-10: 1-4104-5056-2 (hardcover)
  1. Women—Texas—Fiction. 2. Widows—Fiction. 3. Ranchers—Texas—
Fiction. 4. Texas—History—19th century—Fiction. 5. Large type books.
  I. Title.
  PS3560.E527S559 2012b
  813'.6—dc23   2012021922

Published in 2012 by arrangement with Bethany House Publishers, a
division of Baker Publishing Group.

Printed in Mexico
1 2 3 4 5 6 7 16 15 14 13 12

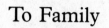

To Family

PROLOGUE

Caldwell County, Texas
August 14, 1878

At an hour when every other God-fearing woman of Caldwell County was either elbowing her snoring husband or sleeping undisturbed in her spinster bed, Rosa found herself sneaking toward a barn that was not her own. She was a trespasser whose goal was to get caught — a terrified stalker whose prey held her future in his hands.

Holding her skirt up and away from the piles of manure, she crept closer with a pounding heart. Surely anyone inside could hear it.

What was she doing here? Returning to Mexico didn't seem so bad compared to the shame of what she planned to do. True, if there was anyone who could help her, it was this man. And if there was anyone she'd like to visit with or work beside, it was he. But alas, he didn't return her regard. He'd purposely avoided her for over a month now. Yet here she was, in the middle of the night, with instructions to go to his bed and ask for money.

Rosa's hands shook as she pushed against the barn door. How had it come to this? How had a respectable widow found herself in such a humiliating situation?

1

"Rosa, sit down. The way you pop up like that scares the grits out of me."

Rosa Garner had only met Aunt Mary Garner that morning at the train station, but she could already tell the woman expected obedience. Blushing, she squirmed between the barrels and the crate of chicks to reclaim her seat in the crowded wagon bed.

"But did you see that house? It's big enough for a hundred people." After a month-long journey from Mexico, Rosa could contain her excitement no longer. She craned her neck to see over Aunt Mary and her mother-in-law, Louise Garner, who shared the bench seat.

Aunt Mary shifted her substantial weight on the bench, causing the wagon to lean. "That ain't a house, it's a hotel, and we don't need you falling out. After all Louise has been through . . ."

"Don't scold her, Mary. She's suffered right alongside me." Louise smoothed her black mourning gown, keeping her handkerchief crumpled tightly in her fist. "We're both widows, you know."

Rosa pushed against the barrels that threatened to squash her as the wagon rocked along and continued to marvel at the elaborate buildings lining the busy street. What they lacked in color, they made up in size, hulking over her like the mountains of Mexico, her homeland.

Hard to believe her husband, Mack, had grown up here. Hard to believe he'd never return.

"Wave, Louise," Aunt Mary said. "You're attracting attention."

Huddled together in front of a dress shop, two women whispered behind idle hands, but it wasn't Louise they noted. Rosa pulled the neckline of her blouse higher and sighed. She'd chosen her clothes with care. Her white blouse was whiter than any she'd seen since crossing the Texas border. She'd worked days embroidering the line of poinsettias that adorned the collar and the embellishments on the gathered sleeves, but she doubted it was her embroidery work they objected to.

The emerald skirt had been saved for today, too — the day they reached Caldwell County and met Louise's family and friends. Rosa was determined to make a good impression. Louise had coached her for weeks on manners and etiquette, and she couldn't disappoint her mother-in-law, not when it meant so much to the older lady.

Louise waved and startled the women into returning the gesture. "So where else do we need to go? I'm anxious to get to the home-place."

Aunt Mary turned into an alley and ticked off their progress on her fingers. "We've been to the bank, the mercantile, and the feed store. Last stop — the courthouse."

"I'll be relieved to have that behind us. After all, how much can the taxes be?" Louise held onto the dash rail. The road had washed out between the two buildings, making the going treacherous.

"You left Caldwell County for a reason," Aunt Mary said.

Yet Rosa had trouble reconciling the descriptions she'd heard of a struggling desperate town with the bustling prosperity she saw before her. According to Louise, she and her husband fled Caldwell County with their son, Mack, to protect him from the lawless situation called Reconstruction. Hearing extravagant tales of the silver mines of the Sierra Madres, the Garners leased their farm and went searching for riches. But instead of a fortune, Louise lost her husband and son and gained *nada* — unless she counted Rosa.

Before Louise could answer Aunt Mary, the wagon lurched, tilting down at one corner. In a move surprisingly nimble for her girth, Aunt Mary somehow got her feet over the box side and onto the ground before she was tossed out. At the same time, Rosa skidded on her backside down the sharply angled bed, a barrel rolling right behind. It slid onto her skirt, twisting her as she struggled to remain upright. Her feet tangled in her hem, leaving her pinned against the hard side of the wagon bed.

Her heart was racing, not just from the suddenness of the accident but from the horrible sensation of being trapped, smothered. Too many collapsed roofs, too many cave-ins at the mine had left Rosa with eggshell nerves, but she wouldn't succumb. Lying on her back, she pushed against the barrel, desperate for room, fighting for breath.

"Rosa! Are you all right?" Louise reached around from the front and helped shove the barrel away from her daughter-in-law.

Rosa crawled to the side of the wagon and swung her legs over. Using Aunt Mary's support, she slid out of the wagon box, careful not to land on the wheel lying beneath her.

"I'm fine." Hiding her shaking hands, Rosa caught her breath. She hadn't been trapped. There was the sky. There was air. She looked around, trying to get her bearings, feeling crowded between the tall buildings in this town of Lockhart, Texas. No time to panic. Louise needed her help. If her terror would pass, she could turn her thoughts to the problem before them.

The empty axle hovered a few inches off the ground. Rosa walked to the back. Just as she suspected. The opposite corner was elevated, wheel spinning errantly midair.

Aunt Mary huffed. "It's that sorry pin again. I keep telling George to take it to the blacksmith, but looks like I'll be doing it myself."

"We'll go with you." Louise climbed down. "After weeks coming out of the mountains on the back of a burro, then all that time on a train, I would welcome an opportunity to transport *myself* for a change. A stroll sounds delightful."

"You're going to leave the wagon here?"

Rosa asked. "With all our supplies in it?"

Louise looked to Aunt Mary for an answer.

"She's right. You can't afford to lose a cent's worth," Aunt Mary said.

Rosa nodded. "I'll stay behind."

Louise tucked a strand of red hair behind her ear. "You're certain you don't mind? Then, if it's fine with you, we'll return shortly. Remember what I taught you, and don't speak to any strange men."

Aunt Mary rolled her eyes at the advice. Obviously not all *gringos* were bothered with the niceties that consumed Rosa's mother-in-law. Or maybe customs had changed during the ten years Louise lived in Mexico.

Rosa watched the two ladies. Tall Louise and stout Aunt Mary looked nothing alike, but the way they related reminded her of sisters. True, their husbands were only cousins, but kin was kin, and they needed all the help they could get from Uncle George and Aunt Mary. Rosa and Louise couldn't even get to the homeplace without assistance.

So the pin had broken? Rosa assessed their predicament. Even with the necessary part, the axle was too close to the ground to get the wheel on. No one could lift the

14

wagon loaded down like it was, but if the weight was shifted . . . She scrambled up the side. They'd come this far. A broken pin wasn't going to stop her.

Rosa grasped the burlap sack of beans and lugged it up the incline to the back of the bed.

"Appears you've run into trouble."

Rosa looked up to see a bearded man. She'd been properly introduced to only two men since arriving — Nicholas Lovelace, the spoiled son of the lumber mill owner, and Deacon Bradford, the manager at Simpson's Mercantile. This man was neither, so she ignored him, as she'd been taught.

"Nothing to be afraid of, miss. I was going to help, that's all."

"Are you bothering this lady?" another man asked, entering the alley. He launched a stream of tobacco juice against the side of the building and extended his hand to the first.

"Naw, just offering my assistance, but she ain't too receptive."

The bags of flour were slick and tightly filled, making them hard to grasp. Rosa rolled them, one at a time, up the bed and wedged them between the beans.

"Maybe she don't speak English."

"Probably not. Pretty thing, though. Wish I could get the missus to wear something like that."

"What are you boys doing?"

Three of them now? Rosa blew a strand of ebony hair out of the way and grasped the bars of the chicken crate. Bending and walking backwards, she lugged it to a chorus of frantic chirping, then stood and stretched her back. Why were they gawking at her? She knew what she was doing. Each trip across the bed of the wagon brought it more level.

By the time the front end of the wagon lifted, money was exchanging hands. No wonder there was such a crowd. She'd stumbled into some sort of wager. Whatever the stakes, the men seemed to be entertained.

From her platform on the wagon bed, she saw Louise and Aunt Mary crossing the street with the blacksmith. She waved. Rosa thought they'd be surprised with the progress she'd made, but Louise looked stricken.

Plowing her way through the crowd of men, Aunt Mary was the first to reach the wagon. Her mouth hung agape as she stared at the perfectly situated axle, but Louise wasn't concerned with the wagon.

16

"What is the meaning of this?" Louise gestured to the crowd, which, with shuffling feet and thinly veiled smirks, began to disperse.

"I leveled the wagon."

"With all these men looking on?"

Rosa dropped from the wagon and studied her slippers. "I didn't talk to anyone. I didn't climb or whistle. I didn't do anything you've warned me against."

Louise put a hand to her forehead and closed her eyes. "Rosa, you created a spectacle — just what I most wished to avoid. The sooner we get you out of town the better. Perhaps we should visit the courthouse at a later date."

Rosa bit her lip. She'd followed the rules and still made a mess of things. But Aunt Mary came to her rescue.

"Stop fretting yourself over niceties, Louise. Your taxes might bring you to ruin, not some innocent blunder. Now, let the blacksmith see to the wheel while we go to the courthouse. Hiding from bad news don't make it no easier."

—

2

"One hundred and sixty-six dollars? How are we supposed to come up with one hundred and sixty-six dollars?" With white knuckles, Louise grasped the brass rail bolted to the countertop in the tax assessor's office.

Rosa took her mother-in-law's arm. She had no idea how much that amounted to in pesos, but it was enough to turn Louise's skin pale. Enough to make Aunt Mary speechless, something that hadn't happened since she'd met the woman that morning.

"We leased out our farm before we left for Mexico. We had no idea the renters had abandoned the property and stopped paying the taxes. It's not my fault." Louise twisted her hands around the smooth brass rail. "Unless God works a miracle, there's no way two widows can make that much money by August fifteenth. That's three months . . ."

The buxom girl behind the counter fiddled with the ink-splotched apron that covered her starched shirtwaist. "I'm sorry, Mrs. Garner. The account has been delinquent for four years. It's a good thing you came back from Mexico when you did —"

"Don't you get smart with Louise, Molly Lovelace. I'll have a talk with your ma," Aunt Mary huffed.

"I'm not being smart. I'll get the ledger, and you can see for yourself."

The ladies didn't protest, so Molly turned on her heel, but not before sending Rosa another peculiar look.

So this was Nicholas Lovelace's sister? The dapper young man had given Louise an account of his sister while escorting them on their shopping errands. Evidently Miss Lovelace hadn't purchased her fine clothing from the dry goods stores they'd visited thus far. They were more extravagant than any Rosa had ever seen.

"I bet she wouldn't shift a wagon load in public," Rosa said.

"If she could gather a crowd as big as yours, she would." Aunt Mary hitched her skirt higher over her soft belly.

"Ladies!" Louise scolded, casting a warning glance at the approaching clerk. Molly brought the oblong book directly to Louise and led her to a bench against the wall. She pointed to a column of numbers stacked as neatly as the leather-bound volumes behind her. "It says right here."

Rosa itched to get a look at the figures, but it wouldn't do to push the elegant Miss Lovelace aside.

With brow furrowed, Louise bent over the ledger, then straightened and closed the book. "What does it matter? If God wants us to have the money, then no power on Earth can prevent it. We mustn't despair."

Aunt Mary raised an eyebrow. "True, but —"

"So Mack is really gone?" Molly interrupted.

"Yes, I'm afraid so." Louise turned to Rosa. "Molly and Mack grew up together. Her mother, Adele, is one of my dearest confidantes."

No wonder Molly's eyes filled with tears at the mention of Rosa's husband. No wonder she felt free to inspect Rosa so closely.

"Mack missed you and your brother immensely when we left." Louise handed her the ledger. "I apologize for causing a scene, Molly. You were only executing your position in this office. We expect any child of Thomas Lovelace to be the best at their profession."

Molly leaned forward. "You haven't become reacquainted with my brother, Nicholas, have you?"

"He followed them from store to store, talking up a storm," Aunt Mary snorted.

Rosa smiled. Nicholas Lovelace might not be industrious, but he was entertaining and informative.

Louise stuffed her handkerchief into her reticule. "I was glad to see him regardless, just as I am you. We didn't come back to the best circumstances, but we made it here, and I refuse to believe the situation is as dire as it sounds."

Silence. Molly and Aunt Mary's eyes met. Between the sophisticated career girl and the farm wife, Rosa guessed they agreed on only one topic — Louise and Rosa didn't stand a chance at raising the money. She prayed they were wrong.

Molly's manners recovered first, having been utilized more frequently than Aunt Mary's. "At least you're home, Mrs. Garner. Your family is here for you."

Louise managed a weak smile. "I do have family, but Mary and George have a house full of young ones."

"I offered to let you stay with us," Aunt Mary said.

"But you don't have room. Besides, you're trying to make ends meet, too. Not easy with seven of you under one roof."

Aunt Mary nodded. "You know, I think Weston's taking a herd on the trail, but he might be able to put you up. He's still got that big place his pa left him when he died in the war. There is plenty of room for the family at Palmetto."

"Weston Garner?" Molly squeaked and hopped off the bench. Her mouth opened and closed a few times before she found words. "Oh no. That wouldn't do. Not at all."

Her blue eyes traveled from the ribbon holding Rosa's hair behind her neck to the black slippers on her feet, missing nothing in between. "That would be disastrous indeed." She wrung her hands. "Mr. Garner hasn't been social for years. I've tried to . . . Well, let's say he's not fond of company right now. Unapproachable, even. You might get a roof over your head, but I doubt it. He values his solitude."

"My nephew would welcome us," Louise protested. "We were very close. He and Eliza are the closest family we've got."

Rosa could still hear the voice of Mack's father, Eli, encouraging him to follow his older cousin's example. Mack had spoken of Weston as being big and strong, but serious — something Mack could never understand.

Aunt Mary shook her head. "Now that I think of it, it's a bad idea. Weston ain't been himself since his wife's death. Just as dear as ever, but forget I said anything about going to his house. If worse comes to worst, you'd be better off sharing a room with my girls."

Molly nodded a bit too eagerly. Rosa moved closer to Louise, convinced something was afoot. Meeting her eyes, Molly turned a slight pink. Her story was verified by Aunt Mary, but it still didn't ring true. What was the girl afraid of?

Round Rock, Texas

The barbershop bell rang as Weston Garner opened the door and then again when he bumped his head on it while crossing the threshold.

The barber took the razor handle out of his mouth. "Sorry about that. I need to hang the ding-a-ling higher."

Weston dropped his hat on the hall tree. He'd taken a quick dip in Bushy Creek before reaching town, not wanting the odor of the Chisholm Trail to precede him like every other drover strutting down the streets. If he'd time, he would've washed his clothes. They sorely needed it, but town was too close for them to dry on his back and too close to lollygag without them. A man his size attracted enough attention as it was. Still, with his shaggy dark hair and rough beard, he sure could use a spit and a polish.

"We're working fast as we can. One of us will get to ya in a minute if you have time to wait."

"I have all day." He had all day, all week, all month. No one was waiting for him at home. Might as well sit a spell. Weston headed to the only empty seat in the shop and fell into the cushioned chair.

He already regretted his decision to leave the herd and turn back early, but not from concern over his investment. Those four-dollar steers were worth ten times that when they reached the butchers up north, and the cowboys could push them on up to Wichita without him. He didn't need to mollycoddle his ranch hands, but maybe he should've stayed longer. On the trail he'd found some peace. Would it endure when faced with the memories that haunted his home — Palmetto?

Finding an open jar of pomade, Weston took a whiff but was disappointed. Bear grease.

The barber returned with steamed towels. Tilting Weston's chair back, the man covered his face. Weston sunk into their heavenly warmth. After weeks of scanning the horizon under the Texas sun, his eyes relaxed; his wind-burnt skin was soothed. He'd kept up with the younger fellas during the day, but sleeping on the ground was another matter. He'd be snoring soon if he wasn't careful.

Lord, he prayed as he settled in, *things are fixin' to get hairy. I don't rightly know how to be the man you want me to be. I thought I had it figured out before Cora, but that didn't work out so well. How do I start over?*

He didn't realize he'd fallen asleep until the barber lifted the towel from his face.

"Now, how about that beard? You want a trim?" The spindly barber mopped up the excess moisture from Weston's face.

"Go on and shave it all off."

Despite the shaving soap, Weston could've dozed off again if it weren't for the conversation between the two men to his left.

"So ya finally caught up with her?" the man nearest Weston asked.

A cultured voice from the corner seat answered, "Yes, she was trying to catch a train to Ohio. Ignorant wench. I don't know how she made it this far without someone telling her what to do."

Weston's jaw clenched. He shifted in his chair, just then realizing how small it was for his large frame.

"Don't move," his barber warned.

The men continued.

"Women! They don't appreciate nothing."

"Precisely. Her father insisted I marry her, and then she runs off. As if he wants her back." There was laughter all around.

"Why don't you just let her go?"

"Because that's what she wants."

Weston tried to lean forward, but the straightedge razor scraping his neck made him think twice. He wanted to get a look at those two. Between towels, shaving cream, and a hovering barber, he couldn't tell who they were — just that he could whop both of them if he needed to.

"Where's she now?"

"At the hotel."

"You ain't worried about her running off again?"

The soothing voice belied the words. "No. She won't be running anywhere for a while."

If it were Caldwell County, Weston would be honor bound to say something, but correcting strangers usually led to violence. Men might talk tough and mean no harm, but they didn't do it in front of him without some reckoning. Especially about a woman. But he was far from home and eavesdropping on strangers. Not a good place to start a confrontation.

The barber across the room finished a haircut and cleaned the customer off with a stiff brush. Sounded as if the two men next to Weston were leaving, as well.

At least three men made their way to the door. The bell rang as they walked out. Weston looked, but in vain.

The barber parted Wes's hair and smoothed it down to get a straight cut.

Weston cleared his throat. "That fellow talking about his wife, you know him?"

"Naw, and glad I don't."

They fell silent while the scissors snipped and clumps of dark hair dropped quietly to the floor.

"He's from somewhere south of here, but definitely a Yankee — I ain't judging, just saying he's not been here long enough to lose his accent. Think they said he's from south of Lockhart."

"Lockhart?" Weston bolted upright in his chair. Jay Tillerton! The voice, the attitude, suddenly rang very familiar. Come to think of it, Tillerton and his wife were from Ohio.

"Was that fellow tall, narrowed shouldered? Schoolteacher type?"

27

The barber wiped his scissors on his apron and began to backtrack. "Oh, I wasn't paying no mind. Besides, people say a lot of things they don't mean."

But they shouldn't.

"I'm calling it quits." Weston jerked the sheet off his neck, sprang up, and fished for money in his pocket.

"Aren't you gonna let me finish? I only got half done."

"Sorry. Gotta catch up with someone." He tossed him a coin and hurried to the door.

"But your hair —"

"I've got a hat."

Weston strode down Georgetown Avenue, watching both sides of the road, looking for the man. If Tillerton was headed home, he should've come this way. Weston stopped at the corner of Lampasas before the absurdity of his behavior caught up with him.

Chasing a neighbor down the streets of Round Rock? What had gotten into him? Probably wasn't Tillerton at all. He turned west toward the livery stable to get his horse, Pandora, being too embarrassed to go back to the barbershop.

If he wanted a fresh start, he'd made a poor beginning. Yes, he needed to get involved, but there had to be a better way.

This type of erratic behavior would earn him even more sympathetic glances and subdued voices. He wanted to stop making people feel uncomfortable. He wanted to enter a room without dampening the gaiety. If he was going to rejoin society, he needed to quit taking everything so seriously.

Besides, hadn't he already proven he was no help to damsels in distress?

3

Prairie Lea, Texas

Before the sun reached its zenith the next day, the ladies' wagon had rolled onto the farm situated on the west fork of Plum Creek. Rosa stretched, glad she wouldn't be sharing a bed with Louise and Aunt Mary again. The crowded hotel was better than the train, but she was ready for a place to call her own.

As they broke out of the piney forest, the prairie expanded before them like a giant quilt that hadn't been perfectly smoothed. Verdant fields stretched before Rosa. In the mountains, the green ran vertical: vines, trees, and giant cacti. Here it raced to the horizon, dragging her imagination to the future.

The road split and they took the left branch.

A clump of shade trees huddled in the otherwise cleared plot. As the wagon drew near, Rosa could see that they were gathered protectively around a whitewashed two-story house. Her mother-in-law's tear-filled eyes were all the confirmation she needed. They were home.

"Oh, Eli, you should be here with me," Louise choked into her hankie, her red hair escaping the bonnet, causing Rosa's thoughts to turn again to her own late husband.

Mack grew up here. This farm was his, and she couldn't lose it, not after she'd robbed him of his happiness.

Rosa had taken what belonged to another and had paid for her folly. Everything had been ripped from her hands except this farm, Louise, and her new faith. That was all she'd managed to salvage.

Sitting at the Garners' table in her Mexican village, Rosa had heard stories about Jesus and stories about Texas until, in some way, they were connected. Jesus would keep her safe with Louise. Jesus would keep her safe at their farm. But Jesus might not be concerned with a poor Mexican girl on her own.

And if it weren't for Louise, she would be on her own. When the Garners first rode into Ciauhtlaz, Rosa's parents encouraged her to help the *Americanos*. As a leading family of the village, it was their duty to extend hospitality to the newcomers, but as Rosa's interest in their religion grew, so did her parents' disapproval.

The memory of her mother's tears as she implored Rosa to reconsider her decision made her own eyes water. Her *madre* begged, she pleaded, but once Rosa refused to worship *Santa Muerte,* Saint Death, her mother relentlessly avoided her only girl child.

Stunned by the thoroughness of her banishment, Rosa clung to Eli, Louise, and Mack — the only family that wanted her.

She would do anything to help her mother-in-law make it here. They had nowhere else to go.

"Is that George?" Louise motioned to the man standing on the shady porch.

"None other," Aunt Mary said as they rolled into the yard.

"I declare, I thought this day would never come." Uncle George bounded to the wagon and helped Louise and Rosa down, surprising Louise with the heartiest hug his long arms and narrow chest could produce. "Don't know how you managed, but you look younger than the day you left."

Louise waved her handkerchief at him. "You rascal. I can't lay claim to youth with a daughter-in-law at my side."

"Ah, yes. But she's barely left the nursery." He smiled and then nodded somberly toward Rosa. "Sorry, ma'am. I shouldn't tease until I've paid my respects. Mack would be right proud that you're standing on Garner land."

"And he'd be plumb irate if you have to leave it," Aunt Mary grumbled. "We can get acquainted over a plow and hoe just as well, but first let's get this wagon unloaded."

She *gee*d to the horse, leaving the others to follow her to the barn. It seemed that with each item lifted over the edge of the wagon bed, Aunt Mary assigned another chore to be completed before nightfall. No *siestas* here. They'd use every hour of daylight God gave them until the house was restored and the crops were sown.

And Rosa's first task? She would follow behind Uncle George, the horse, and the plow to break up the lumps of earth they overturned. The hoe didn't look heavy, but by the time Aunt Mary and Louise carried an earthen water jug out to them, Rosa's back ached and her hands were blistered.

"Uncle George and I have already plowed an acre. We are working *rapido*, no?" Rosa took a drink of spring water, not minding when it splashed down the front of her green blouse.

Uncle George fanned himself with his hat. "Louise, I don't know what you'd do without this girl. I'm glad you brought her home to us."

"She's a gem — the one consolation I have from our disastrous Mexican venture. She's not very big, but she works circles around me."

Louise's words pleased her. Rosa knew she might not be the smartest, richest, or prettiest woman around, but she could work. If hard labor could earn a place in this community, she was guaranteed success.

Aunt Mary plopped her thick frame directly on the ground next to her spouse. "Louise and I ain't doing too shabby ourselves. We've cleaned the downstairs and hauled that mouse-infested feather tick to the burn pile."

"Yes, and I'd better get back inside. This sun will ruin my complexion." Louise picked up the water bucket by its rope handle to carry it back to the kitchen.

The sun was gathering strength, but Rosa didn't fear its rays. Her complexion would only glow richer. No freckles or liver spots to worry about.

Poor Louise.

Mack had always vexed his mother about her Irish complexion, an oddity in Rosa's village. He was constantly teasing someone, surrounded by giggling village girls. Had he not reveled in their attention, perhaps his father wouldn't have reacted so strongly. Had Netnetl — that pagan girl, as Eli described her — not been so beautiful, perhaps Eli would have had more patience.

For Rosa, agreeing to Eli's suggestion came as easily as plucking a ripe mango. No man in her village wanted a wife who had turned her back on their traditions, so her choices were few. Still, she never would have consented to the marriage with Mack had she known how strongly he objected to it. But she was foolish. Rosa believed what she wanted to believe — that Mack would love her.

With a sigh Rosa got to her feet. After having been a wife for less than a month, she'd now been a widow for almost a year — a long year. Was it wrong to dream that someday a man would cherish her? Shouldn't gratefulness to Louise override all discontent?

Rosa followed Uncle George to the garden plot and was soon back in the swing of things, swinging her hoe, that is, while he turned the ground.

"Don't overdo it, Rosa. This heat will get to you before you know it. Besides, we could use your help at our place when we're done here. It's shearing season and the pay is decent."

Her blade sunk deeper with each stroke. "I don't know how to shear sheep, and I can't accept payment, especially after all you and Aunt Mary have done for us."

"You'll learn quick enough, and as foreman for Weston, it's my job to hire the help. I have to pay someone. It might as well be you." He pushed past her to complete the row.

Handling sheep sounded much more interesting than handling a hoe. Rosa would never catch up with him, but maybe she wasn't supposed to. Uncle George would finish this evening, leaving her a couple of days to break up the clumps and scatter the seeds.

On his next pass, Uncle George had a request. "Would you mind bringing the water jug out again? No hurry, but I could use a swig."

Rosa dropped the hoe and flexed her hands. Would she mind? She smiled. Anything to break the monotony.

Skipping past her baby chicks and into the kitchen, Rosa found the dingy house

36

transformed. Louise and Aunt Mary had whipped the abandoned homestead into submission, from the cobwebs that had graced the corners to the mouse droppings on the floor. The stove and basin sparkled. Even the parlor was tidy, although faded. She poked her head into Louise's room but found it empty. They must be upstairs.

Her foot was on the first step when she heard Aunt Mary from the room above. "The town incident really wasn't her fault, Louise. Those men knew better."

"Yes, but they wouldn't have done that to you or to me when we were younger. They treated her differently."

Rosa heard a screech as something was pushed across the floor, then Louise continued. "I felt like part of an exhibition driving through town."

"Nonsense. Everyone is surprised to see you back home. That's all."

"Back home with a Mexican daughter-in-law?"

"Naw, they see Mexicans every day. That's not why people stare at her. She's beautiful, Louise. Did you see how Molly's feathers ruffled when I mentioned Weston? She's considered herself his intended for a couple of years and doesn't relish the thought of you two at his place."

37

So that was Molly's concern? Rosa crossed her arms. Once Molly got to know her, she would realize how unfounded her fears were. Rosa's objective was financial, not romantic.

"Weston and Molly? Really? I suppose Adele is thrilled," Louise said.

"She would be if Weston would give Molly the time of day. Poor girl. It's a one-sided affair, best I can tell, but that doesn't keep her parents from pressuring her to snatch him up."

"Who can blame them for trying? But what can we do for Rosa? Makes me wonder if I made a mistake bringing her all this way. Maybe it was selfishness. She's a help to me, but I don't know what kind of future I can offer her. Opportunity won't come knocking often."

A mistake? As if a bucket of cold water had been dashed in her face, Rosa's vision cleared. If her trip to Texas was a mistake, Rosa was out of options. And her dreams of finding someone to love didn't sound likely in Prairie Lea. She straightened her shoulders and pushed up her sleeves. Louise must not regret bringing her. Give her an opportunity, and she'd make the most of it.

Eating dinner on the long bench between

seven-year-old Susannah and her five-year-old sister, Ida, Rosa felt more at home than she had since crossing the Mexican border.

It'd taken her three days to get the garden in, and then she'd made the short walk with Uncle George and Aunt Mary to their sheep ranch across the creek. That morning their daughters waited anxiously in braids and bows to meet their new cousin. From the start, Ida insisted on holding her hand, but Susannah, a mature young lady, was content to shadow Rosa around the barn as she learned the ins and outs of shearing season. At first the boys, Samuel and Tuck, had ignored her except for stolen glances. By the noon meal though, they were trying to outdo each other with tall tales of Texan proportions.

"You boys are full of beans. Don't believe anything they say, Rosa." Uncle George wiped the last of the meaty juice out of his bowl with a chunk of cornbread.

Across the table, Tuck beamed. "But I taught her how to tie up the fleeces. That wasn't a fib."

Aunt Mary rose and collected the empty dishes. "You must've taught her good, Tuck. She's keeping up like an old hand."

It was Rosa's turn to beam. "Thank you, *señora*." Rosa hopped up to dip a curtsy and wink to the girls, who giggled into their little aprons.

George rose and walked to the open door. "I don't know where those cowboys are. I thought they were coming out to help today. Good thing we didn't wait on them."

"Cowboys!" Mary swatted at a fly with her dishcloth. "Bunch of no-good rabble-rousers! Rosa, if those boys show up, don't you have a thing to do with them. They aren't fit company for ladies."

"That includes our oldest son, Bailey, most days, but the ladies don't seem to mind." George stood a moment longer and then roused himself. "Well, let's go, boys. Them sheep ain't gonna crawl out of the fleeces by themselves." He shuffled toward the door. "You coming, Rosa?"

She didn't hesitate. Rosa loved to handle the greasy warm fleeces, so heavy and soft. Staying inside on such a beautiful day would be a tragedy. The sky was the same brilliant blue as her blouse, the coreopsis crowded around the barnyard gate as bright as the yellow embroidery she had whipped into her clothing while lounging during languid Mexican evenings.

As she passed through the gate, there was a commotion ahead of her.

"Tuck! Catch her! She'll lead them all out!"

"I'm trying, Pa."

Caught by surprise, Rosa stepped out of the way as a heavily fleeced ewe barreled past her red skirt, Tuck hot on her heels. To her horror, the whole flock was following behind. She raced to the end of the wooden gate and lifted and rotated it into place to halt the exodus, but it was too late to catch all of the runaway sheep.

Tuck managed to head off the followers, but the lead ewe made a beeline toward her home pasture. Samuel and George were there in an instant to help Tuck turn the flock.

"Sorry. I let them get by," Rosa gasped as she raced past them after the lone fugitive.

Once clear of the yard, she lengthened her stride. Her legs stretched and greedily ate up the fresh grassland between the errant animal and her. The crisp spring air was invigorating. On the long train ride home, Louise had taught her not to fidget, to sit properly and move gracefully, but she hadn't explained what a lady did with raw energy. If the answer was chasing sheep, then Rosa was behaving perfectly.

The wily ewe slowed to a trot as it entered a copse of trees. Mimicking Tuck, Rosa stalked around the trees to get in front of the animal.

Weston spotted a house on the hill. He hadn't been there since he and the owner had traded bulls. He couldn't remember which bull he'd obtained in the bargain, but he did recollect the man's two daughters — silly things, whose faces looked like they'd been in seed ticks. Sure enough, as he approached, he saw one young lady on the porch. She dived inside and returned with her sister. There they stood, whispering behind their hands as he passed.

Well, that wasn't unusual. When he'd been a young man, it was hard to separate the belles who were interested in his estate from those who were preoccupied with his looks. Since then, the years had wiped away the smooth naïveté of his adolescence, leaving a weathered countenance — not exactly what most young gals were hunting for, but it didn't matter. He'd removed himself from the marriage market, to the expressed displeasure of matchmakers throughout the war-torn state.

Love, marriage, disaster — that's how it read in his book. He wouldn't put another woman through that no matter how handsome they declared him to be.

Then again, he shouldn't be vain. The two girls were probably laughing at his hair, but if he stared at ladies in the same manner, he'd have some explaining to do.

He tipped his hat as he continued on the road toward home. No, not home, not yet. If he remembered correctly, Uncle George would be in the middle of sheep shearing. They'd be grateful for an extra pair of hands. Yep, a trip to Uncle George's might keep the regrets away a while longer.

He and God hadn't been on speaking terms until lately, primarily because of Wes's guilt. Should he blame God for the tragedy or himself? For a time he told himself he'd rather be in the dark than to know he was liable, but he finally reached a point where nothing else mattered. He'd tried a life separated from his God, and it was no way to live. He'd rather be a son who was chastened than a stranger who was ignored.

On top of that, his sister, Eliza, would soon return home from a trip he was too yellow to take. He should've gone to St. Louis and taken Cora's mementos back to her family. Five years mourning was long enough, but instead, Weston had found excuse after excuse. No more. Time to get back in the saddle and start living. He couldn't go home and be the same man who had left.

Approaching the property line, Weston didn't see any ewes in the north pasture. Shearing must be underway. Pleased at the chance to stay away from Palmetto for a couple more days, he let Pandora have her head. His mare must have anticipated a feed sack, for she covered the last leg at a brisk gallop, and soon they were on family land. But was it too soon?

Maybe he should have taken more time to figure it out before turning Pandora south again.

Too late now.

A flash of red caught his eye, and at the same time Pandora's ears twitched. He pulled up the reins. Someone was stalking through the trees. A woman crouched low was sneaking forward, her back to him. Who was she and what was she doing at George's? He turned Pandora and crept slowly behind her, not wanting to announce himself until her intentions were clear.

4

The ewe startled when she saw Rosa in front of her.

"That's right. Outsmarted you, I did. Time to turn around and head to the barn." Rosa bent forward and waved her arms wide, trying to look much bigger than she was. The ewe bleated a warning at her. "No, old woman, I'm not moving. You're going to turn around. . . ."

But the ewe didn't listen to Rosa's instructions. Lowering her head, the animal charged directly toward her. Determined not to step out of the way this time, Rosa held her ground until the sheep ran between her legs and caught in her red skirt. Falling forward, Rosa wrapped both arms around the cushioned body and was carried backward out of the trees and into the open field. She threw her weight to the left and toppled the ewe.

There they lay, side by side, Rosa's arms

still around the south end of the squirming beast. Now what? How could she get the animal home? Rosa gasped for breath. Between the running and the wrestling, she was winded.

She heard a horse nicker, then a man's voice. "If you're hurt, I'll help. If not, I'll pretend I didn't see anything and go on."

At his voice, the ewe struggled harder to get to her feet, but Rosa held on tight. "I'm not hurt, but I need to get this animal to the barn."

Huffing, she tilted her head to get a look at the speaker, Aunt Mary's warnings about cowboys still ringing in her ears. Besides an uneven haircut, he didn't look scary. Instead, his looks were very nice. Pleasing even. Aunt Mary's warning would go unheeded in the face of this handsome cowboy. She couldn't believe the man before her was deficient in any way, or at least his rugged face convinced her to give him the benefit of the doubt.

Speaking of appearances, what must hers be? Lying on the ground embracing a dirty ewe? Rosa stifled a groan. His eyes were averted, but she wasn't taking any chances. She pulled her legs up, hoping they were hidden by her skirt.

"I'm afraid she'll run off if I let her go."

"What do you propose? Are you going to lie there until she falls asleep and then drag her back?"

Rosa felt like she was talking directly up his horse's nose. "If you have a suggestion, I'm willing to listen." She blew some loose wool away from her mouth. "I'm not going anywhere."

The stranger studied the horizon a long moment before answering. He didn't seem rude, but he had yet to get off his horse and assist.

"You're here to help George and Mary?"

Her face grew red as she nodded. Lots of help she was, lying in a pasture.

"Did I miss dinner?" He untied his bandanna from around his neck, wiped his face, and met her eyes for the first time.

What was wrong with this man? "Yes, you missed dinner. *Señor,* my arm is going numb under this animal *ridículo.* What should I do?"

"Let her go."

"I can't let her go. She'll run off."

"No she won't. She'll follow me. She knows me."

Rosa tried to read the man. As much trouble as she had catching the sheep, he'd better not mislead her. She released the ewe and rolled to avoid its sharp hooves. The

47

animal scrambled away from Rosa but didn't go far from the man and his horse.

Rosa stood and dusted off her skirt. What a mess. Between her soiled clothes and his shaggy appearance, obviously they'd both faced some tough times. Maybe she should have compassion on the wayward laborer. Her eyes flickered over him one last time. After accepting help from Louise's family, she was pleased to be in a position to help someone less fortunate.

"I could fix you a plate, if you'll come to the house." She clasped her hands behind her back. Would he take charity from a señora?

He nodded. "Let me get this girl to the barn, and I'll be there directly." He turned south with the ewe following meekly behind.

As Weston approached the corral he heard the bleating of the lambs confused by the loss of their fluffy mammas. Suspiciously they sniffed the ewes, not believing that the lively animals bounding out of the barn, weightlessly celebrating the lifting of their burdens, belonged to them. He opened the gate to let the stray in, then provided Pandora with her long-awaited feed sack. At least she was happy to return.

Turning toward the house, he saw the

woman in the doorway, but she darted inside when he spotted her. Funny that she'd be embarrassed now. She didn't act ashamed before. If she was a *pastora* — a shepherdess — and accustomed to doing a man's job, wouldn't she know more about sheep? Besides, she sure wasn't dressed for sheep wrestling. Stepping into the shaded room, he watched her prepare a plate of cornbread and stew. It'd be cold, but Weston wasn't accustomed to pampering.

He took a seat at the table and hung his hat on a stave of the ladder-back chair. The lady slid the dish across the oak table to him.

He lifted his eyes from his plate to where she stood. "Are you going to stand there and watch me eat?"

She shrugged. "Until I think of something better to do."

Her answer amused him. No coquetry, no guise — just an honest, intriguing expression. Comfortable. She didn't seem anxious for him to leave, but she was giving him his space, too. Didn't make any demands. But something about her made him want to dig deep and find the man he used to be. He was home and determined to do it right this time.

"Do you mind if I say grace?" he asked.

She rewarded him with a genuine smile. "What's your name?"

"Rosa."

She obviously wasn't schooled in proper introductions, not that he was surprised. The memory of her lying in the grass with her arms and skirts around a ewe didn't lead him to expect much etiquette.

"Rosa." He tried it once for himself and then bowed his head. His fist clasped and unclasped on the table before he began, his voice a little rusty. "Heavenly Father, thank you for a safe journey and thank you for your patience and mercy." He paused, silently confessing how much he needed that mercy. "Lord, I pray your blessings for Rosa, and please bless this food and the hands that prepared it. Amen."

"Amen," she echoed.

Weston attacked the food with gusto, stealing glances at her as she tidied up from the noonday meal. The women must have gone straight to the barn after dinner. Having finished wiping the countertops, she moved to the table, working away from the occupied end of the bench.

He ought to be getting to the barn, but if he could have come up with a reason to stay in the kitchen, he might've. The lady darted around like a dragonfly, never landing

50

anywhere long but catching his eye with her brightly colored clothing, bracketed with patterns that mimicked the latticed wings of the creatures.

True, the colors might be a little dingy from her spill, but that wasn't all that captured his attention. The broad neck on her blouse exposed more skin than he was used to seeing before evening — and then only if the ladies were dressed for a social. As she scrubbed against a stubborn drip of beans, he noticed her delicate collarbone, which was exposed to the very point it met her curved shoulder. And the hollow at the base of her neck . . . really! How did Mexican men get anything done during the day if their womenfolk flitted around the kitchen dressed like that?

He pushed away from the table and carried his bowl to her, even more pleased that she hadn't been hurt handling his livestock.

She was a pretty girl, no doubt about it.

"Thank you, err . . . miss."

"Ma'am." She lifted her chin and straightened her back.

All right, he stood corrected. She was a pretty woman.

He grabbed his hat on his way to the barn and turned his mind to the task ahead.

■ ■ ■ ■

After she cleaned herself and the kitchen, Rosa waved Ida into the house to pass along a message to her mother. No sense in Aunt Mary worrying herself over supper. Rosa would make sure the hardworking crew had a hot meal waiting for them.

By the time the pungent aroma from the cook fire wafted through the yard, the day's work was completed. The girls ran through the house with more enthusiasm than the food merited.

"Uncle Weston is here! Uncle Weston is here!" Susannah grabbed the stack of plates while Ida hopped from one foot to the other.

"He is?" Rosa squeaked in an attempt to match their excitement.

She twisted her hair up off her damp neck and pinned it. Pulling a peach cobbler from the oven, she used her apron wadded in her hand for protection against the hot cast-iron skillet, careful not to graze the darting girls with the bubbling dish.

"I can't wait to meet him."

And that was true. Weston and his sister, Eliza, were the closest blood relatives left of Mack's — his first cousins. But even beyond that, she was curious to meet this man who, though younger than Uncle George and Aunt Mary, was spoken of with such respect.

"I declare, Rosa, what have you been cooking? I don't know when this kitchen has ever smelled so good!" Aunt Mary bustled in straight from the pump to dry her still-dripping hands on the kitchen towel. She leaned out the open window. "Yoo-hoo, George. Grab the tea canister, please. Susannah, did you get enough mugs? Help your father."

Fanning herself, Aunt Mary opened each of the wood-framed windows to let out more of the heat from the stove. Finding her efforts futile, she took four dishes off the table and carried them back to the counter.

"We'll let the young'uns have the kitchen tonight. It's hot as blazes in here, and there's no use in crowding around the table. I'm eatin' on the porch."

The men filed through the door, dragging more heat in with them. George had the sparkling glass jar of amber tea hugged snugly to his chest. Rosa's eyes widened at the stranger close behind him. Would Aunt Mary let the cowboy eat in the kitchen with the family? But he was listening intently as Samuel told him about his new six-shooter.

"Tomorrow I want to show you how fast I am on it already."

"Accuracy comes before speed. How's your aim?"

"Not bad. It's better when I slow down —"

George cleared his throat, interrupting Samuel's admission, and brought the room to order.

"Rosa, I'd like to introduce my nephew, Weston Garner."

If the cowboy hadn't stepped forward with hat in hand, she'd still be looking for the man she'd heard so much about.

"Mrs. Garner, it's a pleasure to make your acquaintance." He was more decorous than he'd been a few hours ago but just as handsome. "I apologize for my lack of manners earlier. I didn't realize you were kin."

Aunt Mary gave her a questioning look.

This was Weston Garner? No wonder he didn't get off his horse to rescue the hired help. Molly's words rang in her ears. Yes, he had kept his distance, and yet . . . But he was waiting for an answer.

"And I didn't realize you were Louise's nephew. I'd always pictured someone . . . groomed?"

"Rosa!" Aunt Mary covered her mouth.

"No, I didn't mean groomed," Rosa stammered. "Maybe that's the wrong word. I meant to say I didn't expect Weston Garner to have mangy hair." She tilted her head and studied him. "But it's only on the one side, so maybe it isn't that bad."

Rosa was unprepared for the hoots that erupted from Samuel and Tuck. Uncle George just about lost his hold on the tea canister. Mary laughed tears, and Weston donned his hat, pretending to hide his offending hair.

"Oh my, oh my." Aunt Mary choked as she caught her breath. She wiped her face with her apron as they came to their senses. "Honestly, Weston, what in the world happened to your hair?"

"Well, I was at a barber's in Round Rock when something came up. I had to skedaddle before he finished." He accepted the tin plate his aunt offered him.

"You've looked like that since Round Rock?" Aunt Mary asked.

"It wasn't that bad with my hat, but then I stopped for church, and of course I couldn't go in with my hat on . . . so I tried to trim it up with my knife. . . ."

Uncle George interrupted him with guffaws of laughter. "I don't think that improved matters."

"No, sir. It didn't." He pulled taut the

jagged locks and grimaced.

Enough time had passed that Rosa could breathe again. Hopefully they would forget that her rude comment had started the whole cacophony. She filled her plate last and followed Aunt Mary outside.

First impressions weren't her strong suit.

By the time the bats were swooping in the twilight, dinner had been greedily consumed, as only outdoor laborers can, Aunt Mary no exception. Rosa watched Weston stretch his long legs out along the edge of the porch, where he and Uncle George sat, and lean against the support beam with fingers laced behind his head.

He sighed.

"I haven't had cobbler like that for years. That wouldn't be Aunt Louise's recipe, would it?" He looked toward the ladies in the rocking chairs.

Rosa swept the crumbs from her worn skirt. "It is. It's the only dessert she's taught me, so far."

"Well, she's a good teacher."

Aunt Mary got out of her rocker and gathered the dirty dishes but wouldn't let Rosa follow.

"No, you sit down, young lady." Aunt Mary motioned through the window for her girls and handed the stack through the doorway. "Susannah and Ida will clean up. Are you going back to Palmetto tonight, Weston? I'm afraid we don't have any spare beds in the house."

"The barn's fine. Been sleeping outside for weeks now and don't mind it a bit. If y'all are going to start shearing at dawn, I don't relish a long ride home and back."

"Then, George, why don't you grab the lantern and come with me? I'd feel a heap better about Wes holing up in the haymow if we'd chase the spiders out first. I think some new ones moved in since you visited last." Her smile showed that she clearly enjoyed teasing her nephew.

Rosa watched the older couple take the lantern and swing it in wide arches through the dark yard. Uncle George was lucky to have a helpmate like Aunt Mary. In fact, they were all lucky to have each other. Their kinship consisted of layers and layers of affection and respect — like the corn husks wrapped around a tamale. How could Eli and Louise have ever left this place?

With a groan Weston leaned, reaching off the porch, and snagged a stick. When she looked again he was producing long curls of bark with a short knife.

"It was nice of you to lend them a hand

this week," he said.

She drummed her fingers against the arms of her rocker. Watching him whittle brought back bittersweet memories that she'd rather not examine. She cleared her throat. "I haven't been much help, I'm afraid. Aunt Mary offered to pay me, but I can't accept. It took me most of the morning to learn what I was doing, and this afternoon . . . well, you saw how successful I was."

What was he carving? Would he whittle the stick down to a small cross, bore a hole through it, and hang it on a leather thong? She shook her head. He wasn't Mack.

"Thank you," she said.

"For what?"

"For not telling them about the sheep accident. Samuel and Tuck would have it spread countywide by daybreak. I have enough trouble fitting in already."

He waved her thanks away with the bare stick. "You had the situation under control. Considering you just rolled into town and still have the taming of that homestead ahead of you, I can't believe you have time to do more. We appreciate the help."

"I'll take any paying work that comes my way. I don't know if we'll be able to live on our crops alone this year." Louise wouldn't think that was ladylike at all, discussing finances, but this man seemed to appreciate a sensible conversation.

Another chip, shorter and thicker, sprang from his blade. "Aunt Mary told me about the fix you're in. I wish I could promise that it'll be all right. I mean, you're family, and we take care of family. . . ." His voice dried up and cracked like the thirsty ground. He swallowed hard and finished. "At least we try."

He squirmed on the hard porch a moment, laid aside his whittling, and then became very still. As if gathering his courage he declared, "And we will try. Mrs. Garner, if you're looking for work, let me know. We'll figure out a way to keep you employed on Garner land. If you stay here, we'll make sure you aren't harassed, but a young lady like yourself could run into trouble elsewhere. Can you promise me that you won't work on another farm? It'd put my mind at ease."

She stopped rocking to study him again. He'd wasted no time establishing the boundaries in his territory, but to be fair, it was his territory. She was the newcomer. She'd judged him correctly from the first. He was no ordinary cowboy. He was a man who brought peace and order to his surroundings and possibly wrath on those who disturbed that peace. It was easy to see how he'd earned the respect of the community.

"Mr. Bradford asked me to embroider on some linens he sells at his store — pillowcases, tablecloths, and the like. He noticed the handwork on my blouse when we first arrived at the mercantile."

"Mr. Bradford is a fine Christian man. You won't have any trouble from him. I'm more concerned with your working with a group of cowboys."

"Then I appreciate the warning. I won't hire out anywhere else." Her rocker creaked as she resumed the movement. "Louise was right. You feel that the whole family is your responsibility."

Weston shook his head. She heard him bump against the post as he shifted his weight. "You've got the wrong idea. Aunt Mary told me all that you've done for your mother-in-law. How you left your father and mother and your homeland and came to live with people you didn't know. That was brave. What I'm doing is nothing compared to the risks you've taken."

"But still, I can see why people speak so highly of you." To her surprise, his expression couldn't have been more stunned if she'd slapped him.

He took a shaky breath. "Please don't

think too much of me. God knows I'm not that strong. I'm afraid your secondhand opinion won't hold up to first-hand knowledge."

A chill wind swept the porch, heralding a storm to come. Rosa watched as the stars dimmed on the horizon, obscured by an approaching herd of clouds. In the last glimmer of evening light, he looked uneasy. Why? Yet the uncertainty was real, and he didn't seem capable of false modesty. If he was confessing a weakness, she had no choice but to believe that he was involved in a struggle of great magnitude. A struggle she couldn't trivialize.

With his face turned toward the pasture, he sighed as the grass began to whip in the breeze. He didn't seem to notice the tall stalks bending double under the hand of the rising wind. Where was he? If she had to guess, she'd say it was a place he'd been often — a place full of memories and pain.

Weston might be wealthy and influential, but she still saw the wayward stranger that had stumbled across her path. She didn't think it was arrogance that kept him distant. It was fear.

Rosa desperately wanted to leave the rocking chair, wrap her arms around him, and hold him like she would any hurt child, but he wasn't a child, and he wasn't hers. She would ask God to comfort him and strengthen him to be the man she'd heard tell of. That was all she could do. But it was everything.

5

Why was this man so hard to track down? If Molly Lovelace had known she'd be traveling out to George and Mary Garner's today, she would have worn light muslin. Her fitted afternoon gown was already uncomfortable. Of course, riding shotgun in her father's lumber wagon wasn't exactly a luxury either.

Just another feat in the long series she'd performed to win a man who had her parents' approval. This man in particular. Finding a husband wasn't that difficult if a girl lowered her standards, but Mother and Father expected more. And if he had to be rich, he might as well be handsome.

She ran her finger under the high ruffled collar to keep it from rubbing as they pulled up to the house. Taking off work and catching a ride home hadn't been easy, but Weston hadn't seen her since he'd taken his herd up the trail, and she hated to deprive him any longer. He might forget how badly he needed her.

"Nice of you to call on Mrs. Mary." The driver let a stream of tobacco fly. "Y'all ain't exactly cut out of the same cloth."

"You're right. I'd much rather visit your family. How did the dress turn out for your wife?"

The man flashed her a toothless grin. "Right purty. That gown of yours makes her look like a young thing again. As purty as her wedding day."

Wedding day. Even the driver's wife had had one.

Molly stopped fiddling with her collar and mustered all the dignity a woman riding with two-by-twelves could find. The rumors better be right. If Weston wasn't here, she'd be spending a long morning alone with cantankerous Mary.

After the wagon rolled to a stop, she climbed out unaided and removed her bonnet. A quick touch to her topknot and the wisps of blond hair framing her face and she was ready for presentation. Now, where was he? Knowing Weston wouldn't be in the house, Molly turned to the barn, pleased to hear his voice. Although she couldn't make out specific words at first, she recognized the timbre, low and calm. He was murmuring, soothing the animals, no doubt.

"Mmm, good girl. That's how you do it. Don't be afraid to come a little closer."

One last touch to her hair, the production of the perfect smile, and she walked through the open barn doors on the newly swept floor. Sure enough, there he was.

Weston was kneeling, holding a sheep of some kind on its back, and on her knees with her forehead almost touching Weston's was that Mexican woman, Rosa.

Molly gasped. Weston glanced her way but quickly returned his focus to the shears Rosa wielded.

"That's right. The closer you can cut it the better. Whoa, girl, easy there. I've got you. Nothing to be afraid of."

Molly's arms dropped to her sides. Were the endearments meant for the woman or the sheep? She couldn't be sure. Both Rosa and the ewe trembled. Rosa continued to work the giant scissorlike tool with her face turned from Molly. One look at the outlandish getup and Molly knew it was Rosa, all right. No one else would wear those bright, loose clothes.

"I hope I'm not disturbing anything." Molly tried to sound sweet, but Rosa jumped at her voice, and the shears clattered to the floor.

"You weren't until now," the deep voice replied. Keeping his hold on the animal, Weston rose halfway and then settled down a little closer to Rosa. "Keep going. You're doing fine."

"I think I nicked her." Rosa wrung her shaking hands. Seeing Molly, she adjusted the wide collar of her blouse.

Oh, the floozy. Now she's worried about her gaping neckline?

Weston ignored Molly and drew Rosa's attention back to their task. "The ewe was startled and moved. It's not your fault. I'll hold her still so you can finish."

Picking up the shears, Rosa stretched as far as the tool would allow. Still, Molly thought she was closer to Weston than necessary. Suddenly, the beast sprang up, leaving its fleece on the floor, its naked hide an unappetizing gray.

The animal barreled toward her. Throwing her arms across her face, Molly shrieked and ran out of the doorway, only stopping when she bumped into the rain barrel.

"Are you all right?" Rosa came to her side immediately.

"Yes, thank you." Molly opened her eyes, disappointed there was no other savior inquiring after her safety. "I must have looked very foolish running from a sheep."

66

Rosa smiled. "You'd look even worse if you didn't. Believe me."

The rest of the day was excruciating. Having no inclination for shearing, Molly sat on a crate and watched Rosa and Weston at work. She braided Susannah's hair and then Ida's, played with the kittens, anything to pass the time, but her comments directed at the shearers only earned responses from Rosa.

Already determined she wouldn't leave the ranch without Rosa, Molly strained her eyes at the empty road and waited for the lumber wagon to appear on its way back to the mill. The sooner she got them separated the better. Weston's deep lullaby wrung her heart, and she wasn't nestled against him like Rosa managed to be. Giving an attempt with the shears crossed her mind, but it was impossible. Her gown was so tight she wouldn't be able to bend over without fainting.

Molly's mouth quirked. Fainting? Could that work?

"There you go," Weston said. "Oops, you missed a spot." He pinned the sheep with his knee. "Don't be afraid to scoot a little closer. You aren't going to hurt anything."

He meant scoot closer to the stupid animal! Molly wanted to shout, for Rosa misunderstood. She shifted until she was leaning over his lap to reach the difficult spot. Just as Molly located a pile of hay to faint into, she saw a look of horror cross Weston's face.

Wait. There was hope.

He jerked his hands off the ewe and fell back on his heels, leaning as far away from the woman as possible. The sheep scrambled up with her fleece dangling from her back.

"You let her go?" Rosa asked.

"Yes. No." Weston took the shears from Rosa and cornered the animal. With a few quick snips the fleece was removed, leaving a jagged tuft of wool along her spine.

"Do you want me to tidy that?" Rosa asked from the floor.

"No." Weston wiped his hands on his pant legs. He seemed to be searching the rafters for something. "Aren't you getting tired? Miss Lovelace has waited all day for a visit. Maybe you should entertain her."

Molly hopped off her crate. "I could see you home, Rosa. No need to wait for the wagon."

Weston gave her a look of gratitude that made the whole day worth it. Yes, there was hope.

Rosa hated to leave Aunt Mary's before they finished shearing, but Weston had paid her the full amount and sent her on her way. He'd insisted. Just as well. Working in close proximity to him had tried her nerves. She'd gotten so wrapped up in her task, she hadn't noticed how close she'd gotten to him until a whiff of peppermint reminded her. For a man who wanted to keep his distance, he sure looked good close up. To make matters worse, Molly and her eagle eyes hadn't missed a thing.

But Molly didn't seem to hold a grudge. She gaily chatted about everything and nothing as they strolled, leaving Rosa alone with her thoughts.

Rosa noticed the approaching buckboard first. The driver's features were mostly hidden by his large felt hat. He was dressed like the city men in San Antonio, not the local cowboys. She didn't recognize the woman at his side, either. With her chin down, her face was completely obscured by the long-slatted bonnet.

Molly stopped. "Oh, it's the Tillertons. Have you met them yet?"

Rosa shook her head.

"He's nice enough, but his wife is an odd bird. Not very friendly."

Mr. Tillerton saw the women and his blond moustache stretched with his lengthy smile. "Good day to you, Miss Lovelace."

He tipped his hat and looked cheerfully puzzled. "It's not often I encounter ladies on foot in this neck of the woods. Do you need assistance?"

"No, we're fine, but allow me to introduce Rosa Garner. Rosa, Jay and Anne Tillerton."

He tipped his hat, as was proper, but his eyes lingered overlong, which was not. Yet it was understandable considering the circumstances. Rosa certainly didn't look like a Garner.

His wife looked up just long enough for Rosa to make out a young face hidden in the shadows of her bonnet. No smile. No scowl. Just an accounting of her surroundings before she retreated to the sanctuary of her own company.

"Another Garner? From where do you hail, if I might ask?"

"From our place, the sixty acres just to the north of the crossing," Rosa replied.

His eyes darted behind them as if he could see the farm through the foliage. "Don't tell me you're my neighbors! You're the Garners that left for Mexico?"

Neighbors? She thought Mary's was the closest farm. "Yes, sir. I married Mack — Eli and Louise's son."

"Welcome home, welcome home. That place gives such an aura of family. It was an absolute shame to see it vacant, but now you've returned to fill it with love and laughter." The man rattled off the niceties effortlessly.

"I don't know about that." Molly shook her head and produced a perfect pout. "Eli died in Mexico, and so did Mack. Meanwhile, their renters here skipped town and stopped paying the taxes a couple of years ago. Now it's up to Louise and Rosa to come up with the back taxes before August."

Rosa's mouth dropped open. Did Molly have to tell him everything she knew?

"My goodness!" His hand covered his heart. "May I offer my sincere condolences and well wishes for your future. Please don't hesitate to ask for assistance. We're just over the fencerow. Now, if you'll excuse us, my wife has been under the weather lately. The doctor has prescribed rest, and that's what I intend to provide."

The young lady must have felt unwell indeed, for she did not respond in word or gesture, much to Rosa's disappointment. She dearly hoped Mrs. Tillerton's odd behavior was due to her illness. What good would a neighbor be if she wouldn't even acknowledge them?

"What did Dr. Trench diagnose?" Molly asked.

"Dr. Trench? Yes, you probably talk to Dr. Trench, don't you?" He picked up the reins again. The horses startled a bit at his touch. "Dr. Trench wasn't available, but we were advised that it could be contagious. She needs seclusion, but don't you fear, Mrs. Garner. You won't lack for companionship. Before the week is out, I'll come pay a visit. Anne's illness won't keep me quarantined." The man gave her a look she couldn't quite decipher, but it reminded her of the men who'd watched her unload the wagon.

With another tip of his hat he urged the horses forward, and the wagon disappeared down the shady decline toward the creek.

"Mr. Tillerton's a pleasant fellow. Like he said, you can call on him if you need something. You don't need to traipse all the way to George's or Weston's for help." Molly's smile brightened even more. "There's my wagon. I suppose you can cross the creek alone?"

Rosa nodded. "You really didn't need to walk with me."

"Nonsense, I'm happy to see you closer to home."

And Rosa believed her.

6

June 1878

"It is good to gather in the house of the Lord." Reverend Stoker greeted the congregation. "And to remember the Sabbath day, to keep it holy."

As if she could forget. Rosa counted off the Sundays on her fingers. All in May had passed. By evening one would be gone in June. She bit her lip. They hadn't wasted a single day, but their occasions for profitable work were growing scarce.

Rosa squirmed on the pew, trying to get comfortable sitting atop the tangle of padding and wires that made her black skirt bunch so oddly. She loved the Sabbath, but it reminded her that another chunk of days was lost, another week had slipped through their fingers, and the white crockery jar in the pantry had fewer coins in it than when she and Louise had started saving for the taxes.

She tried to focus on the reverend's words. His message about Elijah and the widow should've given her hope, but unlike Louise, who noted every word and even braved a tentative amen, Rosa didn't foresee a miracle in their future. They'd sheared sheep, were raising chicks, and had planted crops — they'd had a busy month and would need to be busier still if they wished to be profitable. She had linens waiting for her to embroider and sell at Mr. Bradford's store, but preparing the thread was taking longer than she'd expected, especially when Louise had insisted she sew "a suitable mourning gown" for herself. Why worry about propriety when they could soon be homeless? The service concluded with Rosa feeling exhausted. Time to get back to work until the next Sabbath forced her to slow down and contemplate the deadline rolling toward them.

"What's wrong?" Louise asked.

Rosa ducked her head. Everyone else left church refreshed, or so they said. When would she experience the peace she'd heard about?

"It's just this bustle. The person who invented it must hate women."

Louise took the misdirection like an iguana after a chick. "Ten years ago they were round. I'll have to learn to take smaller steps. Our skirts were never this tight in the front!" She looked at Rosa again. "Still my little Rosa, but more foreign than ever in your widow's weeds. However, the dress becomes you. I know the black isn't to your liking, but it brings out the sheen in your hair. It makes you look older, too. I wouldn't say that to just anyone, but it doesn't hurt for you to appear more mature. People look at me askance when I tell them that you were Mack's wife."

Rosa dropped her gaze. Her age wasn't causing the scandal. Although she'd seen several Mexicans about town, she'd seen none in church. No wonder. They probably didn't feel comfortable there. Most of the ladies were polite, but the few who weren't were hard to ignore.

At least with Aunt Mary around, Rosa didn't worry about cruel comments. No one wanted to cross Mary Garner.

"Rosa, dear, your dress looks mighty fine on you," Mary said, coming beside her, along with some other women. "I don't cotton to the black, but you do what you gotta do."

"It's beautiful." Adele Lovelace smiled warmly.

"And proper." Clara Cantrell sniffed, her

75

eyes barely skimming over Rosa. "I've worn this same dress since Lee's surrender, but I'll do my duty. Nothing's more unbecoming than a lady failing to pay her respects to her dearly departed."

Louise shuddered. "Rosa's respectful. You can count on that."

Rosa twisted one of the black ribbons on her bodice. If only respectability was as easy as changing the color of your clothing. Habits and attitudes weren't altered so effortlessly.

The ladies ushered Rosa to the back door, each describing the dish they'd brought to the potluck about to commence.

Aunt Mary stopped in her tracks. "We forgot the tablecloths."

"I'll get them," Rosa volunteered. All Louise and she were contributing was one sack of tortillas. She didn't want to walk outside empty-handed.

"They're in the closet under the steeple," Clara offered as they headed out the back to the grounds.

Rosa wormed her way through gatherings of curious lollygaggers to get to the small door to the right of the entryway. The musty smell and dim light stopped her in her tracks. Could she go in there? She looked around the sanctuary. Everyone she knew had already gone outside. Everyone except Weston.

He saw her immediately. Excusing himself, he left a knot of men and crossed the sanctuary to reach her.

"You look lost."

She gripped the doorframe with one hand. "Either I'm lost or the tablecloths are, and we need to find each other."

He nodded but didn't proceed. Rosa realized she was blocking the way. With a deep breath, she entered the small room and moved to the rickety staircase as he ducked through the doorway. The only light that entered the room was from the circular stained-glass window above them in the steeple.

Rosa needed every ounce of determination to keep from running out the door. Memories of being pinned to a dirt floor by a wooden beam overwhelmed her. Rosa didn't remember the earthquake that had flattened her home, but many times she'd relived the vivid panic of her world tumbling down around her — a feeling that the mine cave-in only intensified.

Searching for tablecloths was more than she could manage. There really wasn't room for them both to move without being crowded. Weston took up the empty space between the shelving. Rosa watched the colored diamonds from the window skim across his back. She wouldn't think about the tight walls, or that the only way out of the room was blocked. Instead, she named each of the colors in English, then Spanish, then Nahuatl. Red, *rojo, chilti.* Blue, *azul, asolti.*

"There must be a leak. Smell that mold?" He dug through a wardrobe of linens. "Smells like a cave."

A cave? Rosa found herself backing up the staircase. She needed air. Perhaps the little window would push open. If she could pop her head out . . .

"Hold on there. Where are you going?"

He must think she was crazy. She *was* crazy. Why couldn't she just stand still?

She gripped the railing with both hands, wishing her voice wasn't so shaky. "I don't like caves."

Understanding lit his face. He closed the door of the wardrobe, making more room for her. "No, ma'am. I don't suppose you do." He offered her his hand. "You don't need to be in here. You could wait —"

He straightened suddenly. Weston looked over his shoulder to the door, then back at her, eyes murderous.

She stopped breathing. What was wrong?

Then she heard the women's voices.

"It takes a lot of nerve to flaunt your brown daughter-in-law at church, the way Louise did today."

"I couldn't agree more. She's not even a *Tejano*. She's straight from the mountains of Mexico."

Weston made a move for the doorway. Before she could think, Rosa grabbed his arm with both hands and pulled him back. Silently she shook her head, her eyes never leaving his. If he went out there, they would hate her for life. He couldn't embarrass them on her behalf.

"And did you hear about the scene she made in Lockhart? From what I hear, she put on quite the show for some of the men."

A sob of protest rose in her throat, but she swallowed it down. Rosa released his arm and stumbled backwards, trying to get away from the hurtful words, but there was no room. Nowhere to go.

"For crying aloud," he muttered. He held his hands out to her, and then clenched them closed. Rosa understood. There was nothing he could do.

". . . prancing around in that wagon like it was a stage. And did you hear about her clothes?"

Rosa sat on the step and buried her face

79

in her hands. It was hard enough to hear them, but Weston heard them, too. What must he think of her?

He took a step toward her and stood at her side. The tension emanating from the man was palpable. He didn't move, but Rosa could feel his frustration.

"Harold saw her in Lockhart. He said she was wearing some native costume. Her skirts didn't even reach her ankles."

Rosa felt his hand on the top of her head. It wasn't a caress. More of a blessing, an anointing of peace. She leaned her face against the balustrade and wished for more. She wanted to be held. She had traveled so far and endured so much. She was adrift, with no anchor, no harbor. She wanted to be cared for. Protected.

But she understood his reluctance. If her reputation wasn't already soiled, getting caught in a dark closet in his arms would ruin it forever. He was protecting her, after all.

The murmuring stopped. Rosa heard their footsteps going away, but neither she nor Weston moved. Finally it was silent. He went to the door.

"Are they still here?" Rosa whispered.

"I think everyone's gone." Weston stood before her. "Are you going to be all right?"

She got up and went to the doorway. "I need to explain —"

"You don't need to explain anything."

"But at Lockhart . . ."

He raised his hand. "Let's make an agreement. You don't believe what people say about me, and I won't believe what people say about you."

Rosa's mouth dropped open. So he knew?

He grimaced. "That's what I thought. You've been here only a few weeks, and you've already heard my story. Well, most of it's true, no doubt, but I'd like a chance to make my own poor impression. I don't need anyone's help." He stepped out of the room into the light. "Besides, moving a wagonload doesn't sound nearly as scandalous as wrestling sheep. Those women will have to come up with a better story if they want to change my opinion of you."

"Thank you." She smoothed her hair, remembering his touch. "Thank you for staying with me."

"You're family." And he didn't offer any more explanation. "Now, I didn't see any tablecloths. You?"

"No."

"Then let's move on." Weston stepped aside to let Rosa precede him. Out of the church and through the crowd she went,

81

trying to school her face into more peaceful lines. Finally she located Louise.

"We couldn't find any tablecloths." Rosa couldn't help but search the unfamiliar faces and wonder who was spreading tales about her.

"We?" Louise looked behind her.

Rosa spun around, but Weston wasn't nearby. He was at the hitching post, preparing his horse for departure.

"You aren't staying for the potluck?" Jay Tillerton leaned against the hitching post and fiddled with his watch fob.

Weston let his actions answer for him. He wasn't in the mood for small talk with Tillerton, but there was one thing he'd like to set straight.

"How's your wife?"

Tillerton yawned and dropped his watch into his vest pocket. "Her health is superb. Now as to her spiritual condition, I have my concerns. If you'd be so kind as to pray —"

Weston cut him off. He had no use for the manure Tillerton was spreading. Something stunk.

"Did she take a trip recently? Seems like I might have run into her at Round Rock."

The man's nostrils flared. "You must be mistaken. My wife eschews crowds. They make her extremely nervous."

Weston didn't move. He didn't blink. He couldn't thrash old church hens, but by George, this man was fair game.

"I'm sorry to hear that. Perhaps my sister and I could visit? We could bring the reverend if you think it'd do some good."

Tillerton forced a smile. "That's a generous offer. I'll be sure and mention it to her, but don't be disappointed if she declines. You know how temperamental women can be."

"Then maybe we'll swing by unannounced. A surprise visit might suit her better."

Sensing his safety hung by a thread, Tillerton stepped back and raised his hands in surrender. "Do what you must. You're welcome anytime. If you'll excuse me . . ." He sulked to the protection of witnesses.

Weston untied his leather reins from the post and led Pandora away from the other mounts. He couldn't stay there. He needed to simmer down.

Since when had Tillerton started attending church, anyway? He swung up on the horse's back, knowing how wrong his attitude was but not caring enough to change it.

Change was hard. You give God an inch,

and He takes a mile. You talk to a man, and next thing you know you're chewing on his lies. You look for tablecloths, and you're trapped with a woman in a closet.

Weston gritted his teeth and tried to release some of the frustration he felt over the little señora. Nothing got under his skin like feeling helpless. Nothing rankled like watching somebody suffer, but what could he have done? Rosa didn't want him to interrupt the women — and he understood why. In the long run, it'd be harder on her. And Weston couldn't have walked out with Rosa. If those gossips saw them exit a darkened closet together, then what would they say?

He took a deep breath.

All sorts of scandalous things. They might accuse him of luring her inside. Of wanting to hold her. Of daydreaming about how she would fit in his arms, how she would feel pressed against his chest.

He broke out of town and spurred Pandora for speed. He'd have to be more careful. He couldn't stumble into those situations if he was resolved to stay single. He couldn't subject another woman to the pain he'd inflicted on Cora.

Nothing he could do for her, but Mrs. Tillerton, that was another story. Perhaps he'd go ahead and make that call before her no-account husband had time to interfere.

"Would you like to serve the beans? Just a scoop each, half a scoop for the young ones, and be careful with the handles. That just came off the cook fire."

Rosa nodded to Aunt Mary, eager to make herself useful. She needed to do something besides guessing who'd condemned her. She wanted the newness to end. She wanted to be treated the same as all the other residents of Prairie Lea.

She had to admit, the ladies hid their feelings to her face. The women came by to meet the Mexican daughter-in-law of their friend, to present a slight dip of the head and a word of condolence, which left her uncertain who was being snake-faced. Several even took the time to share a memory of Mack — whether it was his spelling-bee performance, a rodeo trick he'd learned, or a kind word he'd shared.

Easy to remember the good. Rosa had adored Mack from the first day he'd ridden the shaggy burro into Ciauhtlaz, and she'd hoped he would someday care for her, right up until the end.

Seconds before the end.

Was it really love? Surely, for how could it

hurt so much otherwise? But widows were allowed to relish the sweet memories and toss the pits on the burn pile. No one would guess that the lone pit from their brief marriage would burn her night and day.

She swirled the beans and watched the steam rise. There were too many concerns for today to dig through yesterday's waste. These women, for example — Rosa wanted to believe they were sincere, but it was impossible to discern who wasn't. She sighed. Maybe over time they'd give her another chance. If she could be "respectable," like Louise insisted, they'd forget the wagon incident sooner or later. That is, if Weston didn't tell them about her wrestling the ewe. Or about the two of them hiding in the closet together.

The ladle clanged against the pot. Poor Louise. Rosa was sure she would disappoint her.

The church lawn blurred and was replaced by scenes of a fifteen-year-old *señorita,* the toast of the village, celebrating her *quinceañera.* She heard again the hearty cheers that erupted from the townspeople as she left her doll at the altar, symbolizing the transition from childhood to young womanhood. Then her father led her in the promenade around the square — his cherished daughter. Adored by her mother.

And in a few years she was forgotten.

Louise, Louise's family, and Louise's God represented her only salvation. They hadn't forgotten her. Not yet. But if the family that gave her birth and the town that celebrated her could cast her out, how precarious was her position here as a penniless stranger? She didn't want to know.

She wouldn't leech off another's labor. The spoiled darling of the mountains would work from first light to full darkness to earn her bread. No time to play her flute, no time to dance, because no one could pay the price for her.

She dipped beans onto the waiting plates. Music and dancing weren't necessities. A home was.

Just a few more weeks of uncertainty. If they could pay their taxes, they'd have a measure of security. Until then, she'd serve these people in any way she could in the hope that they would appreciate her enough to let her stay.

Among the strange faces in her line appeared one familiar, Deacon Bradford, the store owner and Louise's old friend.

"Looks like you made good use of that black fabric." Mr. Bradford held his plate away from his melon-shaped belly.

"I can't wait to start on the linens."

"Already? I'm surprised you're ready for that job."

She folded back a sleeve to keep it from the messy edge of the kettle. Ready or not, they needed the money. "The wool is spun. I still have to dye it."

"That sounds fine, but there's no hurry. Don't feel rushed." He picked up a yeast roll. "It's a great comfort to your mother-in-law having you by her side. That Louise, she's always inspired fierce loyalty in those who love her."

"What?" Yes, Rosa loved her mother-in-law, but —

"Nothing." He dropped the roll back in the basket. "I do need to find her, though. There's a shipment at the store that will interest her."

Rosa watched the oddly behaved store-keeper hurry away. Was every man in this town addled? She started to push her hair behind her ear but couldn't with her sticky hands. Thinking that no one was looking, she stuck a finger in her mouth and cleaned it of the sweet sauce.

"Taste good?"

Rosa didn't place the man immediately, but then she remembered the walk with Molly.

"Mr. Tillerton, I should have expected you here. It seems everyone I've met in Prairie Lea attends." Goodness, but his eyelashes were pale. They almost made his eyes look watery.

"I'm pleased I didn't disappoint you. To be honest, this is my first Sunday here. Fie on me." He laughed, not the least bit ashamed. "I know what you're thinking, but who wants to listen to people tell them what to do all the time?"

"I guess I can understand," she allowed. "Learning how to behave here has been a challenge. I'm constantly embarrassing my mother-in-law."

"You, my fair lady? An embarrassment? How so?"

"If I told you, then I'd be breaking a rule, no? Some subjects are not discussed between men and women. Ask Louise." She took the ladle and stirred the beans again, wishing that he'd never started this conversation.

Mr. Tillerton stroked his moustache. "Very wise, but what do you do if a man is so ill bred as to speak of improper subjects?"

Rosa understood this part of her instructions. Propriety had a lot of gray areas. Punishment did not. "If I can ignore the comment, that's best, but if the man talks to me directly, I must slap his face, or he won't think I'm a lady."

Mr. Tillerton's eyebrows went up, as if this was new information to him. "I see. That's good advice, but I have a question." He leaned across the pot. "If a woman confesses that she's been insulted, won't people assume she encouraged the man? Isn't she somewhat to blame for the recklessness?"

"No. How could she —"

"But she'll be judged, regardless. The truth might seem unpleasant, but you'll learn the rules. If you need to slap a man, then go ahead, but never ever tell someone you were compromised, or you'll never be considered respectable again."

Rosa narrowed her eyes. "I don't believe you."

"Men stare at a woman, and no one blames them. The woman is at fault, even if all she was doing was shifting a wagonload, right?"

She faltered and stirred the beans again. He was right. Why hadn't the women been mad at their husbands for standing in an alley watching her? Why hadn't Louise scolded the men instead of her? While it didn't seem fair, it did sound accurate.

Holding his half empty plate out to her, Mr. Tillerton motioned to the beans. She slopped a mess where he indicated. "I just want to protect you from disgracing yourself. It's only a kind of game we play, to be honest." He grinned. "A pinch here, a kiss there. There's no harm done, unless someone protests publically. That's being a poor sport."

"I don't see how —" she started, but he only laughed at her and walked away.

Rosa watched his lanky form, disturbed by the rules as he interpreted them. Louise hadn't explained the situation as clearly, but Rosa had noticed that no matter the situation, it was the woman in the wrong. A lady shouldn't swear. A lady shouldn't draw attention to herself. A lady shouldn't show her ankles, or too much of her neck. Women couldn't even feed their babies if there was a man around.

And the men? They got away with murder.

7

From where he sat atop Pandora, Weston's
nose filled with the soot still bellowing out
of the smokestack. His brother-in-law, Jake
England, had left him to keep an eye on the
buggy while he fetched Eliza and her trunk
from the train. Whatever he could do to
help. Slowly but surely he was getting
involved again.

Take the Tillertons, for example. He'd
gone directly after church to check on Mrs.
Tillerton, and the tales were true — she
wasn't the least bit friendly.

She didn't seem hurt, either. At the first,
when he'd heard the gunshots, all sorts of
terrible suspicions assailed him, but then he
saw her striding across her field, arms full
of quail, and he could only reckon nothing
was amiss. Decent shot, if nothing else.
'Course, she was a bit jumpy. When she saw
him she dropped the birds, and before he
could blink he'd found himself in the sights

of her shotgun. Not a lot of conversation to be had looking up the business end of a double barrel, which was what she evidently preferred.

She was younger than he'd imagined and curt, but her terse greeting had relieved his suspicions. Whatever crimes he'd blamed Tillerton for hadn't occurred. Maybe they hadn't been in Round Rock. Or maybe the barber was right — Tillerton had exaggerated.

Oh, that all his concerns were so easily dismissed. He strained for a glance of his sister. He owed Eliza much more than a train-station greeting and luggage toting.

Although motherless since a typhoid outbreak when she was a child and orphaned in adolescence, Eliza had worked with him to maneuver the estate through the perils of war, reconstruction, and the depression that followed until it was again harbored in the safe bay of prosperity. When they were young, Weston could do no wrong in his adoring sister's eyes, and how she saw him was how he viewed himself — infallible. As she matured, Eliza became the person most likely to hold him accountable when he strayed and the most likely to influence him for the good.

How hard the last few years must have

been for her. Not only did Eliza suffer the loss of her best friend, she'd also endured Wes's detachment. Yep, he'd pretty much been poor company since his wife, Cora, had died, but now he wanted to make amends.

He flicked a horsefly off his pant leg. Eliza didn't seem to hold a grudge. Her sanity had been preserved by the arrival of a smart-mouthed cowhand named Jake, a powder keg of optimism ready to blow away any darkness that threatened their happiness. He was as essential to Eliza's well-being as the cheering sunshine and the inspiring poetry she enjoyed, and Wes was grateful to him.

At breakfast that morning over sausage and eggs Jake had reminded Wes that they were going to Luling to meet Eliza at the train station. As if he could forget! The day he'd been dreading — dreading and anticipating — but he needed to be there. Hiding was getting him nowhere.

Through Eliza, he'd returned Cora's mementos and heirlooms to St. Louis. Small comfort for her parents when they'd lost their daughter. Did they know how he'd grieved — was still grieving? Would they acknowledge his penance or require more?

Weston watched as the passengers took

their first shaky steps off the train. Some flew into the arms of loved ones. Others strode away, business waiting elsewhere. Finally Eliza appeared in the opening. She paused at the bottom step, waiting for Jake to reach her and offer his hand.

Even from his position off the platform, Weston could tell she looked tired. Her burgundy gown was crumpled, and the smile she had for her husband couldn't disguise the weariness lurking around her eyes.

He had to smile at their embrace. Like him, his sister had inherited their father's height. Even in her stockinged feet she stood eye to eye with her husband. With her boots on, they made quite the pair.

Eliza spotted Weston in the crowd and strolled over, arm laced through Jake's. Weston swung out of the saddle to receive her welcoming hug and peck on the cheek.

"Well, get a look at you." She stood back, hands on her hips. "Jake says you've been on the trail, driving cattle like one of the boys."

"Tattletale."

Jake waved him away. "Forget Wes. You have some explaining to do. Something's different." He stepped back and held her at arm's length. "Did you have a growth spurt or something? Take a new tonic?"

Before Weston could figure out what he was talking about, Eliza hushed him. "Jake England! Keep your thoughts to yourself, please. I'll tell you about it when we get home."

"Tell me what?" He dropped her arm and fixed her with a penetrating stare. "Don't make me wait. I ain't a patient man."

"Let's go, Jake." She picked up her satchel and held it out to Weston, who dutifully placed it in the buggy, but Jake didn't move. He perused her slowly with a more critical eye.

"Good gravy!" she exclaimed. "You aren't going to be satisfied until you publicly embarrass me, are you?"

Jake pushed his hat back for a better view. "Come to think of it, you're looking a little thicker all around. Now, either you found some grub that you really cottoned to, or . . ." He finally met her eyes.

"Or?"

Jake squinted. "You ain't joshin' me, are you?"

Weston choked on air and started coughing. He'd expected news when Eliza returned, but not of this nature. Sometimes it was good to be wrong.

"I might be teasing. You'll just have to wait

96

until September to see if I'm telling the truth or not."

"September?" Jake counted back on his fingers as a silly grin spread across his face. "You were with me in December, right?"

Grimacing at Jake's rowdy "yee-haws," Weston made his way to the growing pile of luggage to give them all the privacy available at a train station — privacy that Jake didn't need, obviously. Weston hoisted the trunk onto his shoulder. It was their mother's old trunk, the brass studs aged and rubbed shiny once again.

How he wished his parents could have lived to see their first grandchild. It was hard to believe this baby would never know Davy and Dorothea Garner. Now he'd be playing the role of both uncle and grandparents. Of course, Mary and George would do their part, too.

By the time Weston had the buggy loaded, he had already decided what type of pony the child would ride.

As they reached the road home, the dread he'd been carrying returned. Eliza's joyful news wouldn't spare him from the painful memories her trip would dredge up. He was ready to get it over with, but Eliza hadn't broached the subject. She was still filling her husband in on the news of their new young'un.

"I feel strong for the most part. My stomach gets sour if I don't eat enough — or if I eat too much — or if I smell something foul — but I feel healthy in between times." She shrugged. "I've found the best thing to do is to keep food nearby."

"You knew before you left, didn't you?" Jake accused.

"I hid it as long as I could, but you were bound to figure it out sooner or later."

"And then I wouldn't let you go?"

"Would you?"

"We better change the subject," Jake huffed, "before I get riled. So the trip wasn't too hard?"

Eliza paused, her forehead creased. "It was tiring physically, but I have a fondness for St. Louis. After spending two years at the Academy, I have many memories there. I enjoyed visiting my former classmates and had an extended stay with Aunt Clarice, who I understand sings as well as Mother did." She looked at Weston. "I wish you'd been there to tell me if it was so."

Weston lifted his chin. He wasn't proud of his decision to send her alone, but it was too late to change it now. "Sisters often favor each other."

Eliza strummed her fingers on Jake's leg.

"Well, you're not going to rest easy until I tell you about Cora's parents, so let's take the bitter pill first. Seeing them was more painful than I'd expected. They're still torn up over her death. Naturally they would be. I can't imagine how they must feel. . . ." She instinctively covered her child, as if to protect it from the dangers of the world. "They weren't prepared to see me."

Weston looked straight ahead, bracing himself for what was to come. Did they rail at him, curse him, threaten him? He'd entertained all those scenarios over the weeks she'd been gone but knew they couldn't blame him any more than he blamed himself.

"In a way, they didn't act as I anticipated. When I got there, Mrs. Smock greeted me warmly, just as she used to when Cora and I were at the academy. We visited about my journey, took tea. Mr. Smock was there also, but I could tell they were troubled. They didn't know what to say. When I handed Mrs. Smock the valise, she began to weep, and Mr. Smock thanked me for coming all that way." Eliza dared a glance at her brother.

"Go on," Weston said.

"Then the conversation grew very puzzling. I don't think they meant to be hurtful, I really don't. They just had questions. And you can't blame them. They must have agonized all this time, wondering but afraid to ask."

Eliza looked to Jake. He nodded, and she continued.

"They wanted to know her state of mind, naturally. I assured them you'd done everything you could. You'd consulted a doctor, a parson. You'd tried medicine and prayer. I thought it important for them to know that Cora wasn't alone in her struggle."

Weston shifted in the saddle. "And?"

"I'm sorry, Wes. I wish it were otherwise. I wish . . . I wish I didn't have to tell you. . . . They asked about you, if you'd been cruel or unfaithful, if you'd started drinking." Eliza blinked up at him. "And then they asked if you had any reason to want her dead."

Weston closed his eyes, one hand gripping the saddle horn. He wanted to put the spurs to his horse and race to the horizon. He wanted to run to a land where no one knew his awful tragedy, but he'd already tried that, both figuratively and literally, and it had brought him no peace. He was staying to see this through. God had placed him there. Until He told him to leave, he would stand his ground. Eliza had spent the last three months setting things right so that he could heal. He would hear her out.

He looked at her worried face, already filling out because of the new life she carried. She'd done this for him.

"Please don't despise them, Wes. If you could've seen them . . . They didn't want to ask, but they needed a resolution. My answers satisfied them, relieved them even. They never wanted to think poorly of you."

He swallowed hard. "I'm not guilty of what they accuse me of, but I'm responsible nonetheless."

"And that's the problem," she said. "They told me about your letters. You placed all the blame on your shoulders. What were they supposed to think? It's no wonder they've had suspicions. You've acted like her blood was on your hands. Why would you tell them that, Wes? You don't really believe it, do you?"

Weston removed his hat and ran a hand through his hair. Would Eliza and Jake despise him for his weakness? He had never let them see behind his mask before. During Cora's sickness he took care of every detail. He supervised her meals, threw brave soirees to entertain her, even when she showed no interest, planned daily outings — all the while refusing to show anyone, even Eliza, how worried he was. He'd kept up that act until the day he stoically chose the songs for Cora's funeral, and from then on the mask of indifference never slipped. Only to Cora's parents did he share his fears over his culpability.

"I guess I do. She relied on me, and I let her down. I'd hoped her folks might offer me forgiveness."

"You don't need forgiveness for her death, but you might for the way you've been carrying on since then. Just think of Mr. and Mrs. Smock. How were they supposed to heal, thinking they'd allowed their daughter to marry a beast?" She fanned herself with her handkerchief. "At least they know the truth now. As far as I can tell, they were relieved to hear that you might be suffering from misplaced guilt. It's just like my brother to think he's omnipotent — capable of controlling every emotion and action of those around him."

No, Weston wasn't all powerful, but he knew who was. Where had He been? Was he even allowed to ask that question?

He rode in silence as Jake and Eliza's little buggy jostled across the prairie and through the sloughs that threatened to mire it down.

Jake grunted to his wife. "You did all you could for her folks. Sounds like it ain't your

102

problem no more."

"It never was Eliza's problem, Jake. It was mine. I've been so consumed with my own grief that I haven't stopped to think how my behavior has affected everyone else. I thought my misery was accomplishing something."

About time he was honest with them, and with himself.

"I still don't know . . ." he continued, "I still don't know how this all works out, but I'm going to try. I've been miserable, and I've done my best to make y'all miserable, too. I'm sorry, Eliza."

She waved the apology away and folded the delicate handkerchief. "I know this isn't easy for you."

"No, but you were right to force my hand. It hurts. I hurt, but I can't keep pretending that nothing matters. It's just . . . I'd hoped it would get easier."

"We're here for you, partner. We'll always be here, and things will change. You won't always feel like this," Jake said.

Eliza's smile shone bright through her unshed tears. "And don't be afraid of change. Changes are coming."

8

Rosa couldn't make the chickens lay eggs, and she couldn't make the crops grow faster, but she could sew.

Carded, spun, and dyed — the wool was finally ready. She lovingly caressed the skeins of thread as she pulled a chair to the front porch, took one of Mr. Bradford's crisp, clean pillowcases in hand, and got to work. Rosa didn't pause to measure or consider placement; she'd had long enough to plot this design.

A string of hibiscus blooms connected by a lively green vine and, hovering above it, a violet-crowned hummingbird — that's what she would embroider. She'd noted the colors on a silk parasol of Molly's, and when she saw the same shade of rojo worn by Mrs. Lovelace at church, she knew what color the hibiscus would be. Singing as she went, she fashioned a melody of which she hoped her hummingbird would approve.

Louise stepped from around the side of the house holding a shovel.

Rosa paused. "Are we planting more?" She hopped to her feet and laid aside the pillowcase. "Good. I don't think we have enough —"

"No, we're not planting more. We're out of seed." Louise jabbed the sharp end of the shovel into the soil. "I wish I knew how much our crops will bring. We probably won't know until the day arrives."

"Until then, we'll do all we can," Rosa said.

"And pray it's enough. You get started on those linens. I'm going to the cellar to see what needs killing in there. From the way the wind whipped up, we might need it tonight."

"Cellar? The hole in the ground?" Rosa shuddered as she sat. Putting dirt above your head before you were ready to stop breathing was tempting fate. "Do you need help?"

"No, honey. I know how you hate being crowded. You do your fancywork. We want something to take to Deacon next week." Louise rolled up her sleeves and stomped resolutely away to face whatever critters were denned up at the bottom of the stone steps.

Why did they want to go below ground? You couldn't drown or get buried standing above soil. But Louise had forecasted the weather correctly. That morning had been hot — unusually hot with a stifling wind from the south, but now, although the cool breeze was welcome, it was relentlessly charging from the north, capable of carrying off any loose thread Rosa left outside her basket. The western sky was full of towering clouds that looked like the piles of fleeces she'd bundled at Uncle George's, and they were sailing closer and closer to their homestead.

Also sailing closer was a carriage with two occupants. Rosa strained to see who they were. Only family or neighbors rolled down their road, so a passerby always meant a visit of some sort. As they turned their matched bays up the drive, Nicholas Lovelace stood and waved his hat. "Hello, the house," he cheered while his sister jerked on his coat-tail to pull him down.

They squabbled all the way to the porch. "You must excuse my brother." Molly held on to her hat until they rolled to a stop. "When he leaves town, he quite forgets his manners."

"Oh, it's just Rosa. As if she knows any-thing about manners," Nicholas drawled.

"That's no excuse for you to be a Philistine. Really. What would Mother say?"

Rosa shrugged prettily while Nicholas stuck out his tongue. She laughed. Although a man full-grown, he was as playful as a child.

"Won't you come in?" she offered.

"No, we mustn't interrupt your work." Molly tilted her head and inspected Rosa's clothes. "No mourning gown on today? I heard you were stunning in black."

"Where did you hear that?"

"Don't look at me." Nicholas set the brake and flinched at an ominous clap of thunder. "I was shocked to see you decked out like a widow."

"But I am a widow, and I have a nice dress, thanks to your sister. We sized Molly's pattern down until it worked perfectly."

Molly sat a little straighter and seemed to suck in her stomach.

"I'm glad you could get it small enough to fit you, Rosa." Her bottom lip jutted, but then with a shake of her head, her good humor returned. "Is Mrs. Garner here? The other Mrs. Garner, I mean. I declare, we have no shortage of Mrs. Garners around here, do we? Louise, Rosa, Mary —"

"But there's always room for one more, right sis?"

107

Molly dimpled. "We really can't stay long, so please make our excuses to Louise. I also need to apologize to you. I'm afraid I wasn't at my best during the sheep shearing, but I wanted you to know I'm delighted to have another young lady in the vicinity. I think we should make every effort to become the best of friends."

"Thank you for coming." Rosa clasped her hands behind her back. Was Molly sincere? She *had* expended a healthy effort to ride so far with a storm approaching. Maybe the girl liked her after all.

"Nick, let's go. The storm's going to catch us if we don't hurry."

Nicholas crossed his arms. "Then let's go home. We won't outrun this storm if we ride out to Palmetto. They aren't expecting us anyhow." He rolled his eyes at Molly's cold stare. "Stop looking at me like that. I swear, you could shrivel a grape into a raisin."

"But that was the whole point of coming out today. If we turn around now, all we'll accomplish is ruining my new gown in a downpour."

With effort Nicholas released the brake. "Got to get to Weston's before the humidity frizzes her hair." He winked at Rosa. "Too bad we can't stay here. It's a sight more comfortable lounging in your parlor than sitting all straight-backed at Weston's. I'd send Molly on alone, but escorting her about the countryside is my only excuse to not work at the mill today. Good deal for me."

"Come back anytime." Rosa couldn't help but like the thickset man. He was steady, the same every time she talked to him. He didn't pull her close one minute and run away the next. Not that she was judging anyone, but it was a comfort to know where you stood.

So they were going to Weston's? Rosa waved good-bye to the young man and the fair-haired buxom lady on the front bench of the wagon, her yellow leather boots peeking out from under the skirts blown by the wind.

Had Weston's first wife looked like Molly? If so, they would've made a striking pair — the kind of match that makes people anxious to see their offspring. One could pick them out of a crowd as belonging to each other.

Rosa looked nothing like Molly Lovelace.

Rosa was dark and lean. Her body was petite and lacked the roundness of Molly's figure. Like as not, her straight black hair could be found pulled back in a knot at the nape of her neck. Molly's hair was braided, curled, teased and tortured into performing all manners of amazing feats. She put a hand to her face. Would anyone here think her pretty?

Yet, perhaps she was better off than Molly. At least she didn't have false expectations. Rosa pitied the girl. Unless there was an understanding already in place, her chances of becoming a Mrs. Garner didn't look promising.

How easy for a woman to pin her hopes on a friendly smile, an expression of concern, or a shared moment. Rosa thought of Mack and how he'd always teased her as he whittled on a pendant. He was making it for his sweetheart, he'd said, and winked. How big should it be? Should he carve his initials in it, a heart, a rose? Oh, the hours she'd pondered those questions and their significance.

Rosa gathered her embroidery before the rain began to fall. If only she could warn Molly without being accused of having ulterior motives. Rosa could tell her what it was like to be married without love. Yes, she'd never admit to Louise that her marriage had been lacking, but neither would she accept an arrangement like that again. Mack might've been a wonderful man, but because of her, he was an unhappy one.

She pushed the picture of Mack from her

mind, but another man with expressive eyes and a bad haircut wasn't so easily dismissed. No wonder Molly had her cap set for him. He was strong, rich, and well-mannered, which matched with the practical girl's husband checklist. She knew all that before meeting him.

What Rosa hadn't expected was a man she could spend all day looking at: the crinkles around his eyes when he smiled, his determined, stubble-covered jaw, and his mouth . . . lips that were meant to smile a lot more than they had recently. And that was probably what made him so intriguing. Every account she'd heard had portrayed Weston as a confident man of means and a community leader who was devoted to his family, and that's what everyone, including himself, wanted to believe. How could everyone else miss the insecurity that tracked across that handsome face when he heard himself praised? Molly thought he was moody, but did she really know how wounded he was?

Weston was strong of body and character, but he seemed to fear the reputation he'd worked so hard to earn. Rosa thought of his words, that he hoped she wouldn't lose her good opinion of him, and then she remembered her resolve. She would pray for him.

She'd pray that God would bring to him a friend who would help him heal, who would allow him to occasionally shrug off the mantle of family messiah and tend to his own wounds. She'd pray that God would take his weakness and turn it to wholeness, so he could be a safe haven for his family.

And while she was at it, she'd pray that Molly would find another man and leave poor Mr. Garner alone.

9

"I can't believe they didn't stay. They have no business trying to make it to Weston's. They're going to get drenched, if not worse." Louise bustled into the kitchen, motioning for Rosa to follow. She took the kerosene from the pantry and topped off the hurricane lantern, filling the kitchen with the scent of fuel. "You run upstairs and get some quilts, but hurry down. And stay away from the windows."

Rosa scurried upstairs and grabbed two blankets off the quilt stand. As she passed the window a violent motion caught her eye. The rain hadn't started yet, but the treetops were swinging around like the tip of a whip. The panes in the window rattled, as if they too were trying to flee the approaching onslaught. Where did that wind come from? She'd never seen anything like it.

In the kitchen, Louise laced on her dirty boots. A basket of biscuits and a can of peach preserves rested on the table. "We need to secure the yard." She pulled hard on the long laces. "Don't leave anything out there that could blow away . . . or worse, blow toward us."

Rosa nodded, dropped the soft quilts on the table, and ran to the chicken coop. When she opened the coop door, the muggy odor surprised her. When had it grown so humid? The chickens were already huddled inside, skittish but strangely quiet. Their dark speckled feathers quivered as they gathered close together. She closed and fastened every door, window, and peephole she found. The coop, the privy, the barn — all closed tight before the first fat raindrops fell.

At the first drip, Rosa thought a June bug had splat on her arm, then another, then another, but the large wet splotches were rain, thrown down with a vengeance. She ran toward the house, only to meet Louise on her way out.

Pointing, she yelled above the din, "Rosa, get those buckets in the barn! We can't leave anything that might blow through a window!"

A wooden bucket blow through a window? But Louise sounded frantic, so Rosa did as she was told, even though it meant lifting the heavy crossbeam in the barn doors again. The drops were falling faster and faster, plastering themselves over her bare arms and making her clothing heavy.

"Wait!" Louise stopped her from pushing the beam into place. "I forgot the ax." She slipped inside the barn, reappeared with it in hand, and dropped it down the open mouth of the cellar on their way back to the house. Rosa filled her arms with quilts and waited in the protection of the porch for Louise to pull the door closed. Lightly at first, then in growing intensity, Rosa heard a pinging noise. Something was hitting the house. To her astonishment she noticed small white balls hopping in the lawn.

"Hail!" Louise took a quilt from Rosa. "Cover your head and run."

She didn't need to be told twice. The fierce blast drove rain right through her clothes. Chunks of ice stung her skin as they were hurled from the monstrous clouds above. She'd never known such fury existed. Reaching the crude gap in the ground, Rosa paused, her throat closing up as surely as the ground could, but Louise didn't wait. A bump from her mother-in-law sent her into the hole. Rosa stumbled on the slick stone steps and caught herself against the rock wall on the way down, with Louise right behind her pulling on the door, fighting against the gusts until it almost slammed on her head, then sliding the bolt into the wood frame and plunging them into darkness.

Rosa huddled on the dirt floor, afraid to move. The stale air made the room seem even smaller than it was. As sure as the beam crushed her when she was a child and cut off her air, now panic constricted her lungs, making breathing a struggle. The sound of the bolt played over and over again in her mind. She was locked in. Underground.

Lightning raced through the cracks between the door and frame and made it possible for her to see Louise fumbling with the phosphorus match to light the hurricane lamp.

"Surely they stopped at Mary and George's! They wouldn't try to go all the way to Weston's. Why didn't they stay?" Louise's voice shook in the darkness. Finally a flare lit her face, and she adjusted the wick, illuminating the damp den. "I don't know how I could face Adele if something happened to them."

Rosa pulled herself against the crumbling wall. With the quilt wrapped around her, she forced herself to answer. "I'm sure they did. Molly wouldn't risk ruining her dress."

Louise huffed. "If it meant getting holed up at Weston's for the night, she might, from what I gather." She searched for a dry corner of her blanket to mop up the streams of water running down her face. "Just as well, I suppose. He'd keep her out of trouble." The door rattled against the bolt with each gust. The thunder rumbled unceasingly, punctuated by closer lightning strikes that made Rosa's hair stand on end.

Louise set her supplies on an empty shelf that held preserves in better days and wiped them dry. "Forgive me, Rosa. I shouldn't be talking about Molly like that. She's a good girl. I'm just frustrated with her."

Rosa nodded. Louise would be the last to think poorly of someone and the first to lose control of her tongue, but Rosa wasn't concerned with idle words. Not while cornered underground. "What's the ax for?" Rosa asked, trying to ignore the intensifying squall outside.

"It's in case we get trapped down here." Her voice held no sense of panic.

Rosa produced enough for both of them. "Trapped?!"

"If a tornado heads this way, we could have the whole house sitting on top of that door in the next hour. Not that the ax is foolproof, but it'd increase our odds of getting out."

Rosa wished she hadn't asked.

"Don't worry. They aren't as common as you might think. Remember how the train sounded? As long as you don't hear that, we can ride it out down here. The storms do enough damage above, but only a tornado would pluck us out."

As if listening for its cue, the wooden door strained against the bolt holding it down, but this was no gust of wind. Rosa startled. Was that a voice? Above the clamor she heard someone yell. They looked at each other in surprise, and then Louise leapt to her feet. "Did they come back?" She fumbled with the latch.

A rush of rain blew in. Rosa turned her face to avoid the blinding gust. When she looked again a single set of cowboy boots, slick and shining in the lantern light, descended the steps behind Louise. They didn't belong to Nicholas, and the soaked canvas pants stuck to legs too spindly to belong to —

"Do you remember Mr. Tillerton, Rosa?" Louise used a voice better suited for a plush drawing room than the desperate straits they were in. The man pulled the lock into place, halting the malevolent force that entered with him, and shook like a *lobo* flinging water off his wolfish coat.

His eyes flashed, aroused by the fury of the storm he'd just battled. "Sorry to arrive unannounced like this. I got caught away from home."

"I'm glad you found us." Louise offered her blanket to him, but he gallantly refused. "Did you get your horse in the barn?"

"No, ma'am. There wasn't time. The hailstones are coming down hard, and the lightning is striking close by. I rushed in to determine that you were safe."

He took the lantern from the shelf and sat next to Rosa, keeping the light at his far side. "Don't worry about the storm." He laid a hand on her shoulder. "You'll get used to them, but I've got to say this doesn't bode well for your garden. These hailstones will decimate the young sprouts."

When had he seen their garden? She felt more and more crowded. With a bounce of her shoulder, she dislodged his hand.

"Our sprouts? Surely you're not wishing ill on us, Mr. Tillerton?" Louise's indignation was clear, even through the near darkness.

"Absolutely not! It's a brave thing you are trying to accomplish here, and I wish you success."

The storm had reached its climax, every

ear-splitting crash ringing like the gavel of the great white throne judgment signaling the end of the age. Rosa's nerves teetered on the edge of control. She pulled her knees to her chest and wrapped her arms around them.

Without warning they were plunged into darkness. "The lantern!" Louise cried.

Rosa's arm was grasped firmly through the quilt. With skill Tillerton's hand followed her arm to her knees and brushed downward, fumbling through her skirts. She rolled away from him with a gasp and kicked back as hard as she could, gratified to make solid contact.

"Uff!"

Then she heard nothing but the fading rumbling outside.

"I'm sorry. The lantern is on the other side of me," he said. "Give me just a minute."

Rosa made no reply but scrambled away, feet tangled in the quilt. He mustn't find her again.

"What's happened? Do you need another match?"

"No, ma'am. I've got it." The flame sputtered to life. He held it aloft to expose Rosa crouched against the shelving, every muscle taut, ready for battle. Like a rabbit trapped in its lair, she had nowhere to run, but she would fight with what puny weapons she possessed — her fingernails, her teeth — if she had to.

Louise pulled her quilt tighter around her. "It's going to be all right, Rosa. I know you hate little rooms, but you're safer in here than in the storm."

"And you left your quilt behind in your panic, Mrs. Garner." Tillerton held it out to her.

Rosa shook her head. If that was the game, she wasn't playing. She might not tell anyone he'd insulted her, but she wouldn't go along with the charade.

She shivered in her wet clothes. The shelving dug into her back, but she wouldn't move closer to him.

Outside, the storm weakened. Rosa could hear the rain cascading down, but the thunder stomped its way further down the road. The worst had passed.

Without waiting for Louise, Rosa scrambled across the cellar and forced open the door. Bursting out onto the yard, she gasped like one deprived of oxygen. How dare he lay a hand on her! The rain was drenching her, but she wasn't going for shelter. She'd rather fight in the open. She wouldn't be trapped again.

Louise appeared, followed by Tillerton.

121

"Rosa, what are you doing? Let's get to the house."

"No! Not until Mr. Tillerton leaves."

"Rosa!" Louise's quilt dropped from over her head. "That is rude. You apologize at once."

Tillerton's clothes were plastered to him, his bony frame looking like a wet cat's. "She's just overwrought, Mrs. Garner. I refuse to be offended. Now, if you'll excuse me, I should go comfort my wife. She'll be concerned if I'm not home soon."

Louise nodded and scurried to the house for shelter. Rosa waited until she was out of earshot and then called out, "Tillerton!"

He turned, his fake smile still fastened on his cruel lips. "What? Do you want more?"

"You will never treat me that way again. Do you understand me? Never!"

His eyes roved over her wet dress, making her nauseous. "Pulling a married man aside to have a private conversation? Tsk, tsk. What will Louise think?"

Rosa looked over her shoulder. Sure enough, there stood Louise under the shelter of the back porch, arms crossed, lips pinched tightly together.

He swung into his saddle. "Don't take it so hard. I didn't make the rules. You'll learn how to play."

Rosa stood her ground until he had crossed the pasture and was no longer on their land. She had survived her first prairie storm but discovered there were perils more dangerous than tornados.

The lightning passed and the hail ceased, but the rain still soaked his slicker when Weston started out. Poor Pandora. She couldn't understand why he took Smokey and left her behind, but she didn't care for high river crossings, and he would span at least one tonight.

The clouds behind Weston threw their flickering light on the soaked landscape before him. Riding across the rolling prairie he was exposed to the world . . . and to the heavens. He spent a moment studying the turbulent June sky. There was nowhere to hide out here. He was a solitary figure, completely removed from human contact.

Which was fine with him.

Oh, he did what he was supposed to do, else people would ask too many questions. He went to church on Sunday, and he ground out a prayer over supper, although Jake had taken on that duty after hearing the same weak platitudes for months on end, but Weston knew he was trying to disguise the condition of his heart. To be honest, he was hiding. The Bible said that God is truth, and Weston wasn't ready to face the truth.

The white and tan speckled hides of his cattle were visible, peacefully sheltered under trees along the swollen creek. Longhorns could take care of themselves. Still, Weston wouldn't sleep easy until he'd checked on his livestock after the storm.

Protection was a big deal to Wes. If he had a ewe stray from the flock, he brought her in. If he had a new ranch hand learning the ropes, he'd keep him from any real danger because Weston would hold himself responsible if the greenhorn got injured. Most of his life was spent, in one form or another, protecting those under his care.

He worked across the pastures, finding nothing but downed branches and swollen streams. From the western forty he could see George and Mary's house. Everything looked to be in good condition. Did they know the barn door was open?

As he approached the homestead, he saw a carriage under the lean-to. Lovelaces? What were they doing out here? He stopped, chewed over his options.

"Ain't you going to come on in and sit a spell?" George called from the barn.

"Thought I'd check on the sheep."

124

"Already did. They're fine."

Weston maneuvered the horse to where his uncle sat by a lamp. "What are you doing in the barn?"

"You see that carriage?"

"Lovelaces?"

"Yep. That's what I'm doing in the barn."

Weston climbed down and got a feed bag for his horse. "Is it too warm in the house?"

"It's warm, that's for certain. Mary has a hard time being hospitable to those two. She can overlook a lot of flaws, but laziness ain't one of them."

Weston shook out his slicker and hung it on a stall divider. "To be fair, Miss Lovelace is as enterprising as her father. Now, Nicholas is another story."

"But Molly is helpless in a kitchen or on a farm. That's all Mary cares about."

"She's been employed at the courthouse for a couple of years now. You should have her cipher for you sometime. She's amazing." He settled himself on the ground next to George.

"I'm surprised at you. I thought you didn't care for the girl."

Weston leaned against the support beam. "There's nothing wrong with Molly that the right man can't fix. I'm not that man."

"And why not? She comes from a good

125

family. She gussies up pretty. You could straighten her out."

"I'm not the right man for anyone." They sat in silence. Raindrops splashed into the puddles forming around the barn. Weston wasn't ready to leave yet.

"How was Eliza's trip? I heard she made it home," George said.

"Her visit with Cora's parents wasn't easy." Weston took off his hat and set it on his knee. "I wish there was something I could do for the Smocks. I'm willing to take responsibility, but it doesn't bring their daughter back."

George tossed his straw away. "Weston, we were all there. We saw what happened. It wasn't your fault. She pulled further and further away from everyone. No one could help her."

"God could've."

George pulled his knees up. "Well now. Are you blaming yourself or blaming God?"

Weston shrugged. Could he admit to blaming God? He knew better. But he also knew that God read his heart. His silence wasn't hiding anything from his Creator. "That's where I've been stuck. God could've stopped her, so why . . . why didn't He? Did He not care? Did He not care what happened to her . . . or to me? But blaming

God doesn't get me very far, does it?"

"You know the answer to that."

Weston got to his feet. "Yet there should be a reckoning. Someone should pay for what happened." He paced across the damp dirt floor. "I was doing all I could for her. I thought she'd get it right in the end. Maybe I wasn't trying hard enough. Maybe I should have seen the warning signs, but I didn't until it was too late."

And so he was exacting vengeance on himself. He didn't deserve happiness. He didn't deserve peace. How could he laugh and love when his wife was cold and buried? Justice required more.

"Someone did pay, son. Jesus paid for all our failures. Maybe it was sin, maybe weakness, or maybe Cora was the victim of a corrupt, fallen world. God took all those possibilities and settled the account on them. And you know what He gave you? Life. Refusing to live ain't doing God any favors. He must expect more from you or you wouldn't be here."

Thunder rolled in the distance. "It isn't easy after so long. I feel like every time I stick my neck out, someone puts their boot on it, but I'm going to see this through. Yet my biggest contribution might be keeping my distance so that no one else gets hurt.

127

That's a possibility."

"Maybe. Just make sure it's God's call and not your own fear. Although I can think of one contribution I'd appreciate tonight. Since you're already out in the rain, would you mind swingin' past Louise and Rosa's? Make sure they rode out the storm?"

Weston nodded and got on the horse. Somehow he knew when he left Palmetto that he'd end up at the ladies' house, one way or another.

His horse was unfamiliar with the road past George and Mary's, since they'd had no reason in years to travel it across the creek. Smokey felt his way cautiously. When they reached the bank, the water was swifter than usual, curling around the horse's legs and splashing the cuff of Wes's trousers, but they crossed and made it to the dark house.

From the looks of things, damage was slight. A few shingles littered the yard, a chair on the porch had toppled over, but there was nothing that couldn't wait till morning. The cellar door was flung open, hanging crooked on the exhausted hinges. Good. At least they weren't trapped underground.

He turned Smokey to the back side of the plot to make a complete circle before he headed to bed.

■ ■ ■ ■

Rosa paced the room vigorously, trying to burn off the outrage coursing through her veins. Louise had hung their wet clothes on the backs of the kitchen chairs and provided rough dry towels to ward off the chill, yet still she trembled. Maybe her agitation was heightened from being trapped underground, but Mr. Tillerton bore most of the blame. No question, he had acted on purpose. Hadn't he warned her at church? At church!

Rosa stomped her foot at the memory. According to etiquette, she'd handled the incident correctly, but she wasn't satisfied. She wanted to run through the streets of Prairie Lea and howl that she'd been insulted, but she suspected the blame would land on her. Again.

She flopped on the bed, lying back against the headboard, the ore of her anger melting down to silver determination. She would get through this. Death, widowhood, relocation, and financial ruin; what was a nasty churl compared to everything else she faced? Yet her heart was heavy. She lived in a corrupt world, and he was a thorn that proved it. When would there be relief? Was life on Earth always this hard? Would there be any restoration before Christ returned?

The melancholy longing caused her to reach for her *tlapitzalli*. Her fingers traced the bird-shaped carvings on the clay pipe as her eyes filled with tears. Putting the flute to her lips, she poured her angst into it, where it was transformed into a low, haunting song, and her heart prayed the words of David she had memorized:

I will sing of mercy and judgment:
Unto thee, O Lord, will I sing.
I will behave myself wisely in a perfect
    way.
O when wilt thou come unto me?
I will walk within my house with a perfect
    heart.
I will set no wicked thing before mine
    eyes:
I hate the work of them that turn aside;
It shall not cleave to me.
Mine eyes shall be upon the faithful of the
    land,
That they may dwell with me.

"Lord, please bring the faithful to dwell with us," she whispered. "Bring those who will help and protect and keep the evil ones far from us. May your Kingdom come and

130

do not let the wicked prevail. Please keep me strong. Louise needs me and I'm already getting discouraged." She stopped to blow the lamp out and snuggle under her covers. *How can we do this without help, Jesus? We need your help.*

Smokey's ears twitched as they passed along the side of the house alerting Weston that he had missed something. Was that a bird? No, it sounded like a dove, but it was sustained. No bird sang like that. The music led him to an open window above him. He didn't stare, worried that Rosa might appear and see him — or that he might see more of her than he intended. He steered Smokey under the oak tree, where he couldn't see or be seen and lingered to listen to the auditory salve, to let his prayers join the chorus of praise currently underway. What he had to say couldn't compete in meaning or beauty, but maybe his prayers would be accepted as part of the harmony.

The heavy drops of rain caught in the giant leaves fell with every breeze. He'd been granted a private concert. Sorrow welled up with the lifting of the melody, wringing out his every pain and letting it drip away.

But as painful as the message was, there was resolution. Hope floated in the final notes before they faded, and the square of warm light went dark for the night. He sat, relishing the shared solitude, and wondered how she knew the song in his heart.

10

Dirt under her fingernails, dress sodden at the knees, Rosa knelt and fingered the battered seedlings. The lanky sprouts bent double, but they weren't broken. A few more days of brilliant sunshine like this one promised to be and they would bypass their former height without a doubt.

"The chickens seem to have come out ahead." Louise plodded through the marshy yard, wiping her hands on the faded gingham apron. "They didn't fancy that storm, but with all the earthworms it uncovered, they're enjoying the feast. How are the crops?"

Rosa shrugged. "I don't see any roots exposed or many stems broken, so there was probably no harm done. They're still green. They'll pop back up, no?" She scanned the long rows she had hoed, proud of the tangles of emerald spreading in the median of each. Their work was paying off, but would it be enough?

"I wonder how George and Mary fared." Louise pulled broken limbs to a burn pile.

Rosa did too. She headed toward the dilapidated picket fence to help Louise dislodge a large tree limb that had fallen in the night. With a grunt and a step backward, they disentangled the branch, the sudden release causing both to stumble a few feet.

"I don't know. Come to think of it, I'm surprised Mary hasn't sent George over to check on us, but he's probably got his hands full tending Wes's sheep this morning. They're likely scattered to the four winds."

Rosa removed the broken twigs protruding from between the slats. "Why are Weston's sheep on Uncle George's farm? It is Uncle George's farm, isn't it?"

Straightening, Louise craned her back in what looked to be a satisfying stretch before answering. "Yes, it's their farm, but just barely. According to Mary, they came close to losing it a few years ago when the property taxes jumped clear to the moon. They scrimped enough greenbacks together to pay them, and George set out to Lockhart with the money, but it never made it."

"Was he robbed?" Rosa had heard that Texas after the war had been a dangerous place.

"Yes, but it was legal." Louise shook her head. "Seems that George had developed a taste for poker while in the brigade. He hadn't had much chance to play since then, and all that money was just burning a hole in his pocket."

Rosa started to express her shock, but Louise quickly amended, "I don't want you to think poorly of George. He's a good man. We've all got our weaknesses, and evidently gambling is his. But how was Mary to know? He rarely went to town, so it hadn't come up before. I've known him my whole adult life and would have never thought it of him.

"So, to make a long story short, Wes leased their ranch from them. He took the lease money to the courthouse himself and paid the taxes, so there was no danger of them losing the family land. Wes keeps his sheep out here, where George and his boys can take care of them."

"How sad for Uncle George!"

"Well, that's what family's for. I think the setup bothers Mary more than it does George, though. Specially since it's put Weston in a bind. He's got a lot of land, but cash is hard to come by. Something for us to bear in mind if we aren't caught up by August." She smiled. "We'll just have to make sure we aren't in that position, won't we?"

The horizon held Louise's attention for a troubled moment. "Mary told me they're saving to invest in longhorns again. She thinks after this spring they'll lease back only part of their land to Wes and run cattle on the rest. Could be that Weston would want to lease our land, but I can't offer it unless George and Mary bow out first, so pray they have a good summer, too. If they get enough money together, we might be saved."

She paused as she caught a glimpse of a sharp black buggy crossing the creek. "My, my, looks like we have company. Don't say anything about leasing. It's too early to give up. We still have time." She hurried into the house, leaving Rosa alone in the yard with her arms full of twigs.

Rosa deposited the branches in the growing pile next to the laundry line and went through the kitchen door. By the time she'd washed up at the spigot, the guests were in the parlor, where she could eavesdrop easily.

A woman's voice she didn't recognize wafted into the room. "It's hard to believe that they are never coming back. Both Eli and Mack. I'd always imagined that one day they'd return to this house."

"It's a bitter world we live in." Overcome by sorrow, it took Louise a minute to remember her manners. "And I haven't had a chance to speak with you about your own tragedy. May I offer my condolences?"

The deep voice that answered sent a shock through Rosa's chest. "Thank you, Aunt Louise. I appreciate your thoughts, although my loss isn't as recent as yours. How are you managing?"

Wasting no more time in the kitchen, Rosa entered to see a young dark-haired woman in an ill-fitting gown place her hand on Weston's arm. He didn't finish the sentence. Upon seeing Rosa, he stood but didn't meet her eyes. She knew she wasn't much to look at this morning, but after all they'd encountered together, why was he acting like a total stranger?

"Eliza, this is my daughter-in-law, Rosa. Mack's wife." Rosa held out her hand as she'd been instructed and was pleased to find a pair of sparkling eyes appraising her from under fringed bangs and highly arched eyebrows.

What would the other woman think? Rosa had chosen her stained red blouse for work in the garden, but it was still a strong color for her. Would she appreciate the handiwork on the seams or only see the dirt? And Rosa's hair was twisted up and off her neck in an artless knot, completely unlike the tight curls that framed Eliza's face. She was so out of fashion, but Eliza didn't seem to mind.

"Look at us. So formal." Eliza laughed as she leaned forward for a cheek-to-cheek hug. "This is how kin behave."

Weston didn't follow suit but swung his hands behind his back, making it clear that neither the hug nor the handshake was necessary. "It's nice to see you again, Mrs. Garner."

Rosa searched his face for some twinkle of recognition but found only formality.

"Oh yes, Weston told me an amusing story, but I forget. Where did you meet?" Eliza raised her eyebrows.

Rosa followed Louise's lead and took a seat. "When I went to help Uncle George and Aunt Mary for the sheep shearing."

"Oh, you were the one at the sheep shearing!" Eliza's eyes danced with mischief. "I just wish I could have been there. Sounds like you made quite an impression."

Rosa gasped. He'd told her about the old ewe? But Weston quickly set her straight.

"Your evaluation of my haircut was something I knew my sister would enjoy."

Rosa breathed an internal sigh of relief. Louise would never recover if she heard about her attempt at corralling the rogue ewe.

Eliza went on. "I just wish I'd been there to see it. I can only imagine. Alas, he didn't wait. He had it trimmed before we arrived. Do you think it's a vast improvement?"

Rosa's mouth twitched. He would keep her secret safe, and although she was grateful, she knew whose team she was on when siblings bantered. Sisters had to stick together.

She dared to study him for a long moment, taking in the clean-shaven jaw and the freshly trimmed sideburns framing his handsome face. Rosa screwed up her mouth in disapproval. "No, I'm sorry to say it isn't much improved, but I don't think the barber can be blamed."

"Rosa!" Louise gasped as the girls dissolved into giggles. "I don't know what's gotten into you. And you, Eliza Jane, you haven't changed a bit, always tormenting your poor brother. Doesn't he have enough on his plate?"

Weston shook his head. "You're wasting your time, Aunt Louise. If Eliza hasn't profited from the correction of Aunt Mary, Mrs. Lovelace, and the whole staff of the

St. Louis Ladies' Academy, a mere reprimand won't be effective. The die is cast, and now we must endure while she raises a family of hoydens just like her."

"A family?" Louise's hand flew to her chest. "Is there a family to go with this Mr. Jake England that we've yet to meet?" Her eyes scanned Eliza's figure speculatively.

Eliza's happy face turned a shade happier. "Not yet, but there will be this fall." Then under her breath she added primly, "Although who can say if it'll be a hoyden or not."

Louise looked to Weston, but he adjusted the trim on his Stetson, refusing to acknowledge Eliza's latest comment. Rosa bit her lip to stop the grin that threatened to emerge.

Clearing his throat, Weston restored some decorum to the parlor by addressing his aunt. "So it's been a decade? It's hard to fathom you've been gone that long."

"I can't believe I spent ten years in Mexico either, but when I came back and saw how much had changed, it seemed I'd been gone a lifetime. When I left, you were still green behind the ears and Eliza hadn't put her hair up yet." Louise smiled fondly at the girl. "You grew up without my permission. Yes, the largest shock is with the young folks. My generation just plods along, nothing new, unless you're Mary and get a few December surprises from the stork. Besides that, everyone is just as they were the day we pulled down that drive, heading for Mexico with a wagon brimming with hope, dreams, and my little family." She reached into her apron for a hankie and dabbed her eyes.

"And you, Weston, tell me about your own sweet wife. Cora? Was that her name?"

"Was that her name?" How he hated to hear *was* describing his wife. So final. So permanent.

"Yes, ma'am — Cora Smock. Her people are from St. Louis — which is where we met. She was actually at the academy with Eliza." He floundered. How could he put together the bare bones of the story without disturbing the sensitive, painful truth?

"Cora and I were the closest friends," Eliza interrupted, "and her parents entertained us while Wes was in town to see me." Thus she began the colorful narration, leaving Weston alone with his memories:

True, Cora was stunning — the consummate mistress of the soirees held in her parlor. But what most impressed Weston was her poise. She was capable, gracious, and welcoming to all. She didn't simper like

141

Eliza's other academy friends. For a slender lady, Miss Smock had broad shoulders, and her hands, although soft and white, were ample — definitely large enough to handle reins.

Here was a woman who could stand by his side and meet the challenges of life without flinching.

Difficult to believe his first impression of her was so tragically mistaken. Yet, that wasn't completely fair to her, either. Had she stayed in St. Louis, she would probably have remained the unflappable hostess and gone on to lead a rich and fulfilling life. Yes, she was poised and she was capable, but only in her own element. Just as a strong rye might grow well in one field and turn spindly in another, she'd been transplanted from the soil that nourished her and dropped into a hostile environment.

And he was the one who'd uprooted her.

Rosa listened to Eliza's account, her sharp black eyes not missing the change in Weston. He didn't hear a word his sister was saying. He was somewhere far away. As painful as Eliza's account might be, from the look of despair on his face, his own reckoning was crueler. Eliza told the story of a tragic accident. Weston looked like he was reliving a crime, one of which he'd been convicted.

"But how did she drown in that old pond?" Louise prodded. "The boys used to swim in it all the time. You have to wade halfway across before it gets deep enough. . . ."

Rosa watched, appalled, as Weston seemed to wither, sinking into the faded velvet cushions. She could almost see the spectral accuser hovering over him, listing his shames and failures in a nasty voice that only he could hear. She wanted to end it but didn't know how. Fortunately, his sister was a warrior in her own right.

"She was sick, Aunt Louise, sick and out of her mind that night. We might never know how she became so disoriented, but we do know that she was loved by all and loving to all." She paused, lips pressed firmly together. "Cora would never want the responsibility for her demise to fall on her loved ones."

Louise nodded in sympathy. "I understand, and you can perhaps imagine how much I've tormented myself over the deaths of my men, especially Mack. With Eli, it was unavoidable. How could we predict an earthquake? Every man working the mines took that risk, but with Mack it was different.

"Mack survived the first collapse. We got there in time to see him stumble out, but he wouldn't stay out. He grabbed a shovel and went back. . . ." She stopped and turned her face to the window, her chin quivering.

Rosa tried to pick up the story, but the words couldn't be forced from her throat. She swallowed dust and croaked out a few phrases. "Black powder all over him. Everyone screaming. He came out . . ."

"He didn't come to Rosa or to me. You'd think a newlywed would be more considerate, but no, he didn't have time to spare a thought for her. Not even a word. If he'd given her that, he wouldn't have been in the cave when the aftershock came. Of course, he wouldn't give up on his father. They didn't always see eye to eye, but Mack knew Eli loved him. If only I could have convinced him not to . . ."

Rosa looked up to find Weston's dark eyes on her. She met his unwavering gaze and wondered what he saw. Did he see someone who was unloved? Did he see someone who deserved to be abandoned? She understood that she was no one there in Texas. Not even as important as a beggar, being a foreigner and all. Louise's name and protection were the keys to every good thing that had happened to her since she'd arrived, but was she worth anything on her own?

Mouth slightly opened, she took deep unsteady breaths as she lowered her eyes. Sometimes the fear suffocated her. Daily she looked forward to the new chores they would tackle, but when she thought of the future, bile rose in her throat and her chest tightened. What would happen to them? Louise would be cared for, but how long would these people tolerate her? Who would protect her from the likes of Jay Tillerton?

The parlor fell into silence, interrupted only by the ticking of the eight-day clock, as each of the four family members' thoughts alternated between their own losses and compassion for their kin.

Eliza finally roused the somber group by clapping her hands together and rising. "Despite everything, we have to keep moving. We're still here for a reason, and God doesn't let us save the sunlight for tomorrow." She walked to the piano and absently picked out a melody with her right hand. "Since I returned from St. Louis, I've been anxious to visit, but we came this morning particularly to see how you weathered last night's storm."

Louise sighed, pulling herself back to the present. "Fairly well, I think. A few shingles off, branches down, but no harm done."

Rising to watch Eliza play, Rosa remembered their visitors the night before. "Did Mr. and Miss Lovelace make it to your house?"

"No, but we saw them this morning at Uncle George's. They got caught in the storm and waited it out there last night."

"Oh, I was worried about Molly's dress."

Eliza's head snapped to fix Rosa with a penetrating stare. She shrugged her shoulders wickedly and winked. "Mary loaned her a skirt and shirt. That's what she was wearing this morning, but Wes still got to see the dress, sopping wet and hanging across the line."

Rosa looked down. She hadn't meant to ridicule the girl. She could feel Louise's disapproval. First opportunity she had she would talk to Molly. She didn't deserve to be a laughingstock.

Weston cleared his throat. "Need I remind you that I'm still in the room? Aunt Louise, may I look around outside? Although I don't seem to be hampering the conversation, I'd feel more at ease not being present for it."

"Please do. Rosa and I were gathering broken branches when you arrived. We can finish that ourselves, but if you'd replace the shingles, I'd be beholden to you."

They spent the next few hours completing the work Louise and Rosa had begun earlier. Eliza, not dressed for yard work, volunteered to put dinner on, claiming that their servant Octavia never let her cook at home. By the time the sun was high overhead and steam was rising from the ground, they knew why.

"I started with more beans, but most of them are stuck to the bottom of the pot. If you're still hungry, I'll do some more scraping." Eliza followed the others to the square table.

"No thanks, sis. I don't reckon I'll be hungry for more of your beans." Weston's shirt sleeves were rolled up to the elbows, and the knees of his canvas pants were scarred by the texture of the roof. Once again he could pass for a rough-riding cowboy instead of the gentleman Rosa had observed in the parlor earlier.

"Well, they aren't my favorite, either, but there's really not much in the pantry to choose from. I don't want to pry, but do you have enough to make it till the garden produces?"

Louise's back straightened. "We'll do fine. Next week we're going to Lockhart to buy more goods. Rosa did some fancywork for Mr. Bradford, so we can settle our account and bring home more victuals. Besides, with just the two of us, we don't need much."

Rosa caught Weston inspecting their pantry from his seat at the table. She rose and pulled the curtain closed. Their supplies didn't concern him. They'd be fortunate to raise enough food to get them through the next harvest, but she didn't need his stricken expression to remind her that, in all likelihood, turning a profit was out of the question.

He didn't comment on her gesture but turned to the window instead.

"Your barn is in good condition. Do you have any plans for it?"

Louise snorted. "Plans? Not this year. I think we have our hands full with the garden and getting this place back in shape."

Weston nodded thoughtfully. "Have you ever wrestled with sheep?"

Rosa's foot got tangled with the broom leaning in the corner and sent it crashing to the floor.

"Mercy, Rosa!" Louise put her hand to her heart. "Be careful. You scared the living daylights out of me."

"I'm sorry. I wasn't . . ." She stopped and glared at Weston, but his expression was as innocent as a newborn's as he waited for Louise's answer.

"Eli always ran cattle, not sheep. They take

more looking after, don't they?"

"Yes, they do. That's why I could use your help. I have a handful that got chewed on by coyotes. It's an ongoing problem, and I hate to ask George to care for them because he's too busy with the rest of the flock." He took another bite of bitter beans and choked it down with a gulp of milk. "Maybe you, and particularly Mrs. Garner, would enjoy giving them some tender, hands-on care. I wouldn't want you to get too tied down with them, but if you'd like to wrap your arms around the problem . . ." He focused his attention completely on his bowl of beans. The innocent expression was slipping.

Louise looked at her, a question plastered on her face. The heel of Rosa's boot tapped quickly against the wood floor. He was a devil, but a practical one. She loved her chicks and was eager to try her hand with any other animals available. Besides, there weren't a lot of opportunities for two women to increase their profit this far from town. But would they be expensive to keep?

As if reading her thoughts Louise spoke. "From the looks of things, Rosa is on board, but I don't know if we can afford to feed more mouths around here. Will they graze or do we need to buy feed?"

"They'll graze. In fact, you won't have to

worry about trimming the lawn, just pen them around the house when the grass gets up. I'll send the antiseptic. If you can save them, they're yours. If not, you gave them more of a chance than they had with the rest of the flock."

"Then it's a deal!" Louise sprang to her feet and gathered the dishes. She filled the pot with water and set it on the hot stove to soften the charred remains of dinner. "Rosa, to celebrate, why don't you get that flute of yours and treat Wes and Eliza to a concert? Eliza always loved her music lessons, but she's probably never heard anything like your flute."

"That would be wonderful, Rosa! I'll be in there directly, but I can't let Aunt Louise scrub the pot out. That mess is my doing."

Rosa left the room and clamored up and down the stairs, unconcerned with the ruckus she raised. But when she returned with tlapitzalli in hand, she found only Mr. Garner on the settee, lost in thought.

"Oh, it's quiet in here." Determined not to make any more noise, she silently perched on the piano stool, toes barely able to touch the ground, and mentally ran through her favorite songs. What would they want to hear? What did she feel like playing? Long forgotten songs from her memory took form. Unconsciously she swung back and forth on the revolving stool, pivoting on her tiptoes, eyes lifted to the ceiling in thought.

"Thank you for agreeing to take the sheep." The deep voice interrupted the trilling melody playing in her mind. She stopped rocking as gracefully as she could.

Rosa raised an eyebrow. "You're thanking me for your generosity? You're welcome, I suppose. But why are so many of your sheep getting attacked? Don't you have burros with your flocks?"

"Beg your pardon?" he asked.

"Burros?"

"No, we ride horses."

"I mean to keep the coyotes away. They need burros at pasture with them."

Weston leaned forward, his eyes narrowed in interest. "Really? You think burros are better than sheepdogs?"

She shrugged. "I don't know much about dogs, but burros will trample a coyote or a pack of coyotes. Doesn't matter much to them how many there are. And you don't have to feed burros. They graze with the sheep."

His smile twisted to one side as he looked her over. Something amused him. Was he laughing at her? She surely deserved it. Here she was, the world-famous sheep wrestler

151

telling the landowner how to care for his flocks. They were in a stare off, each trying to read the other, until he nodded. "I don't know why I didn't think of that. I remember a Mexican man who brought his burro to the house once. My bird dog ran out with me, and the burro liked to chase it clean up the steps and into the foyer. Yep, it would make more sense to throw some donkeys in with the flock. I'm afraid the dog food we leave out attracts the coyotes anyway." Leaning back into the faded seat cushion, he crossed his arms. "Then it's settled. I'll try it."

Through the door they could hear Louise and Eliza merrily chatting away. In all likelihood, no dirty dishes remained, but the aunt and niece had much ground to cover before visit's end. Rosa turned her flute in her hands and wondered if some music might remind the two ladies of their family they'd banished to the parlor.

"Make it do the dove song," he suggested.

Her brow wrinkled. "Dove? I don't know that bird."

"Yes you do. I've heard you play it."

"How does it sound?"

He shifted in his seat, and shot her a quizzical look. "I'm not the performer, but if you insist. It sounded like 'coocoo.' " He tilted his head back and hammed up the call a few more times.

Her head cocked like a robin's watching a worm. "That's a *paloma.* You heard me, you say? When did you hear me play a paloma?"

"I think you can do it. You should try."

Shaking her head, she persisted. "You said you heard me. When did you hear me play?"

He pulled at his collar with one finger, and then the words tumbled out like the chicks from the henhouse. "Last night after the storm. I rode out to make sure you . . . and Aunt Louise . . . were all right. Just wanted to check on things. Went by George's, too. I rode by everyone's."

"You were here?" She bit her lip.

"Your window was open, and I heard the music. I could've sat there in the rain and listened to it all night. And now, after hearing your story —" He leaned forward, bridging the space over the hand-knotted rug. His words slowed. "I think I understand better. I think that's why it meant so much to me, because we've both been through —" He stopped suddenly. "I'm sorry if that distresses you. I don't mean to make you uncomfortable."

Rosa kept her eyes lowered, afraid to meet his, and tried to overcome her emotions. *He was here last night? If only he'd been here an hour earlier, how different things would have been.* If Weston had sat by her in the cellar instead of Tillerton, she would have felt secure instead of threatened; honored instead of debased. She wanted to cry at the futility of it all, shocked again by the blackguard's actions. What had Tillerton accomplished besides humiliating her?

After a morning of Weston's presence and Eliza's lively company, she felt safe again. The menace lurking over the next property line had been forgotten, but now the incident was brought back fresh — the humiliation of being used in such a way.

If only she could tell Weston. The muscles of his arms strained his plaid shirt. His capable hands sat idle for the moment, but she was certain they could handle the likes of Tillerton. What would he do if she told him? Would he feel obligated to act on her behalf? Would he put himself in danger for her?

He would.

Last night he rode over in the middle of a thunderstorm to see that they were safe. He came back, first thing in the morning, to check on them again. He gave George and Mary the aid they needed to preserve their land and their dignity. He advised her to only work on Garner land so she wouldn't be exposed to low men. With that record it really wasn't a question of whether he would act for her, but when. He would right a wrong — any wrong — if one had been committed in his territory.

But she didn't want him to know. No use piling more scandal to her already growing list.

"Mrs. Garner, have I upset you?" Worry etched his face. "I apologize if that was uncouth —"

"Oh no." She laid a hand on his arm to reassure him. "Not at all. You . . . you're always welcome here. . . ." He stared at her hand. Was she being inappropriate again? Rosa jerked it back. Her chest rose in a deep, shaky breath as she composed her answer. "It was just the storm. I was scared." She traced a design on her flute with her fingernail. "The cellar, you know. It's so small and dark."

"That's difficult for you, isn't it? I wish I would've been down there with you, if it would've helped."

"You can't be everywhere."

"And yet I feel like I should be."

Rosa had no answer.

"Where did that sister of mine go?" he muttered. "Eliza!"

The chairs scraped across the wooden

155

floor. The table creaked as someone leaned on it to rise from their seat. Footsteps sounded. But Rosa's thoughts were far from the women entering the room.

What would it be like to be loved by a man like Weston Garner? To know he chose you? To know you possessed some precious trait, some beautiful element he held dear? Rosa turned toward the window. She had caught a glimpse of a treasure and didn't want it to vanish unexamined. Would she ever be pursued, instead of fled? Would she ever experience the vast difference between being resented and being cherished?

Hearing Louise's request as from a distance, Rosa put her flute to her lips. Futile questions sowed discontent. She would be fine. One could live without love. She'd done it before.

156

11

"Well, show me what you've got." Mr. Bradford swept nonexistent dust from his countertop as Rosa hoisted her carpetbag onto it.

The moment she'd anticipated for weeks had finally arrived. She prayed her work would be good enough for Mr. Bradford, pleaded that God would make him like it. They didn't have long now, and they were counting on a quick sale. But she needn't have worried.

Snapping the latch open and lifting out a tablecloth, Mr. Bradford whistled low. "Land sakes! If the ladies don't knock my door down to get these, I have no business working retail."

"Does that mean he likes them?" Rosa whispered to Louise.

"Like them?" Deacon Bradford interrupted. "Dear girl, they're exquisite. How you crafted such fine detail with wool thread is beyond me. It makes me wonder what you could do with silk." He pulled the pillowcases out and, after examining the work, placed them with their mates. "And the colors . . . But here is a test." He nodded to a woman approaching the door of the mercantile. Taking a tablecloth and two napkins in hand, he met Mrs. Schwartz, the newsman's wife, who sailed through on a mission.

"Mr. Bradford, I'm looking to acquire a lamp and thought that a painted glass would be just the thing. Do you have any in stock?"

"Yes, ma'am, I sure do, but if you don't mind, would you please hold these for me while I check in the back for the lamps? The linens just arrived, and they'll make a nice display in the storefront — if I can get them there before they sell out." He turned to go but wasn't fast enough.

"These are for sale? They're beautiful." She held a napkin up in the sunlight. "How many come to a set?"

"Um . . . there are only two napkins presently, but for a loyal patron we could specially commission a set. How many do you need?"

"Napkins? Twelve at least. Maybe a few dish towels would be nice in a complementary design. This tablecloth is just the right size already. Can I take it?" She was already fumbling in her purse, lamp forgotten.

Rosa covered her mouth in astonishment. Louise threw an arm around her shoulder and gave her a silent squeeze. They tiptoed to the hardware department to give Mr. Bradford the room he needed to negotiate a price without Mrs. Schwartz seeing them. Rosa didn't mind the anonymity. She'd much rather have gold in her pocket than praise in her ears. Too bad she couldn't pay the county land office directly in napkins and call it even.

As soon as the woman departed, Mr. Bradford found them. "What'd I tell you?" He opened a jar of licorice and offered each of them a piece before selecting one for himself. "We'll have no problem selling these," he said, taking a bite. "If I still had my own store, I'd start selling them to the other mercantiles around. As it is, we might keep you local for now. Once this market is saturated . . . But listen to me, I'm didn't mean to bore you with business talk."

Rosa wasn't bored at all, but he wasn't talking to her. He was smiling over her head at Louise.

Louise dimpled and brushed her red hair back. "I'm sorry, Mr. Bradford. I haven't changed since school. Numbers don't mean a thing to me."

"Does zero mean anything to you, because that's where your account stands now, and I owe you more to boot. Is a dollar fifty fair, Rosa? I'll trade you the work you did on this batch for a dollar fifty plus the balance on the account."

Looking around the store, she saw that a dollar fifty would go a good ways toward buying the supplies they'd come after. With the account paid off, she should be able to put money up from the next batch of linens. How many napkins would she need to embroider to make a hundred sixty-six dollars?

Louise broke into her reverie. "You're more than generous, Mr. Bradford. She'd find something to sew on anyway. It might as well give us some pin money."

Pin money? These funds weren't for trivial purchases, but to keep them from being homeless. Time kept rolling toward August fifteenth, and the money hadn't accumulated. But it didn't do any good to be frustrated with her mother-in-law. God hadn't given the woman a lick of sense about money. Concern over the finances was shouldered by Rosa alone, but she'd have to remember to speak up more quickly in these situations. She couldn't let Louise negotiate for them.

"I do enjoy sewing, but with all the work we have to do in the garden, and now with the sheep, I don't know how much time I'll have. Those things have to be tended to if we are going to keep our ranch." Would Louise take the gentle hint?

Mr. Bradford sure did. "Yes, and depending on how fast you sew, it might be worth your time or it might not." He chewed on the licorice. "Tell you what, Mrs. Schwartz caught me off guard. Maybe she would have paid more for those napkins. I don't know, but I'll try to do better next time. You finish that order at two bits a napkin and then make me a slew of samples with different designs and colors. We'll let them pick the design they want and do only custom orders from then on out. We can charge more that way, and we won't have any surplus sitting around. We can do the same with the pillowcases. Does that sound reasonable?"

"So my commission on these napkins was two bits each. Next time it'll be higher?"

He shrugged. "If they'll pay more."

"Rosa, you know Mr. Bradford will treat you fairly," Louise said. "You can trust him."

"I appreciate your confidence, Mrs. Garner, but your daughter-in-law is sharp. She knows that it's best to get the details before you strike hands." He scratched his chin, probably not realizing that he was still staring at Louise. He blinked as he caught himself. "But there is one more project I'd like her to take on, if you have no objections." Bradford disappeared behind a display of canned goods and returned with a bright rose bolt hoisted on his shoulder. He dropped it on the counter. "What do you think of this color? It's new, called magenta."

Rosa ran her fingertips over the shiny material — too fragile to work for pillowcases or table linens — amazed by how it turned from lavender to pink to nearly violet.

"They say this dye was discovered in Italy, but you've got some of it in those napkins." Mr. Bradford smiled. "I think you like it. Too bad no one else in this town does. They're all afraid to wear it, afraid that the color is too strong for them. They're probably right. So if you'll use it, I'll send a few yards home with you. A welcome-home gift."

"I can take this?" she whispered. Since leaving Mexico she hadn't seen any colors this bold and beautiful.

Louise smiled through tears at Deacon. She unfurled the bolt and draped it over

162

Rosa's shoulders. "You've never had taffeta before, have you? Then it's settled. You must make yourself a gown. This color will be magnificent on you . . . when you're out of mourning, of course. No one else would do justice to this hue."

"For me to wear?" Rosa had never seen anything as exquisite as this shimmering fabric and would've never dreamed of using it all for a gown, but she wasn't going to let them change their minds now. "I will use it. It will be glorious. Thank you, Mr. Bradford. Thank you so much. I can't wait to tell Molly when I have dinner with her. Magenta? Is that right?"

Deacon took a pair of scissors and sheared off a generous amount. "So are you eating with Molly? I'd hoped to treat the two of you to dinner. The noon clerk will relieve me shortly." He wrapped the material with brown paper and tied it up tightly.

Louise's black skirts twisted as she spun to Rosa, eyes bright. "Wouldn't you rather meet Molly without me? I imagine that would be agreeable to everyone, don't you? I'm sure you'll have a splendid visit without having to endure my rambling."

Louise's rambling didn't bother Rosa. It'd saved her from having to converse on many occasions, but from the expression on

Louise's face she could hardly refuse.

Who looked more eager for her answer, Louise or Mr. Bradford? "Go have your dinner with Mr. Bradford. Molly won't mind."

They didn't ask twice. Mr. Bradford handed his apron to the stunned clerk walking through the door, and they were off.

"Mother will be so pleased we had this rendezvous. She really wants us to be friends, you know, since she and Mrs. Garner are so close." Molly dipped her spoon daintily into the creamy potato soup and blew on it from perfectly pouted lips. "And you must have a confidante. No girl should go through life with only her mother-in-law with whom to share her deepest secrets."

Did she have any secrets in this county? Rosa couldn't lace up her boots without someone commenting on the color of her stockings. And if she was the type to share secrets, she'd find someone more discreet than Molly.

"So it's for the best that Louise — oops — Mrs. Garner, I mean, couldn't come. Don't misunderstand, I love her with all my heart, I really do, but this gives us a chance to gossip without her. Now, I've received extensive training on identifying eligible men. Have any of the young bachelors in town caught your eye?"

Rosa couldn't hide her disapproval.

"Don't pout at me, Rosa. I mean, you're still dressed as black as a crow, but a girl must plan ahead."

Molly waved the waiter down for more sweet tea, gave him an effusive thank you, a touch on his arm, and settled into her task of filling Rosa in on the local swains — their attributes and failures. Rosa tried to remember names and descriptions, but they all ran together.

"Molly, by August I may not even live in Texas, and, as you pointed out, I'm in mourning. Don't you think it's premature to be choosing a husband for me?"

"No, I don't. You should be laying the ground work, even now. First, you need to identify a target. Personally, I'd rather you aim for a Mexican. It'd be awful if we found ourselves at cross purposes. . . ." Molly looked up at Rosa through curled lashes. When Rosa didn't respond, Molly continued. "But if you want to expand your options, I understand. Once you've set your cap for a man, you must determine what he likes and where he goes. Men really are simple creatures. Unlike us, they can say what they think, which is quite helpful.

Nevertheless, I think you'd benefit from my assistance. Since everyone is a complete stranger to you, it might take a while to discern their interests."

Especially since Rosa couldn't even discern what "setting your cap" or "cross purposes" meant.

The hovering waiter took their bowls and asked if there was anything else they wanted. Molly requested two pieces of pecan pie and reminded him to place the bill on her father's account.

"For instance, Rosa, if he plays an instrument, you might join a musical society. If he's handy, you might find him at a barn-raising. If he's a lawyer, you could get a job at the courthouse — not a good example. That one didn't pan out."

"But I'm not interested in that sort of courtship. If a man admires you, he should seek you."

Molly rolled her eyes. "What if he doesn't know he loves you? What if he's committed to bachelorhood? Many happy brides have married men who had no plans for matrimony."

"You mean they tricked them?" Was Molly planning something against Weston? Rosa's heart thudded.

"Tricked, swayed, wore down. It hinges

on being in the right place at the right time. One moment of weakness for the poor fellow, and he's committed."

The pies arrived. Rosa poked at the crust, her mind a jumble of alarm.

Molly stared at her. "Aren't you going to taste it?"

Rosa managed to get a lump into her mouth and wash it down with water.

"Mm . . ." She faked appreciation. Her eyes watered and her throat constricted. She couldn't eat another bite without setting Molly straight.

"Never trick someone into marrying you."

"People do. Happens all the time."

"But he won't love you. If it isn't his idea, he'll resent you."

"My stars, Rosa! I'm not going to compromise a man. What do you take me for?" Molly's eyes widened. She shoveled in another bite of pie. "I'm talking about making myself irresistible or setting the mood. About finding what he wants and becoming that."

"I don't understand. What if you catch him? What if he marries you and then regrets it? Would you want that kind of union? You're beautiful and smart, Molly. If a man doesn't appreciate those qualities, you don't want to make a spectacle of

167

yourself hounding him, do you?"

"Beauty is an asset — intelligence a liability. Believe me, if I had any say in the matter . . ." Molly rolled her blue eyes. "Let's just say that until I'm wed, I won't have achieved anything of value in the eyes of my parents. At my age, I'm getting frightfully close to being a disappointment, but don't you worry. I wouldn't do anything to humiliate my family. I do have some pride."

Rosa finished her pie with relief. She wasn't sure what Molly was capable of, but it didn't sound like Weston was in imminent danger. Good thing. The Garner family didn't need two members providing fodder for scandal.

12

"Hullo! Did someone order a shipment of sheep?"

Rosa dropped her embroidery on the settee. A quick look out the parlor window revealed a mounted man waving at her and a flock meandering up the drive to the open pasture gate.

"Louise, you're not going to believe your eyes."

"Land sakes!" Louise still held a wooden spoon in her hand. "Where did all those sheep come from? And what's that donkey doing in the mix?"

Rosa couldn't wipe the smile off her face. He'd even sent a burro. Grabbing her stunned mother-in-law by the arm, she dragged her to the front porch.

"Howdy, Mrs. Garner and Mrs. Garner. Jake England at your service." He tipped his hat with a roguish smile that spread beneath a nose knocked awry, probably by a hostile fist long ago. "I sure hope I'm at the right farm. I ain't herding these old girls back across the creek."

The sheep milled past, driven by two young men. Behind them came a wagon holding two more men, one being young Samuel, Uncle George and Aunt Mary's son.

"My nephew Weston told me to expect some unsound ewes. You've got the correct location, but perhaps you've brought the wrong flock."

"No mistake, ma'am. I reckon there were some extras he wanted to be rid of, ewes and wethers. If it makes you feel better, there're some in need of doctoring in the wagon. We'll get them put up in the barn for ya."

Ignoring the sheep, Rosa watched the cowboys' antics. The wagon driver had kicked Samuel out and was arguing with him over the best way to get the stubborn burro to its final destination. Seeing them squared off, no one could deny the family resemblance. Not only did both boys have Uncle George's features stamped across their faces, but their heated gestures were easily identifiable as Aunt Mary's. Why, she really was surrounded by family! And the man on the horse? Louise pieced it together at the same moment she did.

"Jake England, did you say? Then you're my little Eliza's sweet husband."

"I don't know about sweet," he drawled. "That girl is more trouble than any sweet man could handle." He winked outrageously at Rosa. Evidently, Eliza had met her match.

"Nonsense. I won't have you talking about my niece that way, although I have to confess she hasn't changed one bit since she was a little sprite — sassy-mouthed and bossy. Weston had his hands full after their father died."

"Yes, ma'am, and now the job falls on me." He took off his hat and swung it over his heart. "When you're saying your prayers at night, remember to send up a special request for ol' Jake England. I need the patience of a saint."

"And you're far from it!" The speaker was a lanky young man with hands too big to fit in his pockets. "Welcome home, Aunt Louise."

"Bailey? George and Mary's boy? My, how you've grown!" Louise's words confirmed Rosa's suspicions. Another cousin.

Louise rustled forward, and he accepted the obligatory hug and cheek kiss, much to the amusement of his fellow cowboys, who'd returned from penning the sheep and

171

burro. There they stood, lined up, gawking like they'd never seen women before.

"And this is my daughter-in-law, Rosa Garner. You remember Mack, don't you, Bailey?"

"Yes, ma'am. Mother told me about your loss." They observed a moment of silence, as was fitting, and then Bailey commenced with his own introductions.

"Please excuse me, ladies. I've been on the trail for three months and have completely lost my manners. Anyway, this fellow here is Willie and the youngster there is Rico."

Willie tipped his hat, and then stepped back, but Rico, seeing a fellow compatriot, bounded forward and, with a sweep of his hat, caught Rosa's hand and pressed it to his lips.

"*Mucho gusto,* señorita."

The Mexican youth made an instant impression on Rosa. Initially, she'd thought that both he and Willie were of African blood, so she wasn't prepared for how her heart leapt at the language from her homeland.

Rico was considerably younger than she, as were all the cowboys with the exception of Jake, but she couldn't help but be drawn to him. She wondered about his family.

Where were they? Could she meet them?

Ambushed by homesickness that'd been tightly suppressed, she answered him. "Thank you, señor. Mucho gusto, as well."

"That's not fair." Bailey pulled Rico away from her. "You're in Texas. Speak English so the rest of us can understand."

"The rest of you could never understand." He fanned his face dreamily and made such obvious eyes at Rosa, she knew at once he was only acting for the benefit of his friends.

"Sorry about them, ma'am," Jake interrupted. "They've been out of civilization for too long. We should have given them more time to get adjusted before bringing them out here."

"I'm not offended." Rosa smiled at each of them, boys really. Dangerous, impulsive boys, but boys at heart.

Louise waved them forward with her wooden spoon. "Come on in. At least allow us to get you refreshments before going back."

"No, ma'am. Weston would string me up if I let them in your parlor. Bulls in a china shop, they are, but if we could help ourselves to your water pump, we'd be mighty appreciative."

The June sun had peaked and was relentless. The heat would get worse — at least that's what they'd told her — and she couldn't doubt it, as every day the green spring was burned out of the grass and leaves, the colors fading and fading. The prairie would brown long before the autumn chill stopped the growth, but for now they still could catch a cool breeze in the evenings. Still, it was hard to imagine more heat for weeks on end. The foliage and altitude of Ciauhtlaz hadn't allowed for such misery.

"So, the sheep are at pasture. Those in the field are healthy. Don't know what he had in mind with the donkey. That thing is purt near worthless. Could barely get it through the gate." Jake flashed a grin at Rosa. "Is that for you to ride?"

"No, sir." But she would if she needed to.

"We unloaded the hurt ewes and wethers from the wagon and put them in the barn. They'll need that ointment on their cuts once a day. If they get infected, send over to George's, and he'll get someone to come and check it out. Is that it?"

The cowboys swung into their saddles and headed toward home. Bailey let Samuel hold the reins on the empty wagon, bringing an end to their dispute.

Jake turned one last time. "It was a pleasure meeting you, Mrs. Garner. I'm glad to finally make the acquaintance of Eliza's favorite aunt. And you, Mrs. Rosa. I think I see what all the fuss is about. Good day." He clicked to his horse and was gone.

Rosa watched them ride off before she turned to Louise. "What did he mean by that? I haven't made any fuss, have I?"

Louise put her arm around her shoulder as they walked to the barn to examine their sheep. "No, honey. You haven't made a fuss, but evidently you've caused one."

From his seat on the church steps on Sunday, Weston had an unobstructed view of his sister and Rosa at their places in the serving line. Their foreheads almost touched as they shared some private news over a pot of green beans. No telling what mischief Eliza was up to, but the girls got on splendidly. He was a little surprised. Maybe Rosa would have a calming effect on Eliza.

But the congregation's varied reactions to the señora astonished him. Some had quickly welcomed her into their tight-knit circle, perhaps out of sympathy — both for her and for Louise — and perhaps because she was the tiniest, least threatening filly to ever wander in their midst. If dishes needed washing, she chose the dirtiest. If children needed tending, she held the heaviest. She did her part, and then some.

But a few grew more suspicious with each good deed. They'd already declared their disapproval — Weston remembered who — and Rosa's good behavior thwarted their expectations. If she didn't cause a scandal soon, they'd be eating crow.

Weston mopped up some gravy with his biscuit. Rosa made him proud. She was a quick study. Keeping her on the farms helped, too. Not much trouble for her to get into out there — unless the sheep got loose.

"It's good to see you laugh."

Weston took a second to make out who was speaking amidst the pink flounces and red ribbons. He should have known. Only Molly could pull off a getup like that.

"Good day, Miss Lovelace. That's quite a plateful of sweets you have there."

"Mother always said my eyes were bigger than my stomach." She batted the former and cinched up the latter. "May I share?"

That's what he got for sitting by himself, unsociable. He scooted to the far side of the wooden steps, giving her room to join him. If anyone had a right to his attention, it'd be her. Her family could lay claim to his time whenever they pleased. He'd only started shaving when he joined Mr. Lovelace's rescue attempt for the Texas Mounted Volunteers after the disastrous Sibley Campaign. His father died during the ill-fated attack against the Union at Glorieta Pass, but many local men were saved because of Lovelace's actions. It didn't hurt Weston to talk to his daughter.

"Are those gingersnaps?"

"Sure are." She sat a step lower than he and held out her plate. "I brought them."

They melted in his mouth. "They're my favorite. You made these, you say?"

The smile froze on her lips. "Not exactly. Lola made them."

Her cook. "Well, pass on my compliments to Lola. They're delicious."

Had he done his duty? The steps steamed under the noon sun. Weston wanted to seek shade, but Molly's brother caught him before he could escape.

"Howdy, Weston. Why are you sitting way out here by yourself?"

"He's not by himself. I'm here."

Nicholas rolled his eyes. "What I mean is, he hasn't stayed for dinner in ages. Now here he is, and he's acting like a leper. No offense, Wes, just making an observation."

Molly shoved her plate into her brother's hands. "Here, why don't you finish this off for me?"

Weston couldn't keep his attention away from Rosa. Was it his imagination, or was she troubled? He saw her startle, then drop her serving spoon. She went to the dessert table to stand by Louise, leaving Jay Tillerton holding his empty plate in confusion.

Weston realized too late that Molly was watching him with the same intensity.

"Nick," she said, "why don't you see if Rosa has had any dinner yet. She should get something to eat before they have to start cleaning up."

Nicholas's dimpled cheeks moved up an inch on his face. "Capital idea. And she's already at the dessert table."

Perhaps Weston was mistaken. Whatever had alarmed Rosa seemed to have passed. She smiled brightly at Nicholas as he ambled toward her. Weston couldn't hear what he said, but it must have been funny, for Rosa repeated it to Louise, causing the laughing woman to fling her dish towel at Nicholas.

Molly cleared her throat. "The other night I was reading a volume called *The Mythology of Ancient Greece and Italy,* and I found it so fascinating."

"Really?"

Nicholas brought Rosa a drink. Of course she was thirsty. She hadn't had anything

178

since church started. Why hadn't he thought of that?

"Yes, and several stories caught my attention. I couldn't help but wonder, what's your favorite?"

Rosa took a seat at a long table with Nicholas at her side. She wolfed her food down, probably trying to get away from the oaf as quickly as possible. Nicholas either chewed or talked continuously, sometimes simultaneously, for his mouth never stilled.

"Weston?"

Weston turned, surprised to find Molly sitting by him. How had he imagined that she'd left?

"What?"

"Your favorite Greek myth?"

He shrugged. "I'm not familiar with Greek myths."

"But your horse is named Pandora."

"Eliza named her. If you are interested in myths, talk to her. She likes to read all those old books."

"You don't know any myths?"

Why was the girl so disappointed? "I never had a reason to read them."

Molly flicked a beetle crawling up the step. "Neither have I, evidently."

Rosa had finished eating. She rose, putting a hand on Nicholas's shoulder to steady herself as she slid between the table and bench. Weston winced and then rose to his feet.

"Looks like time to break camp."

Molly played with a red ribbon. "And I didn't bring my apron. Why can I never remember that?"

"Then maybe I can lend a hand. If you'll excuse me."

Making his way around the picnic blankets and long tables toward where Eliza and Rosa were already scrubbing plate after plate, he grunted again at the nerve of the Lovelace boy. Did he mean anything by his friendliness? Was he really going to court her? Weston didn't think so. From what he knew of the man's family, only a first-rate society belle would do, not a young widow without a penny to her name. If marriage wasn't Nicholas's goal, then his intentions could be narrowed to very few legitimate options. He might have a talk with the young man.

Weston gathered empty dishes from a grateful young mother's table and calmed himself. Nicholas hadn't done anything wrong — yet. Surely Thomas and Adele wouldn't permit him to meddle with Rosa.

Yes, he felt obligated to care for the whole herd of Garners, but couldn't little Rosita make things easier on him? The way she looked up at the boy with stars in her eyes . . .

Jake joined him and followed his gaze. "Yep, the boys were pretty impressed with her when we delivered the sheep. They were squirming all over each other like puppies."

"I was afraid of that."

"Looks like you'll need to ride shotgun until you get her safely married off."

Married off? What was he talking about? "I don't think she's in any hurry. Mack hasn't been dead a year yet."

"That ain't gonna matter to those good-for-nothing hands of yours. They're taking to her like calves to sweet feed."

Wes tossed the contents of a mug to the ground. "I'll talk to them. Help them see the light."

"I hope you can think of something to do. Walking around all stiff-necked and on edge like you are has got to be tiring."

"Stiff-necked?"

"Every time you throw a glance in Nicholas's direction, you look like you're judging his hide for boot leather," Jake said.

"Now that you mention it, his hide wouldn't tan well. Too greasy."

"Did you come to help with the dishes?" Eliza splashed her husband as they approached.

"Just came to say hi to my new cousin and make sure you weren't filling her noggin with nonsense."

Rosa ducked her head over her work, causing her silver earrings to swing forward daintily, but she wasn't quick enough to hide her smile.

At least someone was having a good time. They were all having a good time — except for him. Weston slid the pile of dirty dishes onto the workbench. At least he was there, and that was a step in the right direction. He'd known it wouldn't be easy at first.

Eliza took the plates, dumped the scraps past the split-rail fence, and dropped the plates into the sudsy water.

"Rosa and I were just discussing how soon she could put off mourning and get into something besides black."

Weston felt as if he'd been socked right in the jaw. Maybe Rosa was as impatient as the fellows were. Before he could voice his disapproval, she spoke for herself.

"Eliza wants me to get new clothes, but it's unnecessary. This dress is still practically new, and we can't afford anything else. Besides, I wear my old clothes on the farm."

Weston hadn't realized he was holding his breath. His fists unclenched. "I couldn't agree more, Mrs. Garner. You look very respectable in the black." He knew Eliza was staring hard at him, but he wouldn't look her direction.

"We got the sheep." Rosa's eyelashes fluttered downward. "And the burro. Thank you. I love Conejo." There were blank looks all around. "The burro's name — it means 'rabbit.' "

"Because he's so soft and cuddly?" Even Jake acted smitten. Was the whole county going mad?

"No, because of his long ears and big teeth." Rosa demonstrated by sucking in her bottom lip and making her teeth protrude.

Their laughter carried across the grounds. Good. Let Nicholas hear her enjoying herself. Maybe he wouldn't have the nerve to monopolize her time again.

Deacon Bradford strolled across the green with more dirty plates in an outstretched hand. "I appreciate y'all taking over the clean-up duties. Gives us old fogies some time to reminisce."

Eliza turned and grinned at Louise still seated at his table. "Making some new memories, as well, Mr. Bradford?"

"Yes, well, I . . ." He loosened the puff tie around his neck. "We have a lot of catching up to do. You there, Rosa, how's the sewing going?"

"I finished Mrs. Schwartz's linens and made the samples you wanted. They're in my bag."

"That's dandy. I thought you'd have them finished. You don't let the grass grow under your feet, do you? I brought more linens if you're ready for them." Deacon seemed far more comfortable combing the familiar shores of commerce.

"I'm not sure what grass has to do with it, but I'll fetch my carpetbag."

Weston rubbed his chin. Maybe Eliza would like a new tablecloth. Rosa could come out and measure . . . His eyes followed her as she walked past.

Eliza elbowed him. "Looking for something?"

He threw his sister a withering look. "Just wondered if her bag was heavy, but I reckon she can manage without me."

The crowd gradually dispersed as small groups headed out, continuing conversations until the geography of their homes forced them to part.

"You're welcome to come out to the house," Louise called to Weston from Jake's skirt-filled buggy. "Jake and Eliza are going to stop for a bit, and we'd be glad to have you."

Jake pulled up his team, waiting for his answer.

"Thanks, but I'll get on home. Y'all enjoy yourselves." Weston tipped his hat as they traveled on toward the creek, then spurred his horse to the east.

No way would he stroll into that ambush. Just what Eliza needed, another opportunity to make a mountain out of a molehill. Wasn't he having enough trouble finding his way without her complicating the matter?

What was all her talk about Rosa ending her mourning anyway? Was she trying to annoy him?

If he caught the story correctly, and he'd listened intently, Eli and Mack had died less than a year ago. True, things had changed after the war — mourning periods weren't strictly observed now — but why rush her? Didn't Rosa deserve the dignity afforded a widow?

And if Eliza thought that Rosa should be ready to move on, what must she think of him? Five years and he was no more ready to consider matrimony than the day of the funeral. Maybe even less likely now that he'd let his loneliness leech onto him and drain away the cherished memories of being a husband.

No situation he could imagine would tempt him to remarry. He'd learned too well how to remain aloof. He was an expert at it. But even as he rehearsed his resolve, he sensed a change.

Letting the reins go slack, he coaxed the gentle thought out of hiding. His mind had traveled this bitter trail so many times, the ruts had worn deep. He wasn't interested, he argued, but he sensed a calling to jump trail and explore the option again.

How had he concluded he'd never marry again? Had he prayed about it? Had God demanded it from him? No. Not much he'd thought or done in the last five years had been Spirit-birthed.

On the other hand, wasn't this for him to decide? He could make things right with God, but he wouldn't cheerfully tangle with the same grizzly twice. Couldn't they negotiate? He still wasn't ready to enter society. Take today for example. Keeping people at arms' length felt comfortable. He could still be generous and take care of people without really . . . caring. Or so he'd thought.

But God wasn't letting him get by like that any longer.

He couldn't get away from Uncle George's

question. Had God called him to keep his distance, or was he listening to his fear?

Okay, God. I'll agree I'm afraid, and you have the right to call me on it, but let's not start worrying about marriage yet. There's plenty of time for that. Besides, if you just want to see if I'm willing to follow you, then the answer is yes — I'm trying, but I pray it was just a test, like Abraham and Isaac. You really don't expect me to carry it out, right? "Not my will, but thine be done . . . but if possible take this cup from me." Can I pray that like Jesus did?

But then Weston remembered how that prayer was answered and soberly rode the rest of the way home.

13

July 1878

The stifling heat had staked a claim and wasn't relinquishing an inch. The long parched summer destroyed more crops than a round of tornadoes, spreading its damage far and wide instead of only upturning a narrow path. Only by constant vigilance were the garden kept damp and the sheep led to water. And the longhorns — they didn't need much help. They thrived under the harsh conditions.

Catching a glimpse of the sheep through an open window, Rosa smiled. They'd turned out the last ewe from the barn that morning. All had survived and would no longer need the smelly paste smeared over their wounds every day. If they stayed healthy until August fifteenth, the stain on her fingers would be worth it.

She wiped the sweat from her brow with an already moist rag. She mustn't drip on the rose taffeta as she bent over the table. The large steel scissors weighed heavy in her hand. She'd already measured twice. If she made a mistake, there'd be no surplus to draw from. Dress or no dress, she couldn't bear to mar the scrumptious fabric.

Glad to wear her loose-fitting *camisa,* she wondered again at the clothes the ladies chose to wear in this heat. True, on the farm Louise and Aunt Mary wore shirtwaists that were thinner and looser than those they wore to town, but they still had fitted sleeves. She was so careful not to sweat while working on her dress, but what would she do when she wore it in the heat? She sighed. Then again, maybe she wouldn't wear it until winter. What occasion would be grand enough to warrant such a beautiful gown?

The scissors sliced through the material effortlessly, like water bugs across the river, the excess fabric sliding silently off the table and making a puddle of pink on the floor. The window was open, but the cool morning air had vanished. She should take a moment to shut up the house, preserving the temperature as long as possible, but she didn't want to leave her work. She'd dreamt about her dress while she fed the chickens, weeded the garden, and stitched the pillowcases.

But those tasks had priority. Her vanity couldn't derail the slow progress they were making toward their goal.

Louise did what she could. That very morning, she'd left early to help Aunt Mary can tomatoes, expecting a few jars to bring home and a few coins if they sold well in town. It wouldn't be much, but every order for linens, every blossom on the stalks, every chance to help Aunt Mary was a blessing from God. Rosa had learned that lesson at Eli's table: You can sit around and wait for gifts to fall off the tree into your lap, or you can climb the tree and get your gifts yourself. Over time you'll find God leaves most of His gifts in the tree. The chickens, the sheep, and the garden all meant a few more bills to stuff in the crockery pot that sat in the sparse pantry.

According to Aunt Mary, they could replant in the fall and have a winter crop too, but that wouldn't help when the taxes were due. As she spun the material around to start cutting from the other side, Rosa tried to calculate their progress. The sheep were an unexpected boon, but she couldn't guess their market value. Maybe she shouldn't worry. Louise seemed content.

Rosa hated to be negative in the face of

Louise's optimism. Louise was proud of all they'd accomplished. Getting her house cleaned out, repairing it, and even planting a garden were more than the older lady had thought possible without the help of her husband and son. Daily she seemed surprised at how well they were doing, and perhaps they would be if it weren't for the taxes crouching at their door waiting to wolf down their hard-earned money.

Less than two months! Rosa sighed and dropped the scissors into her basket. Why did Louise refuse to face the future? She ignored Rosa's and Mary's reminders of the amount they'd have by August — an amount that fell well short of what they needed.

"God has plans for us," she'd said, squeezing Rosa's shoulder. *"He takes special care of widows and orphans. He won't forget us."*

But what were those plans? Rosa never forgot her sheep, either, but she wouldn't want to share the fate that awaited them.

Perhaps Louise had options she wasn't disclosing. Rosa dearly hoped so. She couldn't see any way their feeble efforts could amass such a sum. She folded the taffeta and wrapped it with the protective brown paper. Standing, she put her hands on her hips and stretched her back. Her worries had distracted her — she'd been so caught up in her thoughts that she hadn't stopped for dinner.

Not wanting Louise to be upset when she got back from Mary's and found the house sweltering, Rosa went from room to room, closing the windows and pulling the shades. She was in the kitchen when she heard a familiar sound, reminiscent of her childhood. It was Conejo braying like burros do, whether in English, Spanish, or Nahuatl. He sounded like he was just on the other side of the barn. Would something stalk the sheep that close to the house?

Rosa grabbed the rifle from behind the kitchen door. Down the porch steps she rushed and across the yard, hoping she wouldn't need the gun. She didn't know how to fire it, but bringing it along seemed wise.

She rounded the barn to find the sheep grazing calmly. Good. She opened the gate before she realized there were two burros in the pasture. No, not two. One was a horse with a man on it. Rosa's arms dropped to her sides in relief, but as he drew closer she recognized the drooping moustache, the sloped shoulders, and the sardonic grin. Jay Tillerton! She tightened her grip on the rifle, holding it across her chest, and prayed

192

she had the correct hand on the trigger.

"What are you doing here?" she asked cautiously. No use getting him riled if he had no devilry in mind.

"Just checking on my neighbors. What's the gun for?"

Her memory of the cellar was too clear to dismiss. She didn't have a gun in hand then, and she wouldn't lay down arms now. She bluffed. "Protection."

Tillerton spat derisively, and raised his eyebrows. "I've got a gun myself." He pushed his vest back, exposing the handle of his pistol. "And I use it when I have to."

"I'll remember that before I trespass on your property." She didn't even blink. If he shot her in her own pasture, there wasn't a jury in Texas that wouldn't hang him. Even she knew that. But maybe he wanted to be civil this time. "How's your wife?"

"She has a hard time staying healthy, that's for sure, but I'll send her your regards." He shifted in the saddle. "I just wanted to make a neighborly visit and see how things are going. Seems like I saw your mother-in-law headed over the creek toward George's this morning. She's not home yet, is she?"

No point in lying. She allowed the barrel to droop toward the ground. "I don't know when she's coming home."

"Left you all alone? Don't you think that's kind of dangerous?"

Rosa didn't answer. She didn't move an inch. Was he worried for her or threatening her? Either way, some instinct told her that she was safer here in the wide open prairie than she would be if he got her into the house.

"I'll tell you what's dangerous," he continued. "It's two women living alone without any menfolk around. But you're not going to have to worry for long, are you? In a month you'll have to find somewhere more suitable to live — some little property two women can handle."

"We hope it won't come to that."

He stroked his moustache. "Of course you do, but in the meantime it pays to be prepared. You see, I've been up to the courthouse. Just curious, I guess. I checked into what it took to buy a county lien, and it's not complicated at all."

"Lien? What has our farm got to do with you?"

"More than you might think. If someone, me for example, can come up with the delinquent taxes due on August fifteenth, the county deeds the property to that person. Simple as pie. Not that I'd want to do that, though. There should be a more neighborly way to handle this situation, don't you think, Mrs. Garner?"

Rosa's stomach revolted. Bile rose in her throat as his words rang true. If they didn't have the money, they'd not only lose the ranch, but they would lose it to him! He wasn't just threatening her reputation, he was threatening Louise's livelihood. At that moment she'd give everything she owned and everything she'd ever own to have the ground open up at his feet and swallow him alive.

"I asked you a question." He looked down at her from the heights of his horse's back.

She refused to answer.

"I want to make a deal with you. Surely we can negotiate a solution that would be more acceptable to us both." His lips spread in an evil leer. "Just because you lose your land doesn't mean you have to move. You could stay here so we could see more of each other." He perused her body from head to toe. "Of course, you'd need to allow calls of a more personal nature. Besides that moment in the cellar, you haven't done much to recommend yourself."

The cellar hadn't been an accident, and he wasn't apologizing. Some ancient Aztec fury boiled over in her veins. From deep

195

inside her gut she bellowed as she raised her rifle with both hands over her head and ran at him, intending to club him to death. His horse startled and trotted out of her range as she swung the weapon like an ax.

"Get off my land!" She turned to run at him again, murder in her eyes. This time she aimed for the horse's legs, hoping to unseat him.

He retreated to a safe distance. "Obviously you don't know how to use that thing. Something for me to keep in mind."

She didn't know, but now was a good time to learn. Her temper pushed her beyond reasonable thought. Her heart raced and a white heat flooded over her body, giving her strength she didn't know she possessed. She was facing evil. It smothered her, taunted her, and threatened to consume her. She raised the rifle to her shoulder and looked down the barrel, not even sure if it was loaded.

"Don't bother," he called. "I'm leaving, but think it over. That'll be the best offer you get. Besides, a woman like you must get lonely out here."

Chest heaving, she kept the rifle pointed in his direction. The gun was heavy, but she managed to hold it steady until he reached the far gully and hauled his lousy carcass off her land.

The sky had faded before Louise returned, escorted by Nicholas. Their carefree voices preceded them, chatting easily until they were thwarted by the locked door.

"Land sakes!" Louise cried as Rosa unlocked the door and let them enter. "It's cooler outside than in here. Why don't you have the windows open?" She removed her bonnet and tossed it on the chair. Going to the window, she tugged it open. "That's better. Is the upstairs closed up, too?"

Rosa's brow lowered. She nodded.

"I don't know what's gotten into you, sitting here pouting. I thought you wanted to stay and work on your dress." Louise continued grumbling as her heels clicked on the wooden stairs, leaving Nicholas standing in the doorway.

"I'd rather poke a bear with a stick than cross an angry woman." He edged his way around her. "But do you mind if I help myself to a drink? It's mighty dry out there."

She didn't answer but followed him to the kitchen, where he filled a cup with water.

"Well, since you aren't talking I guess I better ask. What's wrong?" He took a seat and peered at her over the edge of his tin cup.

What could she tell Nicholas? Tax liens were public record. Surely her good name couldn't be stained by that.

"It's that Mr. Tillerton." She sank into a chair and studied her calloused palms. "He scares me."

"Pshaw." Nicholas waved her concern away. "He's not very scary. Puny, in fact. A jolly fellow, best I can tell, although not much of a rancher. If it weren't for his shop burning up in the fire, he wouldn't have a dime to his name. Nothing to fear."

"His shop burned?"

"Yeah, in the big fire last year. It started at his shop, actually — right after he bought it. Smack dab among the other stores in Prairie Lea. Fortunately for him he had insurance. A lot, actually. Poor folks like Mr. Bradford didn't have any and are still trying to recoup their losses."

"Do you know his wife?"

"His wife? Don't think much of her. If I remember correctly, Father said she used to be a student of Mr. Tillerton's. She caused him to lose his job, some way or another."

"She didn't say much when we met, almost to the point of rudeness."

He nodded. "That's what I've heard, too,

but you won't meet a pleasanter man. Too bad he's shackled to a disagreeable wife. Can't say I blame him for leaving her on the farm." He leaned back in his chair, which protested loudly. "What? Why are you glaring at me like that? What's he done to get you riled?"

Her stomach soured again at the memory. "He was here tonight. He says he's going to get our farm if the lien isn't paid on time."

Nicholas drummed his fingers on the table. "Well, he has an adjoining border, so it's hardly a surprise that he wants it, but it's bad form to boast about it." He shook his head. "I thought he was courteous, but I guess he's just another uncouth Yankee — no manners at all."

"Well, he's not getting our farm, because I won't —" Her hand covered her mouth. Uh-oh. But Nicholas forged ahead.

"Well, I'm terribly sorry he offended you. He probably had no intention of doing so. Don't let him get under your skin."

What about my skirt? But she couldn't say that.

He scooted his chair out and rose to his feet. "There're plenty of good folks around here. You can't let one blackguard ruin your evening." Rosa followed him through the parlor. "But I did bring you some good news. I guess Mrs. Garner would tell you, but I'd rather you hear it from me.

"You're invited to our house for the Fourth of July. We'll have fireworks and the Prairie Lea parade. It'll be stupendous. And the best part . . . you'll have Nick to show you the town."

Coming through the opposite doorway at the same moment, Louise drew up short.

"Oh, Nicholas, you didn't know . . . we've made other plans for Rosa. She isn't going to Prairie Lea."

"Not going? And why not? It'd be just the thing for her."

Rosa ducked her head so they wouldn't see the disappointment on her face. She pinched some dead leaves off the potted African violet and a few that weren't quite dead yet.

"Mary wants Rosa to come to their place. Weston won't let the hands leave the ranch for the festivities, so they're going to cook up something for them. Barbecue, music, and some fireworks, I think. Anyway, she asked if Rosa could come help her and Eliza get it all together. They need her help."

"But you're coming with us?" Nicholas asked.

Louise never stammered. True, she said things she shouldn't, but words usually flowed effortlessly out of her mouth. Not this time.

"I'm coming to Prairie Lea . . . your mother has offered me a room overnight . . . but I may not accompany you during the day." She caught a stray tendril and wrapped it around her finger in the gesture of a woman twenty years her junior.

"Why? What is it, Louise?" Rosa could be more direct than Nicholas, who shared the same skeptical look she had.

Louise swung both hands in the air before dropping them at her side. Rosa fully expected her to flounce off and stomp to her room, but she kept a loose grip on her maturity.

"Mr. Bradford asked if I would allow him to accompany me to the parade and picnic. I accepted. There. Eli has been dead for nearly a year, and Mr. Bradford is an old friend. Make of it what you will."

Nicholas's substantial jaw dropped. Rosa covered her mouth with her hand.

"What? I'm only stepping out with him. It's not a grand occasion."

But was it? Until now it seemed Louise had wanted to recover the life she'd lost, not create a new future. She'd returned to the same house and surrounded herself with her old friends. Surely she didn't think she could remarry and forget all that had happened in Mexico? No, it had to be just a friendly visit. Louise probably lacked male companionship, and Mr. Bradford was an old friend. Nothing to worry about. They hadn't courted when they were young. Why would they now?

"So you'd go out with your fellow and leave Rosa behind to do the work?" Nicholas asked.

Louise's eyebrows disappeared under her bangs. "Excuse me, young man? Mr. Bradford is not my fellow. Besides, Rosa will have more fun at Mary's than she would in town, where she'd have to sit on the sidelines in her black dress and watch the parade go by. At the ranch she can play with the kids, visit with Mary and Eliza, and play her flute." Nicholas's eyes grew wide when Louise whispered, "Don't forget your dancing clothes. I remember how much you liked to kick up your heels in the mountains."

Rosa sparkled. Music, food, and dancing? Why hadn't she said so? Independence Day, indeed.

14

Rosa's stomach hurt — not from the delicious barbecue but from laughing so hard at the antics of the young men who, finding such an appreciative audience, tried to outdo one another in either wit or wildness.

Seated at a long table littered with greasy bones, the men grew louder and louder to draw the attention of the ladies' table.

"Now what are they doing?" Aunt Mary guffawed as Eliza gave her an account of the goings-on behind her back.

"Looks like Bailey's trying to catch a biscuit in his mouth. Willie is throwing it, and . . . oh my! They've picked the dreadful thing up off the ground three times and are still trying."

Even Eliza's cook disapproved. Octavia shook her head and burrowed her creased brow further. "Don't those fools realize we're in a barnyard?"

"Obviously they don't care." Eliza hid her

face behind her hands. "I can't watch or I'm going to get sick."

Mary looked to her husband for help. He was none. George, Weston, and Jake were daring, double daring, and double-dog daring the hapless cowboys to even greater indignities.

"They claim they don't want them to leave the ranch because they'll get into trouble in town, but I think they like to keep them here for sport. George spends all year concocting foolishness to lead them into."

Eliza fanned herself. "I don't think they take much convincing. I'm just glad Jake is finally content to be a spectator and not a participant. Last year he scared the daylights out of me when he jumped off the roof into the trough. He made it, but barely."

"Are you talking about me?" Jake sauntered to their table. "I know you are, because I'm all you can think about."

Eliza rolled her eyes and elbowed Rosa. "You caught me, Jake England. I was just telling Rosa here what a fine-looking, mature, and responsible man you are. At least this year."

"That's what I figured." He laced his thumbs behind his suspenders and stretched them away from his chest. "The boys sent me over to tell y'all that we're going to run some foot races and wondered if you'd like to help."

Now, that sounded like fun. Rosa tightened her hair ribbon before answering. "I'd love to. I just ate, but I don't think it'll slow me down."

"You want to run?"

Why did he look at her that way? He'd just invited her to race.

"Absolutely!" She stood and surveyed the landscape. "How far were you thinking of running?"

Eliza spewed her drink across the yard. "Rosa! Are you serious?"

In a heartbeat their audience grew by half a dozen interested cowboys. Oh no. What had she done now?

"What's this?" Weston looked from Rosa to his sister, who was having trouble sitting up straight.

"Rosa wants to race the cowboys," she gasped.

"Not just the cowboys. I thought everyone was going to run."

Aunt Mary put her hand to her incredibly solid hip. "You thought we were going to run?"

Rosa looked around the table. Stout Aunt Mary had probably never run a step in her life. Dour Octavia wasn't going anywhere

205

fast. That left only Eliza, the most likely candidate, if it weren't for her expanding belly.

"There isn't a race for the ladies?" Rosa dropped to the bench. She hoped Louise didn't hear about this.

"Sure there is." Bailey propelled Rico to the front. "You can race him." Willie and Red pantomimed a race, complete with flailing arms and mincing steps.

"Don't let them tease you, señorita." Rico dusted off his sleeves in a show of dignity. "If there was a race, you would win because we would all be chasing you."

Weston cuffed him on the head. "I apologize for their behavior, Mrs. Garner. They forget how to act around ladies."

"Maybe we've never been around a lady like her." Bailey was trying to help, but Rosa didn't miss the stern look his mother shot him. Anyone could identify the differences between her and the other ladies of Prairie Lea. The challenge was finding things they held in common.

"Y'all say you're going to race, but all I hear is running off at the mouth." Wes gathered the ruffians around. "First one to the north pasture chute and back wins a gold dollar. Take off."

A clamor ensued as they jostled around

the tables, through the gate, and across the pasture, leaving the remaining celebrants choking in their dust. Rosa fanned away the thick air. She'd managed to keep her white blouse clean through the dripping, saucy supper. No use getting it dingy now.

"Let's get this mess cleaned up." Aunt Mary got to her feet and reached for the dishes. "They'll want music when they get back."

George and Jake lifted the long plank to dismantle the makeshift table, giving Rosa little time to clear it. The hastily gathered dishes teetered precariously in her arms.

Weston came to her rescue. Taking the mugs from the stack of plates, he fell into step with her.

"You were really going to run?"

The question sounded nonjudgmental, but she knew a man like him had an opinion. Well, she could only tell the truth. She nodded.

"Did the women race at home?"

The way he said *home* warmed her. She was happy here, but rarely did anyone acknowledge that she, too, had a home — a place where she was special, where she was normal and did everything correctly and properly. Well, maybe distance and time had clouded her memory. Even at home she was considered unconventional.

"Not really, but I liked to."

He pulled the gate open with his boot and held it open with his leg until she cleared the passage.

"Not much chance for a lady to run around here, I reckon."

"Or climb, or throw, or kick . . ." She sighed.

He whistled. "What exactly did you do in Mexico? Rodeo?"

She shot him a sideways glance to see if she should continue. "Not rodeo, although I had to deal with goats from time to time. I also climbed the mango trees with the best of them. Everyone wanted my help during harvest. Sometimes for fun we would hang a clay pot in a tree and hit it with a stick."

"Piñatas?"

She beamed at him. "*Sí*, señor, piñatas, but you all work so hard. Everyone is too tired to have fun." She saw the cowboys, now on their last leg of the race, coming around the grove. "Almost everyone."

The hapless young men sprinted through the yard, red-faced and dripping in sweat. She cheered and clapped with Eliza and Aunt Mary and congratulated Willie for his first-place performance.

Weston held the gold piece between finger

and thumb and dropped it into his palm. "Having y'all tuckered out is worth a dollar."

Willie knotted the coin in his bandanna and stuffed it into his pocket. "We ain't tuckered out. We're just getting started."

"Time for us to call it a night." Eliza could barely get the words out before a yawn interrupted her.

Bailey's guitar stopped mid-melody. The last notes floated up to the owls in the eaves of the barn. "You can't go. Most of the feed is out of the way. Give the guys another minute, and then we'll dance."

Rosa lowered her flute to her lap. Accompanying Rico and Bailey was fun, but couldn't compete with dancing. They couldn't turn in this early.

"You think I'm going to dance?" Eliza laughed at her cousin. "That's not possible, but I'll leave Rosa in my place."

"Rosa's staying? All right, then." Bailey resumed the music.

Eliza's nose curled up. "Good heavens, Bailey! I regret breaking your heart, but it appears your recovery is well underway." She turned to Rosa. "And you're laughing."

"Yes. You're funny and I'm having a good time. Louise told the truth. This is more fun than a parade and fireworks could ever be."

"Well, I'm glad you're enjoying yourself. After all the work you do on that ranch, you deserve a holiday." She patted Rosa's shoulder and made her way out of the barn.

Rosa joined the song already in progress. For the first hour of their improvised concert Rico and Bailey had performed the repertoire of tunes they'd practiced on the trail. Rico played the violin and Bailey alternated between his banjo and guitar, occasionally prompting some rowdy cowboy to dance a jig in appreciation. Rosa skillfully joined in with her flute, familiar with some of Rico's song choices, but able to improvise harmony when she wasn't.

It was getting late, but no one else left, and that suited Rosa just fine. She'd brought her carpetbag to Mary's, which meant she could dance and sing until the sun came up, or for as long as these gringos could keep up with her. She would play until she was out of breath. She would play until her fingers had to be pried off her flute. She would play until there was an opportunity to do something she loved even better.

The song ended with an enthusiastic "yee-haw" from the men. When the hoots and whistles quieted down, Rico stood on a hay bale and hollered for attention.

"Now, for a special treat, I invite Mrs. Garner to join me in *la mariposa*."

Her heart leapt when she heard the name. But could they do it? "Rico, no one dances la mariposa here. Besides, I don't think we have enough dancers to pull it off."

"But of course we do. They don't even have to move. We can make it simple for the *hombres*." He nodded to Bailey. "You play that mariachi song I taught you in Waco. That will be perfect."

"I don't know about this." She hadn't been to any dances in Texas and didn't know what they expected. None of the other women had danced that evening.

Weston came into view. He leaned against a post, watching the proceedings with interest. Surely he wouldn't mind. These cowboys could get rough, but as long as he and Aunt Mary were present, she was chaperoned.

Mary confirmed her judgment. "Honey, you need to dance. You've been sitting here playing for these cowboys for hours. You're going to explode if you don't get out there."

Rosa couldn't suppress the broad smile. Excitement filled her as she set her flute down and laid her shawl aside.

Rico took the stage, the barn floor really,

and announced with a hand to his heart, "This is the butterfly dance, danced by señoritas throughout Mexico to reveal the one whose heart beats with love for them."

Not to be outdone, Bailey called out, "We all love Mrs. Garner. How will this show her anything?"

"If you don't know, then we won't tell you." Rico flashed a conspiratorial smile at Rosa. "Now, all our cowboys need to do is to stand still. Clap with the music, offer your hand to the lady if you will, but don't move. La mariposa, or butterfly, will inspect each flower and decide which it is that offers her the sweetest promise of a future."

Willie objected. "You didn't say anything about us being flowers. Besides, after winning that gold dollar I'd hate to win the girl, too."

Uncle George spoke up. "No one's going to confuse you boys with flowers. Not the way you smell."

"But the butterfly has ways of seeing through all the grime and reading their hearts."

"Oh, Rico," Rosa laughed. "Stop it. You're going to scare them. It's just a dance."

"Just a dance?! Where's your sense of tradition? What have these Americans done to you? Have they drained your warm Mexicana blood from your veins?" He tapped his chin with his index finger. "Maybe we shouldn't do this. Are you sure you can do la mariposa justice?"

How dare he challenge her! She marched to the center of the barn, hands on her hips, and turned quickly enough to make her skirts flare up. With lifted chin, she looked down her nose at the young man and clicked her heels together loudly. "I can dance." And would prove it.

"*Bueno!* Let's see . . . Willie, you stand there, Red, directly opposite. All the hombres face the middle of the square. I'll take the other side, and we need one more." He looked at Bailey but shook his head. "No, you must supply our music. Is there any other bachelor that could win the hand of the señorita?"

Rosa scanned the barn. Everyone left was married. George could step in. Mary wouldn't mind. She was about to ask when she heard Rico call out to Weston.

"Mr. Garner! I forgot you were here. Would you be a gentleman and stand up for the lady?"

"It seems the lady already has plenty of men." Weston didn't budge.

Rosa's mouth grew dry. She searched his face looking for a sign that she should stop, but it was indecipherable. Finally he stepped forward. "But I reckon if the lady wants four partners, she should get four partners." He took his place while his employees cheered their approval.

It couldn't be that bad. Willie and Red weren't known for their dancing. Maybe Weston would teach these yahoos a thing or two. Besides, after their race they'd carried their own stink into the barn. Pleased with himself, he watched her prepare for the first steps and, when she wasn't looking, leaned his nose down to his shoulder to catch the crisp scent of his soap. Yep, still smelled fresh. He might be older than his cowboys, but he was wiser.

Bailey jumped right into the music. He plucked a few notes of the melody, and then the pulsating beat of the dance took hold. Rosa didn't hesitate. First she marched a wide circle around the four men, holding her red skirt in her hand, arm extended, slowly fanning the audience as she passed by, then she cut between her partners in an intricate figure eight, sashaying around first one, then another, her feet sounding out a staccato rhythm as she passed.

Weston couldn't keep his eyes off her. Little minx. She was usually so demure, content to do heavy labor and monotonous tasks. No sign of that girl now. After talking to her that evening, he better understood her frustration. She was a Thoroughbred being made to pull a plow when she should be flying through the territory.

She held her skirt out to both sides and swung it with supple brown arms. She traced quick S's in the air. Colored petticoats were visible with every beat of the music. She dipped. She swung. Silver bell earrings bounced against her neck as she tossed her head.

Rosa's steps slowed as she fixed her gaze on Red. The playful smile settled into a sultry expression as she stalked toward him. Red's eyebrows went up, and a silly grin spread across his mouth. He gaped as she spun around him, swinging her skirt high enough to slap him in the chest. She made one pass, then another while he stared openmouthed in a total lack of sophistication.

Rico wanted in on the game. He threw back his head and yelped like a coyote. "Stupid hombre," he taunted. "He doesn't know how to treat you, mariposa *bonita*. Come dance for me!" He assumed a matador pose, chest thrust out, shoulders back, and followed her path shamelessly with eyes as dark as her own.

Rosa didn't go straight to him, but coyly worked her way through the group. One minute she stared at him brazenly, the next she peeked at him over her shoulder.

"Here she comes, Rico," George called out. "I think you're going to have your hands full." The barn erupted in a chorus of laughter.

Even Aunt Mary got in on the fun, tapping her foot and slapping her leg. "What a show she's putting on. Who knew she had it in her?"

Weston had to agree. And Rico hadn't been fooling. No dancing was required of the men. All Weston had to do was watch. Around Rico she floated, her skirts undulating like a butterfly — no, more like a hummingbird.

Bailey increased the tempo, causing her wings to dart toward the young man and then sweep away. Rico acted the part of a proud don. He raised his hands shoulder height to clap, each sound corresponding to a step she took: a few slow and deliberate, then a spin and dip in rapid succession. The matador didn't move an inch, and for all her rotations their eyes never left each other.

Weston's gut wrenched. Why was she looking at the pup like that? And he was acting ridiculous. Puffing his chest out like a toad. Who did he think he was? But as much as he wanted to deny it, they made a striking couple. Passion to passion, they matched each other. If this miserable dance was going to reveal who loved her, they could end it now. He couldn't imagine a more complementary dance partner for her. But it wasn't over.

The guitar's pulsating melody continued to envelop the humid barn floor. Rosa rounded Rico for the final pass of the set and for the first time during the dance faced Weston.

He saw the uncertainty in her eyes, but before he could understand its meaning, she pulled on the mask and resumed her character. She shamelessly met his gaze, allowing her eyes to go soft and then saucy. She pranced around him once, stepping off her territory before sweeping in toward her prey.

Hands above her head, she snapped out the rhythm with gyrating wrists and swaying elbows. His mouth went dry as she dallied at his side, her left foot pressed tightly against the inside of his right foot, his leg completely lost in her swaying skirts. He clenched his fists, knowing he looked like a fool.

"Oh lands," he overheard Mary say. "He's not happy. Not one bit."

No, he wasn't happy, but he couldn't take his eyes off of Rosa. Her cheeks were flushed, her forehead damp, and heaven help him, he couldn't help but notice how hard she was breathing as she flitted so miraculously close without touching him. He tried not to look at her body, but her eyes were even more dangerous, dark and inviting, knowing and teasing. She was a stranger. Alluring? Absolutely! But not the woman he'd come to respect. But alluring . . . Absolutely! Alluring . . .

"That's enough!" he blurted. Weston strode to the hay bale and yanked the guitar out of Bailey's hands.

The barn went completely silent. The men stood awkwardly in their positions. Rosa's skirts dropped to her side, her mouth fell open. Someone cleared their throat. Straw rustled as the cowboys leaned forward on the hay bales. Weston remained in the center of the observers, holding the guitar at arm's length like a rattler.

He could hear Mary trying to find words, but nothing coherent came out of her mouth. The awful moment stretched until he felt his nerves would snap. Only Rico seemed amused by the situation. Staying out of Weston's reach, he stepped over to Rosa and took her trembling hand.

"Now, señorita, the dance is over!"

Rosa gasped, snatched her hand from him, and ran out the door. Weston dropped the guitar in Bailey's lap and followed her.

"Rosa!"

Her white blouse glowed in the darkness, but she wasn't waiting on him. He ran to catch her before she disappeared into the sanctuary of the house.

"Rosa!" He grabbed her by the arm and swung her around.

"How dare you embarrass me like that!" she spat.

"I'd say you were embarrassing yourself without my help."

Her hand flew up, but he caught her wrist. "Watch it, missy. If this is going to get physical, there's a woodshed back there we can visit. Throwing you over my knee and giving you a good spanking sounds like a fine idea 'bout now."

"Is that how a gentleman acts?"

"A gentleman? I'm the only one with enough sense to call that dance while you still had some shred of a reputation left. What are you supposed to do? See how far you can go with each man? Is that the game? The one who lets you debase yourself the most will be your true love?"

She shot daggers at him. "It's a dance. There's nothing debasing about it. And no, you're so ignorant you don't even know that you . . . that the dance . . ." she floundered.

"What about the dance?" She was hiding something from him. "Did you find him?" He took her chin in his hand and forced her to meet his gaze. "Who is your future lover?"

Was that disbelief on her face? She pushed his hand away. "The lover is the one who stops the dance — the one who won't allow anyone else to be with his butterfly. That's the sign of true love."

Weston staggered to the edge of the porch. He'd played the part to a tee. Sure, he'd watched her too closely, followed her every movement possessively. And he could even admit he was jealous as she and Rico did their duet, but when she came to him, he couldn't laugh it off like Red. He couldn't play along like Rico. She held him spell-bound, and like Joseph of the Bible, he had to flee temptation. He let out a long shaky breath. So now everyone in the barn knew the exact limits of his self-control.

Again, she reached for the door, but he caught her hand on the knob. "Please, Rosa. Stay a minute."

"Why? So you can insult me again?"

"No." He wiped his face hard, hoping to drag his anger away. "So I can cool down and apologize! I know I need to, but you're just going to have to give me a minute before I feel like it!"

She stopped and fixed him with a cold stare. He took a few steps away and hooked his thumbs in his back pockets. His plaid-covered chest rose with deep, long draws as he attempted to catch his breath in the thick night air.

"Rosa, I —"

"What did you call me?" She wasn't giving him an inch.

"I beg your pardon — Mrs. Garner . . ."

She shifted her weight to the other leg and continued to stare him down. How'd he get in this situation? The trollop who'd set him on fire only moments earlier had transformed into a haughty matron. He'd insulted the flirt and had to apologize to the widow.

"Mrs. Garner, my only desire is to help and protect you." Wiping the memory of her smoldering looks from his mind, he focused on the proper, delicate lady in front of him, who currently didn't seem to need help and protection. "If you knew me better, you'd understand that I'm only looking after your best interest. This is a rough land,

and it can be extremely harsh on ladies who are vulnerable, and regardless of what you may think, you are vulnerable." He stepped closer to her, but she took a quick step back. "You're a lady and you're family, and that means, whether you like it or not, I'm somewhat responsible for you. I've tried to take you under my wing —"

"There you go again," she interrupted. "Taking a lady under your wing sounds too . . . too personal. You accuse *me* of impropriety . . ."

"I did not! Merely the appearance of impropriety. And that saying? Jesus said it! It's not inappropriate at all. It's like a mother hen caring for her chicks."

"Oh, so you mean that I shouldn't jump to conclusions if I'm ignorant of your culture?"

Weston watched, fascinated, as she adjusted her demeanor. Obviously she felt she had won the argument. Well, maybe she had, but he wasn't budging from his opinion that she had no business dancing la mariposa, or whatever they wanted to call it, with American men. Tradition or not, Texans wouldn't wait for a translation when they read those looks in a beautiful woman's eyes. Rosa had to be unaware of the effect the dance had on men. She couldn't have meant anything by it. Could she?

Time to bury the hatchet.

"Point taken." He bowed gallantly to her. "I have never seen that dance before, and I am sure that it was danced in good taste and innocence. It was my ignorance — as you named it — that caused me to misinterpret your intentions."

She nodded. "Thank you. I accept your apology."

"But I'm not apologizing for stopping the dance." She frowned, but he continued. "I'm still convinced, Mrs. Garner, that it would be a mistake for you to perform that particular dance again."

Maybe weakness only affected him, but he suspected his brothers would have the same response. She shouldn't be a stumbling block to them. "I won't be the only man who misconstrues la mariposa. I just might be the only one honest enough to tell you. Sorry if that embarrasses you, but please don't do it again."

He didn't wait for her consent. He'd said his piece, and he couldn't get out of there quick enough. Wes turned to go, but she wasn't finished with him yet.

"You should know that your dances would not be allowed in my village."

He stopped, one foot already on the bottom step of the porch.

"What's that?"

"Your dances —" she leaned toward him and added in a near whisper — "I find them shocking."

"Go on." He was intrigued.

"The way you . . . touch. Louise told me that you put your hands on each other. Never tonight did I touch a man."

"No, but you sure looked like you wanted to." He allowed a crooked grin to appear.

"But I didn't!" She threw her hands in the air in protest. "There's a difference."

Tilting his head back, he rolled his eyes. "Are you talking about a square dance? That's ridiculous. Even our waltzes don't compare to what you just did in there." He motioned to the barn, where the music had resumed.

"You mean that you can hold a woman like that and it doesn't mean anything?"

"Yes, absolutely. I've danced with my sister, my aunts, and practically every woman in the county. It's nothing." Seeing her disbelief, he snatched her from the door and dragged her to the porch step. Positioning her on the step, he backed down one so that they were face to face.

"Don't look like that. I'm not going to hurt you. Just pretend I'm a ewe." Rosa narrowed her eyes at him, but he wasn't dissuaded. Taking both of her hands, he dropped one on his shoulder and rotated her right hand, their palms sweeping across each other until the grasp was correct.

"Then we go completely *loco* and allow me to hold your waist . . . like this." Her eyes grew wide at the feel of his hand on her thin shirt just above her hip. To be honest, he was taken aback, as well. Every woman he'd ever danced with had been so tightly corseted that he might as well hug the slop bucket, but not Rosa. He felt the warmth of her skin through the thin cotton fabric. He could tell where her ribcage ended and her pliable waist began.

Swallowing hard, he reminded himself what he was trying to prove. He couldn't sabotage his own argument. They were separated on two different levels of the porch, making it impossible to actually perform the steps, so he improvised.

"Let's do two steps this way." He led her gently, paying heed to the music wafting across the yard. "Then two steps back. Pretty boring compared to your dances, but if we had a dance floor it'd be better."

She stepped woodenly, completely unlike the exotic butterfly she'd portrayed earlier. Her hands trembled. Without thinking he ran his thumb over her palm, but her discomfort only increased. Maybe it was too quiet.

"Mrs. Garner?"

"Yes, Mr. Garner?"

Weston's chest tightened. He forgot what he was going to say. Mr. and Mrs. Garner in each other's arms, dancing the evening away. Wasn't that how it was supposed to be? *Oh, God, please don't cloud my thinking. Let me see this through clearly.*

"I . . . ah . . . I wondered if you enjoyed this evening's festivities." When in a fix, dust off the old ballroom manners. "Are you looking forward to the fireworks tonight?"

She couldn't answer. Obviously, she was flustered. Her lips quivered; her nimble feet hardly moved. "I don't think I could ever get used to this."

"That's a pity," *because I could.* "But if you would like to call it a night . . ." He released her waist and bowed before letting go of her hand, but instead of leaving, she stood rooted to the spot, looking at him in confusion.

"What is it, Mrs. Garner?"

"I'm not sure I should ask this . . ."

"You have my permission to ask me anything."

The wind teased the stray wisps of her hair

and the ribbon drawstring of her blouse, but besides that, nothing moved.

"Is this" — she placed her hand against her heart — "is this how you felt in the barn when I danced for you?"

His heart dropped somewhere inside his stomach. He felt it pounding away in there. She was a straight shooter, this little one, and she had no idea how potentially inflammatory her question was. Their eyes locked. The conversation could take one of two paths: a wide, seductive trail that would be breathless and exciting but leave them with entangled emotions, or the straight and narrow, which required him to love her like a sister and protect her, even from himself. She was his kinswoman. She deserved his best.

"Yes, I reckon it is." He enunciated each word carefully, knowing that he was on thin ice.

"Oh!" Her eyes grew large. She paced the porch a few turns before continuing. "Then I should be the one apologizing. I am sorry. I didn't mean to make you this . . . um . . . what is the word? Alert?"

His mouth dropped open. *Please, God, don't let her talk to anyone else like this.* "That's an interesting choice of words, ma'am." He heard the ice cracking under his feet. It was time to flee again. "I accept your apology. Now, if you'd excuse me . . ."

"But wait! People have dances like this. What if I'm invited? How could I?"

"You don't have to. No one will force you to dance with them, but I wish you'd give it another try. A ballroom filled with people is a much better setting than" — he gestured to himself — "this."

"I don't think so."

She didn't think she'd *try* to dance, or she didn't *want* to dance with anyone else? He couldn't decipher her meaning, but the thought of holding her in his arms reminded him of one more thing.

He scratched the back of his neck and studied his boots. "But if you decide to dance, may I make a suggestion?"

"What is it?"

"Please wear a corset."

From her reaction, she'd been told that before. Her face reddened and she plucked at her blouse, loosening it where it strained.

"I don't know what to say. Louise told me that if a man mentioned . . . well . . ." She tilted her head. "I want you to think I'm a lady. . . ."

"There's no doubt in my mind —" But before he could finish what he'd been about

to say, she'd slapped him and slipped into
the house.

15

Bailey stumbled out of the barn, right into Weston's path, still rubbing the sleep from his eyes.

"Whoa, there. You just getting up?" Weston asked. He couldn't sleep in if he wanted to. His mind had kicked in at daybreak, been spinning ever since.

"Yeah, we were up till about sunrise."

"I'm not surprised. Did it rain last night?"

Bailey yawned, displaying his molars to the world. "Don't think so. Ground wasn't wet when we went to bed."

"That's odd. Sure looks green this morning." Weston pushed against his gun belt, making it ride snug. "But you're probably right. The dew is light and there's no mud."

Bailey blinked a few times. "Nope. No mud. Looks like it always does to me. But you're awfully chipper. What'd you find in your stocking?"

Wes shrugged. He really couldn't answer

that question. Maybe the festivities of the night before caused the unaccustomed feeling of hope, although when he analyzed the evening, he couldn't think of one positive event that had occurred.

"I don't know. Good supper. Fine music. Maybe I needed a holiday more than I realized."

"You turned in early enough. Right after that Mexican dance."

Ah, the dance. An incident he'd like to forget. The looks, the music, the heat — and his gaping like a dumbstruck moron until he threw a fit and ended it. Should've ruined his night, but it didn't. And he wasn't going to dwell on it, either. He didn't want anything to choke out the optimism trying to put out a taproot in his barren heart.

Hungry. Everyone was getting around late this morning. Understandable, considering their activities the night before, but Aunt Mary would have breakfast ready soon.

"Yeah, well, I best wash up before food's on the table. Don't dawdle. Your ma won't be pleased."

Bailey grunted and staggered to the outhouse.

It didn't bother him too bad, the dance. Not since he'd had a chance to talk it out with Rosa.

He rolled up his sleeves and troubled the cake of soap under the spout, enjoying the crisp scent. Was this a new fragrance? He'd have to ask Mary about it. Sure smelled good.

What did Rosa think about last night? Would she want to see him? Their parting was confusing, to say the least. The soap squirted from his hands and landed on the ground. Retrieving it, he picked the bits of grass out of the suds and chuckled. That slap had to be one of the most ridiculous events of his life.

Weston couldn't remember ever being slapped before. Bad words, insults, forwardness — that's what usually earned a smack. No lady had ever convicted Mr. Self-Control of any of those failures. And the slap was so regretful, so apologetic. She wasn't truly offended. He'd seen her mad. If the corset comment had really angered her, his cheek would be blistered.

But he could tell he was getting nearer to the source of his good temper. His reason for hope sprouted from their time on the porch. Since last night he felt he knew her better and admired her more. They'd reached a crisis that could have set them at odds, but through some direct, difficult discussion they'd pulled together. Now he wondered if anyone in the county understood him as well as she did. If there was anyone else who saw him not as who he had been, or who he was, but as the man he was trying to be.

Wasn't that a kicker?

Lord, I can tell things are changing. I don't know where you're leading me, but I'm trying to follow. I'm tired of fighting. I want to smile if I feel like it, fix what needs fixing, and care for your children who need help. Is it all right if I start there? I can't make any promises about the results, but can I start out like a tenderfoot and see how I get along?

If his mood was any indication, God granted His permission.

"I'll take you home."

Weston meant it as an offer, but it came out sounding like a command. He stood, causing Susannah and Ida to bounce on the bench as he left it. Rosa froze with her breakfast dish still in hand. She hadn't spoken a word the whole meal. Thank goodness for the youngsters. They filled the silence succinctly, but Weston doubted George and Mary were fooled. Last night they saw Rosa running out of the barn with him following her like an angry bull. They knew he'd scared her.

Weston heard Mary's boot connect with George's shin under the table. George winced but took the hint. "Oh! Don't bother, Wes. I'll take her. You probably have things to do today."

Nothing more important than spending time with the confused little lady.

"It's no bother. I insist."

Rosa moved like winter sap. She reached for the feed sack apron to start on the dishes when Mary stopped her.

"No. We'll get those." She nodded toward him. "I think Weston means to leave now."

Was Rosa that afraid? She disappeared into the girls' room and came back with her overnight bag. She gave quick kisses to the girls, tousled Tuck's hair, and touched each of the George Garner men on the back in farewell as she walked behind their bench and out the door.

"Uncle Weston, what's wrong with Aunt Rosa?" Ida asked. "She's acting sad."

"She's acting like she has a date with the hangman," Samuel corrected.

Weston hadn't spoken to her all morning. Not that Rosa was surprised. Their last conversation hadn't ended well. She picked at the trunk of the sweet gum tree she was hiding behind. No wonder he wanted to get her alone. After a night of preparation, he probably had scads of lectures for her.

Pandora stood patiently, ripping up mouthfuls of Mary's yard as Weston saddled Smokey. Rosa stayed out of his way as long as she could, but his task was almost complete. He was looking for her now. She might as well take her medicine.

She edged her way to the animals. Was that a smile from him?

"Who are the horses for?"

He squinted at her. "Us."

"I don't know how to ride a horse."

"You said you got bored in Texas, so here's something new for you to try. Come on over. He won't bite." He lowered his chin and peeked out from under the brim of his hat. "I won't bite, either."

Still unsure, she held out her bag to him and tied on her bonnet while he secured the bag to his saddle. To her surprise, he came over to stand toe to toe with her. What was he doing? She couldn't see his face over her bonnet brim. Just his chest. He pretty much blocked any other view. Heat rushed through her body at the memories from the night before. She prepared for him to take her in his arms for another dance, but he didn't. Instead, he wrapped his hands around her waist and swung her up on Smokey's back.

Now Rosa could see his face, and it was red.

"Reckon you didn't have a chance to make any purchases since last night."

She gasped. "Are you talking about corsets again?"

"I was thinking . . . Oh, I'd best keep my mouth shut. Sorry, okay? I've already decided that today's going to be a good day, so let's not get cross with each other."

Just as well. If he wasn't mad after last night, she had no right to be.

She sat crossways in the saddle, just where he put her, then taking advantage of her full skirts, she swung her leg over the saddle horn to sit astride.

He turned his head quickly.

Had she already messed up? "Let me guess, this isn't how ladies ride horses?"

"It's how I ride horses and how you ride burros, so we'll let it be. You don't need to learn on a sidesaddle yet. That can wait for another day."

Rosa released a breath of relief. She didn't want to repeat last night's argument, especially on such a beautiful day. At least her full Mexican skirts draped decently. If she'd been wearing a hobble skirt, then she'd have trouble.

She picked up the supple leather reins and tried to reach the stirrups, glad to have something to do besides invent conversation.

Weston came to her side and reached for her ankle. She didn't mean to jump like that. Really. Why was she so skittish? She stared straight ahead at the sheep-filled pasture as he directed her foot forward and adjusted the stirrup length, fumbling with the buckle in the process.

The silence was unbearable.

"What do I do?" Rosa asked. "Will this horse ride like a burro?"

"He'll follow me. Just don't fall off."

Weston went around to the left side, but she had already moved her foot out of the way. The buckle fastened quickly, and they set off.

Why, it was easy. The motion never halted but fluidly rolled her saddle from side to side. She gripped the saddle horn but didn't need to pull on the reins. Smokey stayed contentedly at Weston's side.

"You're doing great. You're absorbing the movement without bouncing. That's hard to teach people." He observed her a moment more. "You know, after watching you,

I'm inclined to believe your stories about athletic escapades in Mexico. How do you like your mount?"

"He's a lot smoother than a burro." She stood in her stirrups, arranged her skirts, and sat back down.

"You really notice the difference when they gallop. You don't know what true freedom feels like until —"

Gallop? Her eyebrows went up, knees tightened, and she leaned forward.

"Whoa, there!" Weston grabbed her reins and captured her hand in the bargain. "You're not going to try it yet."

"But why not?"

"Because five minutes ago you were too scared to climb on this beast. Remember? I think teaching you to sit a horse is enough for one day." With Rosa's hand under his, he pulled the two horses side by side.

The crunch of the grass under their hooves and the creaking leather sounded small under the vast sky. She watched Weston like she did back in the kitchen during shearing season. Rosa liked the way his shirt hung off his straight back and hugged his shoulders. That was nice. She also liked the way his lasso, rifle, and six-shooters were all within easy reach, available in the split second he needed them. He sat lightly in the saddle, too, efficiently communicating his will to his horse with a feather touch here, a cheeky click there. Mounted, he had a feline quality, smooth and dangerous, like a jaguar that could patiently stalk or quickly strike.

He caught her watching him, but instead of being self-conscious, he winked and went back to monitoring their path. Yes, she was impressed with the man who'd evidently forgotten to release her hand, and who rode so close that their legs brushed with every stride.

They entered the shaded grove lining the creek's path. The fresh scent of pine sharpened her senses just as the cool air refreshed her. He'd been quiet but not moody. His tentative attempts at humor gave her the courage to ask.

"There's something else I'd like you to teach me."

"What's that?"

"You taught Samuel how to shoot a gun. Could you show me?"

"I don't know, Mrs. Garner." He tightened his grip over her hand. "I've seen you angry. Not sure I want a gun in your hands when you lose your temper."

She'd heard a similar sentiment expressed more than once. His smile crinkled his rugged face. Obviously Weston wasn't too afraid of her.

With a tug, she pulled her hand free and let Smokey wander ahead a pace until he stopped near the creek bank. Looking over her shoulder, she called back to him. "Maybe if I knew how to shoot, you'd behave yourself." Her dimples showed. She knew it. Rosa didn't smile wide often, but she could tell he appreciated it. His eyes lingered on her lips, as if he'd finally given himself permission to see her, to acknowledge her as a woman.

She waited as Weston maneuvered his horse around until he was at her side. Unburdened by decorum, his eyes roamed her face freely, saying more than he'd dared hint at before. Her smile softened as he drew near.

"I have trouble behaving myself when . . ." He blinked hard. "I have trouble behaving . . ."

Then he looked away.

The change that came over him bewildered Rosa. His mouth set firmly; his shoulders drooped. With a weary tug, he reined away.

"What's wrong?"

"Nothing." But his tone didn't convince her. "Go on. Don't wait on me."

Go on? How could she go on without him? She bit her lip, but he wasn't looking and couldn't see her frustration. Unsure of how to direct her mount, she let Smokey meander across the low creek and up the bank.

Weston didn't follow. Hoping that Smokey could be directed as easily as a burro, Rosa jabbed him with her heels and kept him facing the house until he reached the porch.

Had she imagined their exchange? Had she misinterpreted his mood? Surely he'd have a ready explanation, or maybe he'd resume from where they'd left off.

The horse seemed taller now. The distance from her feet to the ground had grown. Sure, she'd hopped out of taller trees, but she hadn't seen a woman dismount without help. The proper thing to do — she could just imagine Louise saying — would be to wait for help. But where was he?

Weston's hat appeared over the rise, and she released a breath she hadn't realized she was holding. Rosa smiled over her shoulder, but he didn't look in her direction. Had she offended him?

He arrived in silence, his mouth grim in the shadow of his hat. Without a word, he dismounted and untied the strap holding her bag. He dropped it next to the door and went back to pluck her off her horse. She'd already thrown her leg over and only had to slide down into his arms, but he planted her on the ground without making eye contact.

"I'd best be getting back to Palmetto." He sounded tired.

"Is something wrong? You don't seem . . ."

Weston pulled himself into the saddle. "I'm sorry. Those shooting lessons will have to commence later. You take care, Mrs. Garner." He rode away, dragging Smokey behind him, leaving her abandoned on her doorstep.

No more farewell than that? That was good-bye? She was rooted to the spot, unable to move. He didn't even bother to turn the horses but was riding the loop around her property on his way out. What had she done wrong?

Defeated, Rosa went inside and let the door swing close of its own initiative. She couldn't figure the man out. When he should be mad at her, he forgave. When she responded to his good spirits, he withdrew. What was she missing?

Not trusting her emotions, she ran for Louise. Louise might not have any answers, but her sympathetic mother-in-law would tend to her bruised feelings. She checked

Louise's room first, searching for the nurturing comfort of the only mother she had, but found it vacant. The kitchen was empty, as well, and Louise's bonnet was missing from the peg board next to the door.

Rosa was alone in the house. The stale air had been undisturbed all day. Of course! Louise had gone to Prairie Lea with Deacon Bradford. She wouldn't be home until evening, leaving Rosa all day to fret over Weston's behavior.

But before she could worry about Weston, she had a bigger threat to consider. Had Tillerton seen her?

Still unsure of how to handle the troublesome neighbor, Rosa prayed he wasn't near. She wouldn't endure his advances, but how forcefully could she refuse? Kicking a snake only got you bit.

If only Louise were home.

Conejo brayed. Rosa flew to the kitchen window over the basin. Her burro hadn't lied. Stepping from behind the barn, Tillerton shaded his eyes and peered at the house.

She reached a decision. Rosa would stop at nothing to keep him away. If he came inside looking for her, she'd be ready.

Rosa slid open the drawer to the right of the basin and grasped the longest, heaviest knife they owned. The gun wouldn't do her any good now that he knew she couldn't shoot, and Weston had refused to teach her. But where should she hide?

She flung the pantry curtain back, but shuddered at the thought of being trapped with her back against the shelves. Goosebumps appeared on her arms as she scurried past the windows. Could she find somewhere to hide that wasn't confining? Through the parlor to Louise's room she ran and searched for space under the bed or in the wardrobe. Nowhere seemed safe enough.

The kitchen door rattled.

Rosa froze.

Moving cautiously, she slid around the doorjamb into the stairway. The cold, heavy handle of the knife bit into her palm. She gripped it so tightly her heartbeat vibrated the blade. Silently she backed up one step, then another.

A voice called out, now inside the house.

Maybe he wouldn't be brazen enough to follow her upstairs, but his footsteps rang through the kitchen. She took another step backward, and a board creaked.

Silence, and then the muffled sound of boots on the parlor rug.

No time to hide. He was coming after her, but Rosa wouldn't go without a fight. Raising her voice she answered the challenge. The words flying from her mouth weren't English, or even Spanish. Her mother tongue of Nahuatl, the language she first heard at her birth and would speak even now, at her demise, filled the air. Rosa held her ground at the top of the stairs, where she stood with a death grip on the banister, brandished the cleaver, and called down every curse the millennium-old language had spawned.

But the man who stepped around the corner wasn't her enemy.

It was Weston.

The knife clattered to the floor as Rosa's hand flew to her mouth. She crumpled on the stairs.

Weston holstered his pistol as he rushed up to meet her.

"I didn't know what kind of banshee had hold of you." He lifted his hands as if to take her in his arms, but they changed directions midair and crossed, drawing his chest closed like a locked gate.

His brow lowered. "You're okay?"

She nodded, shaking. Would it kill him to touch her? But he kept talking.

"Tell me, why do you need to know how to shoot?"

He'd come back. He hadn't left without a

good-bye. Maybe his presence was enough for now.

She rocked as she struggled to control her gasps for air. With effort she willed the lines out of her face. "I'm scared."

He waited for her to rise and then clumped down the narrow stairway to the kitchen, leaving her to follow. Seeing the Winchester propped up in the corner, he swung it into his hands and took a long, hard look out the kitchen window.

Knees still unsteady, Rosa dropped into a chair. "Why did you come back?"

He checked the barrel for ammunition, all business now. Obviously there'd be no sympathetic hugs or emotional tête-à-tête. Well, that was fine. If she could nail Jay Tillerton's hide to a wall from a hundred yards, her fears would be squelched. No sympathy required.

"I came back because I ran into a neighbor of yours." Weston studied her, not missing anything. "From the look on your face, I'd guess that my hunch is correct. Where do you keep your cartridges?" Rosa pointed to a white crockery pot in the pantry. He retrieved it and set it on the table.

"When I was leaving, I thought I saw movement behind your barn. Sure enough, there was Jay Tillerton, brazen as Jezebel, waiting for me to leave." Weston pulled a cartridge from his gun belt and compared it with the rifle's loads. They were the same as far as Rosa could tell. He stocked the magazine from the canister and worked the bolt action to chamber it.

"So I asked him what he was up to. He didn't have a real quality answer. Something about checking on your sheep — as if he knows the first thing about sheep." He looked out the window again. "Is this the only gun you want to learn on?"

She nodded. What would be happening right at this moment if Weston hadn't discovered Tillerton?

"I reckon that got me thinking. I asked him how his wife was and if she minded him looking after his neighbors' spreads, and he just gave me a nasty grin. Said he didn't care much what his wife thought. By the time we were done, he allowed that he might as well go home and check on her." Weston laid the gun across the table. "I started thinking of you here by yourself, and how you've never asked me to do anything for you. Why would you ask to learn to shoot?" He took her bonnet from the peg by the door and turned it in his strong hands. "It must be real important to you, and I didn't listen."

No denying it, he'd hurt her riding off like he did, but he didn't owe her an apology. He didn't owe her anything.

"Thank you for coming back. I don't know what would have happened if you hadn't."

He swallowed hard and tossed her the bonnet. "It's not every day I get a second chance. Now, let's make you dangerous."

"One thing first. Do you speak Nahuatl?"

"Nahuatl? Never heard of it."

Rosa smiled. "Good!"

To Weston's surprise Rosa's fragile collarbone and delicate shoulder survived the repeated battering of the gun's recoil. With every strike on the barrel side, she grew more and more confident. Tomorrow she'd be sore, but he hoped handling the powerful weapon would eliminate her worries.

He ate the last bite of the bean-stuffed tortilla and licked the remains from his fingers. Weston hadn't planned to spend all day with her, but as the wait for Louise lengthened, so did his enjoyment. Rosa belonged in the Garner family. She took such pride in her livestock and crops, it was hard to believe she wasn't raised to be a rancher's wife.

She showed him the chickens, big enough

to eat but not laying yet, and the sheep — all healthy and not a coyote to be seen. Their garden was a modest success. It would provide enough produce to make it through the next harvest. Not bad for two women just starting out. And after supper was over she washed up and brought out her stitching.

Before they took the rockers on the front porch, Rosa found some soft rags and oil for Wes, who set out to give her rifle a much needed cleaning. With their work before them, they settled in for a quiet evening waiting for Louise and trying to eke out the last of the light from the summer sky.

Although it'd been difficult to keep his distance, Weston counted the day a success. He'd looked over their farm and evaluated it with a professional eye, making suggestions when he thought they'd be helpful but not allowing the conversation to drift into areas that would be considered personal. Taking a step backward was painful, knowing Rosa had to be aware of the change, but she didn't protest, accepting whatever breed of friendship he offered.

No stumbles caused her to fall into his arms. They exchanged no weighty glances, and most importantly, no dancing occurred. She pretended not to notice the difference and let things be. That was what he wanted, right? To have a wall of defense between himself and any eligible lady?

His spine stiffened and he sat straighter in the rocking chair. He'd exiled himself from women for the last five years. Why did it take so much effort now? Why did he feel as if he were riding the brake down a steep grade? Until this week he thought it implausible he would ever court again. Now, instead of exerting himself to be social, he had to restrain himself. Rosa realized it first, and after seeing the truth mirrored in her eyes, he couldn't deny it any longer. He was falling for her.

Riding along with her hand under his, he felt ready. Maybe he could lay his future before God. Maybe he could loosen his grip and let go.

That's what she'd read in his eyes, and she wasn't mistaken. She fascinated Weston, but when she'd responded to him, he'd turned tail and run. He'd gone yellow.

Disgusted with himself, Weston forced his thoughts to the task at hand. With the ramrod he pushed the wad of cloth through the barrel, but the sharp oily smell brought back memories, just as poignant, reminding him of evenings with his parents when he was young. His father would often bring a gun to repair or clean in the parlor despite his mother's concerns the oil might drip on the rug. He never could understand how she was able to do her needlepoint while watching his father so closely.

Now he watched Rosa loosen the screw and move her hoop over an empty circle of linen. Eliza didn't sew and neither had Cora. Weston was fascinated by the process. He hadn't seen it done since his mother died. The movements were familiar but long buried. He couldn't have said what came next, but each step unearthed memories, pictures of family life he thought he'd lost forever. Even the work on the pillowcase Rosa was stitching looked familiar.

"Where'd you get that design? I've seen napkins like that at Mr. Schwartz's."

"This design is from Zacatecas. I saw it on the way to the train station. It's popular with Mr. Bradford's customers."

"So Mrs. Schwartz bought those from you? That's your work?"

She shrugged. "I did the work. This flower doesn't exist in Texas — unless I plant it on some napkins." She pulled an emerald skein from her bag and separated out a string of floss.

"But they're selling well, aren't they? Clever idea."

She bit off a piece of thread and tied it securely. "Not my idea. It was all Mr. Bradford's."

He studied her serene face and felt himself slipping again. "And you said yes because, after all, you have nothing else to do besides tame a wild ranch, get a garden in, shear sheep, adjust to American life — no wonder you were so bored."

She smiled at his compliment.

"It's not out of boredom I do this. It's out of desperation. I still don't think it's going to be enough. Mr. Bradford has been generous, but we're trying to make up for years of debt in one summer. Unless Louise knows something I don't —"

"Speak of the devil."

"What?!" Rosa looked to the gun in alarm. "Who is the devil?"

"Coming over the crossing. See? It's Aunt Louise and Mr. Bradford." He pointed, glad for the opportunity to distract her. Hearing of someone's problems without volunteering to fix them went against his nature. But he couldn't do that this time.

He'd tried before and it didn't pan out. He wasn't ready to try again.

He managed to smile at the approaching wagon, but the woman next to him disturbed his thoughts. God needed to give him more time.

That's what he wanted. Time. And space.

Caldwell County had plenty of space. No reason to cross the creek until he was ready. Could he do it? Could he stay away? His jaw clenched and he laid the gun down.

Keeping his distance was something he'd mastered.

16

"Are you two still counting money?" Louise bustled past Rosa and Mary with her basket of greens. "Counting doesn't make it multiply. Seems like with all the work we've done, we should have enough by now. Maybe they'll decide that, considering our situation, they should forgive the debt —"

"Just as soon as a leprechaun shows up and leads you to a pot of gold," Mary grumbled.

Rosa shared her frustration. How many times would they have this discussion with Louise? True, Eli had never included his wife in the family's financial decisions, but how could she be so ignorant of matters?

Mary and Rosa had already separated the bills from the coins, which were few. Rosa had the bills on her side of the table. Her eyebrows lowered as she counted them for the third time. "I'm coming up with twelve dollars. What do you have?"

"Maybe another five by the time I get these all figured. I ain't too good with ciphering." Mary looked again in the crock. If she was hoping that, like the widow's jar of oil, it would miraculously fill, she was disappointed.

"Seventeen dollars? Can you believe it? And that's without selling the sheep!"

Mary blew her hair out of her face in a huff. "Louise! I told you, George says that you might get twenty-five dollars for the sheep. That's all. You're still over a hundred dollars short." She picked at some dirt under her fingernail. "So when is the fifteenth? A week from Thursday? George should come that Tuesday for the flock. We'll see what they fetch at market. Then we can take whatever vegetables you have ready into town and see what we get."

"They won't all be ready," Louise protested. "Some need a few more weeks."

"Either way, sister, you need to bring them in. There's no use leaving food behind if . . . you know. You're going to have to live somewhere. Might as well bring your own victuals."

The room went silent as each lady avoided the touchy subject they'd been afraid to broach. As of yet, Louise hadn't taken

George and Mary up on their offer for a room. Likely she would, but it would require considerable sacrifice from the struggling couple. Their large family crowded the house enough as it was. Besides that, George and Mary were beholden to Weston. They shouldn't be taking in more mouths when they themselves were in debt.

"Where's he been anyway?"

Rosa didn't need to ask of whom Mary spoke. She was thinking of the same man.

Louise shook her head. "I don't know. It's been about a month since I've seen him around. For a couple of weeks we saw him right regular. Now, even at church he slips in late and doesn't stay for dinner. I don't know what's stuck in his craw. Seems like he was warming up to people again there for a spell." She turned to Rosa. "You haven't heard from him, have you?"

Rosa grew light-headed. "I haven't." The teakettle squealed. Louise jumped to tend it, but Mary's eyes narrowed.

"Come to think of it, the last time he was out at our place was on the Fourth of July. Seems like maybe something happened that night?" Her weathered face searched for an answer.

Of course Mary remembered the dance. She was giving Rosa an opportunity to explain. But how could she? She didn't understand herself.

"Something happened? To Weston?" Louise set teacups and saucers around. "He seemed fine when I saw him the next night."

"It was nothing." Rosa allowed Louise to fill her cup.

Mary blew on her tea. "Nothing, you say? That's good, because when I saw him he was spitting nails. I'm glad to hear you worked it out."

Louise turned a questioning gaze on Rosa as she took a gulp of scalding tea. Rosa crammed a napkin against her mouth just in time to keep from spewing the burning liquid across the room.

"It's hot, goose. Be careful." Louise patted her back as she choked. "Now, what's this about him being mad?"

Rosa sucked a breath of cool air and wiped the tears from her eyes. "It was nothing. Just a misunderstanding. Everything was fine the next day." She found something very interesting about the wood grain of the floor and refused to look up.

"Well, that's good to hear." Mary pounded the table. "It doesn't do to make enemies in times like these. We need every friend we can get."

Rosa couldn't agree more, but she had a

suspicion that maybe she'd been too friendly. No, that wasn't right. Weston had instigated every moment of their time together. Perhaps she was guilty of enjoying his company too much. Had that offended him? How could she tell, and how could she make amends if he never spoke to her again?

But if he never spoke to her again, there was one sacrifice she'd be more willing to make. "My dress — we could sell it."

"That beautiful pink-violet one?" Mary asked. "But you've never got to wear it."

"Then it's perfect. It'll bring more than a used one."

Mary got out of her seat and came to stand behind Rosa. With strong, sure hands she kneaded her shoulders, working the tension from the younger woman's neck. "Rosa, honey, selling that dress ain't going to solve your problems. You might as well wear it. Wear it and feel like a queen. You just let us old folks worry about this. You're taking it too hard."

Losing it wouldn't sting so badly if they weren't losing the farm to Jay Tillerton. Knowing that he would own the property, could actually sit in this kitchen if he wanted, made it that much worse. But she wouldn't tell them. They couldn't do anything anyway.

Louise sat across the table folding and refolding her hands. The movement caught Rosa's attention, but when she looked to Louise, the older woman had nothing to offer.

Rosa dropped her hands and implored Louise. "We have less than two weeks. Think! What can we do? All we've done and it's still not enough." Rosa's soul was crushing in on itself, collapsing and then collapsing again. She wanted to be a turtle — bury her head in her shell and not have to face the harsh world until all the scariness disappeared. But even in her shell the words echoed . . . *not enough, not enough, not enough.*

The same words had driven her to carry the water from the pump to the garden every day of the long drought. Every drop of water the thirsty plants could hold increased their weight. And until Mr. Bradford ran out of orders, those words kept her straining in the dusk to make a few more stitches before turning in every night, hoping to get a dollar more that week. And worst of all, they caused her to tell Louise she wasn't hungry so she could cut back on the beans she cooked and make fewer biscuits, hoping the staples in the pantry would last longer.

All of that and still it was not enough — but she'd never expected it would be.

"Mary's right. You mustn't make yourself ill." Louise took Rosa's hand. "You need to have faith. This land has belonged to the Garners since the Battle of Plum Creek. We aren't going to lose it. God will have a plan for us."

Rosa lifted her head. "God may have other plans for you, but not for me. I came all the way from Mexico to help you — to live on Eli and Mack's ranch. I left my home. You might have other people who'll take you in, but I don't. I'd be destitute without you."

Louise squeezed her hand. "Rosa, you'll be fine. You've taken such good care of me — I'd never leave you behind. I'm confident there's a solution waiting for just the right moment, and then it'll appear." She brightened. "And maybe it just did. The chickens! I completely forgot about the chickens. Why didn't I think of them before? Mr. Bradford is sure to get a premium for them. Do you think we have a hundred dollars' worth of chickens?"

"You only have twenty-five dollars' worth of sheep." Mary wiped her forehead with the back of her arm.

"But we have twice as many chickens."

Louise smiled and waited for Rosa's reaction to her good news.

Dropping her head to the table, Rosa
covered her face with her arms so Louise
wouldn't read her thoughts.

A waning moon hung over the creek. From
her bedroom Rosa watched it glide from
the corner of her window to the absolute
center. Another sleepless night. Her mind
swirled with possible solutions, but each one
ended in a crockery pot with a smattering
of bills.

The week had dragged on through a painful end. Everything Rosa's eyes fell upon
was another possession she would forfeit,
another place to which she must bid *adios:*
the porch where she sat during the breathless summer nights with her embroidery
basket at her feet, the parlor where Eliza
and she played through their heartache to
form melodies of healing, and the garden
where she blistered her hands. Even the
spooky spare room across the hall had
become part of her domain, tamed by her
time at the spinning wheel and the comforting smell of the wool with which she
worked.

But it was slipping out of her reach.
Rather, the ranch would stay there, and she

would slip away. No difference.

Where would she go? No one had answered that question, and during this, their time of desperation, their circle of companions had grown regretfully thin.

On Rosa's dresser sat an envelope in fine white stationery — a letter from Eliza explaining that Jake had forbidden her to ride for the remaining time of her confinement. She promised a visit as soon as one of the men had an opportunity to drive her over in the carriage. If she waited on Weston, she wouldn't arrive until there were new tenants on the property, but Rosa doubted Eliza's brother had the nerve to tell her.

Then, a few weeks ago Nicholas and Molly had visited, full of news about what had gone on at the Independence Day festivities in town. Molly had artfully pried and prodded but could get no satisfactory news about Weston from Rosa, who was certain that, sooner or later, the story of the mariposa would reach her. Rosa didn't have the nerve, or the skill, to relate the story faithfully while protecting Molly's pride, so she remained mute. Her excuse that she retired before the fireworks didn't help, for Molly was as perceptively acute as her brother was obtuse and seemed painfully aware that Rosa had dodged the questions.

"What was I supposed to do?" Rosa said aloud to the God who created the moon. *"I don't want to make her mad, but I can't lie. Besides, I have bigger problems stewing than an unfortunate courtship dance."*

She held her flute but dared not play it for fear of waking Louise. At least she would get to keep her music. In fact, she was going to have everything she'd carried into Prairie Lea. She'd lost nothing. Nothing except her hopes and dreams of living on the land of their family.

But what right had she to dreams? She'd usurped another's position. For the millionth time Rosa revisited the trail that had led her there. Had committing her life to Christ been a mistake? Absolutely not. Yet that decision had guaranteed her expulsion from her family and her community. Was she supposed to decline Louise and Eli's offer of shelter? She had nowhere else to go, but from there the choices she made grew more and more questionable.

Mack was charming. Mack was kind. Mack needed a wife, and Rosa needed a husband. Should have been that simple. Turns out, Mack hadn't suffered from the same desperation Rosa had. Eli insisted they couldn't continue to live under the same roof without a commitment. Had Rosa known that Eli was less concerned with her welfare than he was with his son's relationship with another woman, she would've refused. Wouldn't she?

Leaning her arms on the windowsill, her head partially out the open window, she tried to appreciate the solitude of what would be one of her last nights at the ranch and pondered her future. How many of her options had been pieced together with the scraps, bones, and remains of real choices? She'd surely never had the luxury of two desirable alternatives. Why couldn't God just once give her a choice that wouldn't lead to heartache and uncertainty?

At first, this move to Texas seemed to be her chance. She'd been filled with such hope that sunny day when she'd pulled up the drive with Mary and Louise, so excited when she first saw the pretty two-story home, so eager to set things right and restore the property to the condition that Eli and Mack would have remembered.

All of those things had happened. They'd restored the ranch. They'd reclaimed the land. Family and guests had filled the house, but it wasn't going to last.

With a sigh she rested her chin on her arms. Sleep had eluded her. The nearer the deadline loomed, the fewer hours of respite she could snatch from the night watch. If only she could see a solution!

She turned the flute in her hands again and hummed a sad melody that begged to be set free. Maybe she could play. She didn't wake Louise the night of the storm, the night that Mr. Garner sat somewhere out there listening to her.

She bit her lip. If only he were there now! Why was he staying away? The soft moonlight lit the landscape. The ground was barely visible through the spreading leaves of the oak tree, but the wide expanses further out glowed brightly.

There. That shadow seemed to move. One step closer, the dark bulk inched to the border of their property. It was a horseman, edging his way up to where the picket fence separated the lawn from the roadway. Was it Weston? She waved before she remembered her lamp was out. He probably couldn't see her, but as she was hardly dressed for company, it was for the best.

Why didn't he come closer? He'd had no scruples about approaching the house before. But he kept his distance, only allowing his horse to broach the boundary by a hoof before making her turn and pace the border in the other direction.

What horse was that? It wasn't Pandora or Smokey. She strained to make out some familiar markings. So intent was she on the horse that Rosa didn't realize she was leaning out the window, Molly's old white gown that she was wearing gleaming in the blue light. Not until he took his hat off and sneered did she see the moustache.

Jay Tillerton!

An icy fear poured across her shoulders, down her back, and into every pore of her body. She froze, unable to move out of his sight, unable to spare herself his vulgar expression visible from across the yard. He was counting the days, and she was powerless to stop him. He knew her anguish, but he offered her a razor-edged lifeline to grasp with her bare hands.

Never!

Forcing a long draw of air into her lungs, she fell back into her room and slammed the sash closed. Her head hurt. She collapsed into her straw mattress and set her flute aside with shaking hands.

Their time was up. She needed to get ready for the move to . . . wherever. Only Louise still held hope, but Louise would never admit they could lose the farm. Rosa needed to look beyond the tragedy and start planning her new life. But hadn't she done that already that year?

The morning of August thirteenth came like an undertaker, right on time but not joyfully anticipated. Following the rising sun, with a lot more enthusiasm, Uncle George and the boys arrived to drive the sheep to market.

"Good morning, ladies." Uncle George stomped his feet on the back porch and motioned for the boys to do so, as well. Rosa thought she saw Bailey roll his eyes at the parental instructions, but he followed suit.

They each gave their aunt Louise a kiss on the cheek, then stood staring at Rosa. She didn't mean to make them feel uneasy, but she couldn't disguise the puffy eyes and drawn mouth the sleepless nights had gifted her.

Well, they couldn't help the mess she was in. She passed a plate of tortillas to the boys, hoping to wipe the worried expressions off their faces.

"Are the bushels of produce you want to sell out there near the barn?"

"Yep, did you bring cages for the chickens? We still have the crates we hauled them in, but they won't fit now."

George looked both directions to his sons.

"Boys, go toss those bushels in the wagon, but don't mess with the chickens. I'll be out directly."

"It don't take all of us to do that," Tuck protested. "And I just cleaned my boots. Can't I stay?"

"Get!"

Tuck stomped out with Bailey and Samuel, leaving George in the kitchen with the ladies.

"Before I head out, let's have some coffee. We've got some matters to discuss." He swung a chair around to straddle the back.

"So you can't take the chickens? Do you think we have enough money without them?"

"No, ma'am, you don't. Not near enough." He took a pull from the steaming cup of coffee Rosa handed him and continued.

"Mary and me got to ciphering last night, and here's what we come up with: Add up the sheep, the produce, and the greenbacks you got, you still come up 'bout a hundred short." Rosa nodded to affirm his reckoning. "Here's where it gets interesting . . . turns out we got ourselves a little nest egg in the bank. We've been saving so we could run longhorns ourselves next year." He studied the inside of the mug for a second before continuing. "You see, we were in the same predicament you're in, but our family came through for us. Now we think it's time to do the same for you."

"Oh, George, do you mean it?" Louise had his arm in a death grip.

"Sure do. Those sheep ain't so bad, and Wes'll probably want to lease our spread next year, too. Besides, if we didn't bail you out, I suppose Mary'd insist on your moving over to our place, and if that happened I wouldn't get a lick of work out of those hands, Bailey included." He winked at Rosa, who sat too stunned to respond.

They weren't going to leave? The land would be theirs? She didn't realize she was speaking aloud until Uncle George answered her.

"I think it's all going to work out. It'll be close. I'm not sure exactly how much is in the bank, but Mary tried to figure the interest, and if the sheep market hasn't softened, we'll be right as rain." He shrugged. "If we're a few dollars short, I'll send the boys over with some cages and we'll run those chickens up to Bradford's. Surely he'd pay top dollar for such beautiful birds."

Louise blushed. "You mustn't think poorly of him for not helping. He said he'd like to, but he's saving to rebuild his store, since it burned in the big fire and all."

"Sounds like he's got plans for the future, the scoundrel!" George said merrily, still relishing his role of deliverer.

"Oh, stop. I couldn't accept his money even if he offered. He's already been more than generous with Rosa's work. Hasn't he, Rosa. Rosa?"

Rosa remained motionless, stunned. All those months of awaiting judgment, and at the last count of the firing squad, the reprieve arrived. Pardoned. Too much to comprehend. The fear was a huge block of ice in her heart, and while George's news was the first warmth in months, it would take a while before it would melt.

She couldn't keep her head from spinning long enough to think the whole process through. George would leave today with the sheep. He would sell them at the auction tonight. Tomorrow, the fourteenth, he would take the money to the courthouse and pay their bill. After that they were free and would never again need to come up with a hundred sixty dollars in three months. Never again would that much be required of them. They'd proved they could run a ranch, hadn't they? They'd raised enough food to live on. Next year they would be self-supporting.

"I just can't believe it. I thought the farm was lost, and now you . . ." Rosa turned shining eyes to George and, before he could stop her, lunged, throwing both arms around his neck.

His eyes rolled sheepishly beneath bushy brows. "Miss Rosa, this is the one part that caused me to shy away from doing this. I didn't want you carrying on about it."

"George, you old fool, you have to let us say thank-you, at least." Louise searched for her handkerchief but gave up and used her apron to wipe away the tears.

"I reckon we might as well get it over with." George patted Rosa's arm as she squeezed his neck. "Maybe being the hero isn't half bad after all."

17

Her pasture spread before her, deserted — the gentle woolly residents driven away the day before.

"Don't worry about them." Rosa scratched Conejo between his long ears. "We'll get you some more little friends to guard next year. Until then you can go to Uncle George's so you won't be lonely."

Next year. She wouldn't believe it until Uncle George came back, and the further the sun trekked toward the horizon, the more worried she grew. What if it wasn't enough? George said they could sell the chickens if they needed to, but would they have time tomorrow, the dreaded fifteenth, for gathering chickens and a ride to Lockhart? At what time did the money need to be at the courthouse?

Those thoughts had kept her up last night. She couldn't float around the house with a song on her lips like Louise until she saw

272

the receipt from the tax office. The tragedies she'd experienced made it impossible for her to ever take anything for granted again, and the longer Uncle George delayed, the more her imagination turned to unpleasantness.

By the time they'd washed the supper dishes, even Louise couldn't hide her anxiety.

"Why doesn't he come by?" She wiped out the basin for the third time. "You'd think he'd come here first, just to let us know."

Rosa's stomach knotted. The chickens had enjoyed the dinner she'd declined. Maybe it had fattened them up a little for their trip tomorrow, for she'd already surrendered to the idea of an early morning emergency ride to Lockhart.

With a slap, Louise threw down her wet rag and ran to the door.

"It's Mary. She's cutting across the field."

Rosa ran too but couldn't see around Louise.

"What? What is it? Let's go!" She tried to worm her way around her, but Louise was rooted to the ground.

"Louise? What is it?" She succeeded in squeezing into the doorway and stopped, as shocked as her mother-in-law.

They didn't need to meet Mary to hear her news. Her arms were dangling slack from her sloped shoulders. Her grotesquely elongated shadow was dragging behind her like fresh kill. Something had gone horribly wrong, and whatever it was, Mary bore the brunt of it.

"Oh, Mary!" Louise dropped to the porch and covered her face in her apron.

Squatting next to her, Rosa wrapped an arm around her shoulders. Mary came to the bottom step, her eyes lowered.

"It wasn't enough?" Rosa asked.

She shook her head but didn't answer.

Rosa took a long, shaky breath. She shouldn't be so upset. She'd known this was coming for months. Surely she wasn't surprised now.

"Thank you for trying. It's not your fault," Rosa said.

"No, it's not, but y'all need to hear the whole account. I need to say my piece before you decide if you want to associate with us or not."

Mary's words sent a chill up her spine.

"Go on." Rosa's dark eyes never left the woman.

"I'll keep it short. Lots could be said that don't need to be said, but you deserve to hear the truth of it from me — since George ain't got the nerve." With a swoop she pulled her bonnet off and smoothed back her hair.

"George and the boys made it to market last night, and your sheep did right well — got closer to thirty dollars for them, so they were pleased as punch." Louise quieted and listened through the apron she clutched to her face. "So George stayed and took the vegetables to market and headed to the bank to get our share of the payment." Mary paused and cleared her throat. She wadded the bonnet in one hand, stiffened her spine, and continued.

"Seeing how we didn't need as much since your sheep did so well, George decided to take the extra and try his luck at cards. . . ."

"Oh no. . . ." Louise lifted her head.

"He said he was just going to wager that extra money, but when he lost some of it, he couldn't walk away. He wanted a chance to win it back. Well, those cardsharps were more than happy —"

"Mary, did he lose it all?" asked Louise.

Mary's chin quivered, and she beat her eyelids rapidly, but then her jaw set. "No, he didn't. He stopped. I may be a fool, but I'm proud of him. There's a lot of blame to heap on George, but he did learn to walk away. He didn't lose it all. We'll still come up short, but you have all your money. Every penny of it. George didn't gamble your money. Just ours. We aim to give yours to you as soon as you've got a safe place to keep it."

"A safe place? I don't want a safe place. This is my home. . . ."

"I'm so sorry, Louise, but it ain't gonna turn out that way. We haven't got long, but you got to make some plans. You have a fair amount of cash, more than you came with. You should be able to let some nice rooms. . . ."

But Louise wasn't listening. She tore off her apron, ripping loose a strap at the neck and one at the waist, and stuffed the crumpled material to her face to muffle her cries.

Rosa covered her ears with her fists, fingernails digging into the palms of her hands. The last time she'd heard that cry was in the hills of Ciauhtlaz. It rang through the hollows of the mountains and echoed against the wall of fallen rock piled over her husband. She felt the sky crashing down on her, pressing her against the wood siding of the porch, holding her down to inflict more blows. Rosa wanted to get away, but where would she go? Last time Louise had presented the escape, but it had proved to be

276

nothing more than another ambush, another cave-in to trap and suffocate her. Nowhere to run now. No sanctuary left.

"Rosa!"

She pried open her screwed shut eyes when she felt Mary's strong grip on her arm. Mary practically lifted her and dragged her into the kitchen. Spinning her around, Mary stepped close enough that their skirts pushed at each other.

"Listen, I hate that it happened this way, that we can't fix it for you, but you can't fall apart. Louise needs you to be strong."

Rosa leaned against the wall, hands placed flat on the cool plaster. She was so weary. She had offered all that she had, everything she was, and it wasn't enough. She would never be enough.

"Let's see if we can get her in here."

Louise's sobs continued to pour through the window with the cool evening air. The light was gone. Morning would come, but there was not another chance. Not for them to remain.

Sprawled across her bed, shoes still on, Louise had finally quieted.

"What are we going to do?" she asked Rosa for the hundredth time while Mary wiped her brow with a cool rag.

"You aren't forsaken," Mary said. "Haven't you been reminding us that God keeps a special watch over each of His children — especially widows? He won't forget you, and He gave you lots of family that loves you. Tomorrow, George will bring out the wagon, and we'll get you moved over to our place. It won't be so bad."

Louise groaned and pulled the cloth over her eyes.

Mary rose from Louise's bed. "Reckon that kind of talk can wait. You two need your sleep. Tomorrow will be busy."

"You aren't going home? What about the kids and George? He'll want you with him tonight," Louise said.

Mary took Louise's hand in hers. "They'll be fine. George will hold it together for tonight. Weston is there to take his flock to the sale barn tomorrow, and wild horses couldn't drag the story out of George in front of Wes." She yawned big and kicked off her shoes. "It's late. Better get some shut-eye."

"Stay with me, Rosa," Louise begged.

Rosa nodded to Mary. "Go ahead. You can sleep in my room."

"Are you sure, honey? You look like the walking dead already."

"I'm sure. I wouldn't sleep well worrying

about her."

Mary picked up her shoes and gave Rosa a squeeze. "You're blessed to have her, Louise. Mack's best day's work was when he got you such a good daughter-in-law." She kissed Rosa on the forehead, tucked her shoes under her arm, and lifted the lamp. "Try to get some sleep now. 'Night, Louise."

Rosa waited until she heard Mary's heavy steps on the stairs before she stepped out of her slippers and lay next to Louise. The breeze was mercifully fresh. At least she was wearing her loose blouse and skirt from home. She was too tired to go upstairs for her bedclothes. Lying on top of the quilt, Rosa couldn't tell through the darkness if Louise was asleep, but her breathing had evened.

"Are you awake?" Louise whispered. When Rosa grunted she continued, "Maybe it isn't hopeless. Mary's right — God takes care of us widows. Surely He's going to do something. Remember Reverend Stoker's sermon about Elijah and the widow? How God multiplied her flour and oil during a famine?"

Rosa closed her eyes. They didn't need oil and flour. They needed over a hundred dollars by sunup tomorrow morning. She had yet to hear Louise make a reasonable suggestion when it came to their financial straits. Too late now.

"And then there was Ruth and Naomi. They were both widows about to lose their farm."

Rosa bunched the pillow under her head and tried to act interested. "And God gave them a miracle?"

"Not a miracle. They had an unseemly plan, but God blessed it. I'm not sure I understand why." Louise sighed. "If only we had a Boaz."

If only. If only they had a dollar for every *if only*, they wouldn't need something called a boaz. If Louise had a better option, she should've spoken up long ago.

Louise propped herself up on her elbow. "Rosa, he's at George's tonight."

"Who?"

"Weston. He always stays in the barn at Mary's when he's there. Do you think he could be our Boaz?" She fell back against her pillow. "What am I thinking? I couldn't ask you to do that. And what would he think?"

"Think about what? What's a boaz?"

"He's the man that saved Ruth and Naomi."

"Saved their ranch?"

"Yes, of course. But I don't condone their actions. Even Mary wouldn't approve."

What had the woman done? If this plan involved petitioning Weston for help, Rosa didn't know if she had the courage. The memory of being left on her porch was too fresh. Too painful. Since that day, she hadn't exchanged a single word with him. She couldn't approach him, not for any amount of money.

But it wasn't just the money. She wanted to save a legacy — to keep the land of a family she loved from falling into the hands of a man she loathed. Rosa ground her teeth together. Her neck tightened against the pillow. Already she could hear Jay Tillerton's boots echoing down the hall, imagine his long, puny body stretched out in her parlor. What wouldn't she do to keep him from winning?

Rosa rolled to her side and got to her feet. Standing, she lifted her chin and wiped the blurriness from her eyes with her turquoise sleeve. How bad could it be? Surely Louise, with her concerns over propriety, wouldn't direct her to do anything too offensive.

"If you think it'd work . . ." She didn't have the strength for another failed attempt.

"I think it would, but what about Weston? What if he isn't agreeable?"

"He can always say no."

Louise chewed her lip as she looked Rosa over. "I don't suppose he would, but if he did, how could you face him? Listen, forget I mentioned it. It was a bad idea. Instead, let's ask the land office for more time. I can't believe they'd really evict two women."

Sometimes Rosa envied her naïveté. Too bad the world wasn't as generous as Louise imagined. But was Weston? Through the wall she heard the parlor clock gong eleven times before she reached for her shoes.

"I'm going to find him. Tell me what to do."

They had nothing to lose. That's what she kept telling herself. Rosa stumbled away from the house. She was numb. Her emotions were worn slick, but she would follow the story just as Louise had told it. After all, Louise had taught her what was proper in this land. She wouldn't have Rosa behave scandalously, would she? As wild as the scheme sounded, it must be like the dancing — shocking to Rosa's ears but part of the Texan culture. Biblical, even. Yet the closer Rosa came to her destination, the more aware she became of the awful disgrace to which she was exposing herself.

She could still see Weston's outraged face

after her dance. What would he say about her coming to him in the middle of the night? She'd promised to trust Louise, but the one who would have to prove trust-worthy was Weston.

Her usually nimble feet thudded like blocks of wood across Uncle George's dew-less south pasture. The outline of the barn was visible against the night sky, and the closer it loomed the harder her heart pounded until, as she entered the barnyard, she was sure that anyone inside could hear it.

And according to Louise, someone was inside the barn.

The warm scent of horses reached her. Silently Rosa crossed the corral in her soft-soled shoes. Her hands shook as she pushed against the barn door.

The weak moonlight streamed in. She stood in the doorway and allowed her eyes to adjust. Weston was there. Bedded in the midst of a pile of sweet, clean straw was a figure, half hidden, but large nonetheless. Rosa scanned the barn. Good. He was alone, just the horses standing in their sleep as if carved in marble.

And no one had seen her. It wasn't too late to turn and go home. She stood on the threshold, undecided. Her eyes traveled the path back to their ranch, which until that very evening had been home. Going back meant accepting defeat, and the terms had not yet been drawn. Who knew where surrender would leave them?

But the dark barn held a future even more uncertain and in ways more threatening. If anyone could help her, it was this man. And if there was anyone she'd like to visit with or work beside, it was Weston, but alas, he didn't return her regard. He'd purposely avoided her for over a month now. He'd completely rejected her.

She shook her head to clear the cobwebs. Although too scared to yawn, Rosa wouldn't be able to hold off exhaustion for long. Her options had expired. If she was going to be humiliated, Weston was the last person on the earth she would want to witness it, but she had to take that gamble.

Rosa judged the distance to Weston's bed, counted the steps in her mind, and then pulled the door shut behind her, plunging the room into darkness.

Maybe it would be easier if she couldn't see him. She took the first step, heart pounding. Should she call out and wake him? No, she'd better do exactly what Louise told her. At least then the other woman would share the blame for her actions.

Rosa's tentative steps brought her closer and closer. The straw gathered around her ankles, but she pressed on. When the straw reached about knee deep, she knew she was there. With an outstretched hand Rosa searched until her fingers touched the edge of a woven blanket. Trembling, she went to her knees and allowed her hand to brush against him only enough to ascertain the difference between heads and tails. She mustn't hesitate or she'd lose her nerve. With her heart hammering away at her ribs, she knelt close to him.

She'd intended to keep her distance, to wait until he woke, like Louise told her, but the straw sloped where it supported his weight and she slid right into his chest. Rosa couldn't budge. Terrified. Her nose pressed against the pocket of his shirt, filling her every breath with the scent of peppermint.

She didn't dare move, even though one arm was thrown across him. Was it possible he was still asleep?

Weston felt her warmth against his chest; her breath burnt a ring of heat near his heart. The lady trembled, so he took her in his arms and pulled her close until they were both burrowed deep in the hay. *Poor child,* he thought through the haze of sleep. *I wonder what's got her so frightened.*

In his dream Weston knew the woman wasn't Cora. Not for a moment was he fooled into thinking that. Yet he was at peace, happier than he'd been in weeks. He tightened his arms around her. Should be improper, but it sure seemed right. Having her there was approved — sanctioned — his heart told him. God gave him someone to protect tonight, even if the mirage evaporated in the morning light.

For a few moments contentment washed over him like the first warm rays of spring. He enjoyed the feel of her against his chest, a feeling denied him for so many years, but as much as he wanted to savor the sensation, he couldn't shut out a persistent impression, faint but growing more distinct, that he should wake up.

With an effort Weston struggled to find his senses. Were his eyes open? It was so dark he wasn't sure. He had to be sleeping because the petite figure remained in his arms. But how did the rest of the barn seem so real? The owl hooted. The hay poked through his collar. Either those things weren't physically real or the woman in his arms was.

Who could it be? But even as he formed the question, he knew. He couldn't go a day, an hour, without thinking about her. And she was in bed with him.

Rosa.

His breathing changed. Oh, this was worse than Rosa had ever imagined. Weston would wake to find her practically on top of him. Would he remember that he'd pulled her there? He moved away slowly, loosening his embrace, and touched her arm. Deliberately, he explored up her shoulder and to her face.

"Mr. Garner?" She could only muster a whisper.

"Rosa? What are you doing here?"

But instead of waiting for an answer, he dumped her on her backside in the hay and scrambled away. She heard him fumbling until he bumped into the stall partition.

"Ow!"

"Are you hurt?"

He didn't answer but shuffled further away, and soon the giant wooden door at the front of the barn swung open.

The moonlight blurred her vision. Rosa looked down at her straw-strewn skirt and trembling hands. Did she look as pathetic as she felt?

"I'm sorry. You were sleeping, and I didn't want to wake you —"

"You shouldn't be here! Do you have any idea . . ." He stomped outside but skidded to a stop and reentered the barn. "The men . . . at the campfire . . . did they see you?"

She shook her head.

"Does Louise know you're here?"

"Yes, she sent me." Rosa climbed out of the haymow. "She wants me to tell you that we need . . . we need your help."

She lifted her eyes to the imposing figure outlined in the doorway. His stern mouth and lowered brows were enough to send her running, but the hand holding the door open reminded her of another Weston — a Weston who'd held her in a gentle dance with that hand wrapped around her waist, a Weston who'd ridden at her side, pleased to keep her in his grasp. Even if he no longer existed, there was still the man who came back to teach her to shoot and sat on the porch until she was safe. She had a chance.

"And you're asking me now?" He looked over his shoulder toward the dark house and repeated, "You shouldn't be here."

"I'm not proud that I am. Don't you think this is humiliating enough? If there was any other way . . ." She cowered against the post, ashamed to present such a sorry sight.

He took a deep breath and turned from

her, rubbing his eyes. Then she heard words not meant for her ears. "I want to do what's right, and I will. Problem is, I don't know what a Christian man does for a woman who sneaks into his bed. Lord, help me."

When he turned toward her again, she braced herself like a defendant, squared her shoulders, and raised her chin. Louise hadn't told her all the details of the story — just that Boaz saved the women and their property. Was she supposed to ask now?

Weston motioned her closer until she stepped into the light.

His gaze roamed her face, surely not missing a haggard crease or her tear-troubled eyes. He shook his head. "What can I do for you?"

And with that question the cold embers of her hope blazed. He didn't berate her for her timing. He didn't point out the obvious flaws in her method. He merely wanted to help her. It was going to work.

"I don't know if you can . . . or if you want to, and I really have no right to even ask. . . ."

"I'll help you. I will. Tell me how."

Rosa took a deep breath, planning not to breathe again until she had laid bare every ugly truth about their situation. "We have to pay the taxes on the farm tomorrow. They are due, and Jay Tillerton is going to buy the lien. If we don't pay, he'll get the land. We don't have enough money. George and Mary were going to help, but . . ." She paused. George's story was his to tell. She wouldn't share it. "They can't now. That leaves only you. No one else can redeem it." She searched his face for a reaction. "You must take it if you will." She kept her voice from breaking.

"Rosa." Her name sounded sweet coming from him. "Why didn't you come to me sooner? After all you've done . . ." He lowered his eyes. "After all you've done, I wasn't there for you, was I? I'm to blame. I didn't offer."

"But Mary said cash was hard to come by, and you'd already helped them."

"Taking care of Louise was my responsibility, and I failed her. I am the one who should be ashamed, not you. I am honored — do you hear me?" He lifted her chin. "I'm honored to help you any way I can."

Weary eyes watched each word as they departed his lips, gauging his determination. He would help. Rosa needed more time, and he could buy it for her.

Oh, she would pay him back. If it took the rest of her life, she would find a way.

Exhaustion and relief conspired against

her. She almost giggled as her knees started to buckle. Her fear had kept her from enjoying a good night's rest for many weeks, but with the stress removed, she was giddy. Nothing could keep her sleepless much longer.

Clear-headed now, Weston forged ahead. "Tomorrow morning we'll go to the bank. Getting a loan in my name will be no problem, and then you'll go with me to the courthouse. You'll hand them the money yourself. It won't be on your shoulders any longer."

Rosa nodded. Tomorrow morning. August fifteenth. She made a move toward the door and held herself up against the frame. What time was it? She listened to the night sounds. The moon hung overhead. The bullfrogs sang their throaty song. Probably just past midnight. Dawn was a long way off, and she was about to drop in the harness.

"No, you're not going back home. You can barely stand up." He glanced toward the house. "Is Mary home?"

"No, she's with Louise."

"Then you're staying put."

Should she protest? Louise's story had ended where Ruth made the request and Boaz agreed to take care of her. Rosa hadn't had time to find out what happened next.

"I don't know what to do. I'm so tired I'm not thinking straight."

"You can't go by yourself. It's too dangerous at night, and we mustn't be caught together this late. You might as well be comfortable." He picked her up and held her lightly against his chest while carrying her over the equipment to the haymow that had been his bed until moments ago. Looking for the most cushioned place, he arranged her to her best advantage and then took his blanket and wrapped it around her.

Once again, the scent of peppermint surrounded her as he knelt and tucked the blanket under her. He was inches from her face when their gazes met. Her chest went hollow at the gentleness emanating from his eyes. And what did he see? Did he recognize her thankfulness? Did he realize that she was in his debt, and between her gratitude and weariness, she was defenseless against him?

"I know better," he said for anyone who might care to hear. "You're safe with me." And he walked away to sit by the barn door until morning.

18

Weston watched the eastern horizon break into gray. It was time. Before he could get to his feet the rooster had already called out his first greeting. It was past time. The animals stirred and the ranch hands, so intuitively sensitive to the livestock, would not sleep much longer. He must wake Rosa and send her on her way before any witnesses awoke.

Leaving the door ajar, he climbed into the haymow with her, cautiously edging his way toward the blanket. She was there, curled on her side with one small hand tucked underneath her head, her turquoise blouse peeking out from under the rough blanket. He brushed her hair from her face, exposing her smooth complexion.

With the back of his hand he stroked her cheek. "Rosa," he whispered. She didn't move. "Rosa, you need to wake up." Her eyes moved under their lids, but she made no effort to open them. He grasped her shoulder and jostled her more firmly. "Come on. I know you had a rough night, but we've got to get you out of here."

Pandora whinnied in the next stall, and Rosa stirred. She blinked drowsily twice and reached to touch his bristly cheek.

"Yes, I'm real." He understood her confusion. He'd been in the same situation just hours ago.

As she came to, Weston read every moment of the night before in her expressive face: fear, shame, embarrassment . . . then the realization that she was saved. Only then did she allow him to help her up.

"I won't bother asking if you slept well."

"Better than the night before." She smiled at him as if he were some sort of hero. But a hero wouldn't have let her get so desperate.

"Go on home and get ready. I'll come by to pick you up. By the end of the day we'll have this straightened out. Nothing else to fret over. All right?"

With a lowered voice he showed her the best path to the pasture, sweeping away from the sleeping ranch hands and hanging tight to the high brush.

"Thank you," she said.

He felt there should be a hug, a handshake

— some connection between them besides the words — but not knowing how to proceed, he let her depart and watched as she covered the dusty barnyard, sliding out the gate toward her home.

Above Rosa the trees burst with the noise of the chattering birds sharing the morning's news. The colors of their plumage grew brighter as the sun rolled lazily over the horizon. Mockingbirds sang a *canción* while the cardinals fussed at the jays who stole too close to their nests.

The light of morning only intensified the guilt she felt. What had seemed reckless the night before was indecent now. Sleeping in the barn with Weston! What would Uncle George have thought if he'd caught her? It made her sick to think of it.

But as hard as it was to forgive herself, she couldn't ignore the fact that it was that day — August fifteenth — the day she'd dreaded for three months, and they were saved. No eviction. No loss. Weston said he would take care of it, and she trusted him.

But what was she going to tell Louise? Spending the night hadn't been part of their discussion. Louise would want every last embarrassing detail, but please, God, not in front of Mary. Besides, she didn't have time to chat. After a night in the barn she needed to wash up. She was going to town!

"I'll wear my new dress," Rosa said aloud and took hold of a slender trunk to pull herself up the bank. "This is the perfect occasion."

A horse whinnied nearby. Too close. Someone was there. Rosa tried to step behind a bush, but there wasn't time.

Tillerton had heard her. Swinging off the horse, he stepped between her and the path to the house.

"I was watching for you. Wondered if you'd make some last ditch effort today, but I thought I'd catch you leaving the house, not coming back to it."

Her eyes darted around looking for some missile, some weapon to give her a chance, but with the bank yawning at her heels, her choices were limited.

His smile mocked her. "Don't have your gun? No, I don't suppose you've been out hunting this morning." His eyes ran down her every curve, missing nothing. "So what have you been doing? Let's see how fine my powers of deduction are. There's straw in your hair." He plucked it out, pulling several thick strands with it.

Rosa gasped and held her hand against her burning scalp. She tried again to sidestep him, but he angled to block her way.

"And there aren't any footprints in the dew leaving your house. You've been out all night." His nose curled as he peered at her. "So, you turned my offer down all high and mighty only to go fishing around for another. Well, did you get a better deal? Were you able to save your ranch?"

Yes, she wanted to gloat. *We saved the ranch from you.* He wouldn't get it. He couldn't take it from them.

He walked around her again, his anger building. "I bet you don't want to tell me who you were with, not that I blame you. It couldn't have been good old Uncle George. If he had any money, you'd already have it. Surely you didn't waste your time on those worthless cowboys. They don't have two coins to rub together. Unless they pooled their money —"

"Get out of my way." Rosa pushed past him, but he wasn't finished. In a grip that would leave a bruise, he pulled her against his weaselly chest.

"I'm not done with you. I thought you protested on moral grounds, but no, you just thought you could do better. Well, I'm an acquired taste that you'll learn to love. . . ."

She wouldn't take any more. Rosa landed

one good blow to his jaw before they both heard the unmistakable click of a Colt's hammer going into position.

Tillerton stepped back and flung his hands into the air. Forcing a jovial smile, he called out, "All right, you caught us. Just having ourselves a little fun."

"Doesn't look like the lady is having fun."

Who was hiding behind them? Rosa didn't recognize the voice.

Tillerton's eyes narrowed as he peered into the undergrowth, looking for his adversary. "Why don't you come on out and we'll talk about it. Or is Mrs. Garner's friend ashamed to show his face?"

"You're the one who ought to be ashamed. Mrs. Garner, go on home. I'll keep this piece of trash from blowing in your direction."

Rosa didn't need to be told twice. Wondering who had followed her, she gathered her skirts and scrambled up the path to the house.

She'd just looked over her shoulder hoping to see who had saved her when the door swung open.

"Where have you been?" Louise practically dragged her across the threshold. "I can't believe you stayed all night. What will people say?"

Rosa rubbed her arm, still sore where Tillerton had grasped it.

"Weston told me to stay. He was worried about me getting caught outside so late."

The wrinkles around Louise's mouth smoothed when her jaw dropped. "He told you to stay? Interesting . . . What else did he say?"

"He's going to give us the money. He's coming this morning to take us to the courthouse. I'm sorry I didn't come home, Louise. I knew you'd be worried —"

"*Shh.* It doesn't matter now. I'm just surprised you followed the Ruth story to the end. Surprised, but happy nonetheless."

"You told me how to ask for the money. That's as far as you got."

"There wasn't time to tell the rest." She shot a worried look over her shoulder. "Mary will wake up soon. Don't fret, child. What's done is done. We'll trust him to do what's right. If he's responsible for your staying, he'll protect your reputation. In the meantime, you're a sight. Get cleaned up. I imagine he'll be here any time, and believe me you'll want to look your best."

Weston was tightening the flank cinch on Pandora when Willie appeared, running full tilt out of the high grass.

"Mr. Weston, we got trouble."

"What is it, Willie?"

"Something's going on here. Something that ain't good."

Willie had his attention. "Go on."

"This morning I saw a woman sneaking out of the barn, this barn here. I didn't know who it was or who she came to see, so I followed her." Willie's eyes darted to the side. "I hate to be the one to tell you, but you need to know."

Weston looked at him with deadly intensity and said it for him. "It was Mrs. Rosa Garner — and she was with me."

"How could you?" Willie's lip curled. "I might be a cowboy, but I know that a woman sneaking out of a barn at first light is wrong, and it don't matter who it is."

Between this former slave and former slave owner, one of them had some explaining to do. Wes couldn't hide behind his status to squelch Willie's questions, but what could he say without hurting Rosa's reputation?

"Willie, I'll tell you what happened last night, and I hope you can keep this between the two of us. Mrs. Garner did nothing shameful. She was helping Louise, and neither of us would want to hurt her reputation."

Willie shifted his weight impatiently from the six-shooter leg to the Bowie knife leg. "Well, that's the problem, boss. We ain't the only ones who know."

Weston strode into the dining room of Palmetto, causing the curtains to fling their skirts as he passed. He wouldn't be surprised if a swirl of dust still followed him, considering the breakneck speed at which he'd traveled from George and Mary's. The whole world seemed in an uproar. Naturally, Eliza and Jake were unaffected, engaged in their usual banter at the breakfast table.

"You keep chowing down like that, and we'll need to get some more chickens," Jake quipped as Eliza sopped up the runny yolk with her toast.

"You keep talking like that, and we'll need to get another bedroom."

"I hate to interrupt, but I've got to scrub up and hit the ground running." Weston kicked his boots off while fumbling with his collar. "I'd be grateful if both of you could give me a minute."

"Weston, you aren't going to undress in the dining room, are you?" Eliza said with her mouth full. "Don't you want some breakfast?"

"I'm hankering for sausage and eggs, but

301

it'll have to be fast. Have Octavia send it up." He pulled his suspenders down over his shoulders and ran toward the stairs.

Wes didn't have time to gauge their reactions. He took the stairs two at a time and raced to his room. Finding his razor and shaving soap in place, he set to the job as fast as he safely could.

"You'd better slow down. You're going to cut yourself."

How'd Eliza get up the stairs so quickly in her condition?

"Thanks, Ma. I'm new to shaving, you know. Now, stop riding me and listen. I've got to go to Lockhart today. Right now, in fact. I'd be honored if you'd go with me."

"Honored? You ain't making no sense," Jake said. "What's the rush?"

"I'm getting married."

No sound emitted from the mouthy couple for a good ten seconds. One noteworthy accomplishment for the day.

Eliza's hand went to her chest in shock.

Jake smiled from ear to ear. "Who's the lucky lady?"

"Mrs. Rosa Garner."

Now it was Eliza's turn to smile. With a squeal she jumped to hug her brother's froth-covered neck. "How did this happen? When? I didn't know you'd talked to her recently. How long has she known?"

"She doesn't yet. That's why we need to hurry." Eliza stepped back as Weston darted into his dressing room. "I need to propose, and then we have to go to the bank, get the money, and take it to the courthouse to pay the taxes on their farm before the end of the business day. We'll be doing good to make it." He emerged wearing a dapper black suit and vest and carrying a stylish bowler. The boots were nonnegotiable.

Eliza dropped onto the bed with her arms crossed. "Hold your horses. What's all that have to do with her wedding? Why don't you just start over?"

And so he did, between bites of sausage and eggs, but the retelling didn't put much shine on him. How had he let them get so desperate? Eliza seconded his thoughts.

"Today is August the fifteenth? That's right. They had to have the money today," she said. "Why didn't I check up on them? How scared they must have been!"

Weston grunted. "And I actually caught Tillerton lurking around their place a few weeks ago. Rosa was terrified. I didn't even ask if he had been there before." Wes wouldn't rest easy until she was under his roof. He'd already had his suspicions about the man. Who knew what he was capable of?

"She probably wouldn't have told you, anyway," Jake reassured them. "She doesn't want to cause trouble for anyone."

"Well, looks like she has, whether she meant to or not," Eliza said. "It doesn't sound like Tillerton to threaten her, but if she stands between him and the land, maybe he's not using his best judgment. She needs to have a husband's protection."

A husband's protection. Those words rang in Weston's ears all the long buggy ride to her house. What good had a husband's protection done Cora? His failure had devastated her whole family. Was it fair to involve another innocent woman before he was ready?

Weston wasn't one for rushing into things, especially not something this big. At every boundary line he questioned whether he was making the right decision. He didn't know if he could risk his heart again, but he cared enough about Rosa to protect her. That would have to suffice for now, because in a way, God had taken it out of his hands. He couldn't call himself a gentleman and refuse to offer her his name — not in the position she found herself. Besides, the last month had been torture. Perhaps his heart was lost already.

Then again, she might refuse him. She only bargained on giving him sixty acres, not a bride.

From her room, Rosa heard Louise's greeting. "Land sakes, come in, come in. Weston, Eliza, and Jake — you're all here! What a joyous company you make. And Wes, you're all dressed up to go to town. How handsome you look! Rosa! Come down. They're here."

She checked her reflection in the hand mirror one last time and descended the stairs.

The scene in the parlor was a lot to take in. Louise, still flushed from the joy of their victory, exclaimed over all the young people, while Mary sat in shock on the piano stool, finally aware of Rosa's whereabouts last night. A moment's guilt crossed her heart, but Rosa shook it off. Today she would celebrate.

Eliza kissed Mary's cheek and patted her shoulder. Even she seemed to be in a tizzy over the last night's activities. Rosa was possibly the calmest of the bunch. To be truthful, she felt like dancing, but she wouldn't dishonor her beautiful rose gown with such immature behavior.

Rosa didn't know who marked her entrance first, but sound and movement ceased in the crowded room. She looked from face to face in wonder. What was wrong with them?

Jake's mouth hung open, and Eliza's hand went to her throat. Weston stood frozen except for his Adam's apple, which bounced a few times before he could swallow successfully.

Rosa checked her black hair, still damp from her hurried washing. It was drawn up in a complicated twist that left her neck exposed all the way to her perfectly fitted bodice. She'd remembered her corset, so what were they staring at?

Louise recovered first. "You are beautiful."

"Amen!" Jake added. "We knew you were a pretty girl, but have mercy."

Eliza had yet to look away. "That color, Rosa. It's so rich, and the way it reflects off your complexion . . ." She looked to Weston and burst into tears.

"What's got into her?" Mary asked. "Have y'all gone mad?"

"No, ma'am," Jake answered. "Eliza's been emotional lately. It's her delicate condition, you know. She'll be fine." He turned to Weston and patted him on the back. "You're up, partner," and propelled him to the center of the room.

Their strange behavior confused Rosa, and she wasn't the only one. Mary frowned stiffly, while Louise smiled at Weston as if he were Sam Houston reincarnated.

Weston cleared his throat. "Mrs. Garner and I will go to Lockhart to pay the taxes this morning. I can't tell you how much I regret not intervening sooner. I, ah, should have stayed in touch, but there's no way to change that. We have to move forward." He looked over his shoulder at Jake, who nodded his encouragement. "So, before we leave, I would like to ask Mrs. Garner if she would do me the honor of becoming my wife . . . today."

From behind him came a terse whisper. "On your knee!"

"Drats!" He dropped to one knee before Rosa and took her hand.

She tried in vain to snatch it back. The spiffy man before her was unfamiliar, spouting nonsense. Where was the tender man who had wakened her that morning? Where was the rancher? Her friend?

"I don't blame you for being startled. That was rather abrupt. Let me try again. I would be honored if you would consent —"

"You can't be serious!" Rosa said.

Weston frowned. "But I am, I assure you. You were observed leaving this morning, so we must get married — with haste."

"Isn't this what you wanted?" Louise's tremulous smile threatened to unnerve her.

What kind of question was that? Married to Weston? Not like this. Not now.

"I asked him for a loan, that's all. We never spoke about marriage."

"But it has to happen," Louise said. "Weston here is a gentleman and will make a fine husband."

Rosa tore her hand away from him as he stood. Why was Louise accepting this arrangement? Had she anticipated Weston's offer? Oh no. What had Rosa led him into?

"Don't act shocked now, Rosa." Mary hopped off the piano stool. "No one's going to believe you weren't party to this. What does it mean in Mexico when you spend the night with a man? You got what you were after. You saved your ranch. Weston's the only one with reason to protest."

Rosa felt her face blazing, humiliation turning into anger. "Ridículo! I didn't do anything wrong. We need money. You all know that. It's the only reason I went — for the ranch. You have to believe me." She scanned the room — Jake, Mary, Weston, even Eliza — no one would look her in the face.

"But last night," Louise said, "we talked about Ruth and Boaz. I thought you'd decided to do like she did and get a husband."

"Ruth and Boaz? Was that your intent all along?" Weston's face turned as white as a corpse. Only the thought of being shackled to her could cause a man such distress.

"No!" Rosa turned to Louise. "You can't force another man to marry me. I won't do it."

"But what can I do?" Louise wrung her hands. "Mary's right. I can't go against propriety, not now that you've been compromised. Maybe it won't be so bad. If he didn't want you he would have sent you home."

Louise's words cut through her like a dagger.

She'd had enough. Turning, Rosa ran up the stairs as fast as her gown would allow. They were all family. They were adults. Let them figure out what to do. As far as she was concerned, Louise could sleep in George and Mary's outhouse. Rosa wasn't responsible for her any longer.

She would find a way back to Ciauhtlaz and never return. She'd worked so hard to be a proper lady, only to stumble into this. Embarrassment burned her face, angry tears caught in her throat.

She barreled through her room. Finding nothing else to throw, Rosa flung herself on the bed, hid her face, and didn't look up, even when she heard the deep voice in her open doorway.

"You're going to muss your new dress."

"I don't care! I'm not going anywhere."

She could sense Weston coming closer. What she wouldn't give for a lock on the door.

"Is this your bag?"

Who else's would it be? But she refused to answer. The clasp snapped open on the bed next to her.

"Looks like we're in a mess, doesn't it?" he said.

"You're not! You don't have to do this."

"Yes I do. I made a mistake letting you stay last night."

If he didn't want you, he would have sent you home." She cringed at the words, face still hidden in her pillow. This time she had no romantic notions clouding her thinking. Mack had flirted with her — raised her hopes. Weston wanted nothing to do with her.

"But we talked about the land — about

saving our ranch. Just a business deal."

"Most business deals are discussed during business hours while both parties are awake."

She peeked around her pillow and saw him gather every piece of clothing hanging on the pegs, every piece except her black mourning gown.

"We need to go if we're going to make it to the courthouse on time," he said. "I'll make sure the deed remains in Louise's and your name. My name won't be attached."

"What about the marriage?"

"Definitely more complicated. That document will make mention of me." He looked behind him. "If you'll tell me where your unmentionables are, I'll pack those, too."

She threw her pillow in his direction and then locked her arms over her head. How could he act as if this didn't bother him? Why was he giving up his freedom so easily?

Not her. Not again.

"Let people say what they want about last night," she said. "I'd rather have a ruined reputation because of one night than force you into lifelong retribution. Besides, half the women at church predicted I'd disgrace the family. No one will be surprised." Her bottom lip trembled, so she bit it. She would not cry, not with Weston being so . . . so . . . reasonable about everything.

"I talked to Willie this morning. He had an interesting story to tell. Seems like you had another way to save your farm, after all." The rocker creaked as Weston eased into it. "Rosa, would you please sit up and look at me? I need to know something. We're getting hitched today either way, but I want you to tell me the truth."

She pushed herself up, hoping she wasn't committing to anything by complying. He rose enough to pick the pillow up off the floor, drop it on the bed, and then wait with his elbows on his knees until she was ready.

"What is it?"

Weston's eyes filled with compassion. She couldn't take out her frustration on him. Not with all he'd done for her.

"Downstairs Louise said you had some plan to secure my help. I need to know, when you came to me last night, did you think I would make you the same offer Tillerton did?"

Rosa looked away, but not fast enough. She couldn't stop the blush from burning her face. She suddenly became aware of their location, her bed and her clothing stuffed in the open valise.

"No! Never! You would never ask me to

do that. And now, because of me, you feel forced to ruin your life, but you don't have to. You have to believe me. I didn't trick you, or trap you, despite what Louise says." She grasped her quilt in iron fists. "I had no idea how the story ended. It was in the Bible, so I thought it'd be all right to go to you and ask for help. I never meant to take advantage of you. Let's go to Lockhart, pay the taxes, and come back — unmarried. Mary can't force us. We must be firm."

"If I didn't respect you, nothing Mary could do would force me to marry you."

Rosa pulled back. "So now you want to marry me? Odd, since you haven't wanted to speak to me since Independence Day."

He looked away. What did she expect him to say? The truth certainly wasn't pretty.

"Regardless, you're in danger here — not just your reputation, but your safety, as well. I think you and I are the only people who've seen Jay Tillerton as he is. The best protection I can offer you is my name."

"But then the marriage can be temporary, right? We'll get it canceled after the gossip dies down."

He stood, dwarfing her tiny room. "I take my vows seriously. We're saving you from disgrace, not increasing it."

But was there any disgrace greater than

having a man who didn't want you? She didn't know what he expected from a wife — this kind of wife, anyway. They needed to be candid.

"I've married for convenience before. Mack was a good man, a great friend. . . ." She took her pillow and hugged it to her. "But I couldn't make him love me. I gave him everything, and still he never loved me. He never allowed me in. And then, at the mine . . ." She paused.

She'd never told anyone this. In the chaos, even Louise had missed her son's last act. "When he stumbled out, I was right there, relieved he'd been spared, but he ran past me to another. Nenetl was her name. He gave her his necklace, a charm he'd carved for weeks. I waited, but he didn't even look my way. I never saw him alive again."

Weston rose and picked up her flute from the table. The clay pipe looked so fragile in his hands. "I can't promise you love, but I can promise you faithfulness. I can promise you'll never have to pretend with me. You'll never have to give more than you're ready for." He wrapped the flute in a shawl and gently placed it in the valise before continuing.

"You know, I determined to never remarry. Last night changed the situation, but it didn't change me. God could heal me — He could make me hope for more — but it hasn't happened yet. Frankly, I'm terrified. I gave my heart once, too, and it wasn't enough."

His broad shoulders looked indestructible in the tailored suit. Hard to believe he suffered the same doubts she'd fought every waking moment of her life. If only Louise had warned her to come back home. If only they had let him be.

"I need to protect you. I want . . ." He struggled to find the right words, and Rosa could tell whatever came next would be the truth, and not a truth he was comfortable with.

"I want you to be my wife. I do. For whatever reason, God brought us here, and He's showing me that you're my responsibility. You belong with me. I don't know how that's going to work out, but I've known that, as unorthodox as it seems, God is in this. I knew it the moment I pulled you under my blanket."

"You were awake?"

He attempted a grin. "I'm as much to blame as you are."

"That's not true."

"A wedding needs to take place today. Maybe neither of us planned it this way, but

315

you're going to have to trust me."

She opened her mouth to protest, but he stopped her.

"Please. Even if you don't care for your own reputation, consider mine. I have more to lose than a ranch."

Only he could make it sound like she was doing him a favor. Well, she owed him that and more, for he was the only truly innocent one in this transgression. Besides, once again her choices lacked a reasonable alternative — scandal from the townspeople or resentment from him. Disapproval or guilt. Rosa slid off her bed, pulled some petticoats out of the drawer, and dropped them into the bag. She wouldn't rest until she'd paid him back.

Swinging the valise off the bed, she took her hat from the washstand and said a prayer that she wasn't making the biggest mistake of her life. But this time she knew the danger. This time she could avoid the pit she'd fallen into before. A ceremony in front of witnesses couldn't change a man's heart.

Nothing could.

They entered the office side by side, and a better looking couple had never passed through the heavy wooden doors. The rose

316

taffeta gown seemed to change from violet to pink as Rosa passed before the windows, holding lightly onto Weston's arm. She'd turned heads throughout town, but she didn't give it a second thought.

She stood within spitting distance of her ultimate goal and was determined to celebrate their success, however sordid, but her resolve slipped with each glance at the man by her side. When she considered Mary's outrage, Louise's confusion, and Molly's sure misery, she lost courage. Weston had even admitted that he'd wished to remain a bachelor — not the reassurance a bride-to-be longs for.

"Mr. Garner! Don't you look fine!" Molly's eyes lit up at the sight of the man. Rosa had to agree with her assessment. His tailored suit accented his strong frame, and his crisp white collar contrasted with his tan face and dark hair. She knew he was an important man, but rarely did his clothes support the claim as much as they did today.

Molly sashayed toward him but stopped in her tracks when she finally noticed the lady on his arm. Her needle-thin brows knit together and then rose in astonishment.

"Rosa?" She laughed. "Oh, my goodness, you gave me quite a scare. I didn't know

317

who the gorgeous woman with Mr. Garner was."

"Molly, we need to talk. Do you think you could take a moment?"

"Certainly, but let me admire your beautiful dress first." Molly came from behind the counter, lifted Rosa's arms, and directed her to turn slowly.

Pirouetting in public? Any other time, Rosa would've refused, but she complied, hoping to delay the inevitable discussion.

Weston's eyes followed her closely. Why was he looking at her like that? Molly wasn't going to believe their story if he didn't stop staring.

"Mr. Garner, can you believe this is our little friend Rosa? She has turned out to be quite the beauty. You better stay close to Mr. Garner. He's the only man I know strong enough to keep all these wild cowboys in check."

"Miss Lovelace! Are you performing your duties?" Mr. Travis called from his office.

"Sorry, sir." Molly fairly skipped back to her station behind the counter. "Was there something you wanted me for, Mr. Garner?"

Rosa leaned across the counter, her feet barely on the floor. "We need to talk."

Molly's face grew ashen. She put a hand to her mouth. "Oh no." She looked over her shoulder at the other girl in the office. "I forgot," she whispered. "Your taxes are due today, aren't they? I should have sent a reminder. I'm so sorry. Do you want me to get Mr. Travis?"

"That's not necessary. Rosa came prepared to pay."

Rosa couldn't pry her eyes off her friend's face. Weston tugged on her reticule. With trembling fingers Rosa untied it and fished out the bills so recently folded into it.

Molly clapped her hands together. "Rosa, that's wonderful! I can't believe you did it!"

"Well, I didn't do it —"

Weston placed his hand at her back. "She is amazing, isn't she? There's not a rancher in these parts who worked harder for his claim."

"Oh, you always know what to say. That's one thing I admire about you, Mr. Garner, your sincerity."

Rosa couldn't go through with it. Molly glided about the office recording the payment while casting sly looks at the man by her side. Molly wanted to marry Weston. The dream was farfetched, but Rosa didn't want its death on her hands.

"Mr. Garner," she whispered low, "this is all that needs to happen today. We don't need to go any further. Can't we just pretend . . . ?"

"I thought we had this settled."

"It's not that . . . it's Molly."

"Molly? Here she is. Thank you for your help." He held the receipt up and read every word proudly. He handed it to Rosa, and she folded it in half, and half again, and tied it securely in her reticule.

"Let's go outside. I'm feeling ill." The situation was moving too quickly. Rosa felt herself losing control.

"Not yet. We're not finished." Reaching into his vest pocket, Weston produced a document. He unfolded it, the thick paper resisting his attempts to straighten it. "Is Judge Rice available? We were just upstairs and filed our marriage license. Now, as soon as Eliza and Jake catch up, we need to borrow the judge for a moment."

"Your what?!" Molly jumped as if Wes had handed her a branding iron, red end first. She dropped her pen. Her eyes darted from one to the other. "Did you say marriage license?"

Weston laid it on the counter. Poor Molly had no way out. She took it gingerly and read it, lips moving silently in disbelief.

"How could you?" Her red-rimmed eyes brought tears to Rosa's.

"It's not what you think, Molly. We have

no choice. Last night, I slept in the barn with Weston on acci—"

"Rosa. That's enough!" Weston snatched the license off the counter.

"But she needs to know I didn't ask for this."

"You didn't?" Molly's curls shook. "You slept with him but didn't want to marry him?" Her voice rang over the land office. The lady behind the counter stared. Mr. Travis appeared in his office door.

"Let's go." Weston took Rosa by the arm.

Molly's voice gained in strength. "Is this the friend who warned me against trapping a man, cautioned me about making a spectacle of myself?"

Weston dragged Rosa, her feet sliding across the floor. "Out! We are going out."

"And worried I'd be stuck in a loveless marriage? Nice trick, Rosa. You sure had me fooled!"

19

Man and wife.

The golden band Eliza had purchased for her weighed heavy on Rosa's hand. Weston had a matching one, and although she couldn't see it under the reins laced through his fingers, it meant this man sitting on the squeaky leather seat next to her was now her husband.

Judge Rice had been almost as shocked as Molly when he'd entered the chamber to see one of the county's leading citizens lined out for a lightning-strike wedding to the stunned *Mexicana,* but he performed the ceremony and offered his congratulations. Too bad the judge hadn't tried to talk some sense into the man. Rosa bit her lip. Despite Weston's insistence, she still felt the wedding ceremony was overkill. People had finally stopped gossiping about her, and then this happened.

But the blame for the chaos fell on her.

Weston hadn't crept into her bed last night. He hadn't been anywhere near her in weeks. She had to make amends.

Riding in the silence, Rosa missed Eliza and Jake's company. Just like the two of them to make things as uncomfortable as possible. When the couple insisted on staying in Lockhart overnight, their burlesque expressions left little doubt as to their reasons. She rolled her eyes. Why would Weston and she need privacy? Being alone would make things awkward, as if the day's tomfoolery wasn't sufficient.

Had it only been a day? Yes, and a day wasn't long enough for a person to go from unattached and unbetrothed to married. She stole a peek at the tense man next to her. Maybe in a marriage like this emotions didn't matter.

"We're nearing the house," he said. First words in miles. "Before you get another chance to announce our nuptials, let's get something straight. The reason and manner for our engagement do not need to be discussed."

"But if we don't explain, people will assume we meant to do this. That we're in love."

He flinched. "And that would be awful because . . . ?"

323

"Because . . ."

"Excluding Molly."

She huffed. "Not fair." Other than Molly, Rosa couldn't think of anyone else it'd hurt.

"Besides, you'd be surprised how many times I've been accused of harboring feelings for you." He drove the carriage off into the grass, avoiding some deep ruts.

"By anyone not related to us?"

He thought for a very long time, and then shook his head.

Jake and Eliza. She should've known. "Wishful thinking on their part."

He chuckled. Rosa relaxed, allowing herself the full bench instead of clinging to the edge. Maybe they would be all right. Why fear him now?

"Weston, I'm confused. You said we wouldn't pretend to be in love, but if we don't tell people —"

"I meant 'pretend' in a physical way, dear wife."

Rosa pulled herself forward to the edge of the seat again.

"Don't pretend to be in love, but you don't have to proclaim from the rooftop that you're the victim of a scandalous rendezvous," he said.

"I'm not the victim. You are. I thought you'd want your name cleared."

He popped the top button on his fancy collar. "Not at your expense. You needed protection, and I do care about you. Many people marry with fewer reasons than that. So no more explanations, please. Telling everyone about last night effectively nullifies our reason for the ceremony anyway."

The buggy slowed at the crest of the ridge. Weston paused at the top, and then with a shake of the reins, he urged the horses onward toward an imposing block of yellow brick.

"That's it?"

"Yep, that's Palmetto."

His face wore the same look of pride that'd appeared at the courthouse.

"You appreciate beautiful things, don't you?"

"Especially when they belong to me."

Rosa declined to comment on the last statement and instead praised the house that grew larger with each rotation of the buggy wheels.

"That house is even bigger than the Lovelaces'."

"It's big but comfortable. You can walk through it without bumping into curios and knocking bric-a-brac off every pedestal, which is how I like it." After a moment he added, "Of course, you're free to decorate however you like."

The graceful three-story towered over them. The front steps spilled out into the drive and were bordered by a low cement wall. Immense lanterns capped each side of the passage, drawing her eye to the oak doors, inlaid with etched glass.

"Louise's old house was just getting comfortable. Something this big could never feel like home."

"Rosa, I apologize about that." He set the brake. "You did everything you could to save your farm, and I took you away from it. I wish it didn't have to be so."

Her head tilted back to take in the height of the imposing structure before her. He wished she weren't there? Now he was sorry? She put her hand on his arm to steady herself. "We'll get it all straightened out soon. I'll go back to Louise before too long."

His countenance clouded. She'd tried to warn him. Fine words and noble intentions didn't keep the fleas from biting.

"Mr. Garner?" Willie and Red moseyed out of the barn and gawked at her.

"What is it, boys?"

Red stammered, "Who? I don't know . . ." He snatched his hat off. "That's not Miss Eliza, sir."

Willie cuffed him on the back of the noggin. "Of course it's not, you knucklehead. It's Mrs. Garner."

Weston tossed Red the reins. "Mrs. Weston Garner now. We've been to the courthouse and are looking for some grub. Can you see to these horses?"

Was this how everyone would take the news? She hoped not. The blank stares and slack jaws would grow tiresome.

Willie snapped out of it first. "Yes, sir. Congratulations, sir! Ma'am!" Even the hat tipping couldn't hide his astonishment.

Rosa smiled at her guardian angel. "Thank you, Willie, for your help this morning."

"Yes, ma'am. And Mr. Garner, sir," he came forward with hand outstretched. "I wanted to tell you I've never been prouder to work for you than I am today."

"Thanks. You're a fine man, and your opinion means a lot to me."

Leaving the men behind, Rosa took the broad steps to the house and pressed her face against a window. Drawn shades gave her no hint of what she'd find.

"You don't have to peek. We can go in." Weston offered her his arm. The fine weave of his jacket delighted her fingers, but as soon as she was escorted across the threshold her senses were inundated on a grander scale.

Although darkness had not yet fallen, the iron chandelier in the entryway glimmered with the light of twelve candles.

"I won't forget this room," she said. "If I get lost, this will be my landmark."

"You won't get lost. The downstairs is simple. On the left we have the dining room. When Jake and I are home, you'll most likely find us in there or here on the right."

Weston rolled open the two doors to show her the parlor. The cozy room had a fireplace and French doors to the front porch. Eliza's piano, the twin of the one stationed in Louise's parlor, hugged the only uninterrupted wall. Rosa marveled at the vivid colors in the wallpaper. Louise's paper must have been faded.

"Ahead is the great room, although with just the three of us here, we rarely use it."

Rosa followed the red wool runner down the hall and through the wide opening.

"You keep dead animal parts in here?" She squeaked. What kind of barbarian had she married? Mounted above the cavernous fireplace, longhorn racks stretched to the high ceiling.

"Just the horns. Mementos of fertile bulls and juicy steaks. Had to be something special to make it on that wall."

Rosa raised her eyebrows. "Hope you don't think I'm something special."

"Don't grow horns."

Without leaving the great room, Weston showed her where the kitchen was and pointed out the only remaining room of the ground floor, the master suite, currently claimed by Eliza and Jake.

He was right. Not too many rooms, just big rooms. They headed for the second floor.

The giant oak staircase wound along the wall like a massive vine. Weston motioned for her to precede him, but the stairs were wide enough that he could stay at her side without crowding her.

"The third floor is one large room. It's supposed to be a ballroom, so it's kept empty. The only dance we've had lately was in George's barn, but it was as popular as lemonade at a temperance meeting."

Why did he bring up that embarrassing episode? His boots echoed hollowly on the wooden steps as he continued.

"The second floor is all bedrooms, and you can have your choice." He gestured down the long hallway and then stepped aside.

Rosa cracked open the first door, afraid of intruding, but within minutes she was floating from room to room exclaiming over ornate furniture or lavish draperies.

"This fabric is so heavy. Glad it's for a curtain rod and not a dress . . . but it's incredibly soft. I keep coming back to touch it. And this table! *Muy guapo.* Can I move it to the room I choose? This one's too dark."

"Certainly. Pick a room and we'll set it up any way you want, but do you smell that? Roast and onions if I'm not mistaken. Octavia must be about done in the kitchen."

His stomach rumbled on cue. All right, then. She needed to make a decision.

"Which room is yours?"

Weston tugged at the bottom of his vest with both hands, pulling it tight against his body. "Uh, you can stay wherever you want."

She bit her lip. If she was guessing based on the minty scent that smelled suspiciously like his favorite candy, it was the corner room with windows on both walls. Entering again, she inspected the heavily canopied bed.

"Is this one of my pillowcases?"

He sucked in his breath. "I believe so."

"You could've asked, and I would have made you one. No use buying it."

"Impulsive decision."

"And this bed . . ." Rosa took the corner

330

post in both hands and shook it vigorously.

"What in the world do you think you're doing?"

"Making sure it doesn't fall. I can't believe you sleep there. I really don't like things over my head. Little places scare me, remember?"

"That's right. You have a phobia."

She swung open the dressing room to expose a row of pants, cotton shirts, and a few suits. "What's that?"

"I was in a hurry this morning. If there's dirty laundry on the floor —"

"No. I mean, what's a phobia?"

"Oh, you had me worried." He propelled her out of his closet. "It means you're afraid of something — like small spaces, so you probably don't want to spend a lot of time in my dressing room, either."

Rosa sighed, exasperated. What frightened her more: being alone in the big house or being too close to this very masculine near stranger?

She turned worried eyes to him. "I don't know what to do. In my town the whole family lived in a room this size. My entire village could live in this house, but I know you Americans like your space. So much space that I feel lonely sometimes." She took her bag from him. "I don't want to crowd you. Show me where you want me."

He hesitated a moment. "There's a door here. . . ."

Weston swung it open to reveal the adjoining room. She'd passed on it before because the beige linens were uninteresting, but that was no problem. She could whip up some more colorful bedclothes soon enough. The fireplace was bordered in marble, and there was a beautiful vanity and mirror. Rosa halted in front of the mirror, surprised by her own reflection. That rose gown must be magic. No wonder he'd been staring at her all day.

He was still looking, watching her every move, trying to read her thoughts, as if a lot depended on her answer.

"I love it."

"You won't feel lonely?"

"It's big, but if you're next door, I won't be scared."

"Then that's where I'll be."

20

Weston pushed the curtain past the glass. Looked like the boys were already up and about this morning. The longhorns needed to be pushed to the north pasture pond today. August had a way of making water precious.

He took his chair and pulled his boots on. Go without something for long enough and it becomes precious indeed. Like companionship. Jake and Eliza had each other. Could Rosa grow into that kind of friend?

The wood floor in the next room creaked. A drawer closed. She was awake. He fell back into the big leather chair to wait.

Cora had never stayed in that room. They had shared the master suite downstairs. Not that it should matter, but it did.

He spun the gold band on his finger and saw again the glittering drawing room in St. Louis, the vivacious bride-to-be shopping for her trousseau, and then the despondent shell that remained after a year of life here at Palmetto. Would he cause Rosa to do the same?

The ring clinked against the chair arm he clutched. He would take care of Rosa. She may never love him, but he'd do better by her than he had for Cora. God help him, his sanity depended on it.

As beautiful as her magenta gown was, Weston was glad that Señora Garner had chosen to spend today in her *ropas* Mexicanas. He'd given Eliza permission to buy Rosa a wardrobe while in town — and she wouldn't come home until she had a trunk full — but now he was sorry. Nothing wrong with the way Rosa looked this morning.

She followed him to the stables, her skirts flashing bright colors, as she struggled to keep up with him. He should slow down. Her strides weren't nearly as long as his, and he had all the time in the world to show her the place, but it felt like Christmas, watching someone unwrap the gift you gave.

Like an invisible wall, the clean, sweet aroma of straw and feed confronted him as they entered the stable. Sunlight filtered through the slats of the building, throwing stripes over the stall dividers. Rosa recognized Smokey immediately and offered him her hand to nuzzle.

"I think he's your horse," Wes said. "Always one for the ladies, aren't you, Smokey?"

Smokey shook his head vigorously but lipped at her hand, showing his preference.

"The other horses are all in the corral, which means the boys are working somewhere near. The tack room is over here. Riding involves more than just the horse. You've got to have a relationship with your equipment, too. Best horse in the world won't keep you from breaking your neck if your cinch snaps."

He opened a small shuttered window to light the closet and took inventory of the tack. Saddle-covered sawhorses, head to tail, each with its own blanket folded neatly in the seat, lined the walls. Bridles, complete with reins and bits, hung from pegs. Stiff coiled ropes also had their place. There was even a shelf of feed bags and bedrolls — everything the horses could need short of a blacksmith and apple.

Rosa hesitated at the door. "I'd rather not go in." She pressed her chest, holding down the ribbon of the drawstring at her collar.

"The room too small?" he asked.

She reached in to caress the cantle of the seat. He hoped the texture of the seasoned leather would help her relax.

"Everything is so tidy. This is the cleanest stable I've ever been in."

He rocked back on his heels. "Well, that's no accident. To keep it like this you have to scatter clean straw and muck it out if the horses have been inside."

"The straw is in the barn?"

"That *is* where we keep straw, Rosa. And then the saddles have to be rubbed down with oil to keep them supple. We don't have to do that but every other month or so."

"When will they need their next cleaning?" She scanned the shelves, searching for something.

"Why? What are you . . . ? You aren't cleaning them."

"Well, I can at least shovel out the stalls. I know how to do that, but should I do it before supper or after? I don't want you to wait on me, especially tonight if you're eating alone."

She had the situation confused. Out of the tack room he came.

"You aren't cleaning stalls. Not on my watch."

Her eyes darted around the barn. "So what is my job here? The house is Eliza's domain, and Octavia wouldn't even let me cook breakfast this morning."

"That's because she made the mistake of letting Eliza cook a time or two, and she doesn't want that to happen again. Listen, you just came off a bronc-busting kind of a day — the whole month actually. Take time to get your feet under you. Relax." He drew an arc in the straw with the sole of his boot.

"But I want to do my share. You gave us a lot of money, more money than we made in three months. I can never repay you for stepping in when you did, but maybe I can help you recoup your loss."

"Loss? I don't consider getting married a loss."

"I'm not talking about being married. Why would you think that?" Her eyes snapped. "I'm talking about the loan you took out for us. Yesterday I was a charity case, but I don't intend to be one forever."

Weston was poised with pointed finger to straighten her out when he heard his name called.

"Garner! Are you in there?"

In stomped an irate Nicholas Lovelace, his ruddy face already affected by the mid-morning heat, with his sister at his side. Terrific! Weston didn't want to get riled, but Nicholas's appearance was like yelling "Sic 'em" to a dog.

"I knew it!" Nicholas huffed. "Rosa, get

337

in the wagon. I'm taking you home."

"She is home!" Weston growled.

"No, she's not." The last word squeaked out as Weston stepped closer. Nick's eyes widened.

The young man had more spunk than Weston had credited him for. Still, there could only be one bull in a pasture, and Nicholas made him see red.

"Nicholas, I'm going to stay here for a while," Rosa said.

"But you don't have to." Nicholas backed out of the stables into the yard, bumping into Molly in his retreat.

"Yes I do. I don't have a choice."

"You do have a choice. I looked it up," Molly said.

"Rosa, why didn't you come to us if you needed help? I wouldn't have made you marry me," Nicholas added.

Molly slapped Nick's arm. "I told you. He's not forcing her. It's her fault."

Weston rolled his eyes. Weren't they in a pickle? Either he ruthlessly took advantage of a penniless young widow, or Rosa snared an innocent man, shameless hussy that she was. How'd they get in such a mess? Time to clean it up.

"First off, Nicholas, you don't have any money. If your pa said that to me, then we might have a conversation, but you haven't made a red cent in your life. You're an adult, and you've yet to put your hand to a plow, or a ledger, or a saw. How about loaning and giving your own money instead of telling others what to do with theirs?"

Weston took another step forward. "As for you, Miss Lovelace —"

"Weston, please." Rosa took Molly's arm. "She has every right to speak her mind. I've been no kind of friend to her. Will you wait on us, Nicholas?"

Rosa had befriended even Molly? Weston's eyebrows lowered as the women moved toward the stable.

How much time had the Lovelaces spent at Louise's? Weston's absence had lasted over a month. Didn't mean Rosa hadn't had other visitors. Might explain Nick's fire.

"You can wait in your wagon." Weston didn't trust himself to stay civil to the man. He needed to meet the ranch hands coming in from the corral and stop messing with this foolishness, but a new thought ate at him as he stomped away.

Yesterday morning Weston had assured Rosa he didn't expect love in a marriage. Whatever she had to offer was more than he deserved. But what about her? He'd given himself little time to consider that she might expect to be cherished, or worse, that she already was cherished by someone else.

He'd insisted they marry. How long did he expect her to wait for him to get his act together?

Molly had trouble dragging her eyes off the beautiful home dominating the estate. She should be the mistress, and if she played her cards right, she might be yet.

It was the blessing of all blessings that she worked at the courthouse. She knew the judges, and a certain Judge Rice didn't mind giving her some free legal advice. Especially after what he'd seen in his office.

"I know how it looks, Molly, but you have to believe I never intended for him to marry me."

Seeing Rosa dressed in her frumpy peasant clothes softened Molly. She didn't really believe Rosa was conniving enough to have orchestrated this affair, but neither was she willing to give up so easily. Of all the men her parents had paraded before her, Weston was the only one they could agree on, and she still held hopes of gaining his regard.

"If you didn't want to get married, there's a way to fix it."

Rosa's eyes narrowed. "I thought so. Weston said there wasn't."

"Weston wouldn't know." She led Rosa into the stable, out of earshot of Weston, Nick, and the cowboys. She unrolled the paper, flattening it on a barrel top and read, " 'An annulment is a decree that a marriage was invalid from the onset. Invalid marriages include lunacy, consanguinity' — that's not it." She squinted over the page. "Here it is: 'or marriages made under threat, force, or duress.' "

Rosa grimaced. "Weston didn't threaten me."

"But you were under duress. You didn't have a choice."

"But I could've said something to the judge. It's too late now. Isn't there something I could do that wouldn't hurt his reputation?"

"Your actions precipitated this event. It's up to you to correct it."

"What kind of nonsense are you peddling now?" Weston entered with his ranch hands following close behind.

Shielding the papers with her body, Molly hugged Rosa, carefully passing them into her hands. "Go on in the house, sweetie. Send word if I can help you."

Weston let Rosa pass between them. His suspenders stretched with each angry breath. Molly watched the cowboys depart with their gear, one by one, and knew when the last one left, he was going to unload.

She might as well get the jump on him.

As soon as Willie was out of earshot, Molly flounced toward him and took his hand in both of hers. "You can't reward her conniving. This is a sham. I can tell. You don't love her."

"And you consider yourself her friend? Amazing!" He pulled his hand free. "Don't try to influence my wife under the guise of concern. I can smell what you're cooking up."

"I don't blame her for what she did. I'm only ashamed I let her talk me out of doing it myself."

"As far as you're concerned, I'm a happily married man. Before you wrangle Rosa into some sort of divorce, don't fool yourself into thinking I'll be grateful. Your brother is already in the wagon, and I expect you to join him."

"After all the years I spent waiting on you —"

"Then I'll not waste any more of your time."

And he stomped out.

Dismissed? Just like that? How had things gone sour so quickly? Her dream squashed in seconds?

She'd declared herself to a man and he'd walked away. Was there anything more embarrassing?

"Well, paint me pink and call me tickled." Bailey stepped out of the tack room, crunching on an apple. "I'm surprised at you, Molly Lovelace, throwing yourself at Weston like that."

"How dare you eavesdrop!" She could feel her bonnet quiver as she thrust her arms down.

"I'm not the one behaving badly. I'm not professing my love to a newlywed."

He'd heard the whole thing? Still withering from Weston's rebuke, Molly didn't have much fight left in her.

"I'm not staying here to be mocked. Excuse me."

"Not so fast, missy. You did a lot of talking a second ago. Allow me a turn. I don't know why you'd set your cap for Uncle Wes. Seems like you might do well to aim for a younger man, but that's your business. One thing you need to get straight, though. I've been watching Uncle Wes lately, and if he ain't in love with Rosa, then I don't know a jackrabbit from a Jersey. I've seen them dance together, I've seen them fight, and I've seen how he watches her when she doesn't know he's looking. So whatever hopes you have can be buried six feet deep. It's over."

"Thank you for your advice," she sneered. "If you think of anything else you need to tell me, please don't hesitate."

"Actually there is something else — I'll be sleeping in the barn tonight if you're looking for a husband. Worked for Rosa." He winked and walked off.

Where did a cowboy like him get the nerve to talk to her that way? And why hadn't she ever noticed before how much he favored his uncle?

Molly dragged her tail feathers to the wagon. She'd endured enough humiliation. She wasn't ready to try again. Not for days, anyway.

21

Rosa sat in the parlor, unsure what to do with herself and the papers Molly had thrust into her hands. The formal-sounding words confused her, and she wasn't about to ask Weston to explain them. She heard the front door open and barely had time to cram them between the sofa cushions before he entered. He pulled the door closed behind him and turned the key. Her eyes widened.

"Are you locking me in?"

"No, I'm locking everyone out! Awfully nice of Eliza and Jake to leave us so we could have some peace and quiet." She caught him murmuring something about strangling. "You want something to do? Go help Octavia pack up the fellows' dinners. The horses are ready. Let's get out of here before another wave of concerned citizens invades."

Within ten minutes they were mounted,

fried chicken in a tin pail, and a jug of spring water tied behind Weston's saddle. Carefully wrapped in cheesecloth, the sugar-covered apple fritters smelled so good Rosa popped one into her mouth before they reached the pasture.

They rode through the tall dry grass, sending field mice scurrying and jackrabbits bounding until they located the herd. Bailey, Willie, Rico, and Red did their best, but the parched cattle stubbornly refused to leave the shade and the puny remains of a creek they'd found.

Rosa watched Weston direct the cowboys, telling them where to position themselves so the cattle couldn't turn back. No one questioned him out here. His word was law. She sat straight in her saddle, amazed to be friends with such a man.

And until this week he'd been just a friend, although a friend she found overwhelmingly attractive. His dark eyes gauged every movement of the procession before him. The reins barely moved as he guided his horse with his legs. She liked when he was busy and she could study him uninterrupted. He'd caught her a few times but never seemed to mind.

But even if he hadn't had the dark Garner looks, she admired him and had sorely

346

missed his company over the last month. She hadn't realized how much she'd looked forward to his visits until they ceased.

Yes, Weston had been her friend, but she'd ruined it. She'd let herself imagine that his interest in her was more than a family obligation. She stood corrected. He enjoyed her friendship but didn't consider her courting material.

Until yesterday.

A handful of steers ambled their way out of the cedars. The cowboys made progress, and Weston worked his way back to her.

Maybe with time their friendship could've recovered, but now it would never happen. They would never have equal footing. He was at her side not because he wanted to be, but because she'd forced her way into his home, his life, his future. Could she repay him, or should she leave before she owed him more?

She could be the best friend he ever had, but no wife.

Once the cattle were pushed from their shelter and pointed north, the cowhands gratefully refilled their canteens, took a few pieces of chicken and a handful of fritters, and followed after them.

"They eat in the saddle?" Rosa was still getting used to the constant movement beneath her.

"They'd sleep in the saddle if I let them, but we can get down for dinner." Weston urged Pandora toward the creek, and Smokey followed undirected.

Ducking beneath the branches, they found a spot unsoiled by the recent denizens, spread a bedroll, and broke out the remaining victuals. Weston dipped his bandanna into a clear pool and handed it to Rosa before washing his own face and hands. Once he settled on the blanket, she passed him a half a chicken and munched on the savory leg she'd kept for herself. He drank deeply from the canteen, letting a trickle glide down his jaw.

"Amazing what a difference a few drops of water make on a hot day." She reached for the offered drink.

" 'Every one that thirsteth, come ye to the waters, and he that hath no money; come ye, buy, and eat; yea, come, buy wine and milk without money and without price.' "

"That's a fitting description of me." Rosa lowered the canteen and wiped her face with the back of her hand. "No money, but hungry and thirsty. Is that from the Bible?"

"Yeah, but it fits all of us, don't you think? Can any of us be satisfied without God? Can any of us afford all that He's given us?"

He motioned to the trickling stream before them. "Those longhorns don't want to leave this creek because it's their security. It's all they can remember. Never mind that it's drying up and will leave them parched. They don't trust us enough to follow." Weston took a fritter from the bundle on her lap and munched on it before continuing.

"I'm learning that I'm a lot like those dumb steers, pleased to stay in the same place and shrivel up. Thankfully, God didn't let me do that. Reckon that's why He's called the Good Shepherd. He showed up with a cattle prod and drove me into new territory — whether I was ready to move or not."

A line of sweat ran from her neck down between her shoulder blades. Seemed like he wanted to talk. Twice she'd heard about Cora's death, but never from him. Was he ready?

"The cattle are going to the north pasture. Is that the pond?"

Weston's face softened as he studied the weak rivulets of the stream. "Until recently I thought my life ended there, too. Everything I wanted to be — responsible, husband, protector — was crushed." He picked up a smooth stone and troubled it between his fingers. "I tried to blame God, but I couldn't talk to Him about it. I'm still afraid He holds me accountable. That it was my fault."

"How could you be blamed?" Not a rhetorical question. Rosa was linked to this man for a time and wanted to know the truth. Was he responsible in any way?

He swallowed hard. "First off, I married her. Cora was a fine city girl, never been out of town at all. I should've considered how hard it'd be for her to adjust. From the first she didn't take to ranch life. She grew listless, bored, and nothing I did could keep her spirits up, but then the next minute she would be frantic, worried about utter nonsense. Maybe I didn't try hard enough. . . ." He tossed the stone and drew one knee up.

"Got to the point that all I knew to do was to call Doc Trench. He got her some laudanum for her nerves — to let her sleep, you know — but then she had to take it more and more. When I finally put my foot down, she thought her life depended on that little vial." He shook his head. "But to see what the medicine was doing to her — draining her soul away until the spark was squelched . . . She became a very, very sick woman."

"You didn't know what to do."

"And I thought she was stronger. I thought

350

we'd just push through, and it'd all be better on the other side. I misjudged."

A mistake that had taken a life. Could there be any greater remorse? Based on what she'd heard from the rest of the family, Weston alone held himself responsible, but that didn't lessen his pain. Was there anything she could do?

Rosa remembered the night on Mary's porch when she'd decided to pray for him. She'd wanted to comfort him then but had no right. Would he push her away now? Would her offer of friendship be misconstrued?

He'd stayed with her in the church closet. He'd returned the day Tillerton scared her. Surely he would understand her desire to console a hurting friend. She decided to take the gamble.

Rosa slipped her hand under his, and he grasped it without hesitation, clinging to it as if it were his most valued possession. They sat and listened to the birds, swishing horse tails, and the distant lowing of the cattle.

"So that's where I've been corralled: afraid to care, afraid to hurt. I accepted my miserly creek as the best I would ever have, because I knew I didn't deserve any better." He rubbed her golden band with his thumb and gave her a half smile. "Then you shoved me out into the scary unknown."

She opened her mouth to protest, but he shook his head. "I told you, God knows what He's doing. You might have misapplied Aunt Louise's Bible story, but this is where I need to be. If it weren't for the circumstances forcing my hand, I don't know how long it'd be before I got my life back."

"You're an incredible man, Mr. Garner. You've saved my ranch and reputation, yet you carry on like I'm doing you a favor. I don't understand."

He squeezed her hand and released it.

"You don't have to. Just be happy." He stretched out full length on the blanket and pulled his hat over his eyes. "And unless you're in a hurry to skedaddle back to the house, I think I'll catch me a little *siesta*."

One eye peeked out from behind the hat. Looking for her reaction? Was he afraid she'd lie down next to him? Probably so after the barn incident, but she didn't trust herself to get too close. Rosa got to her feet quick enough but didn't know what to do next. Hands on her hips, she took the measure of the majestic cottonwood spreading up and over their heads. She walked around it once and found the two lowest branches were within reach. Satisfied, Rosa came back to the blanket and unlaced her boots. She wiggled out of her stockings and thought she caught Wes watching, but when she looked closer, only saw shadows beneath the hat brim. She must've been mistaken.

She hopped to get both hands wrapped around the lowest branch, then laced her fingers over the rough bark and walked her bare feet up the trunk. Hanging horizontally, she took one more furtive glance toward Weston and, seeing the rhythmic rise and fall of his chest, threw her leg over the branch and rotated until she was sitting atop it. The first perch was always the hardest. Once she stood on the branch, it was almost as easy as going up a ladder.

What was it about climbing that appealed to her? Perhaps the giant tree dared her to conquer it. As long as it towered over her, she was not the victor. And after a string of failures, this ancient cottonwood offered a chance for a small accomplishment. Maybe the combination of the mental and physical tests challenged her. Maybe reaching the apex brought her satisfaction. For whatever reason, there was nothing she'd rather do at that moment.

Fearless now with the knowledge that a leafy layer hid her from view, Rosa scaled the tree, unconcerned with modesty. Soon, her blue skirt was tucked into her waist-band, revealing legs the color of bread crust.

As the limbs grew smaller, Rosa slowed her ascent, making sure to have three grips at all times — two hands and one foot, or two feet and one hand. She hugged the now slender trunk and worked her way around to a break in the foliage.

Her breath caught. Before her spread most of the county. She saw Palmetto's impressive yellow bulk against the dry prairie. The creek was just a scratch until it joined with another branch to make a dark scar across the landscape. She tracked the bare wagon trail through the trees to a doll's house resembling George and Mary's. Could those be people? Why, Mary herself was walking with one of the girls skipping to the barn. Fascinated, she watched the mundane scene as if it were something holy.

How little they looked! No more important than the mice that scurried away from Smokey's hooves. Did God see her that way? No, she believed what Eli had taught her — God cared very much. The verse Weston had quoted said God offered to fill her, to care for her, and to love her. Sometimes He used miracles and sometimes He sent His people to bridge the gap. In her time of need, Weston was God's provision for her.

Thank you for him, Lord Jesus. I pray that you'll straighten out this mistake. He doesn't deserve the trouble I've brought him. Help me make amends.

As she scanned the broad landscape, she felt proud to be a part of this community. The people shared a bond here, a bond formed from hardship and blood, and she would do her best to keep it strong. True, she had no idea what her role would be, but she was pleased that the Garners' precious land hadn't fallen into evil hands because of her. Someday she might be a godmother to Susannah's children. She might sew a wedding dress for a daughter of Eliza. As long as she contributed. *Please let me bring some form of blessing to those who have given me so much,* she prayed, looking up at the unbounded sky.

As much as it delighted Rosa to climb, once she reached the top, she wouldn't linger. Couldn't relax in a treetop. So after committing the scene to memory, she began her descent.

Slowly moving from branch to branch, the arch of her foot found hold on each rounded limb. She lowered herself gently through the years of growth until she was sitting on the giant bottom branch. Looking down, she searched for a good landing spot, not wanting to drop barefoot onto a jagged stone. She spotted a pile of rotting leaves before she swung down, and plopped into them — a perfect shot.

The rustle of the leaves disguised the queer noise. There it was again.

"Don't move," Weston ordered.

She froze, the tone of his command instilling her with fear.

She heard the dry grass under the blanket crackle. Weston moved, but she couldn't? Still crouched with her skirt gathered, she obeyed with everything but her eyes, which frantically tried to locate the sound. Another rattle and some leaves fell away, revealing a coiled snake just inches from her bare ankles. She tried not to flinch but had to steal a glance over her shoulder.

"*Shh,*" he whispered. "You can't outrun him. Be very, very still." Weston slid his gun from its holster and smoothly held it level.

Another rattle brought her attention back around. Could Weston even see it? She was standing between the two, and the snake was half obscured by the leaves. She stared at its malicious eyes and flexed neck. Its sinister head drew back tightly; tongue flickered to taste her air. It seemed to take a breath, and then . . . with an explosion it disappeared.

Where did it go? The leaves thrashed, a whip lashing frantically about in them, but the snake was headless.

Wes sprang to his feet, but before he could reach her, she turned and whistled low.

"You did that? You made it vanish? But I was in the way. Did the bullet go between my feet?"

"It was the only clear shot I had." He holstered his gun and checked his hands. They were steady. "You're sure you're all right?"

"All right? I'm amazed! You stopped it from all the way over there." The close call had her blood pumping. She looked again at the deadly whip he'd rendered harmless. "Tuck and Samuel will want to hear this. They say their Uncle Weston is the toughest piece of jerky around. That's good, no?"

Weston turned red underneath a fine sheen of perspiration. Oops. Maybe she should've lowered her skirts before speaking, for they were still tucked into her waistband. "Excuse me. I forgot . . ." Pretty sure that was a serious offense, married or not. She bounded to the blanket and dropped to arrange them over her feet while she slid on her stockings and boots. "You are finished with your siesta?"

"Might as well be with the ruckus you're raising." He laughed nervously, but he managed to smile. Together they gathered the dinner pail and canteen and strapped the blanket to the back of Pandora's saddle.

"I'm glad you woke up. I'd be in a lot of trouble otherwise. Now I suppose I owe you even more."

"You don't owe me anything."

She waited for him next to Smokey and was about to retort when he put his hands around her waist. Perhaps Weston had forgotten how to lift her, because he sure took his sweet time getting a good grip. Her playful attitude melted in the earnestness of his expression.

"I'm not fooling around, Rosa. You're my wife, and you can't work off your debt. I won't accept it."

No, he wasn't fooling around. With the smell of gun smoke still swirling about him, she knew he'd brook no backtalk. Maybe they could discuss it when they weren't alone with his hands snugly around her perpetually corsetless waist. She decided to bide her time until he saw reason.

"I can read your thoughts as easily as if they were branded in your hide." He lifted her onto Smokey's back and handed her the reins. "Be patient, Rosa. We're in it for the long haul. No sense in doing something we'll regret." With a slap on the rump he sent Smokey toward home.

22

Eliza and Jake returned before another night had passed. Good thing. Weston needed to get out to work. Having both Jake and him absent would put them behind. Besides, staying around the house wore him slick. Especially when he hadn't decided what to do with his bride.

Hosting company had always fallen on the ladies of the family. Obviously, Rosa wasn't a guest, but he couldn't leave her stewing in the parlor while he rode his rounds. On the other hand, he didn't want to risk more time alone with her in the fields. Somehow things got messy no matter where they were.

He couldn't woo her. He couldn't offer himself as a legitimate husband yet. Not with the crazy reactions her presence caused. Half the time he wanted to run and half the time he wanted to hold her, but never did he consider releasing her. Someday he'd be ready, and he wanted Rosa there when he did. Selfish.

You add one woman to the table, and the dining room explodes in noise. Eliza and Rosa chattered over each other like magpies. One of Rosa's stories rolled out so fast, she was half done before they realized she'd switched to Spanish somewhere along the way. Would it ever be quiet again? Was that what he wanted?

"Wes, you haven't said two words tonight. You're mulling something over. What's stuck in your craw?"

Jake caught him staring at her. Now everyone had. Rosa went scarlet.

Jake's napkin flew to his mouth to prevent his food from erupting. "Did you see that, Eliza? I bet I know what he's thinking about."

Eliza's eyebrows shot up as she perused both of them. "They certainly are behaving ridiculously, avoiding each other all evening. Not acting like newlyweds should."

Rosa was the first to break. "I don't . . . we're not . . ."

"You don't need to say anything. It doesn't concern them," Weston said.

"I'm concerned." Jake chortled as his brother-in-law glared. "I am. If y'all are already having spats, we might consider moving out. I don't want to raise our child in a hostile environment."

"Jake, stop. You're making me laugh." Eliza fanned her face. "I'm going to have heartburn tonight for sure."

"Well, that's just dandy. Now none of us will be having any fun this evening." He threw his napkin down in mock exasperation. "You're not being a good influence on my wife, and I don't appreciate it."

A hearty guffaw escaped from Rosa, obviously startling her. She clamped her mouth shut before more could escape, but her shoulders shook from the effort.

She amazed him. Her black eyes sparked. Her laugh rang as high as her spirits. How had she endured three months of quiet evenings with only Aunt Louise for company? And before that, she'd survived a long dry trip over hundreds of miles? Seeing her now made it easy to imagine her as the toast of her town — Ciauhtlaz, was it? Despite her quiet demeanor, she certainly wasn't a wallflower.

The evening sun wrapped the room in golden hues as Eliza told about her shopping trip. Jake threw in his own salty descriptions for flavoring when the story ran dull for his taste.

Weston never imagined his family dinners would look like this — his pregnant sister, rowdy brother-in-law, and his Mexican wife gathered around the table — but now he wouldn't have it any other way.

"That trunk is full of clothes for me? I can't afford them." Rosa's face creased.

"Afford them?" Eliza laid her napkin aside. "Wes will get you all the gowns you need. Just don't expect him to do the shopping."

"She's being ornery, Rosa. I'll take you to town next week to get them fitted," Weston offered.

"Oh no. I can alter them myself. Save a little money, no?"

"If you like." Tossing his napkin on the table, he addressed his sister, "Now, you're probably roaring to go. Finally we have a participant for our poetry readings who might appreciate all your schooling. What highfalutin' cultural goods are you going to expire us to tonight?"

"It's *expose*, not *expire*, and I think you'll like it," she said as she got up. "I bought a book yesterday by the poet John Donne. His religious poetry is well-known for . . ." Her voice trailed off as she made her way to the parlor. Since returning from the Ladies' Academy, Eliza had searched in vain for an occasion to make use of her genteel education. Whenever possible she wrangled the men of her hearth into evening readings, for lack of a more suitable audience. Hopefully, Rosa's presence would take the pressure off of Jake and Weston.

As the ladies strolled out of the room, Jake pulled Wes aside. "Did you miss us?"

"Actually, I did."

Jake's face fell. "That ain't right. I'm disappointed in you."

"Rosa can't rope as well as you do. Nice to have you back."

The parlor settee was June-bug green, its upholstery filleted into diamonds by silken strands of lemon cutting through the cloth.

With her index finger, Rosa traced the golden path, turning at an intersection every time she heard an interesting phrase, until Eliza reached the conclusion. Her head swam with the rich sounds and vivid imagery of the poetry. Always a lover of the dramatic, Rosa could feel the meter pounding each strong word into her heart.

"I love all the words that describe doing things. What are those called?" she asked her sister-in-law.

"Verbs?"

"Yes, the verbs in that poem are so powerful: batter, break, ravish, enthrall . . ."

"What's that?" Weston entered, took the

book from Eliza's hand, and inspected the cover. "That doesn't sound like poetry that should be in my house."

"Nonsense, Weston. It's religious poetry from over two hundred years ago." Eliza snatched it from him and smoothed the page. "See, in the first stanza the poet is distraught because there's something standing between God and him, and he can't remove it alone. He wants his relationship with God to be more intimate, but he doesn't know how to move forward.

"Batter my heart, three person'd God; for you
As yet but knock; breathe, shine, and seek to mend;
That I may rise, and stand, o'erthrow me, and bend
Your force, to break, blow, burn and make me new."

Rosa leaned forward. "There must've been something in her life holding her back — a fear she couldn't overcome. She wants to completely belong to God but needs Him to pursue her."

"She?" Weston looked at Rosa suspiciously and seated himself in the armchair by the unlit fireplace. "I thought the writer's name was John."

Eliza came to her aid. "It's a personal poem meant to be embraced by the reader. If the reader is female, she puts herself in the place of the author."

Jake rolled his eyes. "Yeah, Wes. Didn't they teach you that on the Chisholm Trail?"

"Must have missed that lesson."

"Read the last again," Rosa said.

"Take me to you, imprison me, for I,
Except you enthrall me, never shall be
    free,
Nor ever chaste, except you ravish me."

"That's enough," Weston said firmly.

Rosa blinked. Did he really disapprove?

"Sorry," Eliza said. "I forgot to factor in your provincial scruples."

"Sit back and enjoy, Rosa," Jake said with a laugh. "Wes and Eliza are capable of some Texas-sized showdowns. This looks promising."

But she didn't want them to fight. They'd had so much fun during supper. The evening mustn't be ruined now.

Without thinking, she left the settee and found herself on the footstool at Wes's knees. He sat up a little straighter.

"Don't you ever feel that way? Sometimes

it seems every choice I make is a mistake. If only God would just stop the struggle, surround me, and make me do His will, how easy it would be!"

He moderated his tone for her but continued to glare at his sister. "I don't disagree; however, the language in that poem is not appropriate — definitely not appropriate for a parlor, most likely inappropriate anywhere."

Eliza's voice burst through their bubble. "Appropriate? How many times will you use that word in one breath? You forget, dear brother, while I appreciate Victorian sensibilities, especially here on the frontier, God is not Victorian. Prudishness can go too far."

"That poem can go too far. It guides the imagination where it shouldn't go. I'm no prude, but to use explicit imagery to describe a spiritual relationship is unbiblical."

"You need to read your Bible," said Eliza.

"Yes, you do," Rosa agreed. Why were they so riled up? She would end this puzzling hostility. "Eli used to read the Bible to us every night. There's so much I don't understand. Would you read it to us?"

"He'd be glad to." Jake dug for a piece of food in his teeth with his pocketknife. "Wes used to lead devotions at church. You just find a good passage and —"

"Maybe something from Song of Solomon," Eliza suggested. Even Rosa couldn't miss the look her brother shot her.

"Solomon? Isn't that King David's son?" Rosa didn't want to see the fight Jake predicted.

"Yep," Jake answered. "Sure was. He has a nice little book right there in the Old Testament — great reading for married couples."

"Jake, you got any chores to do?" Weston growled.

"Nope. Wild horses couldn't drag me away from this rodeo."

Eliza wasn't done either. "Think about it, Wes. You believe that Scripture is divinely inspired. Why would God include the book if it was something to be ashamed of?"

What were they talking about? Rosa looked to the man who'd never yet failed to help her when she asked. "What is Solomon's Song?"

He put both hands on his face and wiped down hard, almost pulling the day's growth of whiskers out of his skin. He studied the ceiling for a moment before answering. "Truthfully, I don't know that I've ever read it all the way through."

"Why not?" Rosa twisted the unfamiliar gold ring around her finger.

"Well, usually when I study Scripture, I

look for a passage that teaches me how to live. I want to read something that tells me what to do."

"Can't you do what's in that book?"

His startled expression surprised her. He seemed unable to find his voice, so Rosa continued, "Surely God wouldn't put it in the Bible if you weren't supposed to do it, would He?"

Weston scooted his legs far away from the footstool. "You're the expert there, Rosa. Ruth and Boaz, was it?"

"Oh! I . . ." She fumbled for words as her grasp on her ring slipped. The gold band slid from her fingers and plunked on the floor. Her faced burned. She dropped off the footstool onto her knees and frantically skimmed over the rug, fingers splayed in the weak lamplight.

"What in the world?" Weston lifted his feet high as she swept under his chair and retrieved the missing ring.

Chastened, Rosa returned to her spot on the footstool.

Jake's coughing barely disguised his laughter. "Eliza, it's past sundown. Ain't it about time for us to hit the hay?"

"You lead, I'll follow." Eliza dropped her book on the settee, gave Rosa a peck on the cheek, and lumbered out. Jake slowed to slide the double doors of the parlor closed behind his growing wife.

And they were gone.

They'd departed so abruptly that they were down the hall before their voices finished echoing across the parlor. The room was quiet, the doors were closed, and suddenly her position at Weston's knees seemed very intimate. Neither of them spoke. Rosa watched the lamplight. Wes watched her.

"I'm . . . um . . . sorry." He squirmed and once again tried to fit his feet between the stool and his chair. "That was wrong of me. Please don't take offense."

She dared a sideways glance.

"You were right. I shouldn't take sides between you and Eliza. I should know better —"

"I'm trying to apologize."

"But you didn't answer my question about Solomon's Song."

He looked away. "I don't think you're ready for that."

Condescending? Was that the English word? "What do you mean? I've been a Christian for several years —"

"You've been my wife for only a day."

She shrugged her shoulders. "So?"

He scowled, stood, and put some distance between them. "It's been a long day. If you'd like a Bible to read, there's one in the great room. You could take it upstairs, or stay here, or . . . well, do whatever you want, but I'm beat." He backed toward the escape — running from her, and she wasn't even chasing him. "Think I'd better turn in for the night. Will you be all right?"

She nodded, to his apparent relief.

Rosa didn't feel like reading after he left, but she didn't mind exploring some on her own. After he was safely upstairs Rosa located the heavy Bible and flipped through it to see if there were any pictures that would explain the mystery. Naturally, there were not.

23

Weston had known obedience would cost him. Brave words about God giving him freedom and peace flowed effortlessly under the open sky with distant horizons, but put him in a parlor like last week, and he got spooked. He didn't want to get caught indoors any more than necessary. Moving a table and his whetstone to the porch was a minor inconvenience compared to being cornered in a room alone with her. He just couldn't trust himself.

The knife glided over the whetstone with a rhythmic whisking sound. He stopped to test the blade lightly against his thumb and then resumed the motion.

They were married. He still wasn't used to the idea. In his wrestling with God, Rosa had figured into a few conversations already. If God wanted him to remarry he could, in his stronger moments, imagine Rosa as his wife. Not that he'd received divine instruction, but he had a hard time imagining a future that didn't involve his little shepherd-ess.

So why was he so skittish?

Out here, with everything in the hypothetical, he could admit that he cared for her. He could savor memories of their time together and acknowledge their mutual attraction. But when they were roped together, when he could see his own uncertainty reflected in her eyes, he couldn't move forward. Hadn't she been hurt already? Who was he to promise this time would be different? He splashed cool water on the stone. All this agonizing would come to nothing, more likely than not. She was bound and determined to keep her distance, and that might be best for both of them.

The door opened behind him, and Rosa stepped out, bonnet in one hand and a wad of papers in the other. She smiled shyly at him but kept the rocking chair positioned between them.

Before he could stop himself, he'd taken a full appraisal of her appearance, pleased to see her in her Mexican clothing. "You aren't wearing your new clothes?"

"I could change if you think these aren't good. They make me stand out like a jalapeño in cheese."

"Please don't. We have a sight more cheese around here than we need. I'm glad you're here to spice it up."

Her eyes widened and she quickly looked away.

For crying aloud. He could've bit his tongue off for the smart remark. When would he learn?

Rosa waved her bonnet toward the barn. "I thought I'd visit Louise today. See how she's doing. Can I take Smokey?"

He got to his feet. "You don't need my permission, but I like to know when you leave and when you plan to return. Always good to have someone watching for you."

"I don't plan to be gone much past dinner. It feels like rain."

He'd noticed, too. Every ounce of moisture in August was pure gold. "Sounds good, but you'd set my mind at ease if you carried a pistol, as well. You never know when you're going to run into a snake — and they come in several varieties."

Turns out the pistol was much easier to handle than Louise's rifle. Weston insisted on a few practice rounds before she set off, and she complied. After each shot Rosa frowned to see her accuracy wasn't near what she'd achieved on the rifle, but pistols were for close shots. He must have expected an awfully large critter to harass her, because he turned her loose as soon as she could point and fire in the general direction of the target. She worried that she couldn't hit a snake yet, but he assured her that the snake that gave him the most concern would be an easy target.

He watched her ride off, leaving her with more than a tinge of guilt. For her sake, he acted pleased with the arrangement, but even Mack had tried to hide his feelings from her. Weston would regret it soon enough, unless she could free him before things got complicated — if he'd let her. Stubborn as a mule. What was the matter with this family?

The saddle didn't have a convenient place to stow the pistol. After a few near drops, Rosa took it off her lap and tucked it into her waistband.

At least they agreed on the problem of Jay Tillerton. Neither of them trusted the man, but they both figured she was safe as long as she was under Weston's protection. Surely the man was too cowardly to harass a prominent rancher's wife. Still, a pistol could come in handy in a variety of situations.

She patted Smokey's neck as he trotted

toward the ranch. A horse would come in handy, too, when Louise and she were back on their own. Would Weston let her buy Smokey? How much would the horse cost? And the pistol? Her stomach did a funny twist as she remembered Weston telling her of a garter belt with a holster she could wear. He said he'd get one for her in Lockhart, and then took his time studying her, as if he could determine what size she wore under her skirt. There was no way she was going to let that man shop for her. He'd done enough already.

Pistols, holsters, horses — everything cost money. She'd hoped to start work on their winter garden before it rained, but her shopping list had already put her another year behind.

Still mulling over the thought of Weston in Mrs. Leeth's Emporium choosing a lace-covered holster, she almost didn't see the lady crouching along the creek bank. With her basket at her side, she broke the dry ground with a spade and pulled up some wild onions.

"I never thought of looking for onions here," Rosa said.

The lady startled but didn't get up. It was Mrs. Tillerton. Rosa should've recognized her immediately, since she was wearing the same faded gown as before.

"I didn't mean to scare you."

"I beg your pardon." The long slatted bonnet kept her face in the shadows. "I shouldn't trespass. I forget someone lives here now."

"It's not trespassing. The creek is common ground. You're welcome anytime."

Mrs. Tillerton stood and brushed the dirt from her knees. "I have all I need. Thank you." She picked up her basket and followed a rabbit trail through the trees toward her home.

As generous as she wished to be, Rosa couldn't help but feel slighted. Maybe Mrs. Tillerton disapproved of her like the women at church did. Maybe she didn't appreciate having a foreigner living across the fence. Rosa urged Smokey toward the house. They had almost reached the yard when enlightenment arrived. Mrs. Tillerton wanted her farm, of course. That had to be it. The Tillertons had planned to own their place after the fifteenth. A smile crept across Rosa's lips. At least one good deed came of her midnight trek to the barn.

After leading Smokey to the trough, Rosa went inside the house and found it empty. She removed her bonnet and hung it on her designated peg, then opened the kitchen

pantry. It was well stocked: bags of corn-
meal, rice, beans, and sugar lined the
shelves. A barrel of potatoes sat near the
wall, and strings of peppers, onions, and
green beans hung from the rafter. Without
her, the little pantry would be bare. Without
her last minute effort, Louise would be
sharing a bed with Susannah and Ida instead of being mistress of her own ranch.

Had it been worth it? Somehow she'd gotten tangled up with a man that she'd had
no business bothering, but she had saved
their farm.

Rosa pulled the string of peppers to her
nose. The sharp flavor yanked tears from
her eyes. Louise had done her best to come
up with a plan — something was lost in
translation, perhaps — and Rosa willingly
took the task despite Louise's misgivings.
She should've known better, but what else
could they have done?

Of course, their mistakes and misunderstandings hadn't cost Louise anything.
She'd made out like a *bandito.* But the trip
to the courthouse had only temporarily
solved their dilemma. Now that they had
time to think it through, surely a better solution could be found. Pulling a pepper off
and biting the spicy thing, Rosa vowed to
work until she was no longer obligated to

Weston, or anyone else for that matter.

"Rosa? Is that you?" Louise pushed the door open, dropped the slop bucket, and rushed in. "Dear, dear Rosa. Where have you been? I've been watching for you to walk up the path, and here you come, riding by yourself. I've been so lonely. I'm glad you came."

Rosa accepted the hug.

Going to the pump handle, Louise took down tin cups for both of them. "How's Eliza? She has, what, a few weeks to go?"

"Yes ma'am, best she can figure. Jake and Weston have their hands full keeping her from doing too much."

Louise eyed her sharply. "I don't doubt it. Speaking of Weston, how's he doing?"

Rosa didn't answer. She took a seat and picked at her fingernails. How was Weston? He was married, though he'd sworn to never be again. How did Louise think he was doing?

She heard the tin cups drop to the counter.

"I hoped you would've found some consolation by now." Louise sounded tired — and aged. She looked out the window for a long spell and then filled the cups with water. "I thought you two would suit. According to Mary, he'd half fallen for you already."

379

"He must've caught himself."

Louise took a long drink and tossed the contents of her cup into the potted philodendron. "If there was something I could do —"

"Maybe there is."

It only took Rosa a moment to run outside and retrieve the papers from her saddlebag. She dropped them on the table and went to lean against the windowsill.

She heard Louise pick them up and her soft murmuring as she read them to herself. After living at Palmetto, the little white house did seem silent. Almost desolate. Rosa drummed her fingers against the glass pane. She had grown accustomed to Eliza and Octavia's company, plus the comings and goings of Weston, Jake, and the hands. Moving back here didn't have the allure she'd expected. Maybe Rosa could relearn to appreciate the peacefulness of this place.

"So it's not a divorce. It's an annulment, like there never was a marriage?"

"That's what Molly said."

Louise read a little further and flipped the pages, looking for more.

"You haven't consummated the marriage?"

The inevitable question but still awkward. "Of course not." *I made that mistake with your son.* "Molly thought I might have a case if I claimed I didn't have a choice, but is that true? He didn't kidnap me. I've lived under his roof when I had the freedom to leave."

"What does Weston say about this?"

"He wants to let the marriage stand, but if you could see how uncomfortable I've made him, you'd realize he's just being a gentleman. He can't relax in his own house. I'll stay there and work if that will pay off our debt sooner, but everyone would be happier if I could find something profitable to do here. What do you think?"

Louise bounced the papers' edges against the table until they were tidy. "I don't know how we can go against Weston's wishes when he's the only reason we still have a roof over our heads. Between him and Mary . . . well, they were adamant that you wed. Maybe you should go back home and think it over."

"I . . . I am home. I came to turn the garden." The words rushed from her mouth, "We need two harvests a year if we're going to make the tax payment and pay Weston back. We can hardly expect him to give us a flock of sheep every year. I thought we could expand the plot."

Louise tucked a strand of red hair behind

her ear and smoothed her apron over her navy skirt.

Rosa blinked, not trusting her eyes. Navy skirt? Why wasn't she wearing mourning? "Where did these clothes come from?"

"They are Adele Lovelace's castoffs. She knew I needed them."

"Why? What's wrong with your black skirts?" Rosa's voice grew sharp. Something was changing, and she didn't like it at all.

"You know I've been stepping out with Mr. Bradford. How can he court me if I'm in mourning?"

"Courting? I thought you were friends," Rosa said.

"I've always thought friends make the best spouses, don't you? True, things have moved rather quickly, but we've known each other for years, and at our age we don't have time to waste. Besides, he's got the money together to rebuild his store. That's what he's been waiting for. And without you to worry over . . ."

A phobia. Now Rosa knew the word for why it was hard to breathe. She wanted to smash the glass and hang her head out the window to gulp large amounts of fresh air. She paced, kept moving to keep the walls from closing in around her.

"You didn't need this ranch after all. Then

why did you let me humiliate myself to save it? Were you keeping it just in case Mr. Bradford didn't propose, or were you just trying to get rid of me?" Rosa covered her eyes. "Everything I've done has been to help you. To keep us together. And now you have other plans? Now you're telling me it was for nothing?"

Louise dropped into a chair. "Don't be mad. It's family land and should stay with family. You did a good deed, and it could still work out. Weston needs a wife, and you can't live here alone. Could it be that you belong with him? Wouldn't it be wonderful if you two fell in love? It worked for you and Mack."

Rosa's mouth dropped open. How could Louise be so deluded? Blind, optimistic Louise thought that Eli's demands had left everyone satisfied.

"Mack? You . . ." Rosa swallowed.

Louise's mouth turned down, puzzled by Rosa's tone. "Yes. What about Mack?"

This woman had made Rosa her daughter. She'd taught her about family, taught her about Christ, and taught her how to be a lady. Rosa couldn't bring herself to cast any shadow on the cherished memory of her son.

"Weston can't take Mack's place."

Because Rosa wouldn't let him.

It was amazing how much easier swinging the hoe was now compared to her first planting. Rosa's arms evidenced new strength, and her aggravation made the task that much more satisfying.

The unforgiving sun prickled her skin where it was exposed, but a breeze was kicking up, the first in a month. Bent over her hoe she didn't see how close the clouds had crept until the shadows swept across the rows.

"Rosa? If they expect you back, you better get started or you'll get caught in rain. I'll wrap up some dinner for you."

It wasn't even time for their midday meal, and Louise was going to call it a day? But what did Louise care? The success of the ranch had always depended on Rosa.

"It'll pass." Rosa swung her hoe again.

"No. It's moving in rather slowly. It could be around all day. You need to go before the creek rises." Louise's tone was apologetic, but she didn't leave. It looked like she intended to wait until her stubborn daughter-in-law did as she said.

With one last thunk, Rosa pulled the hoe free, took it to the barn, and then strode toward the house, her boots covering the yard in long strides. Why was Louise interfering? Couldn't she see what needed to be done? Now even Louise, who'd always relied on her, was telling her what to do.

Rosa's frustration was at a peak as she entered the tidy kitchen. It didn't help that Louise tried to calm her anger down.

"Don't get upset. You should be relieved that you don't have this responsibility on your shoulders any longer."

"I'm supposed to take care of you. I left my home and family so I could help you. Now you don't need me."

"Oh, honey, I do need you. You know what we've been through. You are my daughter, the only child I have left." Louise pulled her to her side. "If I marry Mr. Bradford, I won't need a ranch hand or a gardener, but I still need a family."

Rosa didn't budge.

Louise tightened her lips and shook her head. "They'll be out looking for you when the rain starts. I bet Eliza is already worried sick." She stepped back while Rosa washed the soil from her hands and watched the dirt swirl away down the drain.

"No matter where I go, you're welcome. That old house of Deacon's will have plenty of room for you, but you have to plan for your future. Don't reject what you've got without thinking it through. You'll break a lot of hearts, and not just your own."

24

The rain was gentle, leaving Rosa soaked but not battered. Using the crate in Smokey's stall to stand on, she pulled the heavy saddle off, letting it fall to the floor.

"Sorry about that," she said to the startled horse. "I'm not as strong as the *vaqueros*." She slipped her hand into the back of the broad brush and began rubbing down her mount, calming him before wiping down the wet leather.

Pandora's stall stood empty, her saddle and bridle gone from the tack room. Was Weston out looking for her? Several times during her ride she felt someone watching her but chalked it up to Tillerton. When she was done with Smokey, not wanting to answer questions about her visit with Louise, she hurried around to the kitchen door, sliding in the slimy mud at the edge of the doorstep.

"Stop right there, Miss Rosa. Don't you

go tracking through my kitchen in those boots." Octavia continued scrubbing on the dinner pans.

Rosa pulled the damp pistol from her waistband and handed it to a disapproving Octavia, then stooped to unlace her boots and leave them on the porch. "I'm afraid I'm going to drip, just the same."

"Don't worry about that. I can throw a towel down. Go on to your room, and I'll bring some warm water for your basin. Don't want you catching cold."

Would the water be any warmer than the rain? But even as Rosa climbed the stairs she had to admit she was chilled. Safe in her room, she discarded the sopping clothes and hung them over her quilt rack once the quilt was snuggly wrapped around her.

She took the rocker by the window and watched the drops splatter lazily on the glass. It was a refreshing rain. The cattle and sheep would find green pasture now. Still water would abound in every hollow. What was the rest of that Bible poem? It was one of Louise's favorites. The next part said that God restored souls. Would He do that for her?

Through all the heartbreak — her family's rejection, her husband's death, financial ruin — Louise had remained at her side.

When she had felt like unraveling, Rosa had knotted the frayed strings of her heart together with the knowledge that Louise couldn't make it on her own.

In Mexico Louise was helpless. Rosa had taught her how to prepare the corn kernels for *masa,* then make the masa into tortillas. She had introduced her to the fruits and vegetables that would feed her men. Louise had needed her, and when the men were gone, she'd needed her more than ever. She had relied on Rosa, but now Louise was leaving — leaving Rosa with no purpose in this new land.

The move to Texas had sapped Rosa's reserves, and when she couldn't carry Louise's burdens alone any longer, Weston had appeared. Not just with money. Even before that. The sheep shearing, the shooting lesson, replacing the shingles. All his help she'd accepted with the understanding that she and Louise would someday reciprocate, but Louise had defaulted. She'd left Rosa to make up the difference alone.

Rosa couldn't tell from her reflection which drops of moisture were tears on her cheeks and which were raindrops on the windowpane. She pulled the quilt tighter. She'd been through the valley of the shadow of death, and God had been with her then.

His rod and His staff had comforted her. But now she was seated at a table with a cup overflowing with blessings, and she was miserable. She didn't belong.

She heard footsteps in the hallway and movement in the room next door. Resting her forehead against the window, she listened as drawers slid open, a chair creaked, and boots dropped to the floor. Her sigh turned into another sob.

She couldn't let Weston throw his future away because of her. Yes, there was an attraction between them, or there had been in the beginning, until he'd made it clear that he had no interest in pursuing it. He'd done the chivalrous deed at the courthouse, but she knew it wouldn't work. He would meet someone else. He would resent her someday.

She remembered his easy laugh when they rode together, his teasing about the ewe — all of that before she'd asked too much. Now he cut her a wide swath, obviously not trusting her, and she didn't blame him. She couldn't claim innocence when her actions had stolen his freedom.

Voices sounded in the hall, followed by a knock on their adjoining door.

"Come in."

She'd never mistake his stride, not even in stocking feet. His wet clothes clung to him, but he brought her the first basin of warm water and placed it on the vanity. She could tell when he noticed her tears, for he halted suddenly.

"Is everything all right? Anything I can do?"

Rosa's chin puckered and she shook her head. "No, you can't fix it. This is my problem." Her shoulders heaved as she fell back into her rocker. She had to figure it out alone. She watched as the windmill spun in spurts, its blades blurring when the rain gusted. She couldn't let her emotions spin her out of control as easily.

Weston pulled a chair next to her, intentionally turned it toward the window and sat as she rocked. He wasn't leaving. If he planned to stay until she stopped crying, she'd better hit a drought.

When the rocking chair halted, he offered her a bandanna, but Rosa had no free hand to receive it without dropping the blanket. He wiped her face himself with the worn cotton rag.

"Blow," he said, then, "good girl" when her nose cleared. She gave him a watery smile, and although nothing had changed, she did feel better.

"I don't know what I'm going to do with you," Weston said at length. "My daddy

391

taught me to help where there's a hurt, and obviously there's a hurt here somewhere. How can I make you happy?"

A powerful blast sent the windmill to whirling again. She willed her emotions down and took a deep breath, pushing all the unsaid regrets out voicelessly. "I have to find my own way. You can't help me, but I will be happy. I am, I mean, already. Of course, I'm grateful." She paused. Her words weren't convincing. The least said, the better.

She sniffed. When he pulled his bandanna out again, she shook her head. "Please don't. That's embarrassing. . . ."

"Nothing to be embarrassed over. Just yesterday Jake had this giant booger —"

Rosa's eyes bugged wide, and she accidentally snorted.

"That's more like it."

Of everything he'd done, moments like this meant the most to her. He didn't run when she was angry, or heartbroken. Hadn't he stayed at her side through the roughest times? This is what she couldn't jeopardize. She needed his strength and his friendship. She'd learn to live without love.

"You remember when we were by the creek?" Weston's low voice held steady under the howling wind. "You listened as I talked about Cora, and then you did something that surprised me. You held my hand."

She blinked, surprised by his words. "I'd wanted to do that all summer — ever since we sat on Mary's porch and you worried that my opinion of you was too high. I wanted to help you, but I had no right."

"You do now."

Rosa nodded. They were friends and had been before that piece of paper at the courthouse caused any confusion. If the ceremony allowed her to comfort him, so be it.

Weston stood, his clothes soaked through, down to his stocking feet. He went to the window, the gray light sharply framing his muscular silhouette. "Remember that Sunday when we were stuck in the closet? I barely knew you then. You heard some hurtful things, and all I could do was stand by and watch you take it."

"You laid your hand on my head."

"It wasn't enough. I wanted to keep the pain away, to shield you from the sting of their words. I wanted to hold you . . . but I had no right."

Rosa trembled beneath her quilt, and tears pooled in her eyes. She looked at him from behind with his soggy socks and curly damp hair, and knew this was her invitation.

"You do now," she whispered and left the rocker.

Weston turned and opened his arms to her. She fell against his chest, her forehead and cheek pressed against his warm, wet shirt. He held on, even as sobs racked her exhausted body. Could he forgive her for her mistake? If he trusted her enough to let her this close, he must know she hadn't tried to hurt him.

They must protect this bond, this delicate balance. Tenderness, understanding, and safety. She couldn't ask for more.

Grasping her quilt in one hand, she tried to wipe her tears off his shirt.

"Don't worry about that. It's drenched through." He squeezed her tight. "Just checking up on a little filly of mine that left the ranch today."

So he had followed her? She thought she'd sensed someone near. Rosa wormed her way closer, not ready to leave.

"I remember after Independence Day." She wouldn't dwell on her fear when he banged on the door of the empty house — when she thought he was Tillerton. She just wanted him to know she understood the boundaries he'd set. "I wanted you to touch me." Rosa pulled back to watch his face. She braved a small grin, having learned the magic phrase. "But you had no right."

His breath caught and his eyes filled with awe. He slid his hand along her jaw and turned her face up toward his. "I do now."

Rosa's eyes widened as he lowered his lips over hers. She wanted to protest, convinced he'd ruin everything, but instead he calmed her. He was so cautious. So gentle. Her stomach fluttered, but she didn't feel threatened.

A kiss — and they'd both survived. No boundaries were broken.

But the next kiss shattered them all. He took her like she was his. Like he had every right, and in terror she realized he did. She tried to turn away, shaken by his desperation, but Weston held her firm, giving her no escape until she was as insatiable as he. Alert? The word didn't even approach what she felt. She dissolved into him. Her bones melted into lava that burned up all her hopes for a companionable relationship.

With a groan, Weston lifted his head and pressed her against his chest until the room stopped spinning. "You hear my heart? You did that." His voice was raw. "How did you get in? I didn't think I would ever . . ." He buried his face in her hair, while his other hand roamed up and down her back, re-

minding her that she was once again corsetless.

"Thank you," he whispered. "Thank you
for giving me permission."

"What?" Her head spun. She wouldn't be
surprised if neither of them made any sense
right now. It was all she could do to stand
upright, and that with his help.

"You told me to kiss you." His chest
heaved against her face. "That took a lot of
courage. Courage I didn't have."

Rosa hated to be the one to pull away, but
with all the misunderstandings between
them, she couldn't let him get away with a
purposeful one. She touched her lips,
surprised they were still there. "I didn't tell
you to kiss me."

"Oh yes, you did. You said you wanted me
to touch you when we were riding after
Independence Day. . . ."

"Not when we were riding. I meant at the
house. You came in, swinging your gun."
She swallowed before she could go any
further. Forming a coherent thought was
painful. Communication impossible. "I
nearly attacked you, remember? And then
collapsed. You didn't even hug me. You let
me lie huddled on the staircase while you
found a rifle."

His flushed face went white. His eyes

flickered over the quilt draped tightly around her and then to the pile of her wet clothes in the corner. Did he believe her?

"At the house? A hug? Not when we were riding?" He looked like he might be sick.

She nodded.

Weston's hands balled up into fists and his arms tensed. His lips disappeared, and he stood as still as a statue.

"Arrrgggghhh!" he bellowed, then stomped back to his room, slamming the door behind him.

At the house, of course. She'd been scared. She'd wanted comforting. Wasn't that what they were talking about? Fear and sorrow? Not desire.

Weston peeled off his clothing and grabbed his towel. He was a fool, and once again, he had run. What stopped him in the first place? Rosa hadn't rebuffed him. Best he could tell, she'd liked it.

Fire raced through his veins again. Only a wooden door stood between them. Was it too late to go back? Had she recovered her senses enough to remember why they weren't sleeping in the same bed? He sure hadn't.

He'd promised her no pressure. He'd told himself he wouldn't get closer without her permission. But what now? The herd had stampeded and there was no corralling them.

His skin was wet, but it wasn't chilled. He scrubbed before wrestling himself into some dry duds. The rain pelted the window and didn't look like it was going to let up. Terrific. He was imprisoned inside — with energy to burn.

He paced his room, with the door to the hallway open, and waited for her to emerge. No way could he plan his words. Coursing emotions washed rational debate away, but they needed to renegotiate. The deal they'd formed back when he'd proposed was hopelessly outdated. Heaven and earth had moved since then, praise God.

But Weston was still terrified. Fear that he might not be ready had kept him paralyzed before. How could he be certain what he wanted? Now, he knew.

Rosa.

And now he realized that knowing what he wanted was even more frightening if he couldn't have it.

He popped a peppermint into his mouth. Rosa wasn't persuaded he could love her. No wonder. He'd flat out told her he didn't want to remarry. Ever.

And she had to notice how he fled every

time she got near. He was right. He couldn't get close and be safe, but maybe safety didn't have the appeal it once did.

Rosa's door opened. She stepped toward the staircase without ever looking to her right.

Weston cleared his throat, causing her to jump. "Do you remember when we were riding? I held your hand."

Her back was as straight as a branding iron. She clutched the banister in a death grip. Without turning a degree, she answered, "Yes. I know the exact moment you're talking about."

"Do you see why . . . ?"

Her chignon bobbed as she nodded and began her descent. "You made an honest mistake. No need to apologize. You've kept your end of our bargain nobly."

He choked out the words before he lost the courage.

"That's fixin' to change."

Rosa's skirt flew as she spun around. Her skin glowed against her yellow blouse. "What?" She ran up, skipping the top step altogether. "You don't know what you're doing."

Weston recognized the embroidery on her blouse. It matched his pillowcase. Maybe he could do a side by side comparison. Shaking his head, he forced the riotous thought from him. "You said you couldn't pretend — that you didn't want intimacy without love. It's time to give me a chance, Rosa."

"There *is* no chance for us. The moment caught you off guard. Both of us, really. That's not love. It could've been Molly, should've been Molly."

"It's never been Molly."

"But it'll be someone, someday. I pray for you, Weston. I pray that God heals you and brings you closer to Him. Part of the healing might mean falling in love and getting married."

"I am married."

Rosa pounded her fist on the banister. "To the wrong woman."

Eliza's voice wafted up from below. "Rosa, is that you?"

"Yes, be down in a minute." She looked to Weston and lowered her voice. "I owe you. We both know how far in your debt I am. If this is a way you've come up with for me to make amends, then be honest. Don't pretend otherwise."

"I'm not Tillerton," he ground out. She knew how to hurt a man. "When I kiss you again, it'll be because you asked me to, just like in there."

"Shh!" She cast nervous eyes down the

stairwell. "I didn't ask . . . All right, fine. If you need to blame someone, then blame me. I'm sorry for tricking you into something so distasteful, but I'll take the responsibility to see that it doesn't occur again. If you can't forget what happened in there, I'm leaving. I won't have another resentful husband on my hands. You won't rue the day I rolled into town."

"You can't go. It'd be a mistake to squelch what could come of this."

"Nothing will come of this besides pain and resentment. Can you honestly tell me that you love me? That you'll love me forever?"

He took a step back. She'd gone all in before he even had a chance to look at his cards. "I, uh . . . I do *care* for . . ."

Her eyes, snapping with fire, cooled to dull chunks of ice.

"Rosa, don't. I don't want to hurt you."

"Then stay away."

"Are you and Weston fighting?" Eliza called. "I wondered what's kept you up there so long."

"Just a minute, sis." Weston crossed his arms. "You can't go back. Speaking of Tillerton —"

"I haven't seen hide nor hair of him for a

week. I don't think he'd dare bother me now."

"What about Eliza?" He was grasping for straws, desperation rolling through him.

Eliza appeared at the foot of the stairs. "Don't make me climb up there. If you're going to fight, come on down. I don't want to miss it."

Weston stepped around Rosa and called down. "We were just discussing your confinement. Did you plan on Rosa assisting you?"

"You're wasting my time with a question like that. What's this really about?"

Rosa sent him a withering look but kept her voice sweet. "I need to help Louise on the ranch. I can't stay here."

"You're not going anywhere in the rain, are you? But next time you go to the farm, bring her back for supper. We'll put her up for the night, and Jake can take her home the next morning." Eliza clapped her hands together. "I have an even better idea. I'm still short some baby linens. Maybe we could go to Lockhart, the three of us, and finish putting the nursery together. It's getting close, Rosa, and there's so much to do. I can't imagine where I'd be without your help."

Weston rocked back on his heels. His
sister did have her moments.

25

"I'm about out of bootlaces," Eliza complained several days later as she stretched on her bed. "If my ankles get any thicker, I'll have to wear Jake's boots."

"At least the weather has broken. It's getting cooler." Rosa folded yet another baby blanket crocheted by the loving ladies of Prairie Lea.

"But the swelling is here to stay."

"You could go barefoot."

Eliza paused only a moment before ripping the boots off and throwing them across her bedroom. "That's the most practical suggestion I've heard this whole pregnancy. You should be a midwife."

Rosa grinned. Thank goodness for Eliza. Rosa needed someone to distract her from the charged atmosphere with Weston.

She blanched when she heard footsteps at the door, but it was only Octavia.

"Miss Eliza, Miss Rosa, your Aunt Louise

is in the parlor."

And she wasn't alone. Beaming at her side stood the balding Mr. Bradford, looking uncomfortable without a countertop to hide behind. "Hello, ladies, how are you?" His wheezy chuckle repeated itself like a crow caw as he shuffled around the room in his eagerness to properly greet the younger women while not leaving Louise's side.

Louise kissed both girls and then frowned. "Weston and Jake aren't here?"

"No, ma'am. They're out. I'm not sure what pasture they're in today."

"That's too bad. I'd hoped your husbands would be with you." She gave Rosa a compassionate smile. Mr. Bradford patted her hand timidly, his own bottom lip drooping in sympathy. "We've come with some stupendous news."

Eliza's eyes danced, and she clapped her hands together. "Do tell."

Louise beamed at Mr. Bradford, who cleared his throat and began, "You see, I have asked Louise, after knowing and admiring her for years, for her hand in holy matrimony, and she has consented."

Eliza's squeals were heartfelt. Rosa's were not. If tears appeared, Rosa hoped they'd be mistaken for tears of happiness, for she did wish her former mother-in-law happiness, but she was certain there was none for her in their tidings.

Congratulations were still flying when Weston stepped in. Rosa's heart hopped like a jumping bean when he looked at her, but Louise intervened, smiling at him expectantly.

"Aunt Louise, Deacon . . . ah, may I guess what this call is about?"

Louise pinched his cheek like the dark-haired five-year-old boy he used to be. "We're glad to see you. It wouldn't be the same without your blessing." And then seeing a man over his shoulder, she called, "Mr. Mohle, is that you hiding back there? What are you doing?"

The man stepped into the room and spoke around his plug of tobacco. "Wes has a carpentry job for me, but congratulations just the same. I'll be sure and tell the missus."

"Yes, congratulations!" Weston added. "But if you'll excuse me, please, Deacon, Aunt Louise, I need to get him started on this job. Don't leave without telling Jake. He's right behind me."

Weston looked Rosa over like he was taking inventory and then led Mr. Mohle out of the room.

"So when's the date?" Eliza was making

up for Rosa's silence.

Louise reached to take Rosa's arm. "I don't want to shock you, but if Rosa approves, we'll tie the knot this Saturday."

"Saturday?" Rosa gasped.

But Eliza giggled. "This family sure doesn't hold to long engagements."

"You're going to be all right without me, Rosa. Aren't you? Deacon will take me to San Antonio for our honeymoon, but we'll be gone only a couple of weeks. When we return, he's going to begin rebuilding his store. We'll want to get everything done by Christmas."

"I think it's marvelous," said Eliza. "Every day you wait is one less day together. Besides, I could drop this colt at any time, and I do want to go to the ceremony."

"Eliza!" Louise scolded. "I'm sorry, Deacon. This girl has spent too much time with her aunt Mary."

"Hello there, what's this about?"

As they shared the news with Jake, Rosa considered her options.

Saturday. She bit her lip. Louise had found a new guardian and would follow him devoutly, but what would Rosa do? Could she live there alone with Jay Tillerton seething the next field over? Before she could think it through, one alternative was taken forever off the table.

Adjusting his suspenders, Jake took the floor just as Weston reentered. "Aunt Louise, Weston, there's a subject I've been meaning to broach. Would there be any objection to me and Eliza purchasing Louise's place? I know I don't have the family name, but we're family, sure enough. I've been thinking about getting our own place now that the young'un is coming."

The walls were closing in on Rosa, but no one could see them snuffing out her hopes, one by one. Instead, hearty congratulations flew from all sides. Eliza wrapped both arms around her scruffy husband's neck while he shook hands with Louise, sealing the deal. Before Rosa could join the obligated celebration, Louise brought it to a halt.

"Wait! What was I thinking? I can't say yes without Rosa's permission. The farm belongs to her, as well."

A split second of silence ensued as all eyes fell on her. Surely she looked odd with her olive skin turned a sickly green. She opened her mouth to speak, but the words caught in her throat.

"Of course it's all right." Eliza laughed and smothered Rosa in a hug. "We'll give Rosa her share of the money, and she and

Wes can have this big house all to themselves."

Rosa watched their faces — eyes bright, smiles wide, not a care in the world. How could she possibly object in the face of their happiness? She tried to hide her despair, but Weston didn't look fooled. He was working his way to her when there was a mighty crash from above.

"Land sakes alive!" Louise crouched down and covered her head. "What was that?"

Weston didn't flinch. "Mr. Mohle."

"What's he doing up there?" Another crash caused the picture frames on the wall to rattle.

"Updating some furniture."

"You hired Mr. Mohle to decorate?" Eliza was incredulous.

Scraping sounds filled the room as something was dragged across the second story floor.

"No, he's fixing my bed." Wes scratched the back of his neck. "He's taking off the big canopy."

"The four-poster bed? Have you lost your mind? Why would you do that?" yelled his sister above the din.

"I decided I don't want it hanging over me anymore."

Louise laughed. "You surprise me,

nephew. I had no idea you got uneasy about such things — but I suppose it isn't that uncommon. Rosa is scared to death of being trapped, too."

Rosa could feel her face go from green to red.

"I guess I'm changing, Aunt Louise, and this room is starting to feel mighty tight, too. It might be time for me to get some air."

"Well, give me a kiss and get back to work, then. We'll look for you on Saturday."

"Yes, ma'am. With bells on."

Getting onto the roof wasn't difficult. The third-story ballroom had large windows in its gables that practically begged Rosa to climb out. Keeping her feet flat on the roof, she sat and hugged her knees to her chest. No one would think to look for her up there.

Although the Englands decided not to move until after the baby came, Eliza's excitement, packing, and planning strained Rosa's ability to pretend she supported the decision. Her tender emotions required some sanctuary from the ruthless joy downstairs.

From her perch she could see much of the Garner ranch. Directly beneath her, Octavia was taking cuttings from Eliza's herb garden while Eliza sat in the shade and mopped her brow. Far in the east pasture she could make out four horsemen — Willie, Red, Bailey, and Weston, no doubt — barely visible above the cattle they were riding among.

Jake had left already. Early that morning he'd taken the wagon to Louise's to help her clear out the house. Louise wanted some of the furniture moved to Mr. Bradford's and some would remain for Eliza. They had offered to give Rosa first choice, but what would she do with the furniture? She'd lived there only three months. Besides, she had no house to furnish anyway. Oddly enough, Jake didn't offer to take her with him. He was probably afraid she'd change her mind — as if she'd agreed in the first place.

But no one cared. They had their plans and were pursuing them blissfully. Rosa had to put the feelings of abandonment and hurt behind her and make arrangements of her own. Being sad wasn't going to change anything.

So what to do?

She fingered the black trim along the hem of her skirt. If the Englands bought the land, she could pay Weston off with some left over, but not enough for a house. Heat

411

curled off the shingles in long waves. She couldn't sit up there much longer. She had to think.

According to Molly, Rosa could let a room at a boardinghouse in Lockhart, but the only person who might hire her would be Mr. Bradford. His store would be in Prairie Lea by Christmas. Moving in with Louise and Mr. Bradford remained her best option, but moving in with Louise didn't hold the charm it once had.

It'd be difficult to leave the spacious house warming her backside at that moment. She'd grown fond of Palmetto. The wide halls, ornate banisters, and six-paneled doors didn't intimidate her anymore. And while they could use more color, she'd grown to appreciate the textures of the rugs, wallpaper, and draperies. Even the stable held a place in her heart, and she hated to give up the freedom she had via Smokey.

Squint as she might, the cowboys were no longer visible, having no doubt sought shelter under the leafy trees surrounding the creek. They must be hunkering down for dinner. The noonday sun blazed above her, doing its best to leave an impression that would last through autumn.

Could she stay here? Without Jake and Eliza's presence, it'd be thorny. Since their kiss, Weston and she hadn't been alone together, but his bedroom renovations didn't bode well. Would he respect her wishes and keep his distance, or would he get skittish again and leave her altogether?

She bit her lip. Tricky. When Jake went to the bank to get his loan, he would pay off Weston's note and then return the difference to Louise and to her. She wouldn't owe Weston anything. Yet, just because her obligation was cleared, that didn't mean she couldn't be profitable to him. Regardless of where she lived, she intended to earn her keep. Would he let her work for her room and board?

With Eliza gone, Octavia would need help with the housekeeping and laundry. Feeding those cowboys was a full-time job. She'd even move out to Octavia's cabin if there was room.

She tapped her toes against the shingles. This plan could work. Weston was a fair and generous employer. She'd still live close to Mary and Eliza without crowding Louise. She wouldn't be a burden to anyone.

Satisfied that she'd found a solution, Rosa edged down to the windowsill and climbed inside. All she had to do was convince Weston that she could earn her keep. That sounded a lot easier than turning a profit on the ranch.

Dinner was ready and waiting on her.

"This child is going roly-poly today," Eliza exclaimed at the end of the meal as her stomach lurched again, making her napkin bounce.

"He or she is getting anxious to meet us," Rosa said.

"I'm anxious to stop carrying him around. I'm tuckered out."

"Take a nap if you feel like it. I thought I'd help Octavia in the kitchen this afternoon. I won't be bored."

"If you're sure." Eliza pushed herself away from the table with an effort and waddled to her room.

By midafternoon, Rosa's plans for the evening meal were well underway. Octavia already had a chicken butchered, so she whipped up some *mole* sauce for variety. She didn't have any masa prepared, so she settled on flour tortillas and a mandatory pot of beans.

When the tortillas were done and the beans were simmering, she took out toward the garden. First she inspected Eliza's herb garden. She plucked a fat caterpillar off a stalk and squished it under her boot. The garden looked well kept but would need tending once Eliza was gone. Next to the herb garden sat the large vegetable patch cultivated for consumption by the human and animal occupants of Palmetto. Could she handle a plot that size?

The garden lay fallow after the summer harvest, but with early plowing she probably had time to get the seeds sown by herself.

Rosa's mind raced as she considered the possibilities. Now that she could drive Smokey, maybe she could even plow by herself. She fairly ran to the barn to look over the plow. Was it too heavy for her?

Weston didn't expect to run into Rosa in the barn, but there she stood in her new town-bought clothes, messing with a plow. Her goldenrod dress had black piping that ran from her shoulders to her waist, just in case he didn't notice her curves. Much too pretty to be fiddling around in a barn.

Her large sleeves swayed as she tried to drive the plow blade into the hard-packed earth of the barn floor. He didn't like the looks of this.

"The kitchen smells delicious." He approached warily, afraid she might bolt again. "Octavia says we have you to thank for that."

Her black eyes followed every step he made toward her. "Thank you. I miss cooking. I hope Octavia doesn't mind if I do it more."

"It's your kitchen, but you might have to prove yourself before she trusts you. What are you doing out here? Are you looking for something?" Wes double-checked one of the straps for wear.

"No. I'm planning the garden. I'd love to put some different herbs and peppers out. And the big garden — I think I could plow it. This isn't that heavy."

The look he gave her should've made the words unnecessary, but he said them anyway. "You're not plowing like a field hand. Not on my property."

"Weston, things have changed. Your note is paid. I don't owe you anymore. We don't have to be stuck in this sham —"

"It's not a sham to me," he gritted through clenched teeth.

"You've made yourself clear on that, and I'll honor your wishes. If getting an annulment is against your principles, we can leave things like they are on paper, but our contract is over. I paid you back. We can't call this a marriage, when neither of us had a choice."

"But if this is where we find ourselves, shouldn't we make the best of it?"

She winced before he realized what he'd said.

"Someday you'll regret you settled. I'd like to negotiate a new contract now. You paid for sixty acres and a bride, and you got neither, so I'm giving you a refund." She dug the plow blade further into the ground. "But what about your end? Remember that night we met? You asked me to only work on Garner land, so I'm coming to you first. Will you hire me, or do I need to find another employer?"

Was that a threat? He knew she wanted nothing to do with him, but surely she wouldn't run to complete strangers. Why was she so desperate to get away? But if she wanted to talk business, he welcomed the familiar language. About time he had an advantage.

"You aren't plowing. What else can you offer?"

Her eyes darted about. She looked worried. "I'll do all the housework, mending, and help Octavia in the kitchen."

He unbuttoned his pocket and found a peppermint while he pretended to consider her answer.

"Eliza will need help for the next month or so, but after that? I won't dirty the house much if I live alone."

She leaned hard against the plow. "I can work outside. You saw me shearing. And I'm strong. I'll work anywhere. I'm even getting good on Smokey. Maybe you could teach me —" A wind gust caught her skirt, forcing her to release the plow to smooth it.

"Why would I hire a woman to do a man's job? Think of something else. What did the women in Ciauhtlaz do?"

"They spent most of their time taking care of their children." Her hand covered her mouth, but it was too late.

Children. Somehow in the flurry of their marriage, Weston had overlooked the possibility of a family. He'd only thought about protecting her and her reputation, but now as she moved further and further from his grasp, he realized that he might also be burying the chance of carrying on the Garner name. For all his protestations to God about maintaining bachelorhood, he'd never relinquished his dream of having children.

Rosa came to stand by him and watched a sparrow hop along the fence rail. "I shouldn't have said that."

"It's all right." He shoved his fists deep into his pockets.

"You want children?"

His advantage had vanished. He smiled at

418

the carefree bird even though his heart was breaking. "Very much."

"You'd make a wonderful father."

He looked deeply into her eyes and was disappointed by what he saw there: compassion and concern, but a solid determination to remain distant, as well.

He shook his head to clear the thoughts whirling inside. "I give up. You want to renegotiate? Here are your choices: We can have a sterile, distant relationship. You've taken my name and are my wife, but we'll live as strangers, *or* you can throw your lot in with mine."

He stepped closer and bent, trying to get a glimpse of her downturned face. "Maybe together we can be brave, Rosa. We'll let loose of the past and see where we land, but if we do, this talk of leaving must end. We can't build trust while you have one foot out the door. Sure, I have more than you, and I intend to give you so much you won't ever be able to buy your freedom. For better or worse. Can you live with that?"

All he could see was the smooth part in her black hair. She wouldn't look up.

He stepped back. He'd asked her to give him a chance, and she'd refused. Time was up. Happened to men everywhere, every day. Only difference — he was already married to her.

"You're sticking to your guns, huh? Fine." He dusted his palms on each other. "I promised that I wouldn't leave you, and I won't send you away, but if you want a business relationship, then you've got it. Starting now, you'll keep yourself busy. If I need you, I'll let you know, but don't expect me to treat you any differently than the fellows — worse even, because I can't be accused of fraternizing with my female help. Forget that we're married. I'll never mention it again. You got what you wanted. You win."

He felt like a child stomping off, but he did anyway, trudging through every puddle before him.

26

The spicy scents brought back memories of home. Spooning the dark sauce over the golden chicken, Rosa tried to replace her feelings of loss with feelings of attachment. She might not belong to the family, but she definitely belonged with them.

How she could've used one of those hugs Weston had a right to, but in his negotiations he never mentioned love. The shame of an annulment, the practicality of having a wife and children — good reasons to stay together, but not what she was looking for. She'd asked him for love once before, and the terror on his face humbled her. She couldn't cross that line again. The pain of rejection would send her running, and she didn't want to leave. She wanted to be here.

Rosa relished the weight of the ceramic tureen of chicken in her arms, a small gift to the people she'd grown so fond of. Octavia followed her into the dining room with the cloth-wrapped tortillas in one hand and a bowl of beans in the other.

"Yee-haw!" Jake said. "I couldn't believe my nose when I walked in. Fiesta tonight."

"It's all Mrs. Garner's doing." Octavia filled their empty glasses with sweet tea.

"Not true. It was a two-woman job." Rosa carried the tureen back to the table and found her seat. "And if you've never eaten this before, I'll be glad to show you how it's done. You'll notice there's no silverware on the table."

"How quaint! It won't matter anyway. I drip everything on my belly." Eliza laughed.

Octavia stepped out as Jake prepared to return thanks, but Weston stopped him.

"Hold on a minute. Rosa, weren't you going to eat in the kitchen?"

She kept the smile plastered on her face, even though there wasn't a hint of humor in his eyes.

"Why would she do that?" Eliza asked.

"She wants to. That's where Octavia eats." Weston might as well have worn a mask.

All eyes turned her way. He wasn't jesting. Her throat closed, rendering her unable to confirm or deny his story. Without a word, Rosa gathered her glass and plate in trembling hands and walked to the kitchen through their shocked silence.

The door swung closed behind her, muf-
fling Eliza's heated conversation with her
brother. For a split second Rosa almost
railed against him, too. Her embarrassment
tempted her to lash out, but logic reigned.
She'd asked for this. As much as it hurt, he
was doing what he'd promised — what
she'd requested.

"Why are you in here? Ain't you eating?"
Octavia mumbled around a mouthful of
chicken.

"No, ma'am. I don't feel like it." Rosa slid
her plate across the counter and tossed her
tea in the slop bucket. "Have a good night."

The sunlight lingered, but Rosa turned in
for the night. She closed her bedroom door
and dropped onto her bed. The stuffy room
seemed warmer than usual. Octavia hadn't
been upstairs to open the windows for the
evening. She probably did that after supper
while they were in the parlor. What else did
Octavia do that she didn't know about?
More importantly, who kept Octavia company when her work was done?

Rosa searched for her sewing basket. An
employee should stay busy, but the basket
wasn't in her room. It was probably down
in the parlor. Soon Eliza would have the
poetry book before her and would be reading to an unappreciative audience. Jake

would be on the settee with Eliza, and Weston would be in his chair. Would he kick his legs up on the empty footstool since she wasn't there?

She picked at a pink hibiscus she'd sewn into her coverlet. Rosa loved the evenings when the men came home and the house was filled with their deep voices. The stories they'd shared, the jokes, the plans, all of it made her feel like she belonged. But she knew better. Weston had welcomed her, but she couldn't live here as a guest. She needed some reason to justify her presence. Some reason that didn't involve him personally.

Rosa rolled off the bed and pulled her flute from a drawer of stockings. The night promised nothing but sorrow and loneliness. She would learn to enjoy her own company. First she opened her window and then played the songs of a home that a young girl with a bright future once knew.

Try as she might the only songs she remembered were doleful melodies not played since the night of the thunderstorm. She sighed, refusing to give in to desperation. This wouldn't be an easy transition, but she should count her blessings.

As far as laborers went, Rosa wouldn't suffer. Many slaved from dawn to dusk and weren't compensated fairly. Many endured overseers who were cruel and oppressive. Her employer, on the other hand . . .

She remembered another song, took a deep breath, and started the forlorn tune. Her employer was a good man — one who'd tried to correct her mistakes and pay for her errors, but she couldn't rely on his charity. She didn't deserve his help. How she longed to make it right, but an annulment was the only remedy she could fathom. Barring that, she had to resort to keeping as far away as possible.

The loud knock on her door startled her. She looked at her window. Darkness had fallen. They must have left the parlor by now. Smoothing her gown, she called out, "Yes? You may enter."

But the door didn't open.

"It's Mr. Garner. Would you kindly desist with the flute? It's late and you need to get up early to start breakfast."

So unexpected was the request, it took her a moment to compose herself. "Yes, I-I will."

"Thank you."

"Good night," she called, anxious for conversation, but there was none. Footsteps faded into his room, and then silence.

Rosa had no choice but to lie on her bed and watch the twinkling stars mock her.

■ ■ ■ ■

"I don't like it, Weston. It kept me up all night — that and indigestion." Eliza lowered herself onto the settee with a groan.

Weston pushed the curtain aside to watch Rosa ride away from the house. First light and she was already out the door to begin her day's work. "I don't like it, either, but what choice do I have? She insists I treat her like a servant, or she'll leave."

"What if she left, Wes? You weren't exactly planning on marriage this summer. Would it matter so much?"

Rosa's small figure rode steadily as Smokey carried her farther and farther away. What if she never returned? Could he pretend she was just another cousin? Could he banish his hopes, or would they dog him continually?

"It would matter very much." He dropped the curtain and turned to face his sister. "I'm scared, Eliza."

"Of her leaving?"

"Leaving, staying — I don't know which scares me the most." He fell into his chair. "I want to give her everything, but I can't promise her an easy relationship. I can't promise her that she'll be happy. I tried that with Cora and failed."

"Guaranteed happiness? That's her demand?"

"No, but with her history, I'm afraid to offer anything less. I can't let her down. Mack only married her because Eli made him, and he let Rosa know how displeased he was over the arrangement. Rosa never forgave herself for complying."

"Why should she feel guilty? Mack could've refused."

"She doesn't see that. Maybe he didn't mean for Rosa to take it so hard. Maybe he would've adjusted and done right by her, but then he died, leaving her to wonder what she could've done differently."

Eliza raised an eyebrow. "Sound familiar?"

"No one forced Cora to marry me." But the words had scarcely left his mouth before he saw the parallel. Of course, no one had forced her. She'd chosen her course with less interference than Mack had. Yet once they were married, Weston felt completely responsible for her moods. Where had her accountability lain?

Cora had declined, mentally and physically. She'd lost the will to live. Had she chosen that path, or had she been dragged down it against her will?

"I can't blame Cora. It wasn't her fault."

427

"Yet you blame yourself. You see so clearly the splinter in Rosa's eye, but you've missed the beam in your own. Rosa can't afford to offer her heart again — not before you're ready to accept it." Eliza pointed at him for emphasis. "If you want to suffer from guilt, let it be for not kissing her senseless and pledging your undying love. Never under-value the persuasiveness of a grand gesture."

"You and your sentimental twaddle." But Eliza was right. His regrets had crowded him into fresh offenses — like carrying out the first half of her suggestion without of-fering the latter. Rosa had allowed, nay participated in, the kissing, but when she'd asked for love, he'd hedged. No wonder she didn't trust him. "Unfortunately, she's made up her mind. She'll have to make the first move now. And you — you can't get involved. She'll leave if she feels pressured."

"I wouldn't pressure the poor thing. These things must be handled with a delicacy I don't possess. I just wish you'd get it settled. You're keeping me on tenterhooks, and I'm uncomfortable enough already."

With what threat had Eliza's compliance been secured? Rosa clicked to Smokey, hop-ing to hurry the patient animal along. It must have been an impressive warning, for

Rosa had fully expected Eliza to protest her new position. Loudly. Of course other events competed for her attention. Moving the furniture to Mr. Bradford's and Louise's personal items to Adele's, where she was staying until the wedding, kept them all busy. Any spare time was spent preparing for the baby. Whether they had a deal or not, Rosa would have worked like a hired hand this week anyway.

Smokey's horseshoes clicked on the hard-packed road, never slowing down. Cleaning out the vacant house for Eliza's eventual move had taken longer than she'd expected. Back at Palmetto, Louise's unfinished tablecloth lay folded in her sewing basket, and the wedding shower was tomorrow.

She cringed at the man who appeared as she broke out of the trees. Definitely no time for the likes of him.

"Who do we have here? If it isn't Mrs. Garner, Mrs. Weston Garner." Tillerton's voice was smooth and pleasant — just like a tasteless poison. "I've meant to congratulate you. You sure didn't waste your time with the small fries, did you? Went straight for the big catch."

Falling in beside her, he went on. "I'm not surprised that Mr. Garner was game for a romp in the hay. I'm sure you were tempting enough. What amazes me is that ring on your finger. Poor man." He lowered his voice to a stage whisper. "There was a witness, wasn't there?"

"Nasty man, leave me alone." With her heels she prodded Smokey to a trot, but Tillerton stayed at her side.

"Yes, you women flock after the uncultured Philistines. My whole life I've played second fiddle to the big, strapping illiterates who don't know the difference between Darwin and Dickens. Then I discovered that the ladies prefer rough handling. You treat them badly, and they come back for more. Sometimes they even — what was the rumor? — hunt you down and crawl into bed with you."

But Rosa wouldn't flee. She had the protection she needed at hand. She had to take care of herself. Weston wouldn't follow her around anymore.

She glared at him. "You know, at the church you sold me a bill of goods. I didn't know any better then, but I think you lied to me. No other man acts as crudely as you. No one else has insulted me. Makes me think the rest of the story was hogwash, as well."

He bowed with his hand on his chest, leaning forward in the saddle.

"Mrs. Garner, I underestimated you in many ways, but in particular, your intelligence. To my shame, I'll admit I was only having a bit of fun with a young single lady. Just teasing you. Let me assure you, as a married woman, you have nothing to fear from me."

That was more like it. Rosa didn't trust him any further than she could spit, but if he could keep from leering at her, maybe she wouldn't have to shoot him.

"Thank you." She tried to think of something civil to say. She'd spent a lot of time composing insults, but those wouldn't work now. What would Louise say? "I haven't seen your wife about. Is she well?"

"Yes, but she remains reclusive. If only I could entice her to enter society. She might step outside occasionally, but in general she doesn't even want to leave the house."

"Really? I saw her out just last week at the creek bed. She didn't stay long, but —"

"You've spoken to Anne?" Tillerton's jaw clenched. "That's odd. She didn't mention it. Makes me wonder what else she's hiding from me."

And without another word he spurred his horse, leaving Rosa behind to wonder.

Rosa regretted burning her finger on the

skillet that afternoon. It made the needle-work nigh impossible. She also regretted that Octavia wasn't more of a talker. She didn't appreciate Rosa's wry observations nearly as much as Eliza did. By the time the potatoes were cooked through, Rosa had learned to keep her comments to herself. Yes, she had a lot of regrets, but she was doing her dead level best to make amends to those she'd wronged.

A plate of gingersnap cookies had mysteriously appeared in the parlor. A second embroidered pillowcase awaited discovery in Weston's room at the moment. And with her first wages she planned to buy some peppermints from Deacon.

Not much, but she hoped he'd notice. Despite their disagreement, she intended to serve him faithfully. She wanted what was best for him even if their friendship couldn't survive in close quarters.

She jabbed her needle into the tablecloth she was embroidering for Louise's new kitchen. Just a few more stitches and the red border would be done. It was a good thing her sewing wasn't as big of a tangled mess as her heart. How had her concern for Weston caused so much pain?

Rosa jumped when he appeared in the doorway, hoping she hadn't been speaking aloud. His clean butternut shirt was still crisp, not yet soiled by the day's labor. He crossed his arms and leaned against the wall, his presence emanating a force she had to handle with care.

"Willie's going to plow on Monday. Do you know what seeds you want?"

She dropped her hoop to her lap. "I haven't got it all planned yet. When do you need to know?"

"Now would be good. Jake's taking Eliza to town for Louise's shower. He's going to ride to Lockhart for me and pick up any goods we might need."

"Louise's shower?" She looked helplessly at the fabric in her hands. "How am I going to get there?"

"I thought you'd want to go to the wedding. You can't really take two days off in one week."

Not go to the shower? What would Louise think? But he was as cool as a line of trout. She took one more stitch, tied a knot, and bit off the thread.

"What excuse will Eliza give?"

"As mad as she is, I suppose she'll brand me a monster."

Rosa folded the tablecloth, smoothed the heavy square, and pulled a ribbon from her basket to make it presentable. She placed it

433

in his hands. "I don't mean to hurt you."

He looked at the floor. "There's nothing new to say. This is what you've chosen, so we live with it. Eliza can take your gift to the shower, and you'll ride with me to the wedding tomorrow. In the meantime, unless you had other plans, I'd like to see the upstairs bedrooms aired out. They haven't been tended since spring, and we'll probably have guests once the baby arrives."

A cheerless relief descended upon her. He hadn't put up much of a fight, but she wasn't surprised. She knew if she gave him some space to think it through, he'd realize he didn't need her.

After dictating a seed list to Jake, Rosa hurried to the second floor. Since the first night she'd arrived, she hadn't had a reason to visit the spare rooms upstairs. Taking brass polish, rags, feather dusters, a broom, and all the linens she could carry, she started at the back of the hall, saving the only two occupied rooms for last.

The rooms weren't messy. The fireplaces hadn't been lit since the last cleaning, so the grates only received a quick wipe down. Chasing the dust from every embellishment on the heavy furniture took more time than she'd expected, but she enjoyed running her fingers through the wooden curlicues, following their meandering way across chairs, headboards, mantels, and picture frames. These people might not appreciate bright colors, but they sure did like fancy carvings.

Who had occupied the rooms? Did Eli hide under this bed? Did Eliza cry into this pillow over a long-forgotten suitor? She imagined dramatic scenes as she stripped the sheets and shook out the rugs, letting the character of the room dictate the direction of the plot.

Only one room wasn't serviceable. It contained a single bed with a lonely white sheet tossed over the mattress. Rosa lifted it to see what it could possibly be protecting and caught her breath. Laid out from end to end were framed photographs and painted portraits. She pulled open the shade so she could study the sepia images.

They were Garners, all right. The family traits were stamped on the unfamiliar faces, but upon closer inspection she realized they weren't all strangers. There was Mack, grinning impishly with a rattle in his tight fist. Louise was as plump as her new infant. Eli — young, proud papa Eli — stood straight and tall, overlooking his family.

She picked up another picture to find a serious little fellow holding his sister's hand. His head rested against his mother's shoulder, as if all the world's problems were already his own.

"Do you recognize anyone?" She jumped at the low timbre of his voice.

"Quite a few, actually."

Weston drew near to look over her shoulder. "Goodness, I never realized how much Eliza has grown to resemble Mother."

"And yet you both take after your father, too." She handed the framed photo to him and picked up another one, surprised he tarried. "Here's you and Mack together, with the rest of the family. Three generations."

"Let me see." He held the picture before him; his fingers hovered above the surface as he named them. "George and his family aren't in this one — just my grandfather's family. My father, Davy, was the oldest, then Uncle Eli, Uncle Teddy, and Aunt Elizabeth, who is Eliza's namesake. Uncle Teddy died in the war and Aunt Elizabeth never married but moved back to South Carolina to teach school."

"So then the only grandchildren were you, Eliza, and Mack."

"Yes. My parents had two infants that died, and now, with Mack gone . . ." The lines framing his handsome face stilled.

He was the only male Garner of his

branch remaining.

Rosa studied the determined look on the elderly lady seated among her offspring. Tightly curled gray hair peeked bravely out of a severe bonnet. Her husband, the Garner patriarch, was flanked by his three sons, all of them taller than he. She leaned across Weston to touch the image of his *abuela* and wished that she could've met her. Her hands were blurred in the daguerreotype, probably from trying to keep the grandchildren still for the duration of the exposure.

This whole *familia* without any Garners to represent them. Eliza's children would be their only progeny walking the earth. When the mine collapsed and the blood of two of their sons was spilled in the Sierra Madres, Rosa could do nothing to stop it. Would another family line end before her eyes, as well?

She could never atone for her behavior. The awful realization weighed heavily on her heart. Weston wasn't the only one hurt. She'd altered the destiny of this whole family when she compromised his good name.

I'm sorry, she wanted to cry to the assembled chorus looking back at her through the glass, but the only one she could make amends to was the man standing at her side.

■ ■ ■ ■

Supper that night did nothing to ease the growing sense of despair she felt for him. While Octavia organized food for the next day's wedding luncheon, Rosa served Weston solo. She pushed through the dining room door with the platter of pork chops, unprepared for what she saw.

A sob caught in her throat, soundless. He was there alone. No one to talk to. No one who would listen. The long table shone like glass but reflected nothing save a solitary chandelier and bare ceiling. When other families gathered, chatting and sharing, he sat abandoned. His chairs stood empty, mocking the man who couldn't fill them.

Weston looked away when she slid the frightfully overloaded platter in front of him. He remained motionless. As a servant, she had no right to intrude on his thoughts. He had set the boundaries and she had agreed. She returned with a pitcher of tea and added a drop to his full glass, not wanting to leave him friendless in the vacuous house. He thanked her and, with a sigh, moved a piece of meat to his plate, giving her no excuse to stay.

Back in the kitchen Rosa sat and picked

at her food, noting each clink of the silver on the china in the dining room. Why hadn't she made dessert? It would've given her one more minute to serve him — one less minute to contemplate what a disaster she'd caused.

Silence and space, Weston had treasured those commodities recently, and now he had what he'd desired.

With his elbows on the table, he took another unwanted bite of chops. Rosa would notice if he didn't touch his food, and he had no issue with her cooking. No, she excelled at every task she'd attempted — maybe not on the first attempt, but it didn't discourage her from trying again.

Just another thing he loved about her.

Weston set his fork down and clasped his hands together.

He did love her. Morning, evening, happy, sad, hungry, full — he loved her. He wanted to crow it from the weathervane — he wanted to hide it as if it were his deepest flaw — and perhaps it was. He should be embarrassed to love someone who didn't welcome his attention. Not wise. Or pleasant.

But he had a right to love, didn't he? Whether or not she returned his affection, he was free from the accusing doubts that had held him for so long. If she gave him nothing more, that gift guaranteed his devotion.

All he could do now was pray that Rosa was suffering from the same loneliness that plagued him. He didn't know which hurt worse, her absence or her humiliation. He hoped God would redeem his actions, as imperfect and imprecise as they were. The Lord knew he took no pleasure in the situation. He'd rather take a bullet than send her out of the kitchen again. The look on her face had diminished him in some manner, and until he came up with a better solution, part of him was lost.

He pushed his plate away, and his chair scraped across the floor. Before he made it through the entryway, she caught up with him.

"Are you finished? Is there anything else I can do for you?"

If she were truly his servant, he'd have to dismiss her. The eagerness on her face, the leaning toward him in anticipation would drive him to distraction.

Weston cocked an eyebrow. "I won't need a servant for the rest of the evening. You can do as you wish."

She peered around him into the empty

parlor. Biting her lip, she stepped backward until her back pressed against the wall.

"You're going to sit in there by yourself? When I think of the nights ahead of us . . ."

If his eyebrows were elevated before, he was sure they were now almost leaping off his forehead. "You know my preference." He wouldn't ask her to reconsider, but he waited breathless in case she might.

"Your preferences can change," she said, "and I refuse to burden anyone. If I thought we had a chance . . ." She wrung her apron.

He was so tempted to help her, to try another "grand gesture," but with effort he restrained himself. Seeing her wrestle with her feelings for him was a gift from God. Now, watching from the other side, he recognized her fear — and he saw the love he hoped would force her to confront it.

Trust me, he wanted to urge her, but he hadn't been trustworthy until recently. He had to give her time.

They'd reached an impasse. The empty parlor held no charm for him, but he would shield her from the persuasive words already on the tip of his tongue. He'd made his offer. Nothing to do now but to pray and wait, so he walked away.

Alone.

27

Buggies, wagons, and horses dotted the already crowded churchyard. Not a bad turnout on such short notice. Had Rosa been in a happier state of mind she might've appreciated the show of support the town had bestowed on her mother-in-law, but such observations were impossible in her present condition.

Wearing her rose taffeta, her wedding dress, had been a mistake. The last time she'd worn it, Weston couldn't take his eyes off her. This time he wouldn't look her direction.

With disinterest, he helped Octavia and her out of the buggy and passed Octavia the basket of covered dishes to be delivered to the Lovelaces' warehouse for the luncheon. Then, without turning her way, he started off.

Rosa watched Octavia stride toward Mill Road. Where was she supposed to go?

Where did she belong on days like today? Rosa lifted her chin. Louise's family had accepted her before she'd ever met Weston. She belonged on the pew with them.

She skipped along, trying to catch up with him. If she'd known he'd be so firm, she might have worded their agreement more carefully. She'd wanted to save their friendship, to have a relationship free from forced obligations. Instead, they had no relationship at all.

Strangers.

Rosa hadn't thought she'd miss him so much. He said he wouldn't ask her to reconsider, but would he mind if she did?

Louise looked beautiful. Adele Lovelace had surprised her with a perfectly tailored amethyst suit that highlighted her copper hair and strawberries-and-cream complexion. Rosa had heard that Deacon had done his own preparation, but not to his personal appearance. He'd spent the last week cramming his house full of utensils, notions, and every dry good available at a mercantile. According to Uncle George, they could live six months just selling the wares in their pantry.

When the vows were read, Rosa couldn't help but steal a glance at her husband. How she wished he had said, and meant, those words to her instead of the contractual agreement they'd entered. His hand rested on the pew next to hers — large and capable — warm, if she remembered correctly. As if she could forget. Did she still have the right to clasp it, or had she given that up when she bought her freedom?

What if they had a chance? Was this what she wanted? *He* was what she wanted, but on what terms? She'd objected to the circumstances of their marriage, but she'd never objected to the man. Since she'd first met the cowboy with the scruffy hair at Aunt Mary's, she'd yearned to know him better, and the more she knew, the more she admired. And the more she feared she didn't deserve him.

Her heart pattered like castanets. The moment, the promises, the declarations of loyalty — she didn't want to observe them alone. She only moved an inch, just far enough to brush her littlest finger against his, but he couldn't mistake her intent. Not far, but it took all the courage she could muster.

His eyes flickered up, unreadable but steady. She held his gaze until she grew unsettled, but he didn't move away.

If only he would take her hand. She waited, praying he would give her some encouragement. She couldn't go any further on her own. He'd said they could be brave together. It was his turn.

His hand disappeared. With a start, Rosa realized everyone was standing to congratulate the new couple as the pianist played. She got to her feet, her chest hollow. Diligence, independence, self-sufficiency — it was surprising how many places in her heart remained empty, even though she'd acquired those virtues. Like the seven thin cows of Pharaoh's dream, the lack of love and companionship had swallowed up all her accomplishments.

But Weston hadn't abandoned her this time. He waited on her to join him, offering his arm for the brief stroll down the street.

She slipped her hand into the crook of his arm and squeezed tight, wanting to feel more than cloth. She wanted to feel him — to hold on as long as he'd let her.

"Rosa!" Aunt Mary waved as they entered the warehouse, swept clean for the occasion. "Can you lend Molly a hand at the serving table? I'd feel better if someone could help her. She's liable to make a mess of Adele's table buntings."

"Yes, ma'am."

Weston stopped by her side.

"They need me." Why did she feel like she

needed to apologize?

"Then go."

Of course. She should release his arm and go, but she wasn't ready. Not ready to go any further, but not willing to go back.

She couldn't stand there and cling to him forever. Molly was waiting.

They parted and Rosa found her station.

"Considering I haven't seen you at the courthouse, I suppose you're still wed." Molly licked a finger to freshen a blond sausage curl. "I was going to be gracious and say how much marriage agrees with you, but I can't. You look horrid."

Molly might be upset with her, but at least she was honest. "I feel horrid. I'm in such a mess."

"It's hard to sympathize with you when you've got everything I wanted." Molly's rolls hit the plates with a viscous thumbprint pushed through them.

"I don't know if it will ever be straightened out — the pain it's caused everyone, the awkwardness. Then on top of it all, Louise gets married and sells the farm. We didn't have to do it like this."

Molly narrowed her eyes and bit into a roll. "You really don't want to be married to him?"

Rosa spotted the object of their conversation across the room with Jake, George, and Bailey, listening to some tall yarn. She didn't deserve someone like him. If she agreed to be his wife, she'd be constantly faced with her inadequacies — constantly reminded that he'd stooped to accept her.

"It'd be simpler if I wasn't." Simpler, but better? If only she knew.

"Well, don't fret. Maybe someone will persuade him to free you."

Not exactly what she wanted. Before she could correct Molly, Ida flung her arms around Rosa's knees and buried her face in her skirt.

"Aunt Rosa!"

"Don't, Ida," Susannah warned. "You'll get her dirty."

But Rosa wasn't concerned. She knelt and pulled Susannah close, as well. "I've missed you girls. Why haven't you come to see me?"

"Ma says it isn't a place for children," Susannah replied primly.

Molly's head jerked, making her curls bounce. "Why would she say that?"

"Because they're newlybeds," Ida lisped.

Oh dear. Another roll turned to dust in Molly's fist.

Rosa smoothed the little girl's hair with a shaking hand, repressing any images the word conjured. "Let's find your mother. I don't have much idle time anymore, but maybe you could come over to make cookies. You'd like that?"

Bless their sticky little hearts. Susannah and Ida protected Rosa from uncomfortable conversation throughout the reception. No one wondered at Weston's distance as long as she was surrounded by children, but Rosa found it difficult to keep up with all their chatter. She was too busy tracking her husband to eat the food on her plate. Did he recognize her behavior during the ceremony for what it was — an offer to meet him halfway, to do as he asked and give them a chance?

Chance wasn't the right word. Chance suggested they might not suit. Rosa knew better than that. She knew the moment she dropped her guard, she would be his. The question was, how could he really want her?

"Mrs. Garner! I'd like to converse with you." Nicholas sauntered toward her table, all gussied up like a city slicker. He took the bench opposite her and waved a curious Weston over to join them.

"I want to apologize for my remarks a month ago. Obviously you didn't force Rosa to marry you. And you were right on the money for what you said to me. I deserved every word of it. I thought it through and decided to make some changes." He took a biscuit from Ida's plate and devoured it before continuing. "After lengthy discussions with Father, I have branched out on my own. The new company, Nicholas Lovelace Transportation Specialists, was just awarded the contract to maintain the new railroad track in Caldwell County."

"That's wonderful!" said Rosa.

"Well done," Weston added.

"He took my biscuit," complained Ida.

"Furthermore, I'm traveling to the Texas and Pacific Railways headquarters in Marshall to make a bid for any further line laid in the county."

Weston clapped Nicholas on the back and congratulated him again, completely unaware of Rosa, desperately trying to catch his eye. "Sounds like you're well on your way to upholding the Lovelaces' entrepreneurial traditions. Hats off to you. No hard feelings?"

"None, of course!" He shook the offered hand. "Not as long as you keep my little friend here happy."

Now he noticed her. Weston smiled tentatively, perhaps the first genuine smile toward her since she'd returned his loan.

Ida made a smooching sound while Susannah puckered up her lips and batted her eyelashes.

"Girls!" Rosa gasped. She set her cup down too firmly, causing punch to splash on the table. She didn't dare look in Weston's direction, but Bailey saved her further embarrassment.

"Weston!" Bailey had an arm wrapped around a nervous Deacon Bradford. "Don't we have some business with the new groom?"

"If you'll excuse me." His gaze lingered longer than Rosa expected before he turned to go, but he kept his thoughts to himself.

The September afternoon heat was nothing to fear, as they were sheltered from the sun by the expansive warehouse roof. The men disassembled the tables and the women gathered the dishes as the fiddler rosined up. Louise and Deacon would dance first, and then if the local auctioneer was done with his pipe, he'd do his duty as caller for the square dances. The freshly sawn planks had been moved to the edges of the giant structure, and the bay doors were swung open wide to catch every breeze available, a necessity if there was to be dancing.

Dancing? How she'd love to. The sets forming before her eyes didn't look quite as intimate as the dance Weston had tried to teach her. Maybe she could try a square dance, if no one had any objections. She fidgeted at the outskirts of the group, unsure of her boundaries — unsure she wanted any.

At her core, Rosa always believed Weston was her friend and protector, even when he stopped coming around. Their unexpected wedding had tested their bond, but somehow Weston insisted it'd survived, stronger than ever. Maybe he wasn't absolutely sure of himself, but if he'd forgiven her this much . . .

She shivered as she thought of their one and only dance. He'd encouraged her to try it again if she ever had the opportunity. Would he repeat his offer?

Rosa found Deacon, but Weston wasn't with him. Weston was standing by the cake, carrying on a tête-à-tête with Molly. Rosa's stomach wrapped around her lungs and squeezed. Molly? Didn't Molly say something about persuading Weston to release her?

While Rosa couldn't hear their conversation, she could clearly read every dimple, every flutter, and every bounce as Molly presented her case. *Shame on you,* Rosa scolded herself. She shouldn't have given Molly permission to get involved. She needed to talk to Weston, *pronto.*

Rosa tried to worm her way through the crowded warehouse but lost track of them. Straining to look over tall shoulders, she didn't see Louise until she appeared at her side.

"Rosa, give me a hug in case I get carried away and forget. I can't leave on my honeymoon without saying good-bye to my daughter." Louise crushed Rosa into the chrysanthemum bouquet pinned on her chest. "You're content, aren't you?" she whispered in her ear. "You can come with us if you must."

"No, ma'am. It's going to work. I'll see to it, but hurry home. I'll visit when you return."

Satisfied, she nodded. "I think we did all right for ourselves, after all, Mrs. Garner."

"Yes, Mrs. Bradford, we did." She sounded more confident than she felt.

Rosa scanned the crowd, a swirling mess of people as some left the dance floor while others scrambled to find a partner for the next set. Why wasn't she taller? She couldn't see past those directly in front of her. She weaved her way toward the back of the warehouse, where the dirty dishes were stacked to be cleaned after the party.

Finally she spotted him. Weston's dark head appeared above a tall stack of two-by-twelves to her right. He hadn't wandered far at all. To her horror a hand appeared on the back of his neck — a delicate, manicured hand that laced itself through his hair for a moment before disappearing.

Rosa's feet refused to move. There had to be some mistake, but the words she heard spoken in Molly's husky voice left her no room for denial.

"Mr. Garner, I cannot allow you to take further liberties. I should have known better than to be lured here by you after the way you ogled me."

A chuckle resonated over the sound of the music, and his head dipped again.

Darkness narrowed Rosa's vision to only a point of light in a black tunnel but didn't completely block out the hateful sight. She watched, mesmerized, but there was no mistake. Molly's hand was again at the back of his neck, holding on for dear life. Were her knees going weak like Rosa's had?

She couldn't stay. Her emotions boiled over, and there was no limit to the damage she could do. She mustn't make a scene at Louise's wedding. Stumbling, Rosa made it outside the insufferable warehouse before she gagged and tossed her dinner into the ditch. On her hands and knees in the tall grass, she gasped for breath as the music played on.

Adrenaline coursed through her primed body. As much as she'd like to rip out Molly's thick curls, she was ready to run.

A quick glance told her no one was looking. She headed for the closest building that would shield her and angled toward the creek, keeping away from the road.

Being right had never hurt so much. She'd come so close to trusting him. Why couldn't this have happened last week? Last month? Why now, after her hopes had been resurrected?

But as devastated as she was, she recognized it as providential. Better now than a year from now. He owed her nothing. She'd begged him to leave her alone. She'd done everything she could to steer him toward Molly.

She knew he wouldn't settle for a marriage of convenience. He'd tried to protect and be faithful to her, but he couldn't turn his heart from his true love. Shouldn't she of all people understand? After a month of resisting Weston, she was ready to throw herself on his mercy in a weak moment. Fool again!

The idiotic stays slowed her down. She clawed at her waist in desperation, but the only remedy would be to shred her beloved taffeta gown. She was forced to slow her pace.

Until she got her bearings, a vacant home called to her, offering her sanctuary, a home that had provided her with a roof and a bed when she was a new immigrant. She would go back to where she first began her life in Caldwell County and form her plans.

Rosa plunged through the growth on the banks of the creek, going down into the heavy shade. The brush gripped her wedding dress, leaving it in shambles. No remedy. She had to cross further up to avoid being spotted from the bridge. Her dress would be destroyed either way.

Lifting her skirts, she waded through the knee-deep creek. The cool water ran down her ankles, filling her boots, but she didn't care. Everything was ruined. Her dress. Her marriage. Her life. She sloshed across to a bank that was higher than she'd expected. Digging into the soft soil, she found exposed roots to grasp and pulled herself up, right into his path.

"Is this the meeting place for errant wives?" Tillerton's moustache curled up on one side.

"Get out of my way." Rosa's fists clenched. She'd unload on him with both barrels, and have no regrets.

"So the little Mexican girl thinks she can boss me around, huh? Talking down to me now that you're such a fine lady? Too bad Mr. Garner isn't here to back you up."

"He's right behind me."

Weston wasn't. He was with Molly. Her throat lurched again. She didn't care what happened to her now. He would be free, but her sense of justice left no room for a victorious Tillerton.

"Yeah, that's why you're off-road, traipsing through the creek while the rest of your family are at the wedding. He knows exactly where you are, does he? See? I'm having the same problem. My wife's gone missing, too. . . ." His piercing eyes scrolled their way down her bodice.

She read his intentions but wasn't quick enough to avoid him.

He grabbed her by the arm. "I guess one woman's just as good as the other."

Rosa screamed, twisted, and kicked, but he was ready for her this time. He shoved her backwards off the dark loamy bank, and she toppled, head over heels, to the bottom, hitting every root and stone along the way.

Before she could get to her feet, Tillerton had her by the hair and was dragging her backward, her heels bouncing along the ground. She heard him enter the water first, and then she was on her back, her skirts floating up around her while he brutally crammed his hand in her face and pushed her under.

Rosa thrashed and strained but couldn't get to the surface. Every panic she'd ever experienced culminated in horrific terror, but this time it wasn't just a small space. She truly was suffocating. Her heart battered her chest, every beat a plea for oxygen. She pushed against his arm with both hands, digging her fingernails into his hairy wrist, but he was relentless. With a sob, she relinquished the air exploding in her lungs, and only then did he lift her to the surface.

She inhaled immediately, and then sputtered out the creek water that was trickling into her gaping mouth.

"Stop fighting me. You hear?" He clenched her jaw in a vice grip, his wet lips inches from her face. "You'll play along or I'll —"

She was never one to cower and definitely not today. Rosa screamed in his face and was instantly thrust under the surface again, this time with a mouthful of water. Her chest heaved. She tried not to expel the precious air burning in her lungs. With her feet she swung about trying to locate his knee, his leg, anything to cause him pain, but his grip over her face only tightened.

The water churned around her as she struggled. A swirling mess of hair and skirts and bubbles, all was moving. Only the hand choking the life out of her was steady.

With a shove he plunged her to the very bottom. Rosa's head hit the creek bottom as Tillerton lunged, but his grip no longer hurt her. He lay across her, dead weight. With all the strength she had left, she pushed against him with the current of the crimson water and rolled out from under his body. She exploded to the surface, gagging and coughing, but able to finally make use of the magnificent air that had been denied her.

Rosa crawled to the bank and collapsed, trying to make sense of her salvation. Only then did she see the battered woman holding the pistol.

Mrs. Tillerton stood uncertain, as skittish as a rabbit sensing danger, her stained dress torn at the shoulder. Her eyes darted both ways, and seeing no one, she scurried to Rosa and knelt at her side.

"I didn't plan to kill him. I was only running away. If I'd wanted him dead I could have done that any day." With shaking hands the young lady slid her pistol into a tattered garter under her skirt. "You're breathing, aren't you? Then I better go."

"Wait! Where are you going?" Rosa gasped, her hands clutching fast to her rescuer's arm.

"I don't know, but I need to get away from him."

Still panting, Rosa turned her head to look at the floating body caught in the brambles. "He's not going to bother you anymore."

Rosa heard her name called across the water. She flopped on her back. "You saved my life. If you stay, we can help."

The horses approached quickly. She heard Red say something about the gunshot, and Weston's voice answered. The girl crouched, her head cocked to gauge their proximity.

"Please stay," Rosa begged again. "At least talk to Weston. You'll need money for your trip." Violent coughing overtook her.

"There they are," Bailey announced, and with a rush the three mounted men surrounded them.

Weston slid off his horse and immediately knelt next to her. The shock on his face was awful to see. How she wanted to cling to him, to comfort him, but she couldn't. Not while the picture of Molly's arms wrapped around his neck still danced before her eyes.

"Are you hurt? You're . . . you're breathing?"

She nodded and pulled herself up again,

459

feeling stronger every minute.

"Weston, you'd better take a look at this," Bailey said.

Just behind him, Bailey pulled Tillerton's body from the red eddy. He dragged it to the bank and flipped it over, revealing a jagged hole through his leather vest.

Red whistled. "Mrs. Tillerton?"

She didn't respond. Their eyes traveled from the gunshot wound to her. Both Tillertons were silent.

"What happened?" Weston mopped the trickles of water from his wife's face with his bandanna.

"That man, that brute, attacked me. He told me to stop fighting him or he would drown me. Then he stopped." She didn't go any further, not sure what the girl wanted her to say.

Weston turned to Mrs. Tillerton. She lifted her face so they could all see her black eye and swollen cheek. Rosa knew Weston well enough to guess he'd want to put another slug in the man just for Mrs. Tillerton's sake.

"You're a brave woman, Mrs. Tillerton. You saved my wife's life, and that puts me in your debt. I don't know what went on between you and your husband at home, but Judge Rice won't blink an eye over this incident. You have enough witnesses to clear you immediately."

She made her way to a blackberry bush and retrieved a satchel from under the thorny branches. "Then can I go on home? You'll send the sheriff by? I don't want to stay here with him any longer."

"Sounds reasonable. Bailey, take her home. Red, why don't you ride back to the warehouse and get Sheriff Colton." Wes looked at the dead man again. "Clean shot, by the way."

"Yankees know how to shoot, too," she said.

"I remember."

Bailey turned to help Mrs. Tillerton onto his horse, but she'd straddled it before he could reach her.

Rosa had another spasm of coughing, not as severe as the last. Without waiting for her consent, Weston pulled her tightly to him. His lips brushed her ear.

"When I saw you there on the ground, drenched, I thought it'd happened again." She felt him shudder. "You can't imagine how awful . . . But you're still with me, right? You aren't hurt?"

Cautiously, she touched the back of her head, but there was no bump, only tenderness from being dragged by her hair. She shook her head, the wet tendrils sticking to her face. He waited for his next question until they both caught their breath.

"Why did you run away?"

28

Rosa stiffened. She couldn't condemn him for doing precisely what she'd expected. She'd even sicced Molly on him.

"I wanted to be alone, I guess. Wanted to go home." She searched his face for signs of guilt and found none.

Weston stood and looked down at her, arms crossed, brow lowered.

"Well, let's get you there, Mrs. Garner."

She picked at a bald dandelion cap. "My home is just across the creek. That's where I'll live until Louise and Deacon return."

"It's empty."

"I don't care."

"You don't have any dry clothes."

"I. Don't. Care."

"Get on the horse."

Rosa started to crawl away, but he was too quick. Lifting her from the ground, he tossed her like a sack of potatoes across the withers of a strange mount, then hopped in the saddle. He kept a heavy hand on her bustle to keep her from squirming off.

"You can't do this."

"Apparently I can. I'm taking you home to Eliza. After what you've been through, you aren't going to sit alone in a vacant house tonight. She'll take care of you."

Oh. Was that all?

The saddle horn bit into her already sore ribcage. "Please, Weston. You're hurting me."

He stopped the horse and helped her roll over, right into his arms. "Is this better?"

She didn't answer. The rocking of the horse bounced her against him, but she would not melt into his chest. She would not take comfort in his embrace. Him. Her. No blurring between them.

They crossed his property line. The lights of Palmetto glowed warmly against the blue prairie. Only a few more minutes, and she'd never have to be this close to him again. She'd do what it took to get their marriage annulled. His qualms about his reputation wouldn't sway her now.

Weston cleared his throat. "Rosa, we need to talk. I haven't been honest with you."

She bumped against his chest again, and during the brief contact felt his pounding heart. So he'd worked up the nerve? She braced herself for his confession.

"Last week, you asked if I loved you, and I didn't tell you the truth. Maybe I didn't know the truth, but I do now, and I'm sorry I didn't say it sooner."

What? Not what she was expecting. "I have to stop you before you lose all credibility. You're demeaning yourself. Please don't."

He loosened his grip on her, but no, he wasn't finished.

"I *am* going to say it. I love you, and it isn't demeaning. It's right and . . . and sacred. I had so many opportunities to tell you, so many times that I left you to wonder. I'm sorry. Even today, I didn't reach for your hand when I should've. But if you'll give me another chance —"

"Stop, please." She leaned as far away as she could. "Yes, I'm guilty of intruding into your life, but I've tried to make amends. I've tried to leave, but you've kept me bound. Well, not anymore. I'm free now, and I'm going. Please let me take memories of an honest man with me."

He stung. Like he'd swallowed fire ants, he hurt and he couldn't reach the injury, but it kept burning and burning.

How had he been so wrong? Weston

could've sworn he'd seen signs of thawing, but he'd misjudged. He'd gone and done the very thing he'd sworn he wouldn't — he asked her to reconsider. No wonder she was so mad.

They entered the dining room and caught Jake and Eliza just starting in on their bowls of soup.

Eliza's spoon clattered into her bowl. "Rosa, you're soaked. What happened? Where did you run off to?"

Rosa's shoulders drooped. "I'm really tired. I'd rather not —"

"Tillerton attacked her." Plain talk or nothing. He wouldn't allow any more ambiguity.

"What are we waiting for?" Jake threw his napkin down and jumped up, ready to ride.

"Steady, Jake. He won't threaten anyone again."

Eliza scrambled around the table and took Rosa into her arms. "Oh, you poor thing. Let's get you to the kitchen. Jake, get the tub, and I'll have Octavia fetch her robe and towel. We have to get her warmed up. Soup. Soup would be good."

"I'm really not cold," Rosa protested, but no one heeded her.

Weston headed out of the dining room and into the parlor. Rosa didn't want him around. She'd made that clear. He leaned against the mantel and listened to the ticking of the clock.

What now? He'd been biding his time, thinking that she'd be there when he got the courage. Had he waited too long, or was she never his to begin with? Didn't matter. He was at the end of the trail. First thing Monday morning, he'd ride into Lockhart and see the judge. Who knew what legal wrangling it'd take to annul his marriage, but he owed it to her. She'd never wanted him in the first place.

The gold band on his finger had just begun to feel natural. He rubbed it with his thumb. Soon his finger would be naked again. Unclaimed. Unbound. And he would be free to — what? Wear dirty boots in the house? Go on the trail? Marry?

He shook his head. Rosa was his wife. Although he hadn't planned to propose, he'd never regretted marrying her. Even now. Maybe that ring was right where it belonged.

A little later Weston heard the women's voices from the stairway. He was the man of the house. Protector. Rosa still lived under his roof, and he was honor-bound to see that she lacked nothing. He took the stairs two at a time and knocked on the open door.

"Come on in." Eliza fumbled through Rosa's vanity and called back to her. "I can't find your comb. Where is it?"

"I have a brush," Rosa said. "Please go to bed. You're getting overwrought."

"Well, why shouldn't I? I almost lost my sister today."

When he stepped into the room, Rosa halted her reply midbreath. She pulled the belt of her robe tight and studied the floor.

"Weston," Eliza huffed. "I'm going to have to run downstairs and get a comb. Rosa's hair is ratted frightfully. Will you stay with her?"

Rosa's eyes bulged. "No need. I'll comb it tomorrow. I don't mind being alone. . . ."

But Eliza had vanished.

Weston turned to avoid staring, but her reflection caught him in the mirror. Her wet locks were spread over shoulders, which still retained a staunch vigil against any approach he might make. He didn't want to add to her distress, so he remained near the doorway. She could hear him from there.

"Don't know why God saw fit to let you go through all that today, but I apologize if I contributed to your trials."

She said nothing.

All righty, then.

He continued. "You expressed your frustration with me quite clearly. Now that I know how strongly you feel, Eliza and I will take you to the courthouse Monday morning. I'll set you up wherever you want, or we can wait until Louise comes home if you need to. Whatever I can do, you just let me know."

He scuffed the toe of his boot along the edge of the rug. What was keeping Eliza?

Weston didn't expect an answer, so he almost missed Rosa's simple thank-you.

"If we go Monday," she said, "Eliza should stay here. She's worn out."

He nodded. Practical as always. "Then we could pick up Aunt Mary on the way, if you'd be uncomfortable riding alone with me. It'd be a good chance for me to talk to her about Bailey."

Silence fell again. A board creaked under his weight. Cows could be heard lowing through the open window. Had they reached the end of their relationship so quickly? Had the reserves of shared thoughts, stories, and dreams been depleted? Was there nothing left to discuss?

Uncomfortable. He started rambling, letting his words fill the empty air like gnats. "Don't much relish talking to Mary. She'll beat that boy, for sure. Probably should wait until George is around to restrain her.

'Course if Bailey's big enough to trifle with Molly, he's big enough to take a lashing from his little ma. Definitely do him some good."

"Molly?" Rosa's tone dripped with sarcasm.

Weston's head snapped up. "Yes, Molly. I shouldn't tell tales, but his folks are possibly the only people at the wedding who didn't see them."

Rosa twisted the end of her belt around her wrist. "But I saw you . . ." Her brow furrowed. "I know it was you. She said 'Mr. Garner.' " She blinked, then her eyes widened, and her mouth turned down.

Rosa's outburst of tears caught Weston completely unprepared.

"What's wrong? What'd I do?"

But she couldn't answer. He stood helpless as Rosa plopped onto her bed and blubbered into her hands. Her sobs echoed through the room and brought his sister flying up the stairs. Eliza tossed a comb on the vanity and rushed to her side.

"What did you say to her, Weston? Honestly! Hasn't she been through enough today?" She pulled Rosa to her, and the tear-streaked face was something to behold. "What's wrong?"

Rosa's chin quivered. "He . . . he didn't

470

kiss her."

What? Weston held his hands up and shrugged, but his confusion didn't satisfy Eliza.

"Tell me what she's talking about."

"I don't know. I was just shooting the breeze. Said something about Bailey and Molly —"

"It was Bailey," Rosa cried and hiccuped simultaneously. She clutched Eliza's arm, and her weeping began to sound suspiciously like laughter. "Bailey kissed her."

Bumfuzzled. He was downright bumfuzzled. Was she hysterical? If not, his sister certainly was.

"Rosa, I don't know what's gotten into you, but you're scaring the living daylights out of me. My nerves are just about shot already, and here you are cackling like a banshee. I've been on my feet all day —"

Weston approached cautiously. "Eliza, why don't you go on to bed?"

"I can't leave her. Not in this condition."

Rosa still held onto her arm, and her shoulders shook — whether from mirth or despair, he couldn't tell.

He helped Eliza to her feet. "I'm more worried about your condition. She's going to be fine."

"But . . ."

"Don't make me call for Jake."

Eliza pouted. She gave Rosa one last uncertain look and waddled out the door, closing it behind her.

He didn't kiss Molly. He didn't kiss Molly. Rosa cast about, trying to remember everything he'd said since then, everything she'd discredited, but the only words she could quote with certainty were the awful things she'd said when he'd told her that he loved her.

He loved her.

Weston picked up the comb from the vanity and ran the teeth across his palm. "Now, common sense, my own pride, and all that's decent says I should leave. You've told me how you feel, but my curiosity will haunt me —"

"Don't go."

He stared at her like she was a yodeling heifer. With a clatter, the comb landed on the vanity. "All right. Can you tell me why you want me to stay?"

Rosa wiped her tears on the sleeve of her quilted robe. "Because you didn't kiss Molly."

He pulled himself up to his full height. "Of course I didn't. Did you think . . . ?" Then a slow grin spread across his face.

"You did. You thought it was me."

She dipped her head, unable to bear the intensity of his gaze.

He laughed. Weston tilted his head back and laughed with pure joy. She'd been so awful to him. No wonder he'd looked so hurt, but not anymore. The crinkles around his eyes had returned. His lips spread in the most beguiling smile as he turned his attention on her again.

"An hour ago you had some mighty harsh words for me. Would you like me to repeat them?" Oh, how he was enjoying this.

"No. I didn't mean to say such things to you."

"You didn't? Then what did you mean to say . . . to me?"

Rosa waited for the tightening to begin. At any moment, she'd begin to feel crowded. The pressure would get to her. She'd fought against having this conversation for so long — from making this confession — she couldn't believe she was standing at the brink.

She put a hand to her forehead, drawing her wet hair out of her eyes, and slid off the bed. "You said you'd been dishonest. Well, so have I." The words had grown comfortable hiding in her heart unexpressed. It would take some effort to release them.

She paced the room, back and forth before him, swinging her robe in agitation as she tried to spit them out. "I lied to you, too. I don't want to be your servant." She stomped her foot and looked at him with eyes wide and scared. "I hate it!"

He stepped closer. "Wonder why?"

"I don't want to just be with you." Her warm blood was rising. "Not like that. Imagining you with Molly made me *loca,* but I couldn't stop you. Not when I was just your employee. It isn't enough. I want —" Her gaze locked with his, strayed to his lips, and then dropped to his hands.

She closed her eyes as a definite peace filled her. No fear. She could do this.

"Did you know today at the wedding I wanted to hold your hand?" she said.

He reached out and took her hands, still shriveled from the bath water.

"You should have. You had the right."

She smiled at their old game but wasn't distracted. "I've never been to a Christian wedding before, and I thought it was beautiful. The church words were better than the courthouse words. I wished someone — I wished *you* would say those words to me."

He anchored her hair behind her ear and let his hand remain against her cheek.

"What was your wedding to Mack like?"

"Nothing like Louise's." Rosa thought back to that day in the village. "Eli performed the ceremony. He read a chapter in the New Testament about love and prayed for us. That was it."

"Sounds perfect. Cora's and my wedding was a huge to-do. Nothing as intimate as yours. I felt like a sideshow freak with all the people staring at me. Of course she was beautiful and happy. That's what was important."

Rosa pulled his hand around and pressed a kiss into his palm. She'd never heard him speak of Cora like that. As if she was a pleasant memory. As if he was healed.

Weston led her by the belt of her robe to the bed. He sat down and pulled her to stand between his knees. He was a little shaky. She smiled tenderly. He had nothing to be nervous about. Taking his face in her hands, Rosa flashed him a wanton look straight from her mariposa routine and quoted to the best of her memory the vows she'd heard spoken before the altar that morning.

"Do you, Weston Garner, take me, Rosa Garner, to be thy wedded wife, to have and to hold from this day forward, for better or for worse, for richer or for poorer, in sickness and in health, to love and to cherish till death do us part?"

"I do," he said distinctly, pouring all the promises he'd made her into those two words.

Unlike the last kiss, she saw this one coming, but she didn't try to dodge it. Still holding onto her belt, Weston pulled her against him and wrapped her in his arms, no apologies and no reserves.

"But that's it?" She gasped at her first chance for a breath. "I don't have to promise anything?"

"I can come up with something if you insist." He held her snugly between his legs and let his fingers trace her wide cheekbones, her jaw, down to her neck and collarbone as he thought. "Do you, Rosa, promise to be mine? To whisper my name in your sleep and blush when you think of me during the day? To remember that you were chosen by me and are loved?"

"Is that all?"

"No, there's more. You can't keep accounts. You mustn't ever run away again, and" — his crooked grin made an appearance — "above all, you will only crawl under *my* blanket if you need a favor. No more finding men in barns. Do you, Rosa, promise me that?"

"I do. You may kiss your bride."

"Um, I intend to."

He was doing just that when Jake called through their door. "Excuse me, Weston, Rosa?"

"There's no excuse. Go away," Weston hollered.

She giggled against him, but Jake wasn't dissuaded.

"It's Eliza. She's going to have the baby. I hate to bother you —"

"It could take hours. Tell her to walk around, and I'll be down later," Rosa called. She couldn't tear her eyes off her husband. She leaned forward and took another kiss, enjoying the freedom to do what she'd imagined for so long. "I plan to kiss you a lot."

"Uh, I can hear you." Poor Jake was still at the door. "Rosa, where's the mop? She said something about her water, and Red isn't back yet. Someone needs to get Dr. Trench."

"Just ignore him. He'll go away. I, on the other hand, am right where I've wanted to be for weeks."

Rosa ran her finger down his chest. "I have to go. Eliza needs me."

"Not as bad as I do." He pulled her to him and kissed her once more with an intensity that left them both shaking. "But you're right. Better get dressed and go down there. God willing, we'll need her help someday soon."

The bundle in Rosa's arms weighed as much as a cantaloupe and smelled even sweeter. She rocked quietly in the great room while the rest of the house slumbered. Little Cora watched her with bright eyes and held tightly to her finger, not the least interested in sleep.

"Your family loves you already, *bebé*," Rosa whispered, kissing her for the hundredth time in her two-hour life. "And it's a wonderful family. You'll never know how lucky you are. First, there's Aunt Louise and Uncle Deacon. They'll be back soon. Then there's Aunt Mary and Uncle George. They have three boys who won't let anyone mess with their princess and two girls who will spoil you rotten. But your favorites will be Aunt Rosa and Uncle Weston, because they already love you the most."

From the window Rosa saw the light of a lantern make its way across the yard. The darkness hadn't yet broken, and family was already coming. With a coffee-scented gust, Mary entered the room.

"A baby already? I'm glad Wes went for the doctor when he did." She laid her shawl aside and wiped her hands on her skirt. "Happy birthday, sweet pea. You like your aunt Rosa, don't you? She's a mighty special lady in this family." Mary leaned in close to coo over the baby and peek in the diaper. "A girl, by thunder! All right, Rosa, you've had your turn. Hand her over and go get some sleep." She took Cora from her arms and pecked a kiss on Rosa's forehead. "Morning will be here soon, and with the sun a whole new day to tame."

At an hour when every other God-fearing woman of Caldwell County was either elbowing her snoring husband or sleeping undisturbed in her spinster bed, Rosa found herself sneaking toward a room that was not her own. She was a trespasser whose goal was to get caught — a blissful pursuer whose prey was within reach.

Holding her nightgown above the thick rug, she inched closer with a pounding heart. Surely he could hear it.

Why had this short trip across her room taken her so long? Her stubborn insistence that he would eventually reject her seemed foolish now, for if anyone would love her, it was Weston Garner. And if there was anyone she'd like to visit with or work beside, it was he. And he had made his position clear.

She and the farm were not a package deal. She belonged to him permanently, irrevocably, and completely.

Her hands were clammy as she pushed against the bedroom door. Mentally she judged the distance between herself and his bed, counting the steps it would take, and then pulled the door shut behind her, plunging the room into darkness.

Maybe this will be easier if I can't see him, she hoped, wondering if he was awake. Her tentative steps brought her closer and closer. With an outstretched hand she slowly searched until her fingers touched the edge of the quilt. Trembling, she lifted his blanket, climbed in next to him, and pulled the blanket over them. She meant to keep her distance, to wait until he woke, but the mattress sloped where it supported his weight, causing her to slide right into his chest.

He could feel her warmth against him; her breath was burning a ring near his heart. She was trembling, so he took her in his arms and pulled her close, until they were both burrowed deep in the feather bed. *Stubborn child,* he thought, *I'm never letting you go.*

Holding his wife, he was at peace. This was approved — sanctioned — his heart told him. God have given him someone to protect tonight and for the rest of their lives.

ABOUT THE AUTHOR

Regina Jennings is a graduate of Oklahoma Baptist University with a degree in English and a history minor. She has worked at *The Mustang News* and at First Baptist Church of Mustang, along with time at the Oklahoma National Stockyards and various livestock shows. She now lives outside of Oklahoma City with her husband and four children.